A Rock 'n' Roll
Lovestyle

Kiltie Jackson

FOR IAN

Who supported me every day on this crazy
journey and never doubted I would make
it to the end.

X

Acknowledgements

I have so many people to thank for getting me to this point that the easiest way to ensure I don't miss anyone is to start from the beginning.

First up is Kym Wood – the best friend anyone could have. She read my very early offering and her kind words gave me the encouragement to carry on and see it through. She pushes me on every day and lets me know her belief in me is absolute.

Another massive thank you goes to my mum and my sister Rosie –both were behind me every step of the way and their constant encouragement helped to keep the old pecker up on the days when I doubted I could do it.

To my dad who asked, every time we spoke, on my progress and told me he was proud of me.

My mother-in-law Margaret who told me I was brilliant – more than once! It helped so much.

To Pam Howes I owe more thanks than it is possible to describe – this fabulous lady has given me so much help and direction. Self-publishing is a daunting step but Pam's patient hand-holding and guidance helped me to make it.

John Hudspith was the poor chap who had to take my error-riddled manuscript and turn it into something clean, tidy and mistake-free. Thank you for the lessons taught and I hope the next one is less painful.

My fabulous cover design is the work of Henry Hyde

who somehow knew exactly what I wanted from the garbled details I provided.

The 'Yo Ass Bitches' are the best bunch of ladies I know – Hilda, Vera & Percy are my jury and so many decisions and choices went through them. Thank you for so patiently giving your opinions when asked – I owe you all a very big glass (or six!) of wine.

Martine Fender and Emma Hyde both deserve medals for listening to me rabbiting on about plots and characters on a daily basis and for giving me their feedback after reading the early manuscripts.

It would be very wrong not to include two fantastic book groups I joined on Facebook – The NotRights Book Club and The Fiction Café Book Club. The members of both are wonderful people who are always generous with their comments, support and assistance. I learned so much just from being a part of these groups.

To my Facebook followers who liked my page and gave me their time and support by just being there – every 'like' and comment gave me the impetus to believe that there were people interested in what I was doing and rooting for me to succeed.

To the Moggy Posse – Princess Moo Moo, Mr McGee, Abby, Donald and Tony who make me smile every day. Mummy loves you big time. xx

Last, but by no means least, my lovely husband Ian who kept telling me I could do it, who became a Weekend Widower as I poured every spare minute into my writing (I'm sure it was a real hardship going to all those football matches!) and who told me from the beginning "Follow your dream and believe in your goal –

it's making you happy." Thank you for everything and for being a part of this with me. I love you – till the end of eternity… And a day! xxx

Chapter One

Oxfordshire, UK

Yup, thought Sukie McClaren, as she switched off the television, that Pete Wallace sure can sing a song. Good looking too! Ok, she admitted to herself, he really was rather gorgeous but, not the sort of man she went for. Far too 'pretty boy' for her taste. Although, she mused wryly, she couldn't really pin down exactly what sort of man she did go for. Thirty-six and still single wasn't exactly evidence of someone with a decisive mind, was it? She gently moved her two black rescue cats, Tony and Adam, from her lap, and got up from her chair. Her fur-babies were really the loves of her life and she adored them far more than any bloke she had been involved with thus far.

She moved across to the French windows and peeked through the heavy velvet curtains to see if the snow, the weather people had hinted at, had arrived. She switched on the patio light but all she could see was the heavy frost on the lawn and a set of footprints across it from a wandering cat or fox. She looked down at the two little black shadows beside her with their noses pressed up hard against the windows.

"Maybe it'll be there in the morning, guys. What do you think?"

The lack of reply came as no surprise. Her boys excelled in being the strong, silent type. That is, until they wanted food! And then they were anything but! She shoo'ed them out of the way, switched the outside light back off, checked the doors were securely locked and pulled the curtains back together. Sukie looked around the room and gave a little sigh of happiness. She'd bought her flat almost six years ago and was still as much in love with it today as she had been when she'd moved in. The day she'd come to view it, it had been love at first sight. It made the extra years of living at home with her mum, all the sacrifices of holidays, third-hand cars and even weekends away with the girls, totally worthwhile. She'd lived like a pauper for the best part of seven years and it had paid off. She had absolutely no regrets.

The flat was one of four apartments in a beautifully converted, Victorian, detached property. Rather than turn the building into six or eight boring flats, the renovator had been more sympathetic to the building's design and had opted to go for four, two-floored apartments instead. Sukie's flat was made up of what had once been the lower ground floor – now her open-plan kitchen/diner and lounge – and the ground floor which had become her two bedrooms and bathroom. Above her lived Jenny and her flat layout was, what she called, *up-side down*. The bedrooms were directly above Sukie's and the living space was one floor up, in the attic. She loved the character of the sloped ceilings and regularly admired them on the nights she spent with Jenny, sitting on her little roof-top patio, as they put the world to rights over a bottle of wine. Across from Jenny lived Rupert, a retired Oxford don. Widowed in his late fifties, he now lived alone and enjoyed weekends away hill-walking. The remaining flat, on the ground floor, was where Sadie lived. The oldest resident of the four, she was a sprightly seventy-five years of age but could easily pass for being much younger. She'd shared some tales of her youth with Jenny and Sukie after a few glasses of wine – "None of this sweet sherry malarkey for me" she would say. "That's for frail, sweet old ladies and I'm not there yet!" It seemed as though she had been quite a girl back in the 'Swinging Sixties' if all she said was true. Jenny and Sukie loved spending time with her, listening to her tales. As neighbours went, Sukie couldn't have asked for better. They all got along well and, having heard some horror stories from her work colleagues, on the problems their neighbours caused, she was very grateful for what she had.

She headed upstairs to the bathroom to get ready for bed and thought about some of her past disaster dates; the accountant who, on their very first date, thought he should advise her on the contents of his underpants. Or rather, the *lack* of content! Seriously? It was not exactly the sort of information which was going to persuade her into finding out for herself. Then there was the wannabe rock star who had yet to become known in his own street, never mind the rest of the music-listening world – turning up half an hour later than the time they'd arranged wasn't going to set her pulse racing with passion. Especially as Sukie was already on a train back home by the time he'd arrived! And to think he'd been annoyed she hadn't waited for him! Hah, no chance!

She began brushing her teeth and nearly gagged as she began to giggle. She'd just remembered the very cute bloke she'd snogged when she'd had a rare night out, clubbing with her old college mates. He'd looked lush, in the muted lights of the nightclub and with several tequila shots under her belt; it was just very unfortunate that daylight wasn't his best friend. Not that she was superficial in any way – had his conversation been witty and his personality sparkling, then she could have overlooked the hooked nose, teeth like gravestones and his extremely hairy hands. But there is only so much conversation one can manage, about the delights of working in a bacon factory, from a pigeon-English speaking Cuban. *That* hadn't been very noticeable in the nightclub either! She rinsed her mouth of toothpaste and looked at Tony and Adam who were now sitting on the window-sill watching her.

"Yes, I'm quite sure you guys would have been very happy for me to have dated Mr Cuban Bacon, given your penchant for the stuff but, as much as I love you both, there are limits to the sacrifices I'm prepared to make on your behalf!" She turned back to her reflection in the mirror and muttered, "You've gotta face it, girl, when it

4

comes to the fellas, you are more of a disaster than the Titanic."

She leant forward to have a closer look at her hair – time to get the roots touched up again. It's all very well having hair the colour of warm chestnuts but the shots of red were a real pain in the butt. Every three weeks the red became grey and every four weeks she was bending over the bath putting another hair colour on her head. And on her hands... the tiles... the floor... And usually all over the shower-head too! It was a task she loathed but she loathed the aging grey hairs even more, so the colouring torture always won out in the end. She pulled out her hairband, ran her fingers through the, now loose, pony-tail and gave her head a shake. As she hadn't had time to straighten it that morning, her hair fell down past her shoulders in soft waves. She picked up a few strands, held them in front of her eyes and squinted at the ends, trying to see if she needed to book an appointment for a trim. Satisfied that she could put off the visit to the hairdressers for a few more weeks, she let the strands drop.

Sukie had a quick glance around her eyes. She was happy to see that the crows were still partying with their feet elsewhere for the moment, which was, at least, payback for the hair. She was in no doubt, though, that one day she'd wake up to find *so* many lines it would look like the crows had thrown a Glastonbury-sized rave. Her days were numbered on this one but, hey, what could she do? She just kept slapping on the various over-priced gloops, which the slick advertisers always managed to seduce her into buying, and hoped that one of them lived up to their hype.

She noticed her hazel-green eyes still looked bright and the whites were still white. No blood-shot, road-map effect just yet. All those hours in front of the PC, staring at spreadsheets, were yet to take their toll. She was also happy to note her lips were still plump and full. She hadn't moved into the 'thinning lips' stage that one well-known actress had moaned about after her collagen implants had left her looking like a guppy fish. The jawline continued to be firm, no double-chin was secretly emerging and her neck hadn't yet disappeared inside folds of saggy skin. All in all, she figured, she was not doing too badly for an old 'un.

She straightened up and went over to the full-length mirror behind the bathroom door. It was a very different story when she looked south of her neckline – pert boobs? What the heck were they when they were at home? Sukie couldn't ever remember her boobs being 'pert'. An ex-colleague had once said that doing the pencil test was a good way to measure if your mammaries were starting to sag. When asked what on earth she meant, her colleague had replied, "You get a pencil and place it under each boob. If the pencil drops, then you are still nice and firm, but if it stays put, then those boobies are on the downhill slope, the emphasis being on down!" Sukie had tried it that night and the pencil had stayed put. In fact, she had managed two pencils, a fountain pen and a biro. She still maintained that, had she had an actual pencil case, she could have also managed the ruler and the stapler! Nowadays, however, she was just twice the age with twice the droop.

She quickly skipped past her midriff – well, Buddha

could have been her middle name. "It's a family trait, dear," her mother had told her. "You'll just have to learn to live with it. Your grandmother had a podge, I have a podge and you have a podge."

"And those are good enough reasons for me to like it, are they?" she'd retorted. A big bottom she could live with – thanks to J-Lo and Beyonce, humongous derrières were now an acceptable fashion accessory – but no-one had yet gotten around to making the sticky-out belly this season's 'must-have'.

Finally, on this polar trip from north to south of her body, she got to her legs. Sukie knew that these were the two items with which she could find no fault. She always got compliments when she wore a short skirt, and that was enough to keep her spirits in good shape for several days. It was nice to know that, despite being on the wrong side of thirty-five, she had nothing to fear every time the micro-mini came back into fashion.

With a last critical glance in the mirror, and a quick pull-in of her tum, she changed into her night-shirt, walked through to her bedroom and got into bed. She had ten minutes to read another chapter of her book before putting her light out at eleven p.m. "A girl needs her beauty sleep," she said to the cats, as they kneaded the quilt beside her. "After all, I'm not getting any younger!"

Chapter Two

Austria

Jordie Ray sighed as he switched off the projection screen. The first song had definitely been flat and the second guitarist had been half a beat behind throughout the whole gig. Most of Joe Public wouldn't have noticed but Pete Wallace most certainly would. Being a perfectionist on the stage had gotten Pete where he was today and the feedback from this concert was going to cause some big rucks. Jordie, as usual, would have to stand by, let the bombs land and then clear up the fallout.

On this occasion, however, he was on Pete's side. Shoddy performances were for second-rate players and Pete would never settle for being second-rate. He believed his fans had the right to expect the highest quality from him at all times and it was an expectation on which Jordie gave his full agreement. This was one of the many factors which had kept Pete and himself together as a team for so long. Too many of today's 'popstars' (he always used the term with disdain) thought that a mediocre singing voice coupled with a pretty face and a tight body were all the requirements needed to become rich, famous and pull loose women. And, more's the pity, they were quite right. Discussing the quantity of these 'diluted wannabes' (also spoken disdainfully) muddying the recording waters for real musicians was one of his pet, soap-box, subjects – nuisance groupies was the other! Wannabes and groupies – the two topics guaranteed to set off a Jordie Ray rant and the two which most of the roadies tried to avoid whenever there was a late-night drinking session. He looked across the screening room at Pete who was sitting quietly, still staring at the large screen even though it was no longer on. He tried to figure out what he might be thinking but knew he'd very little chance of doing so. Pete's 'floppy fringe', as he laughingly called it, had fallen over his eyes, making it difficult to see what emotion he was feeling. Volatile was perhaps too strong a word to use when describing Pete Wallace but he certainly kept you guessing on what to expect from him. Things you would expect to cause fireworks would often be laughed off and small incidents, which barely merited a shrug of the shoulders, could create more havoc than an eight-point-five on the Richter scale.

"Well?" he asked. "Any comment you want to make?" Jordie figured if he got it out in the open now, he might see his bed sooner rather than later.

Pete turned away from the blank screen, pushed his

blonde fringe off his face and his piercing, emerald green, eyes glowered across at him. "Are you taking the fucking piss?"

He assumed a blank expression and waited to see just how high Pete would explode.

Pete continued to glare at him. "Aw, come on, Jordie," he said, "I saw you cringing through the first song. It was so flat it bordered on painful. That guitarist was behind through the whole fuckin' set and as for that bloody choir… How much do I pay them to look so fuckin' miserable? Eh?"

Damn! It sounds like this could be a big one, Jordie mused to himself. Pete's swearing always went up a few notches when he was about to lose his temper.

"The fans don't come to my gigs to stand and watch mardy-faced fuckers on my stage. If they want miserable they can stay at home. Half of that choir looked like they'd rather be in their bed with a cup of cocoa. Don't they realise that practically every person in that audience would've happily given an arm or a leg to be performing on the stage that night?" Pete was fuming. "You had better speak with them, Jordie and get it sorted out. I am NOT taking that mob on an all-expenses paid, around the world trip, for the fucking fun of it. The tour starts in just over three months. That's plenty of time to find a happier bunch of singers. You make sure they know that. I'm not having that shit to deal with for six months."

"I'll get it dealt with first thing in the morning."

"Fine!" Pete heaved a big sigh. "You know what – there are times when I wonder why I bother with all of this. I really do." He stood up from his chair, turned and headed towards the door.

"Pete…" Pete turned back to face him. "If it makes you feel any better, you're right and I completely agree with all you've said. We'll have it all in shape before the tour kicks off, I promise."

"Thanks mate," said Pete, giving him a tight smile. "I'll see you in the morning. Goodnight."

"Goodnight."

When the door had closed behind him, Jordie let out a huge sigh of relief. The explosion had been relatively minor. He'd seen much worse over a lot less. Nothing had been thrown or broken and that was always a good sign.

Pete slammed his bedroom door closed, picked up the first thing he laid his hands on – in this case a wooden hanger – and threw it across the room yelling, "Aaaaaagggghhhhhhh!" as he did so. Then, leaning back against the door, he stood with his head slumped down, his chin on his chest. He rubbed his face with his hands. Sometimes, the pressure was just too much. He often wondered how he coped with it all. He didn't mind writing the music. He could even cope with having to perform it, but he hated how he'd work so hard to get just the right sound, such as the choir tonight, and spend hours going through the rehearsals only for them to then behave on the stage as though they were one step away from being tortured. He knew that anyone watching the televised gig tonight, and noticing the faults, would say he was to blame. Few people ever stood back and looked at the bigger picture. To most, it was very simple. His show, his problem!

He sighed and walked across the room to the vast, hand-carved, antique, four-poster bed. He flopped down across it on his stomach. His brain was buzzing and he knew that, unless he could find a way of emptying it of any thought, he would not see any sleep that night. He rolled over onto his back and gazed up at the hand-woven tapestry above him. Four months ago, he'd finally moved out of the turret bedroom he'd slept in since he was ten years old and into the master bedroom of the family Schloss. He was still deciding on whether to decorate it or not. As beautiful as all the dark, wooden, hand-carved furniture was, and he appreciated that the bed he now lay on was totally unique, it all dated back to his great, great grandfather's day and he, personally, found it very oppressive. Maybe he should ask Kara to pull together some information on interior decorators. It wouldn't hurt to get some suggestions and ideas.

He closed his eyes and tried to empty his mind but to no avail. He forced himself to think of the various exercises his therapist had suggested. He needed to relax – he was far too wound up. Perhaps now was the time to try the flower garden therapy thingy. The one which had had him cringing in his seat when Hannah read it out from her list. Flowers? For goodness' sake, he was a bloke. What do blokes know about flowers? Apart from the fact they're a good way of getting out of the shit with the girls… Oh well, it was one of the last options for him to have a go at, all the others hadn't helped all that much. Let's see how he faired with this one. How did it go again? He imagined himself back in Hannah's room and heard her voice as he remembered her reading out loud to him.

"Picture a garden with freshly mown grass. It's a very quiet garden, with only the sound of birds chirruping and bees buzzing breaking the silence. The sun is shining and the warmth from its rays is soothing. Stand in the middle of the lawn and breathe in deeply, through your nose, taking in the full fragrance of the grass. Hold it for a moment before slowly letting it all out through your mouth. Do this several times, very slowly."

He lay on the bed with his eyes closed, breathing deep and slow.

"Now start to think of flowers using the alphabet. Think of a flower starting with 'A'."

Azaleas are they outdoor plants? Well, they are now... Next, he had to picture himself picking up this flower, breathing in its scent, filling his lungs with as much of the perfume as possible, and walking down the garden to plant it, all the time breathing in its glorious soothing smell. He had to imagine the feel of the cool earth as he created an area in which to plant his azalea. Now he had to try and focus the stress to flow out of his fingers as he pushed the earth back around the roots and base of the plant. Once he'd finished, he had to imagine sitting back on his heels, stretching his hands and arms up above his head, all the while breathing deeply and imagining the mixed heady scent of grass, flower, and earth. Now he had to 'walk' back up the garden and choose another flower, this time starting with 'B'.

"Bluebells," He continued to breathe deeply, holding it and then letting it go. He went through the planting process again. This time he could actually feel his shoulders drop as he finally started to relax.

"C? Carnations,"

His mind started the walk back up the garden but, by the time it came to thinking of a flower starting with 'D', he was asleep.

Chapter Three

Italy

Eduardo Di Santo walked back into the private hospital room, picked up the remote control from the bedside table to turn off the television in the corner, put it back down and returned to the seat beside his sister Sofia's bed. Today was her eighteenth birthday and she had spent most of it in tears. She'd rallied round when the Pete Wallace gig came on but now she was asleep, worn out from all her crying.

He looked at her as she slept and felt like weeping himself. She was so beautiful. Her long dark hair fell around her shoulders. Her long eyelashes rested upon cheeks that were as pale as snow and her full lips were no longer the deep rose pink they had once been. Sofia had been lying in her hospital bed for so long now the colour had slowly seeped from her cheeks and lips with each passing month. This did not, however, stop her from being a true Italian beauty. When she was awake, Sofia had the largest brown eyes. They had once sparkled with glee and mischief. Now they were dull and lifeless.

Eduardo knew he had to be strong for both his baby sister and his mother. As the man in the family, it was his place to support and care for them. Not that he'd cared for Sofia particularly well. If she hadn't disobeyed him that night, by sneaking out to go to the Pete Wallace concert, then she wouldn't be lying here in this hospital bed, broken and disabled. He'd refused her the right to go and, despite all her begging and pleading, he had not given in. The ten-year age difference meant he had the right to tell her what she could and could not do. But she'd refused to listen to him and, on the night of the concert, had collaborated with a friend to get her out of the house. The first he knew of her rebellious act was when his mother called him at work to say there had been a terrible accident.

Now it looked as though Sofia might never walk unaided again. The doctors and specialists had told them she was very fortunate to have regained the full use of her arms and upper body and the fact she had feeling in her legs was a promising sign. It had taken them almost three years, and goodness knows how many operations, to get this far. This, however, was of no consolation to a teenager who had been so energetic and sporty throughout her young life and who'd lived for dancing, swimming, gymnastics and ice-skating. Sofia had wanted to try everything, living her life like a whirlwind as she raced about soaking up all that life had to offer. She'd had no sense of fear and only ever saw the good in everyone she met and every venture she wanted to try.

Sofia had always been the ray of light and the sound of laughter in their home. Eduardo knew he was too serious and too brooding. He blamed this on the father who had walked out when his mother had fallen pregnant with Sofia, saying he'd never wanted one child tying him down, never mind two. Hearing his father say this had impacted on the young nine-year-old far more than his mother had ever realised. It wasn't until he'd walked out that the young Eduardo became aware that his father was one of life's takers – happy for his wife to look after him whilst he sat at home drinking all day. He had looked up to his father and idolised him, the way most boys do, just because he was his dad. Upon seeing the façade stripped away, he'd been left with a deep, burning, loathing inside him and he'd vowed that no-one would ever harm, or upset, his family like that again.

Rosa had struggled through the pregnancy alone, trying to hold down her early morning and late evening cleaning jobs along with her lunchtime waitressing role. As her pregnancy progressed, he had taken over the cleaning roles before and after school, in an attempt to help his mother as much as he could. When he saw how grateful she was for the help he gave her, he had silently promised he would never let his family down like his waste of space father had done. He would always be there to take care of them. For sixteen years, he'd believed he was keeping that promise but, the night Sofia had her accident, he knew a pain greater than he could have ever thought possible. He *had* let them down and, in the subsequent months and years since, his guilt had grown into an intense anger. He often struggled to contain it. He constantly wanted to roar at the top of his lungs, and hit something, anything, he didn't care what, as hard as he could and never stop. This anger, and sense of failure, had slowly consumed him to the point where he could no longer see past it. He had felt like this for over two years and had become so used to its presence within him – a big black, hard core of fury – that, were it to suddenly leave him, he knew he would be empty of any other emotions.

All of this anger he directed towards Pete Wallace. Both his mother and Sofia had told him it was not Wallace's fault that Sofia had been stupid enough to try and jump onto the stage but Eduardo closed his ears to them. He knew Wallace was to blame, totally and completely. He'd seen the videos of the rock star strutting around on stage wearing revealing clothing, flaunting himself, and letting young girls whip themselves up into adolescent frenzies. He'd watched his concerts and seen the way the rock-star flirted with the pretty ones, winking at them and blowing them kisses, making them think they were in with a chance of getting close to him. Young girls in their teenage years were easily excited and Wallace's behaviour was very irresponsible in the way he encouraged them. It was wrong. He was wrong. It had to be stopped before another pretty little girl ended up in hospital, her life over, in the same way his little Sofia's life was.

He'd met Pete Wallace once, the first time he'd visited Sofia after her accident. It had taken every ounce of his will-power and control that day to not punch

Wallace into the middle of the next century. Instead, he'd stood back and watched as he'd smarmed his way into the affections of Sofia and his mum, telling them not to worry about the future, no matter what, he would look out for them and do all that he could to help them through this. It was as though he was doing them some great favour. Well, he hadn't fooled him and he was going to ensure that, one day, Pete Wallace would know how it felt to lie in a hospital bed, wasting away to nothing, just like Sofia was doing now.

He looked at his watch – it was time to leave. He was a Senior Security Guard for a large, national, security firm and was on duty that night. He kissed Sofia lightly on her forehead, taking care not to waken her, and whispered, once again, that everything would be alright.

He was walking along the corridor and the thought of revenge came again. The idea had first sprung up when he'd seen Sofia during the first few hours after her accident. She'd looked so small, battered and bruised and they didn't know what the morning would bring. He knew it was normal for people to desire revenge on those who hurt their loved ones but this usually dissipated over time. In his case, however, it was growing stronger. So strong in fact, that he no longer tried to push the thought away when it came into his mind. He drove through the hospital gates, deep in thought as he ran through the myriad ways he could make Pete Wallace pay.

Chapter Four

When Sukie arrived in the offices of E.G.T. Ltd the next morning, the Pete Wallace concert was, unsurprisingly, the main topic of conversation. Well, for most of the ladies in the office anyway. It was Pete Wallace's first gig in nearly three years and the hype on most of the TV satellite channels, over the last three weeks, had been excessive so it was no wonder most people had watched it.

"Did you see it?" asked Elsa Clairmont, the Chairman and Finance Director's PA and Sukie's closest friend. She cornered her in the kitchen as she was making her mid-morning coffee.

"I gather by 'it' you mean the Pete Wallace gig?" she replied with a grin.

Elsa's passion for Pete Wallace was second only to her passion for keep-fit classes and large metal machines which were supposed to help maintain a tight and trim figure. In Sukie's mind, they were simply modern-day torture instruments which should be avoided at all costs but, under the guise of trying to keep up some degree of fitness, she suffered on them several times a week. Elsa, on the other hand, now lived most of her life around these things. Her excuse was that she needed to be in good shape for the day she met Pete Wallace. After all, with the bevy of beauties that constantly surrounded him, he would pay no attention to a fat little frump like herself, which is what she would be without all this hard work.

Sukie always laughed when Elsa said this. Elsa couldn't be a 'fat little frump' if she tried. She was a petite five-foot-two with the proverbial English-rose looks of flaxen blonde hair and startling sapphire blue eyes. She had the milkiest of skin and a sweet little rosebud mouth. Elsa went to great pains to maintain what God had so kindly given her. Her face and body creams were top of the range, her cosmetics the most expensive – any lipstick costing less than thirty pounds would never grace *her* lips. The clothes which covered the tightly honed body rarely lacked a designer label. And that included the Rigby and Peller underwear.

Sukie adored Elsa and considered her the sister she'd never had. This was made easier by Elsa also having the nicest – and most endearing – personality she had ever come across in another human being. Men met her and wanted to protect her. Most women hated her on sight. They would take one look at Elsa and their own jealousies – and insecurities – flared up, which they then blamed on her. When Elsa was in a pub or club, the men flocked to her side. Sukie, however, was not fazed by

21

this. She'd known Elsa from the tender age of seven when Elsa had had buck-teeth, braces and was the shape of dry spaghetti. They had been best friends forever – through their teeny-bop years of Take That and New Kids on the Block to the cool, affected, period of disdain towards anyone not into Radiohead, Pulp and the Pixies in their late teens. If anyone now could see the photographs of Elsa togged up in baggy jeans and sloppy jumpers – a la Happy Mondays – covered in mud at one of the wetter Glastonbury Festivals, they would never believe their eyes. Sukie had been with Elsa through all of her joys and all of her tears. From the joy of her wedding to her darling childhood sweetheart Harry, to her tears on the day she'd buried him five years later.

"Didn't he just look SOOOO sexy?" gushed Elsa. "I'll tell you now, Sukes, I would NOT kick that man out of my bed for eating ginger-nut cookies. No siree!"

"Is that so?" replied Sukie, smiling. "And just tell me where, exactly, in your house, would the poor fella find a packet of biscuits – ginger-nut or otherwise? You know, as well as I do, that if any food product has even sat on the same shelf as an item containing 'E' numbers it will find no place to rest in *your* shopping basket!"

"I'll have you know the local health shop does a lovely selection of naturally baked products, with no additives or GM ingredients which, may I add, happens to include some very tasty ginger nut biscuits!" sniffed Elsa, in mock umbrage.

"Really? Please do tell when you allowed one of these lucky cookies to enter the temple that is your mouth."

"Ok, ok, if you must know," Elsa laughed, "Mum was over for a visit last week and I picked up a packet for her. I confess I sneaked a crumb or two for a taste when she proclaimed them to be the nicest ginger biscuits she'd ever had. Now, stop changing the subject and get back to talking about Pete Wallace."

Sukie sipped her coffee as she thought back to the previous nights' gig. "Well, on the up side, I thought the gig was good, as far as pop gigs go. I quite liked some of the new songs and his voice does seem to be getting better as he gets older. On the down-side, however, I'm sure the first song was flat and his backing singers looked like they were there under duress."

"Oh trust you, Sukie McClaren, to find fault with things. He was brilliant."

"I'm not saying he wasn't good, Elsa, I'm simply saying there was some room for improvement. You know I don't go for him the same way you do. I like him enough to appreciate his talent but I'm also able to view him without bias."

"Well, I thought he was great!" said Elsa and poked her tongue out at her.

Sukie laughed and returned the gesture. Since the age of seven, they'd always ended their disagreements in this manner. Some things were never going to change.

"I'm glad you enjoyed it," she replied with a smile. "Were you able to sleep afterwards?"

"Eventually... After I'd imagined ravishing a certain Mr Wallace a few times!" retorted Elsa. She picked up her mug of coffee and walked out the kitchen, giving her a wink, a sassy grin and a wave as she left.

Sukie grinned back. It was two years since Harry had died and Elsa was still coming to terms with it. She continued to have trouble sleeping and it was not unusual for her to be wide awake at three in the morning, playing Solitaire on her computer. Therefore, if fantasising about Pete Wallace helped her to get a good night's sleep, then she was not going to be the one to put a downer on it. The very fact that Elsa could even think of another bloke – in a romantic or sexy way – was a huge step forward. Elsa's mother, Jean, worried that obsessing about Pete Wallace was her daughter's way of keeping the real world at bay and holding onto Harry, but Sukie kind of understood that this was Elsa's way of starting to let Harry go. Pete Wallace was a safe crush. She was taking tentative new steps towards fancying someone other than Harry but totally safe in the knowledge that nothing would ever come of it. She didn't feel as though she was betraying his memory. In time, Elsa would have to face up to taking that step back into the real world but, for now, seeing her smile again was enough to keep Sukie happy.

She watched her friend disappear into her office and turned away with a smile on her face. If Elsa was having a good day, then so was she.

The rays of sunlight creeping around the edge of the thick, floor-length, curtains pierced their way into Pete's brain as he slowly opened his eyes.

"Oh crap, not morning already!" he groaned.

He threw his forearm across his eyes to block out the light and lay for a few moments wishing that, just for once, he could have a sleep where he woke up feeling rested and refreshed. Instead, most days, he felt totally shattered. He rolled over onto his stomach, turning his head to the side. The clock on the bedside table blinked at him – 9.15 a.m. He knew he had to get up and get on with it. He'd woken up just after 4 a.m. to find himself sprawled over the bed, still fully dressed. He'd stripped off and gotten into bed but it had taken ages for him to fall asleep again. Now he could feel every minute he'd been awake. A meeting was scheduled for ten o'clock to discuss the press and media interviews for promoting his new album, and he could really do without it. This was the part he hated most about his career. He loved the creative aspect – writing music and working on lyrics gave him the biggest buzz, far more than any chemical he'd ever taken in those drug-ridden years – and he often wished the world would just leave him alone to write. He'd once floated the idea of someone else performing his work to the record company but that had gone down like the proverbial lead balloon. The record executives weren't fools and they knew that Pete Wallace – the voice AND the body – was the cash cow which would keep them in big bonuses and flash cars for many a year to come.

He groaned once more and turned onto his back, finding himself staring up at the antique tapestry on the canopy above him again. He was willing his body to catch up with his brain and find the energy to actually deal with the effort of getting out of bed. He deeply regretted the drug-fuelled roller coaster his life used to be.

It meant he was now too scared to take any form of sleeping tablet for fear that he may end up back on the ride which had caused him, and those he loved most dearly, so much heartache.

As he thought of his parents, he slipped into a light doze. His mind went back to some of the happier times in his life – the Christmas Day he had gotten his train set from Santa Claus. His dad helping him to set it all out while his mum cooked the turkey and cursed the two of them, happily, for getting under her feet as she was trying to set the table. The momentous occasion when his dad had taken him to his first ever football match – he'd been an Aston Villa fan ever since. He couldn't recall the opposition that day but he did remember the sound of the crowd roaring and cheering when the Villa had scored a goal. He was sure that was the day when he first got the buzz of how it feels to be a part of something so big. When the Holte-Enders sing their approval of their team on the pitch, it really takes some beating. His slumbering lips turned slightly upwards as he recalled his mother's gentle bullying as she'd measured up Buzz, Ed, Danny and himself for their first stage outfits when they'd performed at the school disco. She'd spent several nights cutting and sewing those suits so the band would look good for their first proper gig. His small smile slipped away as his sub-conscious prodded him awake with the realisation that she wouldn't have been so enthusiastic if she'd known where her hard work would take them.

A knock at the door startled him back to the present.

"Pete? It's Jordie. Are you awake?"

"Yeah, c'mon in."

Jordie walked into the room with a tray in his hands. "Sal made up some coffee for you. She did it extra strong to get you going. She also sent up some fresh warm croissants even though she knows you won't eat first thing in the morning."

Pete grimaced. "Your Sal is determined to try and fatten me up."

"Well mate, if you will insist on having the body of a whippet what can you expect." Jordie walked over to the bed and handed him a mug of coffee.

"Thanks." He took the mug and inhaled the rich smell before taking a sip and savouring the warmth as it flowed down into him. Nothing could beat that first mouthful of caffeine in the morning. He let out a sigh as he leaned back into his pillows. "I've told her I take after my dad. He was a rake of a man his whole life. You know that. The upside of having his genes is that I can eat like a horse and not put on an ounce. The downside is that two pints of beer leave me legless."

"Is that so? Can't say I'd noticed," Jordie replied, sarcastically. "It's not like I've *ever* had to carry you upstairs to your room because you've sniffed a wine cork or two! Anyway, less reminiscing of fun times, you need to get a move on. Kara's already downstairs. There's quite a busy schedule to get through. The joys of being the golden boy, mate, everyone wants a piece of you!"

"Tell me about it!" Pete grumbled, as he threw back the quilt and stomped across the hardwood floor towards the en-suite bathroom. "Fuckin' tell me about it!"

Chapter Five

Jordie had taken a deep breath, before he'd knocked on Pete's bedroom door. There was never any way of knowing what mood Pete would greet the day with. With a morning meeting scheduled to discuss the publicity for the new album and upcoming tour, he suspected that Pete's frame of mind would not be a sunny one. He'd need to tread carefully, otherwise Pete would go into one of his super-sulks and that would be no use at all when trying to diarise his movements for the next few months.

Walking on eggshells around people did not come naturally to Jordie. He originated from Newcastle-upon-Tyne and the natives there were known for speaking their minds and not pussy-footing about. His mother had had a tongue sharper than any swordsman's rapier and, when his father had suggested she may want to curb it a bit – usually after a run-in with yet another neighbour – she would always reply, "Just saying it as I see it, pet. Just saying it as I see it!"

His mother was a vibrant, loud, happy woman but most of the folks around them knew to keep on the right side of her as her temper was legendary. On the other hand, his mild-mannered father, John, strived hard to keep the peace between his beloved Mags and the surrounding neighbourhood. There had been many surprised faces when Mags and John had first gotten together as a couple. People were further surprised when they'd married and had been amazed to see the marriage flourish. Like most couples, they had their moments but John was not a push-over and stood up to Mags when he felt it was needed. She respected him for this and loved him all the more as a result. Their differences had made them stronger together.

Jordie had been christened David Arthur Ray and, growing up, he'd always known when he was in trouble as his mam would call him by his full name before she walloped him for whatever mischief he'd been caught doing. In his eyes, he'd had a normal childhood – he was well fed, decently dressed, totally loved and, quite often, well disciplined. He hailed from the Scotswood Road area of Newcastle. Terraced streets where everyone knew everyone else and a strong sense of community had prevailed. His father had been a foreman in the nearby Armstrong's factory and his mother had stayed at home, doing her best to keep their small, terraced home in some semblance of order. Not an easy task when she had to share it with three blokes. Well, one bloke – his dad – and her two sons.

His brother, Daniel, was eighteen months older than

him. A fact Daniel often cited when he and Jordie had fought over some toy or another. Daniel always thought that, as he was the eldest, he had first call on any of their toys, even if Jordie had been playing with it first. As Daniel was a 'bit of a bruiser', to use some local parlance, Jordie had learned quickly that fighting back was a useless exercise. If he did, he'd come away with either a fat lip or a black eye and no toy. Not fighting back meant he only came away without the toy. He had been small as a child so the odds of him winning were stacked against him. There'd been no point in making matters worse by trying to defend himself.

As he'd grown older, Jordie had never had the moment where his mam had promised he would 'suddenly shoot up like a beanpole'. His growth had stopped at five feet and eight inches, putting him at the low end of the average height scale. He'd also inherited his mother's temper which meant any comments on his height usually saw the offender staggering away, clutching whichever body part Jordie's fist had come into contact with. At the age of twelve, when he'd been allowed to roam further away from home, he had discovered a boxing club a few streets away. He'd joined up and went on to become their champion boxer. He learnt to channel his temper away from his head and into his fists. His height became his advantage over larger opponents and his resentment over his lack of inches diminished.

He'd left school at seventeen. His education had been average and he'd been an average student so, like most of the boys in the area, it was expected he would join Armstrong's on his eighteenth birthday. With his father being a foreman, it was understood by most that this was the path his life would take.

Jordie, however, had had other ideas. On his eighteenth birthday, he went to the post office and withdrew all the boxing winnings his father had so carefully put away for him over the years. He went home, packed a suitcase and informed his parents it was a big world out there and he planned to see it. He understood his father's chosen path in life but it was not one he could share with him. He had to find his own way in the world and moving away from his home city was the first step he needed to take. He shook his dad's hand firmly, gave his mam the tightest of hugs and stepped out the front door. Daniel and he had never been close as children and had grown further apart as the years had passed. Not seeing him to say goodbye hadn't bothered Jordie in the slightest.

He'd travelled to Birmingham and had looked up the brother of an old classmate. Gary worked on the music circuit and figured he could get him some roadie work. It was a hard life and a hard slog – different towns every other night, first putting together, and then dismantling, the amps, the lighting rigs and the band's gear. But, it got him around the country for free and he was often able to spend a couple of hours looking around their latest location before it was time to move on. It was on his first tour when he'd stopped being David and had become Geordie. Nicknames were the thing, when you were out on the road, and this one had stuck. One night, however, when a large order for fish and chips was being passed around, he noticed that someone had spelt his name Jordie. He'd instantly preferred this alternative version and had been Jordie, 'with a J', ever since.

He'd met Andrew Wallace, Pete's dad, on the night of the European Cup match in 1982. The band he was working for had a gig booked in Birmingham that night. Andrew was watching the game in the front bar as Jordie had been setting up in the back room for the gig later that night. After the sound-check, the band and crew had wandered through to see how the game was going. Andrew was ordering drinks at the bar at the time and had begun chatting to him. Over the next couple of hours, they'd become friends and Jordie would often look him up whenever he was in the city. Andrew had always said, afterwards, that May the 26th 1982 was the best night of his life as, not only had his beloved football team just won one of the biggest trophies in the game, but it was also when he'd met the two people most important to him – his best friend Jordie and his future wife Katya.

A few years after this, he jacked in the roadie work. It had served a purpose. He'd taken charge of a bar in Birmingham and had worked hard to make it the number one, must-go-to venue in the city for new, up-and-coming, bands. His friendship with Andrew and Katya was firmly established and he was a god-parent to their children.

When Pete's schoolboy band had suddenly begun to make a name for themselves, and had started going places, Jordie's experience, and knowledge of the music industry, made him the perfect choice to be their mentor and then later, their manager. This long-standing relationship also meant he'd stuck with Pete, and helped him carve out his successful solo career when the band had, eventually, gone their separate ways.

These days, however, he was becoming weary of this way of life. He'd been in the business for over thirty-five years and he was now feeling tired of it all. He hadn't said anything to Pete; he would wait to see how he felt once this next tour was over. There was no point in upsetting the apple cart just yet.

Chapter Six

"Oh, for crying out loud!" exclaimed Sukie, as she went through the figures on the email she was reading. "When will Sales get it into their thick heads that the accounts department sets firm rules and procedures for a bloody good reason?"

The girls in the office next door heard her loud comments and wondered who would be getting it in the neck today. As their supervisor, Sukie was great. Helpful if they had a problem, understanding when their personal life made work difficult, but an absolute nightmare if you made stupid mistakes. On this occasion, they could smile, it sounded like someone in the Sales department was about to be on the end of a 'Sukie Special'.

She let out a huge sigh and carried on reading, gritting her teeth in despair and anger as she did so. Time and time again the sales boys would promise their new clients extended payment terms while quoting them the lowest prices possible in order to win the business. She was sick to the back teeth of telling them they must stick to their standard payment terms and stop giving the company profits away. Not that they ever listened, of course. They were too busy thinking about their year-end bonuses. What a pity they were also too thick to realise that all their 'wheeling and dealing' meant their bonuses were a lot less than they could be. Now she had a client informing her they would only be paying a fraction of the amount she had been expecting as Andrew Hollings had told them they could have selective payment terms.

Thank goodness this month is not year-end, she thought, there's still time to get it sorted out. With the best part of fifty thousand pounds not being paid, she was grateful for this fact but you wouldn't have known it from the tone of the email she proceeded to send to Andrew Hollings, his boss Carol and her own boss William. "That feels better," she muttered aloud, as she hit the 'send' button. "Nothing like a little bit of spleen-venting to clear a girl's head."

She jumped when her phone rang, the noise startling her out of her thoughts.

"Good morning, Accounts," she answered. "Oh, hi there William, how are you today?"

Sukie was fond of her boss, William O'Docherty, and had a good working relationship with him. He understood the way she worked and had enough respect for her ability to allow her to get on with the job without breathing down her neck.

"Of course you can see me in your office," she grinned into the receiver. "You are the boss after all."

She put the phone down, and saving the worksheet she was working on, pondered on why William wanted to see her. She knew the email she'd sent had been quite strongly worded but she was sure she'd managed to avoid being abusive in it, although, that had been a test of her willpower. She set her phone to Do-Not-Disturb, walked along to William's office and went in, closing the door behind her.

"Hiya Sukes," said William "please grab a seat. I've just read your email regarding Solid Safety's payment terms. Like you, I am not happy about this at all but it has helped me to make my mind up on an issue I've been mulling over for the past couple of hours."

"Would it involve Andrew Hollings, myself and us both being locked in a torture chamber for several hours by any chance?" she asked hopefully.

William laughed. "Well that could depend upon your interpretation of it. It certainly does involve you having Andrew Hollings all to yourself for a few days. He may even consider himself tortured by the end of them."

She leant forward. "Tell me more, my pretty!" she leered, whilst assuming her best Wicked Witch of the West voice. "You have me intrigued."

William laughed again. "You know, Sukie McClaren, you can be very evil when you put your mind to it."

"Well, I do my best. It's what gets me through the day. Now, will you please spill the beans on how I get to make Hopeless Hollings' life as miserable as he makes mine!"

"How good is your German?"

"Very basic," she replied. "Why?"

"Hollings was in Salzburg ten days ago. He's managed to get in the door of Monchsberg GMBH. They just so happen to be in the European Top Ten of large, and rather profitable, businesses."

"Wow! That's brilliant. I wonder if they took their company name from the mountain just outside Salzburg..." she mused.

"Trust you to know that!" William rolled his eyes.

"I have a poster of it on my office wall so of course I'm going to know about it!"

"Well, I believe they probably did as their company logo is a snow-capped mountain. Anyway," William continued, "getting their business would be a massive coup for E.G.T, both in monetary and commercial PR value."

"It sure would. So why am I here? I know it'll be my account to look after, if we get it sewn up, but why are we discussing it now?"

"Hollings received a phone call yesterday from the CEO at Monchsberg. They were impressed with his presentation so did a bit of further research into the company, and the feedback they received, from our other European clients, was very favourable. The result is they want him to go back to discuss details such as quantities and rates, admin support and terms of payment. The potential here is massive! We would really like him to return with a signed contract in his briefcase. That would be a perfect end to the year." William paused for a moment. "I'm trying to come up with a diplomatic way of phrasing my next comment but I know that you'll cut to the bones any attempt I make to be 'nice', so I'm just going to be blunt. There is the potential for it all to go tits up. As much as I like Hollings, I simply do not trust him to get us the most favourable deal. I'm worried he'll allow them to call the shots on payment terms which could be very detrimental to our cash-flow. An account as big as this, will mean a lot of money going out before we see it coming back in again. We need to be sure he doesn't end up crippling us and our cash flow. So, I've decided I'm sending you out to Salzburg with him."

Sukie stared at William, unable to believe what she was hearing. Usually, on big accounts like this, it would be the FD himself attending, not his Credit Control Supervisor.

"Okay," she replied slowly, as she tried to think on how best to respond. "Firstly... WOW! And, secondly, why? It is rather unprecedented is it not?"

"We've got the pre-Year End Board Meeting next week which means I have to be here," her boss explained. "Sukie, if we get this contract we could be looking at their invoice values being over a hundred thousand pounds a week. I need to be sure Hollings doesn't tell Monschberg they only have to make payments in any year divisible by six or something equally absurd. I also need to ensure he doesn't slash our rates so low we won't even cover the administration costs a client this large will incur. Hollings may well be able to sell snow to the Eskimos but he hasn't quite picked up on the fact we can't offer everything for nothing. The company needs you to be there as a form of protection."

William leant back in his chair, picked up his pen

from the desk and fiddled with it as he carried on speaking. "Also, it will be good experience for you to see how these meetings work. As you know, I'm keen for you to take sole charge of the A-Grade accounts. This would likely be the first of many such meetings. The larger clients require a more bespoke service and you'll need to attend to make sure that, from an admin and accounting point of view, we can give them what they want without it being detrimental to the company."

Sukie understood William's concerns. Andrew Hollings was decent enough but he was a salesman through and through. This meant he was hopelessly incapable of understanding the concept of business accounting and the importance of sticking to payment terms. It was no surprise that his nickname, in the Accounts department, was Hopeless Hollings.

"Okay, you're on," she smiled. "I've always wanted to visit Salzburg. It looks so beautiful. Now, I'll finally get the chance to see it for myself."

"You won't get to do much sight-seeing I'm afraid," William informed her. "Monchsberg are located on some industrial estate on the outskirts of the city. Industrial-sized plastic sheeting companies take up rather a lot of space and that wouldn't really work in the town centre."

"Oh!" She suddenly felt deflated. For a moment there she had gotten excited at the thought of finally seeing this stunning city for herself. "So, when are we due to go and for how long?" she asked.

"You'll fly out Monday morning and return Wednesday afternoon or early evening," William informed her.

"Okay!" She stopped to think for a moment, did a quick calculation in her head and realised she had enough holiday left to tack on a couple of extra days to the trip.

"Has Elsa booked the tickets and the hotel yet?"

"No, I had to speak with you first before I could authorise her to do so."

"Oh good!" She smiled again. "Please could you ask her to make my booking on this Saturday's evening flight and returning next Sunday?"

William's look of puzzlement at her request was short-lived as it dawned on him what her plan was. "I get it. You're working on getting a holiday out of this aren't you?"

She gave him her sweetest smile. "I'm sure you won't mind signing off a couple of holiday days for me now, would you? Especially as I'll be babysitting Hopeless for three days... It's the very least you can do to make it up to me." She added some comic-effect, exaggerated, eye lash battings for good measure.

William laughed. "You drive a hard bargain Sukie McClaren. Oh, go on then! As you do give more than most for the benefit of this company, it will be my pleasure to assist you with this one." He smiled at her. "Fill your holiday form in and I'll sign it off. Speak to Elsa to discuss your requirements."

The smile slipped from his face as he became serious again. "Promise me you'll be tough and focused with Hopeless next week. I suggest you call me every evening with a progress report and we can discuss any tactics if things are looking a bit sticky."

"Thank you, William. You're a star and I really

appreciate it. I won't let you, or the company, down."

"I know you won't Sukie, that's why I asked you. Good luck and have fun."

"Oh, *that* is a given! Thank you again." Sukie beamed another smile in his direction as she walked out of the office.

"I'm off to Salzburg, I'm off to Salzburg!" Sukie couldn't help squealing as she dived in the door of Elsa's office. When she saw Elsa was on the phone, she stopped short and held her hands to her mouth to convey she would be quiet.

"Hmmm, yes, I've got that." Elsa scribbled on the pad in front of her as the voice on the other end spoke. "Uh-huh. Yes. That is correct. Absolutely, I can make sure that happens. Ok, thank you. Goodbye." Elsa put the handset down and turned to look at her. "Yes dear, I know you're off to Salzburg," she replied dryly, attempting to quieten her down before the MD came stalking out of his office.

Shocked at Elsa's reply, she stopped pacing about the office and looked at her. "How do you know? I've only just found out myself a few minutes ago."

Elsa pointed to her phone. "It was William on the phone when you walked in. He'd already informed me earlier there would be a business trip to Austria. He called to confirm the details when you left his office. He told me that I'm to make any arrangements you request and ALL costs are to be charged to the company."

"No, only flight costs and two hotel nights are to be charged to the company," Sukie clarified. "All additional hotel nights will be personal holiday so I'll be paying for those. It makes no difference, however, to the company what days I fly out."

"No can do on that score, girlfriend," Elsa smirked, as she typed on her computer keyboard. "William O'Docherty, Financial Director of E.G.T Ltd, has informed me – in no uncertain terms might I add – that you are to be booked into the best hotel Salzburg has to offer, for as many extra nights as you require and all charges will be met by the company. He also told me, to tell you, to consider this a thank you, from the firm, for all the hard work, overtime and loyalty you have given to E.G.T. He said he reckoned this was a lot cheaper than having you put in an expense claim for all those extra hours of overtime you've worked over the years and never claimed back."

She sank down onto the chair in front of Elsa's desk. "You are joking me?" she stammered, shocked at Elsa's words but also really touched that William thought highly enough of her, as an employee, to do this for her.

"'Fraid not, honey!" Elsa looked away from her computer screen and smiled across at Sukie. "I'm already looking through all the five-star hotels that Salzburg has to offer and, I have to say, there are some good ones. I was especially pleased to see that the Riley Group have recently opened a new one right in the city centre on..." She glanced back at her screen. "Mirabellplatz?"

Sukie smiled back at her. "That's right, Mirabellplatz. The Mirabell Palace is there. That's where they filmed part of the 'Doh-Ray-Me' sequence in The Sound of Music. Unfortunately the steps are now closed to the public due to the amount of people who have visited them over the years—" She stopped when she saw the pained look on Elsa's face.

"Elsa? Are you ok? Did I say something to upset you?" she asked, suddenly concerned.

"Nooooooo!" groaned Elsa "Yeeesss! I've just heard you going on about Austria, Salzburg and The Sound of Music for so many years now, and as delighted as I am that you're finally getting a chance to visit, it's really not doing it for me. I can manage without the Sukie McClaren Guided Tour."

Sukie burst out laughing. "Hey! I thought that was the deal! You get to witter endlessly on about that pathetic boy-band 'The Astons' and their now-ex lead singer, Pete Wallace, whilst I get to do likewise with all things Sound of Music and Austria. Are you reneging on this arrangement?"

Elsa pulled a face. "No. I'm just trying to delay the inevitable hours of boredom I know I'll be facing when you return. Please can we put it off until you get back?"

"No problem my little furry friend, I can wait until then if you can!" She was too excited to be upset at Elsa's words

"Oh, trust me, I can wait!" grinned Elsa. "And talking of 'furry friends', may I assume that you'll want me to feed yours while you're away?"

"If you wouldn't mind, Tony, Adam, and myself, would be very grateful."

Whenever Sukie's name was mentioned in the office, three things usually came into people's minds. Firstly, her sharp, and sometimes quite lethal, tongue which could cut a man, or woman, at a hundred paces. Secondly, her complete adoration for her two cats Tony and Adam, and thirdly, her obsession with The Sound of Music – and all things Salzburg / Austria related. She had some prints of the stunning Austrian countryside up on the wall of her office, and had, twice, organised (or bullied, depending on your viewpoint) a coach trip from the office, into the city, to see the Sing-a-Long stage show. Complete with dress-up, of course!

"Feeding the two men in your life will be no problem," remarked Elsa. "You know I adore them nearly as much as you do and it will be great to hang with them for a bit. Shall I do the usual and stay at yours a couple of times, to avoid the place looking empty?"

"Oh, yes please, if it's no problem for you to do so." As she spoke, Sukie walked around the desk and gave Elsa a big hug. "Thank you, Elsa. I know I tell you plenty anyway, but I'm going to tell you again, that you really are *the* best-est friend I could ever have and I adore you like a sister."

Elsa hugged her back just as hard. "Right, let's get on with sorting out this hotel and your flights. I only want the best for my chum!"

Sukie peered at Elsa's computer screen and proceeded to discuss with her the merits of each five-star Salzburg residence.

Chapter Seven

Pete stood staring out of the window wishing this was all over. Small snow flurries were gently falling outside. Today was the last day of November – St Andrew's Day. Had he still been alive, his father would have been out buying his haggis for the evening meal. He leaned his forehead against the cool window pane. "I'm so sorry, Dad, so, so sorry."

It was six years since his parents had both died in a road accident and he still missed them terribly. He wanted to get away from Kara and Jordie and just be on his own. He had a tune floating around in his head, which was so in keeping with how he was feeling right now, and he badly wanted to get it written down before he lost it. When he got a melody on the brain, it made dealing with other things in life very difficult because he had to keep playing the sound over and over in his mind until he had the chance to write it down and make it into something solid. Until then, it would be like a fine Scottish mist – difficult to grab and keep and easy to slip away into nothing.

"Do you want another coffee, Pete?" asked Jordie from the other side of the room where he was filling up his and Kara's mugs.

"No thanks," he replied, walking away from the window and back over to the sofa.

They were sitting in the lounge, in front of the roaring fire. He preferred to do his mundane administration business in here as it was more relaxed. He sat back down, across the table from Kara, his secretary and Girl Friday. She managed his life almost to perfection. He trusted her to always look out for his better interests and she had done very well so far. He looked at her and pulled a silly face – anything to break up the monotony of this meeting. She smiled and made a silly one back at him.

When Jordie returned and placed the mugs of drinks down on the coffee table in front of them, Kara immediately returned to business.

"Right," she said, "we've got the FHM photo shoot sorted, the GQ interview has been whittled down to three possible dates, the High-Hitting journalist, with her wardrobe team, are happy with any date you'll give them and it's been agreed that a freelance writer can shadow you for one week during the tour, with the objective of getting a view of your life on the road. We understand that the written piece will be offered to specific music editors within the music media after we've approved it."

"Good," said Jordie. "Was there any quibble

regarding our right to approve?"

"No, Graeme Collins was fine about it," Kara replied.

"What about local press and radio interviews while we're on tour?" asked Pete.

"I'm collating all the requests as they come in. The plan is to review them approximately one week prior to each venue and inform everybody of the outcome no less than four days before the requested interviews." Kara looked up from her notes and smiled at Jordie and Pete. "This way, we can monitor how things are going with the tour, how many, or how few, interviews you feel up to doing and if there are any you may want to avoid at any given time. It gives us better press control over any incidents that may occur."

"I take it you have the stage diving incident in mind from our last foray into the jungle?" said Jordie, in his usual droll tone.

Pete looked over at him. He knew Jordie loved both the excitement and the buzz that went with touring but he loathed the frenzy which seemed to accompany Pete everywhere he went. From hysterical fans to the circling vultures of the world media, they were always on his back. Sometimes, Jordie had said once, he wished they were back in the early days when they'd been lucky to get a three-line review in the local rag. They may not have had such luxurious facilities like changing rooms, or a proper tour bus, but there was a lot to be said for the fun and camaraderie that developed when four lads were trying to change in a solitary toilet cubicle, or sleep in a mini-van while he drove through the night taking them to the next gig.

"Yes, I do," replied Kara. "Fan-related incidents will always incite the press pack into writing negative material. We know who will rewrite your interviews to create their own spin and we know who we can trust to give a truthful account."

"I still can't believe Sofia thought she could jump from the front row seating area onto the side of the stage. That gap must have been at least ten feet wide and the drop the best part of fifteen feet," said Pete.

Jordie grimaced. "Well, she'd done gymnastics in her younger years. She obviously thought she had the ability to cover that sort of distance. It's amazing what a couple of alcopops can do to the mind."

"How is she getting on?" Pete looked at Kara. "Have we had a progress report recently?"

"Yes," responded Kara. She shuffled through her paperwork till she found the latest feedback from the Italian hospital. She picked it up and, reading aloud, said "Sofia's back and pelvis have healed and she's started her physiotherapy. It's early days but things are looking hopeful. There's feeling and sensation in all limbs and it's now a case of building up the muscles and getting the body used to movement again. After that, though, it will depend on how much weight and strain the pelvic area can handle. Because the pelvis was shattered in the fall, and is now pretty much held together with pins, it may not be able to give adequate support for her to walk again without the use of walking sticks or a frame. The next six to nine months are going to be critical. There have, however, been whispers of some new techniques currently being developed and her doctor, Dr Manto, advises he is regularly checking to see what new procedures he may be able to work with."

"I see," said Pete. "I'm glad she's done well so far. Let's just hope it continues to stay that way. I don't know how I'd be able to deal with it if she's badly disabled."

"She's done so well because of all the specialist care she's had. Care that you've paid for," stated Jordie grimly. "You didn't tell her to jump from a fifteen-foot high seating rig. She made that decision herself. Sofia should be grateful to you for helping out with her medical costs. I'm sure she would have been just as well looked after on the insurance pay-outs. You didn't have to foot the bills, you know, as I have told you many times since."

"I know, I know," he sighed, "but I had to do something. The insurance would only have paid for basic medical assistance. With all the care she needed, the least I could do was ensure she was settled in a comfortable and friendly environment. She's a young girl who made a bad judgement call. We've all been there. There was no way I could just walk away from her. Besides which, my fault or not, the press would have found some way of blaming me." He looked over to Kara. "Can we fit in a visit to her while we're on the road?"

"It should be possible." She looked at the tour schedule. "You're booked to perform in Verona at the end of June, the last Saturday night to be exact. I was going to suggest we arrive there a few days early – maybe Tuesday or Wednesday – to allow the crew to have a few days off. It should be easy enough to arrange a visit to see her. Do you want it to be a private or public visit?"

"Private," replied Pete, "definitely private! I don't want to give the press any reason for dragging the whole thing up again and perhaps causing trouble on this tour. We also don't want other young girls thinking it's a good way of getting to meet me."

"Good call." Kara made some notes on her schedule list.

"Are we finished now?" Pete sighed, feeling as though he was close to losing it.

"Just about, only one last item to discuss." Kara picked up a letter and handed it to Pete.

"We've received a letter from The Riley Group hotel chain, informing us that their latest hotel has recently been opened in Salzburg. It's called the 'Riley Mirabell' and is situated on Mirabellplatz, right in the heart of the city."

She opened the hotel brochure which had accompanied the letter. "It's being marketed as 'a five-star, exclusive establishment merging old Austrian style with modern-day convenience.'" she quoted. "All bedrooms have the usual stuff – bathroom, Jacuzzi bath, mini-bar etc. They also have a traditional ballroom, with a maximum capacity of twelve hundred, along with several conference facilities which can be altered to suit any number from five people to seven hundred. The piece de resistance would appear to be the Roof Terrace bar 'with stunning views of the Salzburg rooftops, the Festung Hohensalzburg and the mountains that surround this beautiful city'."

Kara put the brochure back on the table. "They've written to us because they are our primary hotel chain whenever you're touring or require rooms. They'd like to offer you full use of their facilities, for one week, as a complementary thank you for your loyal custom over the years. Clearly, the hope is that you'll be impressed enough to stay there whenever you're flying in or out of Salzburg, or for having press meetings and interviews which will, in turn, generate lots of free publicity for them."

"The Riley Mira," chuckled Pete, "there's a name to remember easily enough. I suppose it would be handy to have somewhere close to the airport to stop over. The drive from Salzburg, to here, can sometimes be a bit too much when I've had a busy few days. It would also be more convenient to stay the night before an early flight."

He thought for a few moments, a plan formulating in his head. "Tell you what, Kara, get in touch with High-Hitting, GQ and FHM. See if you can talk them into coming to Austria for the interviews they want. If they'll do it, call the Riley Group to accept their offer, book us in and tell them we'll use their facilities for the photo-shoots and interviews which should generate some excellent publicity for them. I'm sure they'll be happy with that. And if they have spa facilities, set me up for some good massages. Try, if you can, to arrange it to be sooner rather than later. I want to get it over and done with."

"I'm already on the case, boss!" Kara chirruped, as she gathered together her files. "I do like it when you're decisive. It makes my job much easier. Off the top of my head, I think I can re-arrange the diary for the next few weeks without too much trouble."

"Right, I've had enough!" He stood up. "I'm off to

do my real job. Making music! See you guys later."

He left Jordie and Kara to discuss his suggestion further and walked through the vast hallway towards the room he called his Little Studio. It was actually the library but Pete felt this room had a special atmosphere and he always had a sense of being comforted when he was in there. He'd tried to explain this to Jordie, more than once, but Jordie didn't get it. He would look at Pete as though he was mad and ask him if he'd been drinking again.

He walked in, closed the door behind him and immediatcly felt himself being enveloped in the soothing atmosphere. He wasn't sure what made this room more special than any of the others in this beautiful old building he called home. Maybe it was all the books on the floor-to-ceiling, hand-carved, solid wood bookcases, which ran around three of the four walls. Pete loved words. He thought they were fascinating, and writing lyrics was the part of his music creating which he relished the most. More than once, when he was struggling for ideas or had ground to a halt in the middle of writing a song, he'd gone to the bookcases and picked a few random books from the shelves. Invariably, after flicking through them for a short time, he would find the inspiration he'd been seeking to get the job completed. He enjoyed reading and had added a great number of books to the shelves himself when he'd moved in. Most of the books, however, had come with the house when he'd inherited it and, therefore, were in German. He was still working on learning the language but couldn't really concentrate for any length of time to get a firm knowledge of it.

The original plan had been to employ a local Austrian housekeeper, who would have been instructed to speak German to him, most of the time, in the hope he'd pick it up that way. But that idea went in the bin just a few days after he'd finally made the Schloss his permanent residence. Sally, Jordie's sister-in-law, had finally left her wife-beating husband – Daniel had been as much of a bully in adulthood as he'd been as a child – and needed somewhere to stay. Jordie cared about Sally and had always felt she was far too good for his maniac brother. Knowing how possessive Daniel was over everything – people and material things – Jordie had felt it would be better for Sally to put some distance between them both.

He'd asked if she could come to Austria with them in the capacity of a live-in housekeeper for a short time. "Just until she gets herself sorted out and back on her feet, you know," Jordie had said.

Pete had agreed and now, three years later, she was just another member of his 'family'. In retrospect, it had worked out very well. The first year of Sally's 'employment' was the same year he had kicked his narcotics habit into touch for good. Sal had looked after him as he went through the differing stages of withdrawal. She'd cleaned up behind him when he would lose his temper over silly, irrational things and wreak havoc around the Schloss. She'd cooked for him when he'd had the munchies in the middle of the night, and she'd held him in her arms when he'd cried heavy tears of self-hatred and recrimination when he realised just what he had done do to his family, and the pain his selfish actions had caused to those he loved and cared for the most. As far as he was concerned, Sally had a home, in his home, for life.

He also had peace of mind when he had to go off and do all the various things his career required, knowing his home was being left in the safest possible hands. Sal cared for the place as though it was her own. She was also madly attached to his two dogs – Oscar and Bosie – and they were equally attached to her. His boys were stunningly beautiful Siberian Huskies. Both were almost pure white with the exception of two little black splodges on each. Oscar had a little black tip on each ear and Bosie boasted a pair of 'black socks' on his front paws. They'd been named after the great Oscar Wilde and the young man he'd been so madly in love with – Lord Alfred Douglas, otherwise known as Bosie. This was his salute to the man who was his most favoured wordsmith. These two pampered beasts were now lying sound asleep on the rug in front of the roaring fire. This was possibly the second reason why he was so fond of this room – it had a vast cavern of a fireplace that, when lit, gave the room a wonderful cosy feeling. This was actually quite an achievement when said room was over twelve feet high and nearly seventy feet square.

He walked over to the corner where some of his equipment was stashed – microphones, stands, guitars and recording equipment. He had a proper, full-blown, fully sound-proofed recording studio downstairs in the basement and it was there that a song was laid down once it had been fully composed and completed. Here in the library, however, was where he worked on tunes and lyrics until they became finished articles. He picked up his acoustic guitar, walked over to sit in his favourite winged chair near the fireplace and positioned the guitar on his knee. He leaned over it and started picking out the melody which had been running riot in his head for the last two hours.

Pete heard a noise and twisted round. Sally had placed a tray on a nearby table and was busying herself with it. She appeared to have a few tears glistening on her face.

"Hey Sal, what's wrong?" he asked, putting down the guitar and moving over to her. He put his arms around her and held her gently.

"Oh, nothing is wrong," she sniffed against his shoulder, rummaging in her pocket for a tissue. "I'm just being silly. I knocked on the door but you didn't hear me so I came in quietly to leave this for you." She pointed towards the tray which had a sandwich and a coffee mug on it. "You were completely engrossed in the music you were playing. It was so beautiful and haunting that I stopped for a listen. It was actually quite sad and it moved me to tears." She grinned up at him. "It's normally the sound of your singing that does that!"

"Cheeky mare!" He smiled back at her and gave her shoulders a gentle squeeze before stepping away.

"I see you were affected by it too," Sal said.

He frowned. "What do you mean?"

"You've also been crying."

He went to the mirror over the fireplace and saw his

face was wet. He had, indeed, been shedding tears as he'd played.

"I'm guessing you're still working on it?" said Sally.

He rubbed his face with the sleeve of his sweatshirt. "Yes, it only came to me today so it's still fresh."

"Well, I look forward to hearing it when it's finished. Although… I may need a box of tissues to hand when I do."

"We'll see how it goes. By the way, Sal, what time is it?" He'd just realised the room was almost in darkness and, despite the large arched windows which overlooked the lake and mountains, there was almost no daylight left. He began switching on some lamps.

"It's after three o'clock. That's why I brought in the tray. I knew you hadn't eaten anything today." Sally moved towards the windows and closed the long, thick curtains. "Kara also asked me to pass on that she has an update on Salzburg for you when you're ready."

He had been lost in his thoughts, and his music, for over three hours.

"Thanks Sal. Could you do me a favour please and tell Kara I'll be out to see her shortly."

"Will do!"

Sally left the room and closed the door quietly behind her. He sat back down in his chair and stared into the fire. Would this empty, hollow ache in his soul ever go away? Six years on, he was very much beginning to doubt it.

Chapter Eight

Sukie looked up at the departures board again. Her flight was still delayed by half an hour thanks to heavy snow in Salzburg. Not that the thought of snow was upsetting her in any way. Not a chance! If anything, it only served to make her more excited. She loved snow and was delighted to think she would see the city of her dreams all shining and white. She pulled out her mobile phone and sent both her mum and Elsa a quick text to let them know about the delay. The two of them would only panic if they didn't hear from her within ten minutes of the plane landing.

She thought back to the call she'd had with her mother the night before, as she packed. She'd been looking at the bomb-site that was her bedroom, with the phone between her shoulder and chin, talking to her mum while sorting out what clothes to take on her trip. Every item of clothing she possessed was either on the chair (definitely going), on the bed (possibly), or on the floor (time for a trip to the charity shop). She was so excited she'd felt like running around the house squealing. But, out of consideration to her neighbours, she'd managed to refrain from doing so. Sukie had cleared it with Jenny upstairs that she would feed the cats in the mornings and evenings when Elsa didn't stay over. Jenny was also happy to stay for an hour or so, at night, to give them an affection fix and playtime.

Sukie had filled her mum in on all that had happened and the two of them had laughed as she'd told her of the mock-battle she'd had with Elsa, when her friend had tried to book her a penthouse suite. Trying to explain that one away to Hopeless Hollings would have been fun. Naturally, the full details of her trip were to be kept under wraps and so, as far as the rest of the staff were concerned, Sukie would be paying for the extra six nights' accommodation herself and she sure didn't earn enough to stay in a penthouse suite in a super posh hotel.

Her mum, Beth, was delighted to hear her daughter sounding so happy. So many times Sukie had said she would go to Salzburg and, every time she began planning it, something came up, usually work-related, which had prevented it from happening. But now, it was all booked and she would soon be on her way. Beth was a big believer in fate and was trying to convince Sukie that there had to be a good reason for her getting this chance, out of the blue, when so many previous attempts had failed.

"Oh, Mum, you know I'm not into all that mumbo-jumbo in the way you are. It's just a bit of luck. That's all."

"But you just don't know, love," Beth had replied. "You're still not married, no children, your job can be done anywhere – you might just find the man of your dreams over there and everything else will fall into place for you. It's not right that you're nearly forty and still single. It's not right at all."

She had tried not to sigh too loudly. It was a conversation she'd had with her mum many times. She now dreaded even mentioning to her mother if she had a date because her mum was straight to the catalogue, looking for a wedding outfit.

"Mum, it's a business trip with a few days of sight-seeing tagged on! I really can't see me bumping into Mr Wonderful while I'm there but, if it keeps you happy, I won't say no to any suitable offers that come my way. Okay?"

Her mum had snorted at that. "It's your opinion of 'suitable' that's the problem, Sukie. If you set your standards any higher, the poor buggers will need a step ladder to reach them."

"Look, Mum, I've told you before. I would rather be single than stuck with someone just for the sake of it. I've seen too many unhappy people who, because they were scared of being on their own, jumped at the first marriage opportunity which came along. I would rather not marry at all than end up being another divorce statistic."

"I just want to see you settled with someone nice who deserves all that you have to offer. It's my job, as your mother, to want these things for you," her mum had replied firmly. "And, if you check out the rules for motherhood, you'll see I'm entitled to give you a hard time about it."

She smiled as she recalled that part of the conversation. She loved her mother dearly, even if she did give her grief about her single status. Just then, her flight was called to board. She stood and picked up her holdall, her stomach flipping with excitement because, now, she really was on her way.

Beth McClaren was also thinking back to the conversation she'd had with her daughter the night before, as she put her phone away after reading Sukie's text. She adored her only child and wished she would meet someone and settle down. Beth had told her so many times that all a mother ever wants is for her children to be happy and settled. 'Settled', of course, meant married with children. Her best friend Laura had often told her that women today were different from when the two of them were young. Back then, most girls worked until they had a husband and, after that, stayed at home looking after the children. Very few women had followed a 'career path'.

Laura also liked to point out to Beth that she hadn't raised Sukie to be dependent on a man, had she? She didn't want Sukie to be so reliant on her husband that she would fall apart and barely cope if anything happened to him or their marriage – this being exactly what Beth had done, when Jim had left her after seven and a half years of marriage, to move to the other side of the planet with his Australian secretary. It might be nearly thirty years since he'd left but she could still remember clearly how she'd gone to pieces when Jim had told her he was leaving. They may have been childhood sweethearts but they weren't going to enjoy an old age together. He was moving on and his plans did not include her.

For many months, she had felt she was living at the bottom of a deep, dark hole. It was only Sukie who'd kept her from totally losing her mind, but every little job she did seemed to take the greatest of effort. These days, she thought, I'd be given anti-depressants and probably offered counselling but, back then, you just had to get on with it and hope that eventually you pulled through. And pulled through she had. But there hadn't been another man in her life again after that. She'd made Sukie her sole focus and reason for living.

As the years had gone by, and Sukie grew up, Beth learnt to let go and find a life of her own. She'd enrolled with a local Adult Learning Centre and had worked hard on developing the few skills she'd possessed. Eventually, she'd succeeded in finding a job. This, in turn, had led to her meeting new people and even being asked out on dates. Beth, however, was still wary and had turned down most of the offers of drinks or meals out that had come her way. On the rare occasions, when she had agreed to meet someone, the relationship was short-lived. After a few dates, her companion always wanted to move things along but she never felt ready for that. She'd only ever slept with one man, and it was going to take more than a few nice meals to make her feel ready to try all that again.

No, she was quite happy to go out on girlie nights with the girls from the office or down to the local wine bar with the office gang if they were celebrating an occasion after work but, cosy little twosomes, with a bloke, were rarely on her agenda. Sometimes, however, she did feel lonely and she missed the feeling of being in someone's arms, being held tenderly and caringly. When Sukie was growing up, she had, at times, really missed having a husband to share the burden with because, no matter how dearly you love your children, they are hard work and she would have appreciated someone else being around to take some of the responsibility off her shoulders. "But," she spoke aloud to herself, "you got through it, Sukie turned out just fine and your life is now full of many good things."

A quick glance in her hall mirror, above the console table, told her that, for a woman in her mid-fifties, she was doing alright. Dance classes twice a week had kept her reasonably trim, and highlights had done a good job of covering her grey hairs. When she made an effort with her make-up, she could knock ten years off herself. She tilted her head to the side and appraised her appearance. Maybe she should take a trip into town next week and treat herself to some new make-up and clothes. Sukie was always telling her she didn't make the best of herself and that she dressed far too conservatively, which added years to her rather than take them off.

Hmmm… she thought, as she turned this way and that looking at her reflection, if I go to that big new department store, I could take up their Personal Dresser service. Someone who dresses women for a living and who won't send me out into the street looking like mutton dressed as lamb.

For all that Beth loved trailing round the shops with Sukie, she always felt her daughter's comments were biased when she said that Beth looked 'great' in whatever outfit she was trying on. Someone completely neutral would be far better and she was sure that she'd benefit greatly from having a professional sort out her wardrobe for her. Having made this decision, and feeling quite chipper for having done so, she went to the kitchen to make a cup of tea and to indulge in a few chocolate biscuits. Well, she was off to a Salsa club later tonight with some ladies from her Salsa class, she'd soon burn off the extra calories then.

"Remind me again why I'm sitting here on this stupid bus, waiting for a bunch of journalists I really don't want to meet, instead of relaxing in the luxury of my deluxe suite at the hotel, being rubbed up and down by a beautiful woman with good firm hands," grumbled Pete.

"Because," replied Kara, "we agreed it would be an excellent bit of PR if you were to come and meet them at the airport and provide the transport to the hotel. With all the photographers, make-up artists, stylists, and the actual journalists themselves, it made more sense to drag out the bus to pick them all up rather than trying to arrange cars and taxis." Kara forced herself to speak calmly, and smiled as she added, "You get to chat with everyone, in relaxed surroundings, ask how the trip went, make friends with them and get them on your side by making them think what a lovely, charming bloke you are. That should then, hopefully, influence the interviews and make them a bit less traumatic. Also, given that they are dragging themselves all the way over to Austria to meet you, rather than you going to London as had been the original intention, the least you can do is give them a decent welcome!"

Even though both she and Jordie had gone over the benefits of this exercise with Pete at least half a dozen times, she could tell he was still unconvinced it was worth it. When it had transpired that the only flight left, with a sufficient quota of availability, was on Saturday night, all of the invited press and media had been booked onto it. This meant everyone would be arriving at the same time. Kara and Jordie had hoped they would come and go on a rotation basis, to avoid Pete getting too overloaded with them all swarming around the hotel together but, with the arrival of the first decent snowfall of the winter season a few days earlier, the snowboarding fraternity had taken up nearly all the flights into Austria. As the new album was due for release in January, and it needed to be promoted, they'd had no choice but to bring the press out in one big hit. Despite all the last-minute planning and stress, this was still a better plan than Pete going to London, which had previously been on the agenda. Doing that meant running the gauntlet of the British paparazzi and she knew Pete would rather gouge his heart out with a blunt spoon than face those bloodhounds.

She looked out of the window and saw Jordie coming out of the airport terminal, the press posse tagging along behind him. "Smile Pete and look like you're enjoying yourself," she instructed. "They're here."

Sukie stepped through the doors of the airport and drew in a deep breath of some lovely fresh, cold and sharp, Austrian air. She smiled to herself with glee as she joined the queue for a taxi. The flight over had been lively and noisy. There had been a large party on board and they'd all been chattering away, shouting to each other up and down the plane. It was ten past eight in the evening and she was growing tired. It had been a long day as she'd had to go out early for some last-minute shopping. Then there had been the drive to the airport – the M25 never got any better – and, of course, the additional hanging around the Departure Lounge because of the delay. All she wanted now was to have a bite to eat, a soak in the bath and then a good nights' sleep. She needed to be fully rested for the morning so she could get in good bit of sightseeing.

Just then, the next taxi rolled up. "Riley Mirabell, Mirabellplatz, bitte," she stuttered in her very basic German.

The driver quickly loaded up the car with her luggage and off they drove. Fifteen minutes later they were pulling into the forecourt of the hotel and she rummaged in her purse to pay the driver. He'd been very friendly on the drive into the city and had recommended a few places for her to visit so she wanted to give him a decent tip. She finally sorted out the unfamiliar Euros and handed them over. The driver thanked her and, having already gotten her luggage out of the boot, wished her a happy holiday and drove off. She turned and noticed a large coach had pulled in behind where her cab had been and that a number of people had already disembarked.

Oh shit, she thought, just what I need, a bloody coach party. It'll be ages now before I can check in and get into my room.

A porter came over to her and, with a large smile, loaded her luggage onto his trolley. He handed her two tickets and explained that, once she'd checked in, she should hand the tickets to the receptionist, who would stamp her room number on them and pass them to the porters who'd then deliver the suitcases to her room. She smiled and thanked him for his help as she put the tickets in her jeans pocket for safe-keeping. The last person appeared to have gotten off the coach and she fell into step behind him. As she drew nearer to the door, she saw a large gentleman in a smart black suit and another scruffy, very-harassed looking bloke beside him. The crowd in front of her were stating their names as they walked past and Scruffy was marking them off on a clipboard that he was holding.

As she drew level, the suit asked her "Name please?"

"Erm, Sukie McClaren," she replied, "but I'm not part of your group."

"I can't see her on the list," said Scruffy to the suit.

"Sorry, miss, you can't come in," said the suit.

"I beg your pardon?" She drew herself up to her full height of five foot five inches.

"Only hotel residents are permitted in the hotel tonight." The Suit spoke politely but firmly.

"I am a resident," she informed him, in the tone of voice which usually sent chills down the spines of those who knew her well.

Scruffy looked her up and down and she knew he was taking in her jeans, casual sweatshirt and coat. She'd only put on a lick of make-up that morning and it would most certainly have disappeared by now. Her hair, despite being in a pony-tail, was in desperate need of a comb as the wind had blown it about and several loose strands were now hanging down around her face. She'd always disliked that she looked so young without her face-paint on and, even more so, when she was dressed in her jeans or casual clothes. Right now, she was not looking her best, and she knew it. This only made her more defensive for she was fully aware that she did not look as though she should be booking into a five-star hotel.

"I'll deal with this." Scruffy elbowed the suit aside and barked at her, "What is your room number?"

"Excuse me?"

"I said 'what room number'?" Scruffy repeated, rolling his eyes as he did so.

She chose to ignore the eye-roll – there was no need to be so rude – and replied, "I don't know, I—"

Before she could explain any further however, she was rudely interrupted by the scruffy one.

"I knew it! I damn well knew it! You lassies are all

the same! Always trying every trick in the book to get close to your pop idols!" He then launched into an angry tirade about groupies and young love-sick girls constantly chasing after their favourite rock-stars, how pathetic they were and why didn't she just get a life and find herself a real boyfriend instead of dreaming over someone she would never have.

"If you have QUITE finished...?" Sukie growled, interrupting him right back. "The reason I do NOT have a room number to give you, you nasty-mouthed little man, is because I have YET to check in. I have, quite literally, just arrived and I could really do without being insulted by someone who looks as though HE grabbed HIS clothes out of a recycle bin and then slept in them for a week. Now, please get out of my way before I feel the need to get REALLY rude."

She could tell from the expression on his face that Scruffy didn't believe a word she'd said and, had liked even less, the manner in which she'd just spoken to him.

"Well, allow me to escort you in then," he said. And, putting his hand on her elbow, he all but dragged her through the doors and towards the reception desk.

"Get your hands off me!" she snapped, as she tried to release his grip on her arm.

"All in good time, missy," he snapped back, gripping even tighter to prevent her getting away from him.

He pushed through the remaining passengers from the coach, stopping only when they got to the reception desk.

"Good evening, how may I help you?" asked the receptionist, as she smiled at them both.

"This *lady* would like to check-in please," replied Scruffy.

Sukie was amazed at the level of sarcasm he'd managed to inject into the word 'lady'.

"Name please?" asked the receptionist.

"Sukie McClaren."

The receptionist typed on her keyboard.

"May I ask how you spell that please?" she enquired.

Sukie spelt her name out for her. She could feel the waves of temper and dislike emanating from the man standing beside her and she just wanted to get away from him as soon as possible. She really was on the verge of losing her temper.

"I'm very sorry but I can't find your name on our system."

She looked at the receptionist but, before she could say anything further, Scruffy dug his fingers tighter into her arm and began pulling her away.

"Now that I've called your bluff, girlie, you can get out! That was a good try but I've seen it all before and, quite frankly, there aren't many tricks left which impress me. You're just another desperate fool who'll give anything a go to get near Pete Wallace. I'm surprised you haven't offered to sleep with me yet, in the hope that'll get you closer to him."

The last sentence was the final straw. Her blood turned to ice as she finally lost the temper she'd been trying to rein in. With one swift move, she drove the rather solid heel of her cowboy boot onto his foot and slapped him across the face with her free hand. The unexpected assault made Scruffy drop his hand from her elbow as he lost his balance and fell, landing hard on his bottom, on the solid, marble flooring.

Sukie rounded on him. "How dare you!" she shouted down at him. "How bloody dare you! Just who the HELL do you think you are?"

Everyone in the hotel lobby stopped what they were doing to watch this free bit of entertainment.

"I have never been so insulted in all my life and, believe me, I have had heard some insults in my time but you... YOU have completely overstepped the mark. You've man-handled me, spoken to me as though I was dirt, accused me of being a groupie, and have treated me like a fifteen-year-old child. And, as if that wasn't enough, you now think it's okay to verbally abuse me! Well I suggest you BACK OFF before I land another punch on that ugly, sour, little face of yours. And, as you seem to think its ok to insult me at every opportunity, I suggest you have one back. The last time I came across someone as obnoxious, and as ugly, as you, he was trying to sell me a second-hand car!"

With that, she turned on her heel and headed back to the reception desk.

"As you were unable to find a booking under my name," she said to the receptionist, loud enough for everyone to hear, "may I suggest you try my company name. It will be either E.G.T. Ltd or European Group Transport Ltd. Thank you."

The receptionist replied, almost immediately, that she had located the booking and, apologising for the confusion, she passed over a booking card for her to complete. Sukie glared over at Scruffy and then, turning her back on him, in a gesture of dismissal, she picked up the pen the receptionist had handed to her.

Pete Wallace had watched the fracas from behind the glass doors of the ground floor cocktail bar, and had been thoroughly amused by it all. He waited until the lady in question entered the lift before walking out into the lobby. Jordie, by this time, had picked himself off the floor and was trying to appear unfazed by the incident although Pete could see the few remaining coach guests sniggering amongst themselves and throwing him looks of amusement. Jordie saw him come out of the bar and, with the appearance of ignoring those still in the lobby, he quickly walked over.

"I can tell, from the smile on your face, that you saw and heard everything."

"Oh, Jordie," Pete murmured in his ear, "it's not very often I have the pleasure of seeing someone get the better of you but, I would say that one had you well and truly tied up like a kipper. If only all my 'groupies' were as smart as her, it would certainly make this job a lot more enjoyable."

And, with a laugh at the look of anger on Jordie's face, he headed back into the bar.

Chapter Nine

Sukie woke up just before eight o'clock, feeling wonderfully refreshed. Despite the debacle of the night before, she was amazed at how well she'd slept. Although she enjoyed travelling, on the rare occasions when she'd managed a holiday, she never seemed to settle very well – sleeping in strange beds always seemed to knock her system out and it usually took several days to readjust. She was also quite surprised that the episode from the previous night hadn't kept her awake. Normally, she would've been mulling everything over in her head until the early hours of the morning, thinking of various retorts she could have made or basking with pride at the put-downs she'd got in. But not last night! Oh no! Once she'd sorted out her room – an unexpected super-deluxe suite which Elsa had booked without letting on – and unpacked her suitcases, she'd ordered a cheese and ham toastie from Room Service along with a hot chocolate – the latter being, no doubt, the first of many on her visit. She'd enjoyed a refreshing shower, while waiting for her meal to arrive, and had just finished dressing when Room Service knocked on her door. She flicked through the channels on her small television as she was eating, and had come across a local weather report which had mentioned it was currently snowing. With a small exclamation of joy, she'd rushed to the windows and opened the heavy curtains so she could see it.

After her meal, she'd found herself yawning widely so got into the large, cosy bed, with the intention of looking through her various leaflets and guide books to plan her sight-seeing for the following day. However, once snuggled up under the covers, she'd begun watching the snow falling outside her window. As she'd lain there, being slowly hypnotised by the sparkling flakes, her eyes had grown heavy and she'd drifted off into a very deep sleep.

Now, however, it was a lovely, clear morning, the sun was shining in a bright, blue sky, and she was anxious to be out and about. She quickly showered and dressed then made her way to the breakfast room and was delighted to see such a vast selection available from the buffet table. After ordering a pot of coffee from the waitress – Sukie adored that she was called Heidi – she made her way over to the buffet.

She was pondering over the vast array of hams, cheeses, breads and pates when a large gentleman on her left looked at her and smiled.

"Guten Morgen," he said, his perfect accent letting her know he was speaking his own language.

"Guten Morgen," she smiled back shyly.

"Ahh, are you English?" he asked.

"Yes, I am."

"And are you having a problem trying to decide what to have for your breakfast, Ja?"

Sukie laughed. "Is it that obvious? I want to try something really Austrian but I'm not quite sure what that would be."

The gentleman smiled again and said, "May I suggest you try that, that, and that," as he pointed to some cheese, ham, and bread. "I think you will like it, although, I should warn you, the cheese is quite strong in flavour."

"Thank you for being so helpful. It's very kind of you." She proceeded to put his recommendations onto her plate.

"It's my pleasure," he replied. "Please have a nice visit and I hope you have a good day." With that, he went back to his table.

Sukie sat down and gingerly tried the food she'd selected. It was delicious. So delicious, in fact, she went back for another helping.

It's a good thing I plan to do several miles of walking today, she thought, as she bit into the Danish pastry which had 'somehow' found its way onto her plate. I'd be the size of the Monchberg within a week if I was to eat this every day for breakfast.

An hour later, Sukie was trawling through her mind, trying to find the bit of wisdom which had enticed her away from the cable car ride up the mountain, to the Hohensalzburg Fortress at the top, and had, instead, guided her feet towards the pathway up the side. At least I can now stop feeling guilty about that Danish pastry, she thought, as she puffed her way up the steep incline.

"Oh wow!" she exclaimed aloud when she walked around a corner and saw, lying beneath her, the rooftops of Salzburg, laid out against a backdrop of mountains. With the snow from the previous night lying on the roofs, and shining in the bright morning sunlight, the sight was utterly breath-taking. Sukie knew that snowy active holidays were not for everyone but she would choose this over a sunny beach any day of the week. Under the guise of taking some photographs, she got her breath back before climbing the rest of the way up to the fortress.

She spent several hours wandering around the museum inside the fortress, taking more photographs and enjoying the beauty, and the history, of the centuries old building. To save some time, she chose the cable car option for her descent back down to the city. Surprised when her stomach let out an almighty rumble, she saw it was after lunchtime so looked for a small café where she could try out some more Austrian fare.

It's amazing the appetite you develop when you climb high hills in the snow, she thought, as she worked her way through a local sausage and mash main course with some sauerkraut on the side. Who would have thought cabbage could taste so good? This was followed by a delicious apple strudel with vanilla sauce. As she paid the bill, she wondered if she'd already worked off the calories she'd just consumed or would a few hours walking around the Christmas markets be required. She decided to visit the markets anyway. You know, just in case!

Okay, if she was being *really* honest with herself, working off the calories was just an excuse for some over-the-top indulgence, as she admired the little wooden cabins which made up the Salzburg Christmas Market. The temptation to spend and spend on the many different toys, candies and trinkets was immense and, more than once, she gave in. Well, it was so hard to resist. The chalets were all lit up, their wares displayed so beautifully and, with Christmas music being piped out across the square where the stalls were positioned, you were totally drawn into the magic of the season.

Eventually, she made her way back to the hotel, strolling through the Mirabell Gardens and admiring the way the discretely positioned spotlights, lighting up the famous statues, also made the snow glisten in the fast-approaching darkness.

She walked through the reception area of the hotel, and considered a quick stop in her bedroom to get changed into something a bit less casual but, espying quite a few casually dressed people heading straight up to the Roof Terrace Bar, she left her parcels with the concierge, who kindly agreed to have them taken to her room, and she made her way to the bar instead.

When she walked in, Sukie saw that most of the tables were occupied, so found herself a stool at the bar. As she waited to be served, her eyes were drawn to the large floor-to-ceiling window, through which she could see the falling snowflakes dancing and shimmering in the beams of light dotted around the outside terrace. The scene was beautiful and she was mesmerised by the sight.

She turned to speak with the barman who was now waiting to take her order.

"Excuse me," she asked. "Would it be okay for me to sit out on the terrace? Is it open?"

"By all means, Fraulein. Please go out if you wish." The barman gestured towards the doors. "The terrace is never closed."

"And may I order a very large hot chocolate?" she enquired with a smile.

The barman smiled back. "But of course, Fraulein. I will have the waiter bring it out to you."

Sukie gathered up her outdoor attire which was lying on the barstool next to her, wrapped her scarf around her neck, pulled her fleece back on and made her way outside. She walked over to the far side of the terrace. From here she could see the high, brooding, fortress in all its spot-lit glory. She swept the snow off the bench seat with her hand, sat down and zipped up her jacket. She turned to face the view in front of her and thought back over her first day in Salzburg. It had been more amazing than she'd anticipated and, as she sat in the quiet solitude of the snowy terrace, gazing with love-struck eyes over the beautiful city, she realised that she was going to find it very painful when it was time to leave.

Jordie saw Sukie, sitting out on the terrace, as he turned away from the bar with his tray of drinks. Remembering how she'd humiliated him the previous night, he snorted with disgust as he walked to the table where Kara and Pete were sitting. In a few minutes, the journalists and the people of their various entourages would descend upon the bar and it would be back to work. There would be lots of handshaking, networking, answering questions (and ensuring the answers being given were the same written down) and, worse than anything else, smiling all the time! Jordie had no problem with smiling, he just preferred to do it with people he knew and liked. The thought of that girl from last night did not make him want to smile in the slightest.

Pete, seeing Jordie's scowl, looked through the window and saw the reason for it sitting on a bench in the snow. He chuckled inwardly as he realised she had rattled Jordie more than he was letting on. Mind you, he wouldn't have been too happy if he'd landed on his butt in the middle of a very busy reception area. It had served Jordie right though. Sometimes he could be too heavy-handed with his protection services. He was quick to acknowledge, however, that, without Jordie, he'd have a lot more troublesome groupies and teenagers to deal with than he currently had.

He watched Sukie for a few more minutes, wondering what she was thinking as she looked up at the spot-lit fortress, before his attention was diverted elsewhere by the group of journalists, and associates coming through the bar doors with a burst of noise and laughter.

Oh well, he sighed inwardly, back to work.

When Sukie wandered back in from the terrace some thirty minutes later, the noise from all the journalists attracted her attention. In the middle of the heaving throng stood Elsa's dreamy heart-throb – Pete Wallace! The scruffy man from the evening before was standing beside him. Upon seeing this, it suddenly dawned on her what all the fuss had been about the previous night. She'd been aware, at the time, that Scruffy had thought she was a groupie, or something untoward, but she'd been completely unaware as to whom his 'charge' was and had really been too tired to care. Although, now she came to think about it, she vaguely recalled him saying Pete Wallace's name, just before she'd lost her temper and thumped him. She could now understand why he'd been so vigilant regarding who was entering the hotel, but it was absolutely no excuse for him to have been so rude.

She was also very grateful that Elsa wasn't here as the sight of Pete Wallace, in the flesh, would probably have been too much for her. She, herself, wasn't the sort of person to have her head turned by 'celebrities' but Elsa was totally different. She'd once let out a high-pitched squeal right in the middle of the Kings Road in London, because she 'thought' she'd seen Mel C from the Spice Girls. The irony was that Elsa didn't even *like* the Spice Girls! How she would react to standing a mere few feet away from Pete Wallace just didn't bear thinking about. Sukie decided that, when she spoke to Elsa later – to check up on her beloved four-footed boys – she wouldn't mention this particular fellow guest. She could almost guarantee that, if she did, Elsa would be on the first plane to Salzburg in the morning. And then Scruffy really *would* have something to concern himself about.

She handed over her now empty mug to the bartender and, with a smile of thanks to him, she walked out the bar, completely unaware that two pairs of eyes were following her departure – grey ones, full of dislike and emerald ones, full of interest.

Chapter Ten

"Oh, that all sounds so lovely, sweetheart, I'm glad you're having a good time. I hope the meeting goes well for you tomorrow. Speak with you soon. Love you." Beth McClaren finished her telephone conversation with her daughter and replaced the handset of the phone. She returned to the kitchen and switched the iron back on to warm up. She only had one blouse left to do and then she could tidy everything away.

It was Sunday night and she was preparing her work clothes for the coming week. She liked to be organised which meant her outfits for the office were all ironed, and put together, every Sunday night without fail. The thought of having to decide what to wear on a daily basis made her shudder. She much preferred to simply open the wardrobe each morning and take out the next clothes hanger she'd lined up, with her complete outfit already compiled upon it.

As she waited for the iron to reach the correct temperature, she looked at the outfits she'd already assembled, hanging on the clothes horse waiting to be taken upstairs. She cast a cynical eye over them and was glad she'd bitten the bullet and made an appointment with the personal shopper at the new department store. These suits in front of her were dire! What on earth had possessed her to buy them, they were so old-fashioned. Then again, they were rather old now. She'd bought them when she'd gotten her first job almost twelve years ago.

When Sukie had returned from college, Beth knew it was time to let go and began focusing on herself. She'd discussed the matter with Sukie and it was agreed that a course on computer literacy would be a good place to start. She had taken to it like the proverbial duck to water. From there, she'd expanded her learning with courses in basic accounting, secretarial, and administration. Once she felt she knew enough to go back into the working environment, she'd applied for a position with a local insurance firm and gotten the job. She'd worked hard, continued studying and was now the manager of the department she'd first started off in.

She stared at the remaining blouse which she'd just picked out of the laundry basket and realised she'd bought these particular outfits to build her confidence. She'd been elated when she'd received the phone call, telling her the job was hers, but this had quickly given way to terror when it hit her that she was going to be stepping hugely out of her comfort zone. The power suits now lined up in front of her, with their nips, tucks and big buttons, had been her safety net during those first few months, when she was finding her feet. She figured that, even if she didn't feel in control, at least she looked in control. What was that expression? Oh yes, 'Fake it till you make it!' Well, she had certainly faked it. And she had finally made it. The time had come, however, to have a makeover and move away from the uptight look she now appeared to favour. With Christmas just a few weeks away, there would be several parties and dinners to attend. This was the perfect time to get a new look. As she ironed the soon-to-be redundant blouse, her thoughts wandered back to Sukie. She really did have to stop going on about her daughter's single status. After all, she was a fine one to talk. No serious relationships in almost thirty years? That was hardly setting her daughter an example, was it? She supposed, by now, she'd become rather set in her ways. How would she cope with sharing her space with another person? That was one of the downsides to living on your own, adapting to another presence would not be easy – having to consider the requests and needs of that person would be difficult when you were so out of practise. And as for sharing the TV remote control…? Well, some things just didn't bear thinking about!

As she was finalising the last of her outfits, she recalled the man Sukie had been seeing during the summer. Hadn't he turned out to be a disappointment? She smiled when the picture of Sukie's indignant face popped into her mind.

"Oh, Mum, he turned out to be a total control freak! I didn't notice it at first – I thought him choosing where we went on our dates was romantic. The first time we had dinner, he 'recommended' items on the menu which he thought I would like. The next time, however, he just went ahead and ordered for me. Without asking me first! I soon put him straight on that, let me tell you, but it all went downhill from there. He began to make snide comments about my friends and how he thought I should see less of them. I'll be honest here, that was when the alarm bells started to ring but, not trusting my instincts like I should, I ignored them. Thankfully, the lightbulb moment came when he arrived last night to pick me up for a party we'd been invited to. Do you know, he actually had the audacity to walk into my flat and tell me the outfit I was wearing was not appropriate and that I *had* to change! And, as if that wasn't insulting enough, he then proceeded to tell me what dress and shoes *to* wear! Well, let me tell you, I wasn't slow in telling him the only thing I was changing was my boyfriend. I showed him the door and told him never to contact me again. Who on earth does he think he is, talking to me like that? No one, and I mean no one, tells me who to see, what to wear and what to eat. I'm the person that I am and anyone who doesn't like it can damn well sod off!"

Even now, all these months later, Beth couldn't prevent the swell of pride that rose up inside her when she thought of that day. She'd been so proud of Sukie for standing up to someone who was one of life's manipulators, and delighted that she'd had the confidence and self-belief to take quick action and eradicate him from her life.

She was folding the ironing board and putting it away in the under-stairs cupboard, when it occurred to Beth that maybe her own single state hadn't been as detrimental to Sukie's emotional development as she'd feared. If it had helped to develop Sukie's sense of self-worth and her belief that relationships should be equal partnerships, then she hadn't done such a bad job in raising her after all.

She gathered up the hangers from the clothes horse and walked up the stairs to put them away. She felt a sense of contentment wash over her as entered the room. Her daughter was okay. She could look after herself and she would find the right man in her own good time. Beth decided she would no longer intrude in that area of Sukie's life and concentrate on her own. After all, the party season was coming up, who knew who she might mcct then.

Chapter Eleven

Kara and Jordie exchanged glances. Pete was working himself up into a right bad temper which they were both powerless to prevent.

It was Monday evening and the three of them were sitting in the still relatively quiet Roof Terrace Bar, discussing the events of the day. Pete had a cardboard beer-mat in his hand and was leaning forward, tapping it vigorously on the table in front of them. He'd had his first interview session with Aggie Wilson, the journalist from the award-winning magazine High-Hitting, and it hadn't gone as well as he would have liked. The problem was that Aggie had consistently asked him the sort of questions he'd answered when he was in his mid-twenties. Now in his thirties, he would have preferred questions which were more in keeping with his music and his thoughts rather than which female celebrity did he most fancy and did he have lucky underwear that he wore for each gig.

The reason for his already bad mood going into overdrive, however, was the revelation regarding the photo-shoot that was to accompany the interview. He did not want to do semi- nude! No matter how artistic. No matter how tasteful. Any kind of undress was no longer an option. When he'd been younger and more of a lad, he'd allowed the photographers carte blanche when it came to their shots. For so long, he'd been either drunk, or high on drugs, and often hadn't realised what was happening until it was too late. He always agreed that the unexpected centrefold in Playgirl hadn't done his career a disservice but, not actually knowing anything about it, until Jordie had come bursting into his bedroom with a copy of the magazine in one hand and the phone, with his seething record company on it, in the other, had been quite a shock. Fortunately, for him anyway, these days he was totally drug-free, and in full control of his drinking, which meant the photo-journalists did not get such sensational shots as they had before.

"I am not doing it!" He growled to Jordie and Kara. "I don't care how much they ask, or how much they pay, I am not doing those shots."

Kara was trying to keep the peace. "But Pete, it will be very… artfully done."

He knew she was picking her words with care, in an attempt to try to diffuse his temper but he had been in a difficult mood all day and didn't have a desire for appeasement. He hadn't slept well last night and his tiredness, mixed in with his hatred of corporate pleasantries, had left him tetchy and grumpy. The interview *had* been rather poor quality, with far too many questions about his past and very few about his future. He was sick of regurgitating his bad-boy days – he'd moved on and wished the rest of the world would let him get on with it. He'd hoped the High-Hitting interview would provide him with the opportunity to show he'd finally matured but, no matter how he'd tried to direct Aggie's questions to more meaningful topics, she'd pushed them to one side and carried on with her prepared set list. The more questions she'd asked, the more wound up he'd become. The photo-shoot remit had pushed him over the edge and he was now past the point of listening to reason. A full-blown explosion was on its way and nothing was going to prevent it.

"Hurrrrrummph." Jordie cleared his throat.

"What?"

"Nothing! Just trying to think what I could say that might turn this situation around. You could suggest chest shots," he mused aloud, "they might go for that."

"Oh puh-lease!" Pete's voice was heavy with sarcasm, "I was doing those when I was eighteen, I really have no desire to do them now."

Jordie suddenly snapped. "Well then, just tell them to stuff the interview and the photo-shoot if it's all too bloody much for you to cope with! Here I am, running about all over the place, trying my best to keep everyone happy, keep everything running smoothly and keep all the journos in good spirits to ensure they give you some good press and it's doing my head in. I, too, have had enough!"

This response was all Pete needed to let rip.

"I'm sick and tired of being used and abused by

people more interested in meeting their own agenda and thinking I'm just another step on their career ladder. Oh yes, I'm sure more nude shots of Pete Wallace will really enhance Aggie Wilson's C.V. No one interviews me with the intention of letting me speak and saying my piece. Oh no, they all just want something that can be turned into a nice little controversial piece that'll flog their papers and magazines. The general public accuse celebrities of using the press to self-promote – well, how fucking wrong they are. The media only promote themselves and we get hung out to dry in the fucking process."

He stood up, threw the now shredded beer-mat onto the table, and yelled at Jordie "I'VE HAD E-FUCKING-NOUGH!"

And, with that, he walked away from their table and stormed out onto the snow-covered terrace, ignoring the shocked and surprised expressions of the other residents sitting nearby.

Kara and Jordie looked at each other for a moment. "Brandy?" asked Jordie.

"Make mine a double!" Kara replied.

Sukie walked into the Roof Terrace Bar with Andrew 'Hopeless' Hollings behind her. The meeting, with their potential new client, had gone well and she'd been relieved to find Andrew was far more on the ball than expected. They were back out again tomorrow, for a full-on tour of the various Monschberg GMBH sites to obtain first-hand working knowledge of the company's requirements. Terms had practically been agreed and, depending on what they came across tomorrow, the contracts would be drawn up and signed on Wednesday morning before Andrew went back to the UK.

At this moment, however, she was currently more preoccupied with trying to figure out who the woman was that she'd stood beside in the lift up to the bar. She'd recognised her face but just couldn't put a finger on her name or where she knew her from. She knew this would sit at the back of her mind and bug her until she solved the mystery. She was generally quite good at remembering names and faces so it was a bugbear when she struggled to place someone like this. Eventually she gave a mental shrug and let it go. It would come to her, it always did.

Andrew had commandeered a table and she took off her coat, slinging it on a spare chair alongside Andrew's fleece jacket. It was bitterly cold outside. A street sign they'd passed, on the way back to the hotel, was advertising the temperature as currently being -6 degrees C. Coupled with the wind that had begun to pick up, it felt much colder than that. She was debating on whether it was too cold to have a hot chocolate out on the roof terrace again when she heard voices a few feet away. A quick glance revealed Pete Wallace having a heated discussion with Scruffy and another woman. As she was about to look away, she saw him get up, yell at Scruffy and then storm out onto the terrace.

Aye, aye, something's rattled his cage, she thought.

Andrew arrived back at the table, having been for a visit to the loo. "Want anything to drink?" he asked.

Ignoring him, Sukie watched Pete through the window of the bar. He was sitting on the same snow-covered bench she'd sat on the night before, with his elbows on the table and his head in his hands.

"Erm... not at the moment thanks, Andrew," she eventually replied, as she wondered how long Pete was planning to sit out there in his short-sleeved T-shirt. "He's going to get very cold," she mused aloud to herself. "Why hasn't one of his cohorts gone out to him?"

She watched for another couple of minutes. Scruffy and his female companion were now sipping on what looked like a couple of brandies. Well, honestly, it's nice to know they care so much!

She let out a sigh of annoyance, got up and walked over to Scruffy.

"Excuse me," she barked down at him. "You do realise your Golden Goose is sitting out on the terrace in just a T-shirt? It's minus 6 degrees out there. Do you want him to catch pneumonia?"

Scruffy looked up at her, unable to keep the look of disdain off his face, and replied sneeringly "Not that it is *any* of your business but, having known Pete for *rather* a long time, I know when it's best to approach him and when it's best to leave him alone to cool down. This occasion is one of the latter."

"Well, there's a big difference between 'cooling down' and freezing to bloody death!" she responded before turning sharply on her heel. She marched back to her table where she grabbed her coat and Andrew's fleece.

"Just borrowing this a moment," she said to Andrew, who was watching her with bemusement, as she walked off towards the terrace door.

Scruffy also watched her go. As he'd said to Sukie, he'd known Pete a very long time and, when he was in the sort of mood he was in at the moment, it was the next best thing to suicide to try and approach him before he had calmed down. Girlie there was about to get a rather big shock and he was in a prime position to see it happen. He turned to Kara and said with a wink, "This should be fun."

Kara watched Sukie walk through the doors to the terrace. 'Well, she's a braver woman than me, that's for damn sure. Good luck to her, I say!"

Jordie sniggered. "She's going to need more than luck!"

Sukie stopped a passing waiter and requested two hot chocolates be brought out to her on the terrace before pushing the door open and stepping out onto the snow-covered area. There was, unsurprisingly, only one set of footsteps and they led straight to the bench where Pete Wallace was sitting. She walked over, stopped in front of him and held out Andrew's fleece.

"Here," she said gently, "it's cold. You might want to put this on."

"No thanks," Pete replied, not bothering to look up. He continued to stare down at the table, with his head still in his hands.

She tried again. "Look, it's freezing out here and you're only wearing a thin T-shirt. You should really put it on."

Still without looking up, he said in a deeply sarcastic tone "And I have said I don't want to. Which part of 'no' did you not get?"

In that moment, her own temper suddenly flared up and, before she could stop herself, she replied in the same tone which had just been used on her.

"Actually, *sunshine*, I personally don't give a monkey's either way if you put this jacket on or not, but, if you end up with a dose of pneumonia, then the chances are, the next time you open your big, stupid gob to sing, you'll sound more like bloody Tweety Pie than Pete – fucking – Wallace. Now I suggest you put this damn jacket on, and that you put it on NOW!" She continued to hold Andrew's fleece out to him.

Pete's head shot up and his jaw practically fell into his lap with shock as he found himself looking straight into the face of Jordie's nemesis. He was so utterly gobsmacked that he simply put his hand out, took the proffered jacket and slipped it on without uttering a single word.

"That's better," said Sukie. Just then, the waiter arrived with the mugs of hot chocolate she'd ordered and she passed one to him. He took it without question.

Sukie brushed the snow off the bench on the other side of the table and sat down, saying nothing as she sipped her own drink quietly.

Pete looked at her, taking in her professional, business-like, appearance. With her make-up on, and her hair properly styled, she looked very different to the whirling dervish he'd seen giving Jordie what for two nights ago. After a few more sips from his mug he eventually said, "You're scary!"

Sukie burst out laughing. "Apparently so, it's been mentioned a few times!"

"I can't believe you just spoke to me like that. I can't remember the last time that happened."

"Well, maybe it should happen more often and then you'll stop behaving like a petulant, three-year-old child."

It was Pete's turn to laugh. "Ouch! Speak your mind, why don't you."

"I usually do. There's less room for confusion that way."

"I didn't know it was you talking to me. I saw the way you handled my manager the other night. I would've done as I was told straight away had I realised." He picked up his mug for another sip of the warming liquid, peered over the top and asked, "Do you always speak to people in a sergeant major tone or are we just the lucky ones?"

Sukie laughed again. "Your manager was rude and fully deserved his tongue lashing. You were being childish and required a firm tone. Do not confuse the two. Neither of you, however, are the first people to receive the sharp end of my tongue and it's highly unlikely you'll be the last." She took another drink from her mug before continuing, "I've learnt to live with being a 'straight-talker'. I tried to curb it for a time, but it didn't go too well, so I reverted back. I'm happier being me. I can't always say the same for those on the receiving end, mind

94

you. They do usually concur, however, that they are rarely in any doubt as to where they stand with me. I prefer the no-nonsense approach."

Pete put his mug back down on the table, trying to place it inside the ring of melted snow its warmth had created. He looked at her and sighed. "That's the problem with this business, too many people are too busy sucking up to you and you rarely hear a truthful word spoken." He jerked his head over his shoulder, "Even those two in there watch every word they say to me."

"I'm sure they don't, it maybe just feels that way sometimes." Sukie couldn't imagine Scruffy choosing his words with care for anyone.

"No, they do. I often see them thinking how to word things before they speak to me."

"Then maybe you should ask yourself why? Do you have a quick temper? Or go into bad moods easily? There has to be a reason for them to behave so tentatively around you."

He grimaced. "I suppose I do have a short-fuse and can lose my rag quickly, sometimes over things which are really not important."

"So, that's something you need to work on. If you want them to feel they can be completely honest with you, without repercussions, then you need to find a way of reining in your temper. If the people you respect have become 'yes' men then I suspect it's because they're too scared of you to be 'no' men. Only you can change that, Mr Wallace."

"I suppose you're right." He shuffled his mug around in the snow on the table, making various ring patterns where it melted. Finally, he put it back in its original spot and looked at Sukie for a few seconds "You're very astute you know. And please, call me Pete."

"I'm Sukie." She leaned across the table to shake his hand. "So, feeling better now?"

"What do you mean?"

"Well, you stormed out of there in a bit of a tizz, if you don't mind me saying."

He looked at her and was silent for a moment before he spoke. "We're doing a load of publicity for the new album this week and I got wound up over it. I hate doing this sort of stuff and always have less patience than I should."

"Yeah, I can get that," Sukie sympathised. "It wouldn't be my thing at all. All those people, asking all sorts of questions, which you know they're going to supply their own answers to because they'll sound better than anything you could have said."

"You're right about that." He looked at her closely, a slightly suspicious look on his face. "How come you've got the journos so worked out then? Are you one of them?"

"Hey! Less of the insults! Please!" Sukie smiled at him. She wrapped her hands around the mug in front of her, trying to pick up some of its warmth and continued, "I've heard stories of what they can be like and I've seen it for myself. I hate how I can pick up two newspapers, which are supposedly describing the same event but they make it sound like two totally *different* events. I loathe how they intrude into the lives of normal, everyday folks, who are facing some terrible, heart-breaking tragedy. I deplore how, when this kind of thing happens, there is some journalist, sticking a microphone in their face and asking them how they feel. And then, when someone tells them to stop, they say 'the public have a right to know'. It all makes me sick."

Pete looked at her. "Well, it's finally nice to meet someone, not in the public eye, who actually understands what it's like. I respect that. So many people today think that being a 'celebrity' is the *only* thing to be. They don't understand how difficult it is."

"You won't hear me saying that, Pete Wallace." Sukie shook her head vehemently as she replied. "I wouldn't want your life for a pension. Sure, the perks you get with it are quite fantastic but the level of intrusion just doesn't bear thinking about. No thanks! I'm quite happy being an unknown little office lackey and long may it stay that way."

She smiled gently at him. "Do you ever wish you'd never taken up singing and maybe been a plumber, or something else, instead?"

"I couldn't do without my music. I'd be happier writing the stuff and letting someone else perform it but the record company won't allow that, so I'm stuck with the role for now." He hesitated for a moment, before continuing. "Usually, I can just about get through the publicity stuff but Aggie Wilson from High-Hitting sent me over the edge today."

"Aggie Wilson! That's who she is!" Sukie explained to Pete about the woman she had seen in the lift. "She's an excellent writer. I really like her articles which is why I recognised her."

Pete sighed. "Well, I don't know why but she's gotten it into her head to interview me as though I'm still a young twenty-something. She even wants 'semi-nude' photographs to accompany the piece. I'm sick of doing stuff like that. I've changed and I want the public to know it. I've grown up a lot over the last few years. It's been tough, but I've done it and I want it to be recognised. It's why I had the argy-bargy with those guys inside – they just couldn't get what I was saying."

"Maybe she's star-struck. Maybe she has little fantasies about the two of you..." Sukie winked mischievously at him.

He laughed at her comment. "Oh don't. That's a thought I could do without. It's going to be bad enough facing her tomorrow, with barely any clothes on, without that one running through my head every time I look at her."

"It sounds to me like you're planning on doing it then."

"I really, really don't want to but I know it will be more difficult to get out of it than to not do it. I shall just have to bite the bullet, along with anything else I can lay my teeth on, and go through with it. C'est la vie, eh?"

Sukie grinned at him. "You're such a trooper. Anything for the masses, yeah?"

Pete straightened up and threw back his shoulders. "Right, I'm sick of thinking about, and talking about, me. Do you mind if we change the subject? What are you doing here in Salzburg? You're quite intriguing and I want to know more about you. I'm also not quite ready to go back into the bar just yet".

"I'm here on both business and pleasure," replied Sukie. "It began as a business trip but, as I've *always* wanted to visit Salzburg, I managed to wrangle a bit of a holiday out of it too, so I'm staying until Sunday. Then, there will be some bloke crow-baring me onto the plane because I already know that I don't want to leave."

"I see. I hope the weather doesn't prevent you from any sight-seeing," said Pete. "We've had a bit more snow than is usual for this early in December. It normally arrives like this in January."

"Oh, it can snow as much as it likes!" she answered with a large smile. "I love snow. I love winter. I feel more alive at this time of the year than at any other. I adore the wintery, Christmassy colours. And that tingling sensation you get in your hands and feet, when you step indoors after a long walk in the cold, is pure heaven. There's no doubt about it, I am one hundred percent a winter girl. Maybe I was a snowman in a previous life."

He smiled and was about to respond when Andrew Hollings appeared at their table, shivering slightly in the cold air. "Sorry to interrupt you both but, could I just retrieve my mobile from my jacket please. I need to phone home before the kids go to bed."

"Oh, Andrew, I'm so sorry. I just grabbed your jacket without thinking."

"Here mate," said Pete, slipping the jacket off and handing it back to Andrew. "Thank you for the loan, much appreciated."

He stood up and looked down at Sukie. "I'd better get back in and face my demons." He smiled at her. The Pete Wallace killer smile, known to melt icebergs at a thousand paces, came hurtling towards her on full throttle. This was the smile which caused teenage girls, and their OAP grandmothers, to swoon alike. Combined with his amazing emerald green eyes, twinkling with mischief, it could very easily be a recipe for disaster. Sukie was glad she was mentally standing a thousand and one paces away because, now, this close up, she could see what all the fuss was about.

"Thank you for the chat and thank you for caring about my health." He paused. "It was nice." And, with that, he turned on his heel and walked back into the bar.

Sukie stayed behind for a few moments to finish her mug of chocolate. She was also still getting her head around the conversation she'd just had with Pete Wallace. She hadn't anticipated *that* when she'd walked out here earlier. It just went to show though, and proved what she'd always thought, being in the limelight is not all it's cracked up to be. Now she knew that to be fact.

She collected the mugs from the table, walked back indoors and went over to the table where Andrew was now chattering away to his wife. She placed the mugs on the table and bent down to pick her handbag up from the floor. It was time to go to her room and enjoy another nice soak in the tub.

As she straightened up, however, she saw Aggie Wilson walk in and go to the bar. Suddenly, a little pickle of an idea entered her head. Not allowing herself to ponder further on the wisdom of her thought, she decided to take action before she could talk herself out of what she was about to try and do. She mouthed goodnight to

Andrew and walked over to the bar to where Aggie was standing.

"Hi there! I'm very sorry to trouble you but I wanted to apologise for staring at you earlier this evening in the lift. I saw that you'd noticed but were too polite to say anything."

Aggie turned to look at Sukie and made a non-committal "Hmmm" sound.

Sukie carried on, a smile plastered on her face. "I was staring because I knew I recognised you. It finally came to me that you're Aggie Wilson, the writer for High-Hitting. I thought your article last month 'A Day in the Life of An Aussie Flip-Flop' was excellent. It was so witty and humorous. I do like what you write, it's very clever."

Aggie, along with most human beings, liked it when a compliment came their way. And being a journalist with an ego, she was prepared to lap it up.

"Why thank you very much," she responded, returning Sukie's smile. "It's kind of you to say so. And yes, I was a bit concerned earlier so thank you for taking the time to explain. I was wondering if you were related to someone on whom I'd performed a hatchet job, somewhere along the line of my extensive career."

Sukie grinned and popped herself up onto the stool next to her.

"Nope, you're quite safe on that one. Although I don't recall reading any of your articles where you've done such a thing."

"Back in the early days, when I was a young hack on the dailies, I did. The only way to get noticed on a tabloid paper was to put in work rich with venom and sarcasm. Nice pieces fell into the file marked 'R' for rubbish. People have long memories though."

As Aggie spoke, Sukie got the attention of the barman and ordered a glass of white wine. She turned back to Aggie and asked, still smiling, "So what brings you to lovely, snowy Salzburg? An article on the day of a wellington boot perhaps?"

Aggie chuckled. "Now there's a thought. Although no, not this time. I'm actually here to interview Pete Wallace."

"Really? Wow! That must be quite a buzz," she replied innocently.

"Yes, I suppose it is. I've had to step in at the last minute. My colleague, who should've taken the interview, fell ill and I was the only person able to come here at the last moment. I was in France, doing some research for an article when I got a phone call late on Saturday afternoon, asking me to step in for Wendy, my colleague. I couldn't get a direct flight so I ended up hiring a car and driving here. I arrived late last night and I'm shattered. Fortunately, Wendy had written out the questions she wanted to ask, and emailed them to me, so I wasn't as unprepared as I could've been. When I do an interview, I usually spend several days doing subject research. This time, however, I'm flying blind and having to follow someone else's remit. I feel very off kilter, I have to say."

"Oh, that's understandable. I watched his concert on the television recently. Did you see it?"

Aggie sighed. "No, I was away on an assignment at

the time. Was it any good?"

"Oh yes! It was interesting to see how he's matured over the last few years. He must be what… in his thirties by now? No longer a silly kid, that's for sure. You must be pleased at being one of the first to interview the all-new Pete Wallace."

"Oh bugger!" Aggie had a look of annoyance on her face. "The colleague I've stepped in for is younger than me and her interview questions reflect that. I wasn't happy asking them but didn't have time to come up with my own. No wonder he was getting shirty with me earlier, he's probably heard them all a thousand times before."

"I hope you don't mind me saying this but, won't it be your name on this article? You need to sort out your own questions. Pete Wallace has grown up and definitely now ticks all the boxes for being a mature adult. Even his music has moved on." Sukie paused as she thought on the best way to press the point home, without being pushy. After all, she was trying to steer Aggie down a different path, not steamroller her into submission. She took a slow sip of her wine, to let Aggie digest what she'd said, then continued. "I like the edge his songs seem to have now. A bit more of 'I've seen life' about them now rather than the 'I'm waiting for life to happen and I'll snog a few cute babes while it does' as he was before."

Aggie looked thoughtfully back at Sukie. "You know, you're right! It *will* be my name on this and I'll be the one getting it in the neck if I don't deliver something fresh. I'm not letting some other publication get one over on High-Hitting." Aggie stopped to think for a moment.

"I'm doing a photo shoot to accompany the interview, with Pete tomorrow. I might be able to slip in a few extra questions," she muttered.

"What? Aw, now I'm quite jealous that you're getting to spend even more time with him doing a photo shoot." Sukie fixed a star-struck look on her face. "You are SO lucky. What type of pictures are you going for? Pleeeeeease tell me you're not going for the bare-chested, wearing nothing but a towel, nude-style shots with glamorous models draped all over him. That is just SO old and past it. I'm sick of seeing photos like that. It's almost as though he doesn't know how to keep his kit on!" She grimaced, and gave mock shudder, as she took another sip of her wine.

Aggie, taking a sip of her wine, just about choked and quickly coughed to cover it up. "Are you a mind reader? That's exactly what Wendy's requested in her email. So, um, what kind of pictures would you like to see of him then?" she asked.

Sukie pretended to think for a moment. "Well, stuff that's more tasteful really and reflects the man he's become. If I was in charge of the camera, I'd have him in some nice chinos, perhaps with a crisp white cotton shirt opened down a few buttons. A hint of chest rather than a lot of chest – you know, the old 'less is more' thing! And, maybe some shots of him laughing into the camera, rather than the well-worn pout and sexiness. I'd like to see him in a nice dinner-suit with the shirt collar open and an un-tied bow tie around the neck. Also, I'm sick of the glamour girls. I'd rather see him giving an old char-lady a huge big hug than a length of spaghetti, with lipstick on, hanging off his arm."

Sukie paused as she thought about how, if she had a say in the matter, she would really like to see Pete Wallace being photographed.

"I'd just like to see him looking mature, approachable and happy. He's done mean and moody for so many years and it has become *really* boring. It would make a nice change." She took another sip of wine, trying to assume an air of nonchalance and hoped her suggestions didn't sound too contrived. She put her glass back down on the bar. "Well, I think so anyway. Maybe that's just me and everyone else still wants the 'mean and moody' look. I don't know. Who am I to judge? I'm just one woman. There are most likely twenty million women who would be quick to disagree!" she laughed as she smiled back at Aggie.

Aggie stared over the bar into the mirror behind the optics for a few seconds. Sukie could almost hear the cogs whirring as her mind digested all that had been said. Finally, she turned back to Sukie.

"There's a lot of potential in what you've said. This really is a chance to get a jump on the other glossies and move Pete Wallace out of his 'lad about town' pigeon-hole and into the 'all grown up' sphere instead. I can almost see the headline now, 'The Boy Becomes a Man'. Yup, it's really workable." A wide grin raced across her face. "Girl, you might just be onto something there. Would you mind if I dwelled on your suggestions and maybe used one or two?"

Sukie raised her glass and smiled sweetly "Be my guest!"

Aggie replied, "I believe I owe you a drink of thanks for that. Please let me buy you one before I head off to hit the internet and redo my whole interview from today."

Before Sukie could decline, Aggie had already turned away to get the barman's attention.

Just then, Pete, with Kara and Scruffy behind him, marched past her on his way out of the bar. He didn't look at her, or catch her eye. "Treacherous bitch!" Scruffy hissed in her ear as he passed by. Kara simply glared at her but said nothing. Sukie looked after them in amazement. What on earth...? But, before she had a chance to chew Jordie's ear off for his comment, they were gone.

Pete couldn't believe his eyes when Jordie gave him a nudge, and pointed over to the bar where Sukie was laughing with Aggie Wilson.

Damn and blast, he thought. Why on earth did I trust her? She *is* a bloody journalist after all. Shit! Shit! Shit! Look at her all smiling and giggling with Aggie. Probably having a good old laugh at my expense, no doubt! I suppose I'll read the full details of our conversation in some newspaper or magazine before the month is out.

Jordie and Kara looked on as the annoyance spread over his face. Jordie was quick to guess what the problem might be. "Ok Pete, what did you say to her?" he asked.

"What do you mean?" he replied, unable to tear his eyes away from the women laughing together in front of him.

"Look son, I've known you a bloody long time and I can read you like a book. You're angry and worried at the same time so I need to know what you said that's making you feel like that."

Pete sighed. "I told her how pissed off I was with having to do this nude / half-naked photo shoot tomorrow."

"Well that ain't so bad."

"I also told her how much I loathed the press and how I didn't like dealing with them. How they're all a bunch of leeches, sucking the bones dry of people like me in order to get some kind of story. Well... not those exact words, but no doubt that's how it will read in the headlines!"

"Bugger!" was the only reply Jordie could make to that one. They all knew a one-liner like that would be dished up as a three-course meal by the media. Being attacked, or slated, for the bloodhounds they were, was something they didn't take lying down.

"Let's get out of here," said Pete, standing up. "I can't bear to watch that anymore."

And, with that, he walked out the room with his head high. He didn't make eye contact with anyone, and avoided looking at Sukie. The feelings of being used and abused were good friends to him. He'd experienced them so often over the years. He just wished it still didn't hurt so much when it happened. Why did he always have to be so bloody trusting with people? And, more to the point, why did people always see him as a way to make a fast buck?

Chapter Twelve

It was Tuesday afternoon and Sukie was walking along the hotel corridor to her room. She couldn't wait to get her boots off and have a nice hot bath before meeting the clients again this evening for dinner. It had been a good day today. Both she and Andrew had been given an extensive tour of the Monschberg GMBH site and they both knew this client was going to be worth a lot of revenue in the months to come. The potential for greater business was excellent. It had been an exhausting day though and she would much rather have ordered some room service and chilled out on her bed, all snuggled up in the rather lush bathrobe the hotel provided. Instead, she had only three hours in which to relax, bathe and get tarted up again before going back out for dinner.

When she opened her room door, she found an envelope on the floor behind it. She picked it up and was busy opening it as she walked into the room. She noticed the smell first. What on earth...? She looked up. The explosion of flowers – it really was the only way to describe them – that was sitting on the table in front of the window, was truly stunning. It was the biggest arrangement she'd ever seen this close up and consisted mostly of roses and carnations in the most amazing shades of crimson, white, and cream she'd ever seen. It was utterly beautiful. She couldn't think of any reason why she would receive a bouquet and wondered if the arrangement had been put in her room in error. She dropped the envelope she was holding onto the chair and walked over to see if there was a card. She finally found one towards the back in a gold envelope, and it most definitely had her name on it. She opened the envelope and took out a thick, gold-embossed card. The writing on it was also beautiful and quite in keeping with the whole glorious experience.

A Winter Bouquet for a Winter Lady.
An Apology and a Thank you.
Please join me for dinner this evening so
I may say both in person.
Room 1020.
Yours most humbly
Tweety Pie.

Wow! An apology? For what? She didn't know what to think. So she didn't. She just sat on her bed and admired the glorious arrangement in front of her.

Earlier that same day, Pete Wallace had been equally gob-smacked. He'd turned up – very reluctantly it had to be said – for the dreaded photo-shoot with Aggie Wilson and had walked into a hive of activity that saw Aggie grabbing his arm, dragging him over to several rails of clothing and holding various shirts, jumpers and tops in front of him. When she saw his confusion, Aggie smiled and proceeded to explain.

"I was having a think last night, after we'd finished our interview and it occurred to me that the details of the photo-shoot for today were really no different from the others you've done for the last fifteen or so years. So, I decided it was time to let the world see how much you've grown up. These are your first interviews in almost three years and it's clear you're no longer the young teenage boy who arrived on our television screens. You've matured into a man and it's time for the rest of the world to see that." As she was talking, Aggie continued to rummage through the rails, pulling out different items for consideration. Turning to replace the psychedelic shirt she'd just rejected, Aggie carried on speaking to him over her shoulder. "Therefore, today, you'll be fully clothed at all times. Do you mind jumping into these for me so we can get started?" and she'd held out a cream cricketing outfit, complete with jumper and cap. "It also occurred to me that some of the questions I asked you yesterday were rather out of date, so if it's alright with yourself, I'd like to ask some new ones while we take these photographs.

Would that be okay?" Aggie stood in front of him with her eyebrows raised.

"Umm, yes! Yes, that would be fine," he responded slowly, still trying to take in this change of photographic direction. It had been the last thing he'd expected. He went behind the screens in the corner and got changed. He pulled the cap on and twisted it slightly to the side. As he walked back out it suddenly hit him like the proverbial thunder-bolt.

Sukie!

She was responsible for this. She had to be. It was *too* much of a coincidence that he'd seen her talking to Aggie last night, just after he'd spilled his heart out to her about how he didn't want to do topless or raunchy shoots anymore, and now, here he was, *not* doing a topless, or raunchy, shoot. He walked over to Kara and Jordie, who'd just come into the room, and were taking in the goings-ons with some amazement. This was not what they were expecting either.

"Kara, I need to you do something for me. Please can you sort out the biggest bouquet of flowers possible – the colours need to be greens, reds, whites, creams, golds; all the colours of Christmas – and have it sent to the woman I was talking with on the roof terrace last night. Her first name is Sukie but you'll need to find out her surname, I don't know it. Reception should be able to arrange for the bouquet to be placed in her room."

Kara stared at him. "What on earth are you wearing? I thought you were going to be in your birthday suit? And why do you want to send that woman flowers? When you saw her last night, you were furious because she was spilling the beans on you to Aggie Wilson."

"I think it would be fair to say that I was wrong," he smiled. "Very wrong indeed!"

Kara's eyebrows disappeared into her hairline. "You're admitting you were wrong? Blimey! You don't get many of those to the pound.'

He tried to explain his change of heart. "Don't you think it's a bit strange that, after I tell Sukie how much I don't want to do this shoot, we see her speaking with Aggie and then, when we turn up this morning, we find the remit for the shoot has been completely altered? Aggie is making a big deal over how I'm now 'so grown up and mature'. That's exactly what I told Sukie I wanted."

Kara looked him in the eye and spoke sternly. "You were saying some pretty nasty things about her, when we got back to the suite. You should be ashamed of yourself."

"I am. Totally! I feel like a Grade-A shit. I need to think of something to write in the card which conveys that."

"Well you're the song writer, Pete. Words are your business, time to do your stuff."

"I'll have a think about it while you sort out the flowers. And Kara, make it a bouquet not easily forgotten please."

"Will do," Kara replied, as he was called over by the photographer.

It was four hours later when he finally got the thumbs-up from Aggie. The shoot was over at last and, he was quick to admit, it was probably one of the most fun times he'd had while being photographed. It had been a blast. There had been lots of laughter and the hour with the little old cleaning lady had been hilarious. She'd had a few stories to tell and tell them was what she'd done.

Kara came over, just as he was cleaning the matte powder off his face, and told him that she'd sorted out the bouquet and had made the arrangements for it to be delivered to Sukie's room. All she needed now were the details to put on the card.

He'd been thinking about this all through the shoot and had finally come up with something he was happy with. He dictated the piece to Kara and she wrote it in her notebook. When he got to the end, she looked up at him with surprise.

"Tweety-Pie?"

"Yup!"

"Care to elaborate?"

"Nope! Private joke." Pete smiled at her. He felt really good today. The change in events had been a total surprise and, it was that which had made it even better. He'd almost go as far as to say he was happy. And that was something which didn't happen very often anymore.

As Sukie sorted out her outfit for the client dinner that evening, she tried to figure out the best way to tell

Pete she was unable to accept his invitation. She was deeply disappointed as she'd much rather be in the company of a young, cute rock star, cracking jokes and having a laugh than having dinner with three fifty-plus Germans, listening to them talking business, and watching Andrew Hollings smarming all over them. Until the contracts were signed in the morning, however, she and Andrew had to keep smiling, and laughing at the bad jokes and pretend that in-depth conversations on the merits of plastic sheeting, were all that they lived for.

If only he'd asked me to join him tomorrow night, it would have been so much easier, she thought to herself as she walked over to the phone. The sooner she dealt with this, the better.

While the phone rang, she tried to think of the best way to appear cool and nonchalant. As if being asked to dinner by a famous rock star was an everyday occurrence for her.

Just then, a woman answered the phone. "Hello. Room 1020."

"Err hello, may I speak to Tweety Pie please?" she asked.

Kara burst out laughing at the other end. "One minute please," she smiled down the phone. Upon hearing the laughter, and the smile in Kara's voice, Sukie relaxed a small bit. She could hear Kara at the other end. "Oh, Tweety Pie, your Winter Lady is on the phone."

She laughed herself when she heard that, and was still chuckling when Pete came on the phone.

"I suppose you think that's funny do you?" he growled at her.

"Oh yes, I sure do!" she replied. "It was your choice to use the reference, now you pay the consequences."

"Thank you for your support."

"You're most welcome." She was still smiling, unable to get her head around the fact she was having cheeky banter with Pete Wallace.

"I gather you got the flowers then?"

"Oh yes! Thank you, they are absolutely stunning! Although, I'm not quite sure what you mean when you say they're an apology? You've lost me there I'm afraid."

Pete was quiet for a second. "Erm, I'm trying to think of the best way to explain..." He took a deep breath. "Okay, I'm just going to plunge right in. When I saw you talking with Aggie last night, I jumped to the wrong conclusion. I thought you'd lied to me and that you really were a journalist. I was expecting to see all that we had discussed splashed over a plethora of newspapers and magazines before the week was out. I called you many names and none of them were complimentary."

In her bedroom, Sukie turned to look out of her window but said nothing.

When she didn't speak, Pete hastily continued, filling the silence. "When I met Aggie today for the photo-shoot, and saw that she'd done a complete about-face on how I was to be photographed, I realised I'd done you an injustice. It didn't take long for me to realise the change was all down to your intervention. Even though you don't know me, you went out of your way to do something nice for me and I feel utterly terrible for being so judgemental. I am very, very sorry. In this business, you get so used to people taking from you, to make their own lives better, it never even occurred to me that you might be doing something to make *my* life better. I really am very sorry."

She heard him breathing on the phone as he waited for her to say something.

Finally, she replied, "Oh, is that all? I thought you were about to say you'd done a hit-and-run on a cat or some other defenceless poor animal. Now *that* would've been unforgivable!" She smiled as she spoke. "Pete, thank you for the apology, it's very generous of you and thank you for the fabulous flowers too, but don't worry about it. I can understand why you'd think like that and I'm just glad I was able to do something to help you. It wasn't difficult and I think everyone will benefit."

"Thank you for being so understanding, I'm still very sorry. This is why I'd like you to join me for dinner. So I can say it to you in person. Please say you will."

"Pete, I can't. I really would like to but my colleague and I are having dinner with our clients tonight and I have to be there. They don't sign the contract until tomorrow so we have to keep them sweet until then. I'm sorry."

Pete was surprised by the wave of disappointment he felt at Sukie's reply.

"Oh, ok then." He thought for a moment, trying to recall their conversation from the night before. "How long did you say you were staying in Salzburg for?" he asked.

"I leave on Sunday morning."

"Would you, perhaps, be available for dinner tomorrow evening instead then?"

"I think, perhaps, I could be." He heard the smile in

116

Sukie's reply and he quietly punched the air above him. He was about to say goodbye when he remembered her comments the night before, about disliking being in the spotlight. "By the way, would you like to eat in the dining room or, if you'd prefer some privacy, I can arrange for dinner to be set up in my suite?"

"Oh, the latter, please, if you don't mind," she replied. "I really don't want to run the risk of appearing on the front page of the tabloids, being cited as your 'new squeeze'!"

"Would being my 'new squeeze' be such a bad thing?" he asked in amusement.

"Too right it would! I'll have you know I have taste when it comes to my men! Now, I have to go. I'll see you tomorrow evening at seven thirty. Bye!"

'What?' He looked at the humming handset in complete surprise and burst out laughing. "The cheeky mare," he chuckled, as he slowly put the phone back down on the hook.

Chapter Thirteen

Sukie sat and stared at the contents of her meagre wardrobe. It was mid-afternoon on Wednesday. The clients had signed the contract this morning, it was on its way back to the UK with Hopeless and she was, once more, on holiday. However, rather than doing more sight-seeing as planned, she was desperately trying to decide what to wear to dinner this evening. 'Dinner with world-famous rock star' hadn't been listed on the agenda when she'd packed her case on Saturday. She didn't want to look too tarty or flirty but, equally, didn't want to look old and uptight either. Since they were eating in Pete's suite, it wouldn't be as formal as the dining room but she wanted to be sure that whatever outfit she wore didn't give the wrong impression. She was not, after all, some groupie – no matter what Scruffy might think – and she was determined not to give that impression in any way.

She pulled on her walking boots and decided a trip to

the nearby shops may be her best option. She recalled
passing some fashion stores over the river on Griesgasse
which might be worth a visit. Maybe some nice dressy
trousers and either a light jumper or a blouse would hit
the right tone. She utterly disliked clothes shopping so
this was not a decision that was made lightly, but needs
must. Besides, she wanted to pick up some gifts and
souvenirs to take home so she may as well do the old
'killing two birds with one stone'. She sent her mum a
quick text to let her know she was still alive and kicking,
picked up her handbag and headed out, mentally
preparing herself for the shopping battle ahead.

Beth McClaren was having the time of her life! Why
had she never done this before, she thought, as she looked
at her reflection in the mirror of the department store
changing-room. She'd kept good on her promise to treat
herself to a personal make-over and, having booked the
day off work, she was now having the best game of
'dressing up' she'd ever had. A quick phone call on
Monday morning had seen her making an appointment
with Fredrick, to be personally dressed. She admitted that
it was a bit of an extravagance – okay, it was more than a
bit – but she was having so much fun, it was difficult to
feel guilty over the cost and Fredrick was proving to be
worth every penny.

Just then, her phone beeped. She fished it out of her
bag and found she'd received a text from Sukie saying

business has been concluded successfully, she was having a great time, and was looking forward to being 'properly' on holiday although she now had to go out to do some clothes shopping as she had been invited to dinner that evening.

Beth was intrigued by the last comment, and wanted to know more but, typically, Sukie hadn't thought to elaborate any further. She wondered if she was a having dinner with a man and desperately wanted to text back, to ask for more details, but she was determined to stick to the promise she'd made to herself on Sunday night. No more interfering in Sukie's life. With a sigh, she replied back, saying she hoped shopping would be less of a chore in Salzburg and that her evening was a fun one. She hit the 'send' button, thinking as she did, on the chance of there being something in the air in Salzburg. It would be the most amazing coincidence if Sukie were to meet the man of her dreams in the city of her dreams. Actually, thinking about it some more, she concurred it would be downright spooky, especially after her making such a remark to Sukie the night before she'd left.

She noticed the time when she returned her phone to her handbag, hurriedly changed back into her own clothes and went to advise Fredrick on the items she'd decided to purchase. She had a hair appointment to squeeze in before going out to the theatre this evening with Laura so it would be good idea to get a wriggle on otherwise she'd be late for everything.

Five hours later, Sukie was standing in her bathroom, putting the finishing touches to her make-up. She didn't normally wear a lot of cosmetics but did like to make the effort for special occasions. And dinner, with Europe's number one rock pin-up, would most definitely be classed as special. After some trawling around this afternoon, she'd managed to find the perfect outfit – a pair of classic cut, charcoal grey, trousers teamed up with a dark scarlet, short-sleeved, light-weight jumper. The colour of the jumper enhanced her chestnut hair and accented her fresh skin tones. It was certainly one of her favourite, and most becoming, colours. Some subtle brown eye-shadow around the eyes, with a lick of kohl liner to give a soft smoky effect, and a gentle, soft red lipstick was all that was required to give the classy look she wanted to achieve. As luck would have it, she'd packed her pair of Icelandic rock, charcoal-coloured, stud earrings and they were a perfect match with the new trousers. They were a small touch but one which pulled the outfit together in a subtle, elegant manner and was completed when she donned her black, high-heeled boots. She looked at the final result in the full-length mirror with a critical eye. She couldn't decide, though, on what to do with her hair – leave it down, pin it up, half-up, half-down...? She lightly tonged the natural waves into more tidy-looking curls and messed about with some grips but still she wasn't happy. Finally, she decided to pin it up slightly at the sides with a few tendrils 'escaping'. She let out a small gasp when she saw the time was after seven twenty-five. That, she decided, would have to do and, picking up her little evening purse – just big enough for a tissue, a lipstick and her key card she left her room and headed for the stairs at the end of the corridor. Well, it was hardly worth getting the elevator to go up two floors.

Chapter Fourteen

Sukie took a deep breath before knocking on the door of Suite 1020. She already knew this suite would put her own executive room well into the shade. The fact there was only one door, in the small corridor, screamed out that this was as exclusive as you could get in this establishment. Sure enough, when Kara opened the door, she walked into a marble-floored hallway with several doors leading off it. The hallway itself was the size of her bathroom downstairs. She managed to refrain from gawping but it was hard work.

Kara smiled as she walked in. "Hi, Sukie, come on in. Pete's waiting for you through here," and she walked towards a door at the far end of the corridor, opened it and stood back to allow Sukie to enter first. When she did, she couldn't stop the gasp that slipped from her lips. The room itself was not too different from her own downstairs, although very much bigger. While Sukie's had a two-seater sofa and a small chair, this room could accommodate the full suite which consisted of two sofas, three chairs and a considerably larger coffee table. What had actually taken Sukie's breath away, however, was the view. The wall which should have been at the end of the room – such as she had in her own room – was instead a floor to ceiling window which stretched the whole width of the lounge. Through the window, she could see the brightly lit fortress, high up on its mountain. The snow was gently falling and, the scene was so blissful, she felt fizzy bubbles of joy welling up inside her. The few table lamps that were lit in the room were subtle enough to only enhance this amazing view. She walked to the windows and gazed out, totally enraptured with what she was seeing. Pete quietly appeared by her side and handed her a glass of chilled champagne.

"I thought you'd like to see this," he murmured quietly. "I saw the way you admired it from the roof terrace earlier this week."

"Oh, Pete, it's too wonderful for words to describe. It's perfect. I really don't know what to say. Thank you." She took a sip from her glass and was delighted to find her champagne was equally as perfect. She dragged her eyes reluctantly away from her perfect view, looked at Pete and smiled. "Now this is what you call a welcome."

She turned back into the room and noticed a small dining table had been set up a few feet to her left.

Pete explained. "The suite does have a proper dining room but the view is decidedly lacking compared to this," he indicated to the window, "so I asked for a table to be placed out here as I thought you would prefer to see your fortress as we eat."

"My fortress?" she asked, with a small frown on her forehead and a smile on her lips.

"Oh, yes, I see a few similarities between you both."

"Look, sunshine," she replied, speaking with a Hollywood-star drawl, "my hips may not be as svelte as they once were but I still object to them being referred to as buttresses!"

Pete chuckled as he explained. "It was more your strengths that came to mind. The fortress is strong and dominating but, also, protective. I believe you have the same characteristics. You have a deep strength within you and know your own mind, which can, I suspect, sometimes be regarded as domineering. I, however, have first-hand experience of your protectiveness so you can't deny that you look after others. People usually look at the fortress with admiration. I think many people look at you in the same way, although, I think you're not aware of it."

Sukie regarded him as he spoke. When he'd finished, she looked at him for a few seconds and then lightly shrugged her shoulders. "Well, that was nicely put. Although I still think you're really trying to tell me I have big hips!" She laughed. "Anyhow, thank you for the comparison... I think!"

Pete walked back into the centre of the room. "I've asked for dinner to be brought up at 8 pm, if that's ok with you?"

"Eight is fine."

Kara walked back into the room. "Pete, that's Jordie and I off out now. We'll catch up with you later yeah?"

"Oh, Kara, let me properly introduce you to Sukie

before you go. Sukie, this is Kara my personal assistant, my Girl Friday and, more often than she should be, my lifesaver. Kara has rescued me from more tricky situations than she should ever have had too. Kara, this is Sukie, who, it would seem, managed to prevent me from potentially singing like a stupid yellow cartoon bird."

Sukie and Kara shook hands. "Pleased to meet you" they chorused.

"Where's Jordie?" Pete asked, looking through to the hallway. "Jordie, you out there?"

Jordie stuck his head around the door. "What?" he asked grumpily, whilst throwing a dirty look at Sukie. She, obligingly, threw one right back at him.

"I'd like to introduce you to Sukie, Jordie, if you can spare a moment?"

Jordie looked at his watch. "We've got a table booked, mate, we need to get going."

Pete sighed. "It's only going to take thirty seconds, I'm sure the restaurant won't release your table that quickly."

Jordie slouched into the room in a manner that left everyone in no doubt he was doing this under duress. He stuck his hand out in Sukie's direction.

"Nice to meet you," he said, his tone of voice totally belying his words.

Sukie touched her tips to his fingers. "Likewise..."

Pete and Kara watched in slight amusement, at the battle of wills taking place in front of them before sharing a look. They both knew Jordie hated being wrong and could be as stubborn as the day was long. It looked like Sukie wasn't one for backing down quickly either so it was no wonder the two of them were locking horns.

"Ok, you guys, off you go, have a pleasant evening. I'll see you later."

As Jordie and Kara left the room, Pete headed over to the music machine in the corner. "Shall I put some music on? Do you have any preferences?"

"I think something soft would be nice, instrumental if you have it?"

"Vivaldi? The Four Seasons?"

"Perfect."

Sukie walked back over to the window while Pete fiddled about with the music. She looked up again at the fortress – was she really as he'd described? Was that how other people perceived her? She was still trying to decide if the character assessment was a compliment or not, when, a few seconds later, Pete was again standing next to her, topping up her glass as the soft sound of violins filled the air.

"So c'mon then," she said, turning to face him, "let's get this apology you think you have to make, out of the way so we can relax and enjoy the evening."

"Ah!" He had the good grace to look uncomfortable. "I was hoping we'd talk about that after dinner when I might've had a chance to impress you a bit."

"It takes more than a dinner to impress me, so I suggest you just spit it out."

Pete looked down and shuffled his feet a bit, before finally lifting his head and looking Sukie in the eye. "After we had left the bar, on Monday night, I said things about you that were, if I'm being honest, incredibly nasty. When I'm upset or angry, I have a mean streak that rises up with a vengeance. I can, and will, say the most horrible and hurtful things imaginable. Naturally, given the bad feeling between you and Jordie, he was only too happy to join in."

"Yes, I'll bet he was! It would certainly explain his comment to me as he walked out of the bar."

"I really am sorry about that. Jordie has always fought my battles with me and would defend me to the end. The opportunity to get back at you was one he was not going to miss." Pete walked over to the dinner table and fiddled with the cutlery laid on it as he continued speaking. "However, while you may not have been here to hear the insults I was throwing around, the fact is, I *was* saying some really evil stuff about you and I'm now *so* ashamed about doing so. When I arrived at the photo shoot yesterday morning, and saw what Aggie was planning, it very quickly became apparent what you'd done. To say I felt, and still feel, really, really awful would be a massive understatement."

"And so you should, I was only trying to help you out."

"I know that now, I just didn't at the time."

"So why are you telling me this? As you've already stated, I wasn't around to hear it so I would've been none the wiser. Why are you apologising when you could have gotten away with keeping quiet?"

Pete looked directly into her eyes, making it impossible for her to miss his sincerity. "I like you. I like the fact you're straight up. You're an honest person and I'd really like us to be friends. I need a friend who I don't also employ. It would be so nice to know someone who wants nothing from me, and who I can trust not to betray me. In the exceptionally short time I've known you, I can already see that having you as my friend would help me to be a better person. I also hope that you'd like having me as your friend, that I can also help you sometimes. You know, the way real friends do. Please... Will you be my friend...?"

Pete's voice trailed off. Blimey, he thought, could I sound any more pathetic? The short time they had spent chatting, on Monday night, had made him realise, however, that he needed to allow more people into his life again. His days of being a virtual recluse were no longer so appealing.

Sukie had turned away and was looking out the window again. Eventually, she let out a sigh, "I really don't know if I can. After what you said about insulting me behind my back when I wasn't there to defend myself, well, it would be very strange..." she stopped.

Pete could see she was more upset than she was letting on. Her lips were pursed and she was blinking rapidly, as though trying not to cry. He didn't speak. To say anything more would simply make things worse. There comes a time, he thought, when you're better off just shutting up.

For a few minutes, the only sound was that of violins, as the music played quietly in the background. Sukie continued to stare out of the window. He walked over to stand beside her – unable to bring himself to look at her, he bowed his head and shuffled his feet about again, feeling very small and rather stupid. He could only remember one other occasion when he'd felt this badly over something he'd done wrong.

The sudden sound of a snort made him jump. He looked up to see Sukie chewing the inside of her cheek as she tried not to laugh.

"What the...?" he started, but didn't finish, as she gave in and bent forward, howling with laughter and wiping tears from her eyes.

He looked at her with a slack jaw. "Have you been winding me up?"

Sukie, walking over and sitting down at the table, managed to draw enough breath to reply. "Your face," she snorted again. "It was a picture. You should have seen yourself. You were so totally squirming with embarrassment. It was wonderful…"

"I'm glad you think so," he replied dryly. "I'm sure you can see why I'm not sharing the joke with you." He actually felt quite miffed that she was taking this all so lightly. He'd just laid his soul out bare to her, practically begging her for her friendship. And all she could do was laugh in his face. He could feel his temper stirring and he fought to keep it down.

"Oh, Pete, relax," Sukie spluttered, as she tried to gain some control.

"Well I'm so glad I made you laugh." He was still quite put out at the idea of her laughing at him, and was refusing to see the funny side of the situation.

"Oh, you did." She giggled again before taking a deep breath to regain some composure. She stood up and walked over to where he was now standing glaring out of the window, placed her hand on his arm and spoke to him with a gentler tone. "Look, I'm not angry with you for the reaction you had because I can appreciate how it must have looked to you. I really *do* understand what kind of crap you have to put up with. I get it. Honest! It's just... I don't often get the chance to wind up a world-wide superstar." She grinned at him as he continued to glower at her.

"You know, you actually looked quite cute as you stood there, scuffing your shoes on the floor. I now know what you looked like as a five-year-old. I'll bet you got away with loads of stuff when you were a kid."

He turned to look at her, smiling up at him, and it dawned on him how rarely anyone ever fooled about with him anymore. When he'd been in the band, they'd played tricks on each other constantly, and were forever taking the piss. These days, however, people were always so serious around him. Sure, Jordie would tease him at times, and share jokes, but the age gap between them meant that Pete always saw him more as a second father, not a close friend he could share all his secrets with.

He started to smile as he remembered how he'd always managed to squeeze his way out of trouble when he was a child. "Well," he replied. "Now you come to mention it..."

Just then the door chimes rang. "Ah, saved by the bell. It would seem dinner has arrived." He smiled at Sukie. "I don't know about you, but this world-wide superstar is starving."

"Me too, so bring it on, dude," she replied. She pointed to a pile of board games she'd spotted sitting on top of a nearby cupboard, and continued, "And then, afterwards, I'm going to whoop your sorry ass at Snakes & Ladders!"

Chapter Fifteen

Jordie looked at his watch as he and Kara made their way up to the suite in the elevator. "Quarter past eleven," he said. "D'ya think they'll be at it by now?"

"How would I know?" she replied. "Why do you always think Pete is going to bed every girl he meets?"

"Because he usually does! And this one is definitely out for something, despite what she says. I don't trust her at all."

"Yes, Jordie, I think we've already established that," she sighed.

All through dinner, Jordie had performed a full character assassination on Sukie. The fact he knew very little about her, was totally irrelevant. Jordie had many great points, Kara mused, but his one biggest fault, was that once he had made his mind up on something, it rarely changed. Sometimes this worked well, especially within business, but, on a personal level, it was more often a failing.

"Well, I hope he does get it on with her and then she'll be out of the way. He never visits the same lamppost twice. She'll just be another notch on that bedpost of his."

"Yeah, whatever," Kara replied wearily, as she waited for him to open the door. She was tired, it had been a long day and she just wanted to get to her room where she could relax on her bed, send her boyfriend a nice long email and forget about work for a while.

They stepped through the door and the sound of laughter flowed towards them, along with Pete groaning "I don't believe it! Not again…!"

When they walked into the lounge, their eyes took in the sight of Sukie, in her stocking feet, doing a chicken dance around the room, as she called out in a very dodgy French accent, "Boring office worker - three, world-wide superstar – nil point!"

Pete was sitting at the coffee table, the Snakes & Ladders board in front of him, his head in his hands and groaning that she had definitely cheated. He didn't know how, but she had!

Kara smiled at Sukie's antics while Jordie simply glowered about being wrong on the two of them being in bed together.

"I'm off to my room," he muttered, and stormed out.

"So, have you two had a good time?" she asked, as she unwound the scarf from her neck.

"Yes, thank you," replied Sukie, as she flopped down onto one of the sofas.

"Yes. Well, apart from being beaten three times at

snakes and ladders by a CHEAT..." said Pete.

"I don't cheat!" Sukie smirked at him. "You're just crap." She flashed him an innocent smile.

"I am not!"

"Are too!"

"Am not!"

"Are too!"

"Enough you two," Kara interjected, "it's like standing between squabbling three-year-olds."

"That's the problem with these world-wide superstars, they just can't accept when they're crap at snakes and ladders," replied Sukie, giving her a friendly wink.

"I'll get you back, don't you worry," snarled Pete, good-humouredly.

"Yeah, yeah. You and whose armies?"

"These armies!" Pete howled with laughter as he waved his hands and arms above his head and Sukie joined him.

Kara looked at the two of them and realised that Pete was actually happy. He was really chilled out and relaxed. And he wasn't drunk either! This was very rare indeed. He always had an air of edginess about him, and never seemed to quite switch off. It would appear, however, that he had done just that tonight although she was quite sure he wasn't aware of it. And she wasn't going to bring it to his attention either.

"Right then," said Sukie, standing up and putting the game back on the pile on the cupboard. "I'm going to love you and leave you, as they say. It's been a long day and I can hear my bed calling me from here."

Pete stood up. "Um, what are you doing tomorrow?"

"Ah, tomorrow is a day I've been really looking forward to. I'm walking out to Schloss Hellbrunn. I've heard it has a rather nice Christmas Market and also a very good zoo."

"You say you're 'walking out' to it, is it far?" asked Kara.

"About three miles, I believe. Or so the bloke on the Concierge desk tells me. I've been shown the route on my map and he told to look out for one or two little surprises along the way. I tried to get him to expand on that comment but he just said I would enjoy the journey more if I didn't know what to expect."

"It sounds quite intriguing," said Pete.

"You're welcome to come along, if you think you like the sound of it."

"Are you sure you wouldn't mind?"

"No, not at all. Your company wasn't as boring as I expected so I reckon I could put up with you for another day." Sukie gave Pete a big smile to let him know she was teasing him.

"Well, just for that, I'm going to come along and be as boring as I possibly can."

"I'm sure you won't need to try too hard!"

"What time are you heading off?" Pete asked.

Kara said, "You've got your last interview tomorrow morning at 10 am."

Pete looked at her. "Oh! How long have you pencilled it in for?"

"Only an hour."

Pete looked at Sukie. "Would it be too late to leave

at 11.30? Do you want to go earlier than that?"

"11.30 will be fine. Call me when you're ready to go and I'll meet you down in the lobby."

Kara tidied some paperwork away while Pete escorted Sukie to the door of the suite.

"Thank you for dinner, Pete. I've had a really lovely time."

"Thank *you*, Sukie, for what you did with Aggie, and for being so gracious in accepting my apology. I'm looking forward to tomorrow."

"Good! I'm sure it will be fun." Sukie gave him a smile, leaned forward and popped a peck on his cheek. "Right, now go and get yourself some beauty sleep. You need it!" She opened the suite door and walked out into the hallway. On the threshold, she turned back to look at Pete, holding the door open with her hand. "Yes," she said.

"Err... Yes what?"

"I'll be your friend." With a quick wave, she was gone, the suite door closing with a click behind her.

"So, now we're alone, how was your night really?" asked Kara, as Pete walked back into the lounge. "Did you enjoy it as much as you said you did?"

He thought for a moment. "Do you know, Kara, I really did. I feel as though I've spent the entire evening laughing and talking but, I can't remember what we were laughing or talking about." He threw himself onto one of the sofas and looked up at the ceiling, before continuing. "Sukie is so easy to be in the company of. She's quite different from other girls, or women, I've spent time with." He paused, trying to think of the best way to describe her. "It's hard to explain. She's not fazed by who I am, or what I do for a living, but she has respect for it. She seems to instinctively know how it all works and understands the pitfalls that come with being in the public eye. Also, she doesn't do that 'trying to be cool' thing either. She's just... relaxed with me. Normal. That's it! She treats me as though I'm normal. That's the best way to describe it."

"So you fancy her then, do you?"

"Ah, now that's easy to answer – no, I don't. Maybe that's why we get on so well because there is no sexual tension. It's actually very nice to be in someone's company purely because you enjoy it and without any ulterior motive going on in the background."

"She's a very attractive woman," said Kara.

"I'm not denying that, but I don't fancy her. She doesn't do it for me. And, there's nothing to suggest that she fancies me either. And I'm really glad about that. This way, I can relax and not have to worry that she might be expecting something more from me."

"Ok! So, to completely change the subject, you'll be delighted to know the MTV interview we'd planned for Friday has been cancelled, meaning we can check-out straight after breakfast. You'll be back home by lunchtime."

Pete sat in thought for a moment before responding. "Kara, could you make enquiries with the hotel manager, or the Riley group, and see if we can stay through to Sunday please. I'd like to spend a few days just relaxing, after all the rush of the week. I could also get some

Christmas shopping done, which would be good, given that Christmas is only a few weeks away."

"I sure can. I don't think it will be a problem. I'll deal with it in the morning."

Kara stood up. "Right, well I'm off to bed now, I want to drop Gareth an email before I go to sleep. See you in the morning." She walked out of the room, leaving Pete standing in front of the window, looking thoughtfully at the fortress on the hill.

Christmas shopping my ass, she thought to herself as she closed the door of her bedroom. The reason you're staying here longer walked out the door five minutes ago. You might not know it yet, Pete Wallace, but that Sukie is getting under your skin. We women can sense these things, call it our intuition. Well I'm not going to tell you, it's far better that you find out for yourself in your own good time.

Jordie lay on his bed, still fully dressed. He could hear Pete and *that* girl, giggling and laughing through the door of his room. The sound of her laughter and voice set his teeth on edge. He couldn't explain to Kara why Sukie irritated him so much because he didn't know why himself. Maybe it was the way she'd humiliated him on Saturday night. Maybe it was her total self-assurance. Maybe it was the way Pete seemed to be behaving around this one, which was very different from any other female he'd had an interest in. Jordie didn't really do introspection but, when he did, he was as honest with himself as he would be to anyone else asking his advice or opinion. Sugar-coating wasn't his style and he could be just as brutal with himself when he needed to be. As he lay in the dark, he tried to work out why he'd taken against Sukie so much and, concluded, it was through fear. He could see Pete was intrigued with her and she would, eventually, get under his skin. This would give her an element of control over him and Jordie didn't like that idea at all. He'd be the first to admit he was a control freak but, he excused, keeping Pete Wallace's life on an even keel – both privately and professionally – was not an easy deal. Pete was a strong character and knew what he wanted but that didn't mean he always went the right way about it. All too often, Jordie had had to clean up the debris which the Pete Wallace hurricane left behind. Sometimes, that was physical debris, where a temper tantrum had resulted in a desecrated hotel room or, twice, un-wrapping his car from a lamppost or tree. Sometimes, it was emotional debris, where Pete's 'love 'em and leave 'em' nature had had more of an impact on some fragile girl's mental state, than he, Jordie, would've liked. Kiss and tell stories in the daily rags were ten-a-penny in this business but, when you threw 'I had a mental breakdown' into the equation, the paper-buying public seemed to multiply. These were the types of stories which resulted in more mud being thrown, and this was the kind which had a tendency to stick, so Jordie had to try and control the damage limitation the best he could. So often, he felt he had too many balls in the air and it was becoming harder and harder not to drop any.

Since the death of Andrew and Katya, he'd been father, mother, manager and counsellor to Pete, and anything, or in the case of Sukie McClaren, any*one*, with the potential to rock the boat, gave him cause for concern. He knew Pete would one day meet someone who he'd finally fall in love with but, Jordie had always hoped it would a/ be someone he could also guide along so that Pete's public persona would not be compromised, b/ be someone who genuinely loved Pete and was not some hanger-on looking to advance their own career and c/ be someone that he, Jordie, actually liked! Someone strong-minded and self-assured – like Sukie McClaren – would be his worst nightmare, as she was the polar opposite of all the above. He was still not convinced that she didn't have some hidden agenda up her sleeve and he was determined to reveal her to Pete as the conniving wench he was convinced she was. He got up and began to get ready for bed, all the time pondering on how he was going to expose the lying little charlatan.

Chapter Sixteen

Eduardo di Santo closed his locker and walked off towards the meeting room on the second floor. Every Thursday morning at 8 am, *RussoRicci* held the weekly meetings where new rotas were handed out, forthcoming events discussed, any new security-based technology introduced and general information exchanged. All staff had to attend. *RussoRicci* was the biggest security company in Italy, and named after the two friends who had conceived it fifteen years ago. Their remit had been to provide close quarter security – all clients would have their own personal security co-ordinator who would create, and install, a completely bespoke security package which catered to each client's own individual requirements. Having call centres was a no-no. Their success lay in the fractured nature of their business. Rather than having large offices in each major Italian city, which outsourced the security requirements for smaller towns to local security firms, *RussoRicci* had multiple offices in the larger cities like Rome and Milan with smaller offices – one or two depending on the location being covered – servicing all other areas, thus ensuring that all security requirements were dealt with by properly trained *RussoRicci* staff.

Eduardo was a Night Supervisor in the Verona office. His diligent and methodical nature made him a perfect candidate for this type of work. He had a team of eight beneath him and they covered a number of the museums in the town. When he'd first started working with *RussoRicci*, he had been one of the many day-shift security guards but, after Sofia's accident, he'd transferred over to nights so that he and his mother could take turns sitting with Sofia during her long stints in hospital. There was also the added benefit of the night shift being better paid. This had been a godsend when they'd had to move accommodation as the stairs in their previous apartment building would have been impossible for Sofia to negotiate on her rare visits home. They now lived in a very beautiful ground floor apartment, with a delightful garden, which was perfect for Sofia to move around in safely. Pete Wallace had created a trust fund for Sofia which provided a substantial yearly dividend. A portion of that went towards the monthly rent but Eduardo's pride would not allow for it to pay all the cost. He insisted on paying half. If he'd had his way, they would not have accepted a single cent from Wallace, but, he'd had to put Sofia's needs first and swallow his pride. Doing so choked him up as much as his anger did. Eduardo half listened to his manager, Fabio Mancini, go through the new rotas and announce some promotions in the Roma office. If only he could get a promotion, he'd be able to tell Pete Wallace exactly what he could do with his trust fund. He hated being beholden to that man, it made him feel inferior and incapable of looking after his own family. It fanned the flames of his anger and made his desire for some sort of payback even stronger.

He dragged his thoughts back to the present and tuned into the information Fabio was presenting on forthcoming events. Despite it being less than a couple of weeks until Christmas, Fabio was sharing the events due to take place throughout the summer months. Not only was additional security required to cover the tourist season, which peaked between June and September, but there was also the need for extra personnel to man the many summer events which took place each year. The Teatro Romano would, no doubt, have a full summer programme and the Stadio Marc'Antonio Bentegodi often played host to music gigs and festivals. In fact, it was the announcement of events taking place at the latter location which had Eduardo sitting up straighter and paying much closer attention.

"… and we can expect Pete Wallace to be performing at the Stadio on the last weekend in June," Fabio was saying. "This event currently holds 'To Be Confirmed' status but we should begin putting plans in place for the extra manpower we'll require. Not only will there be the ticket-holding fans turning up but, we will also have to deal with the ones who arrive ticketless, hoping to obtain one from the various touts who operate at these shows. Therefore, we will need all hands to the pump. Top rates of overtime will be paid to anyone prepared to do extra shifts to help out. I don't need names right away, but, if you can keep it in mind for now, we'll take your details once it changes to confirmed."

Eduardo knew for a fact he would be at that gig. This was what he had been waiting for. Wallace was going back out on the road and that made him a much easier target. It was time to shut this man down, once and for all. Eduardo now had his opportunity. He just had to work on a plan of execution and then chuckled to himself when he realised how fitting his choice of words were!

Chapter Seventeen

Sukie's phone rang at 11.25 am. It was Pete letting her know he was ready to go and that he'd be in the lobby in a few moments. She wondered how the day would turn out – walking through Salzburg with someone as famous as Pete was a scenario she'd never have dreamt of. Elsa probably had, more than once, although she, more likely, would've had them walking on a sun-kissed beach or floating on the Caribbean in a luxury yacht. Sukie had spent some time, the night before, thinking about today and hoping Pete would not be recognised. She'd been totally honest when she'd told him the thought of having her picture in the newspapers or gossip mags was amongst one of the worst things she could imagine. All this celebrity culture, and wanting to be famous, was not for her at all; she liked the privacy which came with the anonymity of being unknown. She thought back on some of the blokes she'd been stupid enough to go out with over the years, and this made her realise there were skeletons in her closet she'd rather stayed in there. Sukie also realised that a couple of them were probably sad *and* desperate enough for their own fifteen minutes of fame, to sell some sordid, made-up, sex story to whatever tabloid would pay them for it.

Yeugh! She shuddered as she closed her room door firmly behind her. God forbid that should ever happen, she thought, as she walked towards the lift.

She arrived in the lobby dead on 11.30 am and was pleased to see they'd be leaving pretty much about the time they had agreed on. At a reasonable pace, it would take roughly forty to forty-five minutes to reach the Schloss on the outskirts of the city. There was a nice scenic path which would take them most of the way there. She only had to find it. And find Pete! She looked around the reception lobby but couldn't see him anywhere.

Ah, the joys of being a world-famous rock-star, she reckoned – always got a phone call to take or an interview to make. She decided to give it five or ten minutes and then she'd call his suite to find out where he was.

She sat in a chair facing the main door and began to do some people watching. She liked to pass the time this way whenever she was waiting somewhere, be it at the airport, train station or bus stops. She liked to observe people and try to work out who or what they were – spotting those who wanted attention by being loud and over effusive to those around them, while all the time spinning their eyes around the room to see who might be looking or watching, or the people who were so sure of themselves, they simply exuded an air of confidence as they spoke with the receptionist, or the concierge, or the barman – they didn't need to scan a room to see who was looking because they really didn't give a damn either way.

As she gazed around, she felt a little prickle on the back of her neck, as though someone was watching her. She looked behind her but couldn't see anyone she knew. She noticed a bloke over by the doors, inside the bar, but he wasn't someone she'd seen before. She looked away but the sensation stayed with her. She looked around again. This time, the bloke in the bar smiled at her. She smiled back tentatively and then realised she'd seen that smile before.

It was Pete!

She burst out laughing as he got off the barstool and walked towards her. He hadn't done anything outrageous but the little he had done was enough to trick the eye. His blonde hair was hidden underneath a black ski cap and the small bit of fringe peeking out was… Auburn? As he drew closer, she could see the famous emerald green eyes had changed to blue. It was just enough to put you off the scent. Anyone looking at him now would think he reminded them of someone but they wouldn't be able to put their finger on who it might be.

"Gotcha!" he smiled, as he gave her a hug and a kiss on the cheek. "This disguise hasn't let me down yet and, so far, I would say its still doing the business."

"I looked at you when I walked in," said Sukie. "It never even crossed my mind it was Pete Wallace in disguise. I've worked out the coloured contact lenses but the hair?"

"A special cap I had made a few years ago. The 'fringe' is a false hairpiece sewn into the lining. I slick mine back, pull on the cap and voila... Pete Wallace disappears and Karl Schultz ees een ze room. And now, Fraulein, I need to ask zat, for today, you must call me Karl, if eet ees not too much trouble." The latter part of his sentence was spoken with a heavy German accent.

She grinned at him. "I will try to keep it in mind, mein herr." She could feel herself relaxing as they walked out the door of the hotel, happy in the knowledge she wouldn't be helping to sell any papers tomorrow.

"How much further is it?" Pete moaned, as they walked along the tree-lined avenue with the sun's rays peeping through the leaves. It was a beautiful winters' day – cold, frosty, and sunny. The sort of day which makes you want to go out for long walks in the country. And that is exactly what he and Sukie were doing, although he hadn't really appreciated just how far three miles was, when it was on foot and not in a car.

"Oh, not that far I'm sure," replied Sukie cheerily, although she looked at the map again and he guessed she was beginning to wonder the same thing.

"Oh, oh, oh... look!" Sukie stopped in her tracks before running up to the gates of a large sandy-gold-coloured building. As she rummaged in her bag for her camera, she explained "It's the von Trapp house." Excitedly, she took a few shots. "Oh wow, this is just amazing!"

He looked on in bemusement. "What *are* you doing? That's the Music and Drama School."

149

Sukie looked at him witheringly. "*This* is the house they used for the exterior shots of the von Trapp family home in The Sound of Music. I would recognise it anywhere." She pointed to the relevant page of her tourist guide which had come out of her bag when she'd put her camera back in. "Look, I'm right. That's another landmark I've found. I wonder if this is one of the surprises the concierge was hinting at?" The smile on her face was one of joy.

"If you're so into the film, why don't you go on one of the many tours that operate out of Salzburg, wouldn't it be easier?"

"Yes, it would," she replied, "but not half as much fun as finding everything myself."

"So, you like doing things the hard way then?"

"Not always, I just like doing things whichever way gives me the most satisfaction. I did think about taking a tour but decided it would be more enjoyable finding the different Sound of Music connections and references by myself, than having some tour guide pointing them out through a bus window and then moving us on like cattle because there's another coach behind."

Sukie put the guide book back in her bag and resumed walking as she spoke. He fell into step beside her. "I prefer to work to my schedule, not someone else's. I've always been like that. According to my mum, I was the same as a child. There was no point in showing me or telling me something. I always had to see, or find out, for myself." She showed him a small scar on her left hand. "That came from being told not to touch the iron because it was hot."

She pushed up her sleeve and pointed to another scar on her elbow, "This one is from falling off a fence I was trying to walk along. There was some glass underneath and I landed on it. I've also got a rather yummy scar on my leg from falling off my bike while trying to ride it with no hands."

"So, you're one of those people who, as my nan used to say, 'just won't take a telling!'" said Pete.

"That would be me I'm afraid," Sukie replied, ruefully. "Mum says I have an independent streak bigger than I am, and will always get me into trouble."

"Has it?" he asked, genuinely interested. She came across as being so grounded, with her head screwed on, he wanted to know more about what had shaped her into the person she was now.

"Well, maybe, sometimes. With hindsight, there have been times when I would've been better off listening to good advice, instead of rushing headlong into situations that, in the end, weren't so good for me. The upside, however, is that there have also been occasions when everything worked out in my favour. If I was being honest, I'd say it was a case of win some, lose some."

"So, you don't consider it to be a bad thing then?"

"No, not at all! I'd rather be independent and rely on myself than be dependent on someone else who would let me down – which probably explains why I'm in my late thirties and have never been married." She smiled at him. "I *don't* consider this to be an issue."

"Would you like to be married?" he asked with some curiosity. Most of the girls he'd met had almost made it a career move to snare a bloke, get married, and have children. And, too many of them, had seemed to think that 'he' was the bloke in question.

"I don't think so. I'm not really fussed about it. It doesn't bother me being on my own – I've got a good life, plenty of friends, financial independence and I enjoy my own company. I certainly don't consider it to be the 'be all and end all' of my life. I've worked with girls who only think about men and weddings and, truth be told, I find it all very boring. I'd like to think that I'm a whole person in my own right and I don't need a fella to 'complete' me. Anyway, I've already got two young men in my life and they mean the world to me."

"Two men?" He looked at her in shock. He hadn't thought of Sukie as being that kind of independent. Although, he hadn't thought of Sukie in *that* way at all.

"Oh, yes! Two gorgeously handsome young men who I adore and, I believe, who adore me in return. They certainly give that impression."

"Oh, well... That's good... I think." Pete didn't really know quite what to say. It wasn't like he was a prude or anything and, goodness knows, there had been enough occasions when he'd had two or more girls dancing attendance on him. He'd just never given any thought to the girls turning the tables.

"Do these young men know about each other?" he enquired.

"Of course they do. We all live together, so keeping it a secret would be difficult."

By this time, him mind was really starting to boggle. This was getting too weird. He thought for a moment. "Hang on a minute...," he said, "are these 'two young men' your sons?"

This was too much for Sukie who let out a howl of laughter. She'd thought Pete had worked out that she was referring to her cats but this was an option which had certainly not crossed her mind. The more she thought about it, the harder she laughed.

"I take it I'm wrong then?" he remarked dryly. He wasn't used to being in the company of someone who laughed at him as often as Sukie seemed to do. She really didn't care about his fame or his job. She behaved towards him as though he was the proverbial boy next door. He'd often moaned to Kara and Jordie about how he wished people would treat him like an ordinary bloke but, now that it was happening, it felt quite strange. When you've spent the best part of fifteen years being told you're the most wonderful thing since sliced bread, it's very daunting to be with someone who seems to think you're not.

"Oh, yes, you are very wrong. My two 'young men' are actually my cats, Tony and Adam. They are *far* better than any bloke, let me tell you."

"Cats! You were referring to your cats!" Pete realised he'd need to sharpen up his act if he was going to be hanging out with Sukie for any length of time, she was winding him up like a clockwork toy.

"Yep, Tony and Adam – and yes, before you ask, they were named after the man himself – and are the most wonderful men in my world and I adore them."

"So, you're an Arsenal fan then," Pete assumed.

"Actually, I'm not, Aston Villa as it happens," Sukieinformed him. "I just admired Tony Adams. He stayed loyal to one club for the whole of his career. That's as rare as hen's teeth these days."

Pete looked at Sukie in amazement. "No way! I'm a Villa supporter too. Blimey! Do you go to the games?"

"I used to go fairly often as a child. My grandfather was a life-long Holte Ender and he'd take me on the weekends I stayed with him and my grandmother. Now, however, not so often although I usually manage about five or six a season," replied Sukie. "What about yourself?"

"My dad took me when I was a kid. We would go every week when they were at home. They were great times. I miss them."

"Why did you stop?"

"The band began to take up too much time. In the early days, most of our gigs were on Friday and Saturday nights so I'd be in a rickety old van on a motorway, heading off somewhere or another. It was no longer possible. I did manage to get some in over the years – when we weren't on tour – but, because of the fame thing, we could no longer go in the stands. We had to stay in the corporate areas and my dad didn't enjoy that. He preferred to be in the crowd, giving the referee what for when he made dodgy decisions, not minding his P's and Q's with the prawn sandwich brigade. So we stopped going and then, when my oma became ill, they moved over here to Austria. Not so easy to visit after that."

"Oma?" said Sukie.

"German for grandmother," Pete replied.

Sukie was about to respond when they walked around a bend and the sight of a glass gazebo in front of

154

them caused her to squeal more loudly than any microphone feedback he'd ever experienced.

"What now?" he asked, half of him wondering if his whole afternoon was going to be full of deafening moments, even if the other half of him was enjoying the unreserved, and unfettered, joy Sukie was having as she made more discoveries relating to her favourite film.

Chapter Eighteen

"I'm telling you, Kara, she walked me for miles! MILES!" Pete was rubbing his feet and checking to see if he had any blisters. He didn't mind a *bit* of walking but Sukie had practically marched the socks off him today. Luckily, he'd been having such a good time, he hadn't really noticed how painful his feet were until they'd gotten back to the hotel and he'd taken his boots off.

"Pfft! Such a wimp!" said Sukie, as she wriggled her be-socked tootsies in front of her.

She was sitting on one of the sofas in Pete's penthouse suite. Pete was lying sprawled along the other, while Kara was curled up on one of the big, cosy chairs. The book she'd been reading when they'd returned now lay on her lap.

She winked at Kara and continued, "No stamina that one. I've seen more oomph in my cats' litter tray than what he's got in him!"

"Given what you've just put me through, I'm getting you checked out to see if you're a secret member of the British SAS."

Sukie looked at Kara again and shot back, "And clearly quite stupid too as he completely fails to comprehend the definition of the word 'secret'!"

Unable to help herself, Kara burst out laughing. It was so refreshing to see someone who did not sit in awe of being in Pete's presence. The more she was seeing of Sukie, the more she liked her.

"Excuse me, young lady! I'll have you know that laughing at your employer is a sackable offence. So please, do try to refrain." Pete put on a stern voice he knew Kara would see through and realise he was also joining in this piss-taking session.

"Oh, please do," she retorted. "Then I can get out of this madhouse and find myself a real job!"

"For that level of insubordination, you are evidently not experienced enough to work elsewhere. I can see I'm going to have to put up with you for a time yet, until you learn some manners."

"Ah bugger!" said Kara. She winked back at Sukie. "And there was me hoping you actually meant it this time."

Sukie looked at Kara. "Has he 'sacked' you before?"

"More times than I can remember but, as you can see, I just ignore him."

"Some folks just don't know how to take a hint..." muttered Pete, a smile hanging on the corners of his mouth. This bantering was fun and it was good to see Sukie and Kara getting along. His new friendship with

Sukie felt really good and it would be even better if the other people in his little circle could also get along with her. This thought made him aware that he hadn't seen Jordie since they'd returned. He asked Kara where he was.

"He's gone back to London for a couple of days," she replied. "He needs to finalise some more arrangements for the tour. He'll be back on Saturday night, ready to assist with your departure on Sunday. The mood he was in when he left, I'm glad to see the back of him."

"Any particular reason for this grump, or is Jordie just being Jordie?"

"He's lost his gloves again."

Pete laughed. "Seriously? He's only had this pair about a week!"

"Hence his bad mood," replied Kara dryly.

He turned to Sukie. "Jordie just cannot keep a pair of gloves for more than a few weeks. He's always losing them." He looked back towards Kara. "Maybe I should have gotten him an industrial sized box of size eights for his Christmas present."

Kara laughed as she replied, "He'd still lose them all by March! Oh, and by the way, he left a message to pass on to you."

"Which is what?" asked Pete.

"Try to stay out of trouble!"

Jordie walked out of the exit at Gatwick Airport and was fortunate enough to find a free taxi immediately. Usually, he would take the express train into London as it was much quicker than a taxi but he had some phone calls to make and appointments to set up, so the privacy of a taxi was better for his needs. He put his small overnight bag on the seat beside him, gave the driver the address details for Pete's house in Notting Hill and then sat back to make his calls.

Thirty minutes later he'd finished finalising his meetings for the next two days and was looking out of the window as the taxi made its way through the London traffic. He really wanted to know how Pete's day out with Sneaky – as he had taken to calling her – had gone. He was hoping she'd revealed her true self to Pete and that he was now packing up his stuff and getting ready to head home on Friday, as originally planned. Although, had that been the case, Kara would've been on the phone, letting him know. Her silence told him that Sneaky was still pulling the wool over Pete's eyes. It's a good thing he had an appointment on Saturday with an old friend who ran an investigation company. He had been unable to find anything about Sukie on the internet, not even a Facebook page or Twitter account, and this made him even more suspicious of her intentions. These days you could find anyone on the World Wide Web. Jordie felt that not being able to do so smacked of deceit and subterfuge. This lack of available information only served to feed his belief that Sukie was intent on digging up some dirt on Pete and getting close to him was how she planned to do it. Well, good luck with that one, girlie, he thought. You'll not get away with this. Not while I've got his back, and not while I'm on your case!

With that thought fuelling his intent, he asked the driver to pull over and let him out. The house was only around the corner and the walk might help to burn off some of the irritation that had been a constant fixture in his guts since Saturday night

Chapter Nineteen

Sukie made arrangements with Pete to go Christmas shopping the next morning before heading back to her room for a hot soak in the bath followed by a light room-service dinner. After all the walking they'd done, she felt a bit achy herself although *no way* was she letting on to Pete about that – having taken the piss out of him so mercilessly, for being such a drama queen, it would've been opening the gates wide for him to come right back at her, so she'd kept her silence and suffered quietly. Some hot bubbles, and the Jacuzzi jets which she hadn't yet tried, should soon ease the aches away.

She was frowning though, as she walked through her hotel room door. She hadn't spoken to Elsa since Sunday, when she'd given her the low-down on her first day in Salzburg. She really needed to call her, to catch up on how her boys were doing and to give her a blow-by-blow account of her week thus far. Elsa wouldn't have expected to hear from her until today, as she knew Sukie was on work time for the first three days of the week. She would, however, be waiting by the phone now, ready to be bored silly, as she listened to her best mate rabbiting on about The Sound of Music again. Sukie had no problem giving her all the details but was worried she'd say something which could give away the identity of who her walking companion had been. In fairness, Pete had not actually *asked* her to keep their budding friendship a secret but Sukie already felt a sense of loyalty to him and didn't want to be gossiping about him behind his back – even if it was with Elsa, who she knew she could trust implicitly.

There was also the issue of Elsa's long-term, not-so-small, crush on Pete. Sukie really didn't know how her new friendship would be received, in the face of Elsa's feelings for Pete and her still fragile state. When Harry had died of cancer, Elsa had broken into a million pieces. Both her mum and Sukie had had to work hard at putting her back together again. Elsa had always fancied Pete when he'd been in The Astons but, since he'd left the band and forged out his solo career, Elsa's crush had increased. Since Harry's death, however, the crush seemed to have become more of an obsession. If her theory was correct though, and Elsa was clinging to this fantastical desire as a means of helping her over the grief of her loss, then Sukie really didn't want to rip that away and risk her friend being hurt again. For the first time since they'd become friends, she was going to have to keep a secret from Elsa. As much as this decision pained her, she knew that – for now – it was the right thing to do.

Now the matter was settled in her mind, she quickly perused the room-service menu and placed an order to be sent up in an hours' time. That would be long enough for her to relax, unwind in the bath and work out what she was going to tell Elsa about her day.

Sukie walked out of the dining room the following morning after having indulged in yet another fabulously tasty breakfast – those Danish pastries really were out of this world and it was a miracle she'd only eaten two – but she was thinking on the chat she'd had with Elsa the night before. Once she'd established her cats were both in fine fettle, and being kept well dosed up with cuddles, she'd gone on to talk about her day out. She'd almost slipped up at one point, when she mentioned the distance 'we had walked'. Elsa had noticed this immediately and had questioned her further on this 'we'. Fortunately, she'd been quick off the mark and told Elsa that another hotel guest, a very nice gentleman, had also been going to Hellbrunn, so they'd agreed to walk there together. She'd used the word 'gentleman' on purpose, hoping Elsa would take this to mean a more elderly man and not ask too many questions. It must have worked because she didn't make any further comments on the matter and she'd managed to finish the call without any further incident. Now, she was going back to her room to get ready to go out with Pete, or Karl, as she expected him to be in disguise again, to explore more of the town and pick up some Christmas gifts at the same time.

"Zwei Apfelstrudel mit Vanillesauce bitte," ordered Sukie shyly. She didn't feel at all comfortable speaking in another language and especially in front of Pete but, having spent a few hours cramming up on some basic German before coming to Austria, it felt very wasteful to not even try to use what she'd learnt. She looked over to Pete as he leaned across the table and whispered, "Now that was impressive. Well done. Much better than I could've managed!"

"I don't understand. If your mum was Austrian, why you don't speak German fluently?"

"I think I could speak it fairly well when I was a child. Mum was adamant her children were going to be bi-lingual but, as time passed, she spoke less and less in German – there's not much call for German speakers in Birmingham – so it was easy to forget what we'd learnt. These days, I find bits of it coming back to me. More so when I'm here in Austria and the language is all around me. When I go out on tour, however, nearly everyone speaks English and it fades again. I keep hoping that, with time, more of it will begin to stick and I'll get a degree of fluency."

"Can you speak any other languages?"

"'Fraid not. I'm one of those Brits who travels the world hoping that everyone he meets speaks the UK lingo and, if not, hopes even more that someone nearby does! What about you, do you speak any others?"

"I'm fluent in Pigeon Everything. Meaning, I can speak the very odd phrase here and there in quite a few languages," she grinned at him, "but I am proficient only in English, Sarcasm and Abuse!"

"Oh yes, I'd quite forgotten about those other two. You must have a Master's degree in both, given how well you converse in them."

Sukie's grin grew larger at his comment. "I'm so glad you noticed that," she said, as she sat back to allow the waiter to put her apple strudel on the table in front of her. She picked up her cutlery and waited until Pete had his dessert in front of him before taking a bite. Closing her eyes, she savoured the taste and let out a small "Hmmmmmmmmm, this is amazing!"

She opened her eyes again, and looking at Pete, said "I'm going to be the size of a house by the time I leave here on Sunday. The food is simply *too* delicious. They'll be charging me for excess weight at the airport!"

Pete snorted, "What kind of house were you thinking of – Barbie house, doll house, Wendy house? Just asking because you are not a large girl by any means?"

"Compared to the skinny birds you like to date, I'm the size of a mountain."

With a spoonful of pudding halfway to his mouth, Pete stopped, placed the spoon back down on the plate and pushed it away. Sukie looked at him in confusion. The atmosphere between them had suddenly become decidedly frosty and she didn't know why.

"What's wrong? What did I say?"

"Once again the junk journalists come to the fore," he replied bitterly.

"I don't get you." She tilted her head, still confused. What was he going on about? She'd seen the myriad photographs for herself – Pete leaving the newest, hottest nightclub in town, with a hot, blonde stick insect wrapped around him, or walking into some designer-chef restaurant, with a skinny, leggy, brunette on his arm. Over the years, there had been red carpet events in Leicester Square with any number of different girls beside him. The girls may have always changed but two things had remained the same – they were drop-dead gorgeous and stick-thin skinny. Elsa would shove the trashy magazines under her nose while asking for an opinion on his latest squeeze.

"Very little of what you see printed in the press and the gossip magazines' is true. Most of those girls you saw with me were set-ups."

"They're what?" Sukie asked.

Pete sighed. "I'm so sick of always having to explain or justify myself to people..." he muttered. He clasped his hands on the table in front of him. "Agents talk to agents, PR reps talk to PR reps and record companies... Well, they don't talk to anyone outside of their own stables. However, they all use established stars to help springboard, or promote, the careers of newcomers onto the scene, be they singers, models or actors. If there's an event, say a film premier for example, then my record label executives may call my agent and say they've just signed a new young singer and they need to have her 'seen' to get her name known, which will boost record sales. It will then be arranged for her to be my 'date' for the night and will guarantee her photograph in any number of tabloids the next morning. She may even be instructed to plant a kiss on me just as the cameras flash to spark a rumour of her being my new girlfriend."

"Oh, my goodness!" Sukie was shocked to hear how

the public were being manipulated in such a way. "Does it ever go any further? When the evening ends?" When she realised what she'd asked, she continued, "I don't mean for you to kiss and tell or anything, I'm more curious as to how you get along with your 'companion' for the evening and how that feels to you."

"When I was younger, it wasn't so bad. After all, it made me look like some hot, young stud, able to pull any number of stunning hot babes." Pete gave her a wry grin. "There aren't many blokes who'd turn down the chance to have a lady-killer reputation and I lapped it up. Revelled in it, even! It took a long time for me to realise I was being used and as the years were passing, and people's perceptions were beginning to change, being a 'man-about-town' was fast becoming more of a slur than something to be proud of. While I would never 'kiss-and-tell', I can say that I spent the night with more than a few of those young ladies. Although, with hindsight, I use that term loosely as they would've been told by their agents to engineer such an event because having **'Pete Wallace's ex-girlfriend'** on their showbiz CV would do wonders for their careers. There are too many photographs out there of women sneaking out of my hotel, or home, in the very early hours and being 'conveniently' snapped by the paparazzi. The same paparazzi who would have received a phone call informing them to be at the location, by a certain time, to ensure they got the shots."

"No way!" Sukie exclaimed, disgust heavy in her voice. "That's awful. Jeez… It's no wonder you dislike them so much."

"It is what it is. It's been going on for years and is

unlikely to change any time soon. That's the nature of the celebrity beast – everyone is using someone else to get them higher up the greasy pole." He picked his spoon up again, "Right, I've had enough of talking 'shop' so please may we change the subject. Tell me more about you. Our conversations seem to keep coming back to me and I do tend to find myself quite boring. All I know about you is you have two cats, and that you like... no, *love* The Sound of Music, are into football and have a right cheeky gob on you! Is there any chance of you expanding a bit more on that?" He smiled at her as he finished eating his strudel.

"Well, I also agree that you are a boring topic of conversation so we have even more in common than we originally thought!" Sukie sassed him on purpose for she'd seen him becoming despondent as he'd given her the inside workings of being a 'celebrity' and she wanted to try and pull him back up again.

Pete let out a snort of laughter as he waved to the waiter to bring over their bill and, turning back to her, said "You really are the cheekiest mare I have ever met. You really, really are!"

As she got her stuff together, and was winding her scarf around her neck, Sukie simply replied, "Honey, you had *better* believe it!"

Chapter Twenty

Sukie tucked her hand into the crook of Pete's elbow, as they left the little café where they'd stopped for some lunch, and steered him towards the pathway that ran along the side of the river, just across the main road from them. "Let's stroll beside the river and I'll tell you about me. Afterwards, we can compare notes on who's the most boring, but, I warn you right now, I'm very competitive and fully expect to win!"

Pete glanced down at the gloved hand lying on his arm and felt the tiniest of thrills go through him. He didn't know why this very small gesture from Sukie made him feel good, it just did. He would think about that one later but, right now, he needed to pay attention to what he was being told.

"Ok, from the beginning... I'm thirty-six years old and my full and proper name is Suzette Catherine McClaren. I was named after the posh pancake, Crepe

Suzette. My dad proposed to my mum over this delightful delicacy and, in memory of that glorious event, I was thusly named. You can probably guess from the tone of my voice that I was, and still am, less than thrilled by this. In my very younger years, it didn't really bother me. It was shortened most of the time to Suze. One day, however, when out shopping with my mum in the local supermarket, she made mention of how I got my name. Unknown to me, one of the school bullies was loitering in the next aisle and heard every word my mum said. Back then, the shelving units in supermarket aisles were puny little things, compared to the massive fixtures you see today, so it was very easy for Sid Miles to move a few cans aside and peer through to see who was doing the talking. Overnight, I became known as Crap Suzette and the name dogged me all the way through the rest of my school years. As you would expect, I came to loathe it with a passion. When I told my mum, she was horrified, and was all set to visit the Head-teacher, but I asked her not to as I believed it would only make things worse. On the day I left school, and with my mother's full blessing, I changed my name to Sukie. As she and my dad had long split up by this time, she no longer felt any need to hang on to the memory." She looked up at Pete. "That is probably my biggest secret, and the worst thing I have to share with you."

Pete looked down at her and said "Aren't kids just the nastiest little sods!"

She laughed and agreed with him. "They can be. Anyway, moving on, as this is my moment in the limelight and this conversation is supposed to be all about me..." She gave him a nudge in the ribs with her elbow, "I no longer answer to Suze or Suzette and woe betide anyone who calls me it. So, consider yourself warned, matey! I went to university as Sukie and qualified as an accountant. However, I found it a bit boring so turned to Credit Control instead. I enjoy this far more but, because of my accountancy background, I'm able to work on larger accounts and provide more information on them with regards to their profitable status. My position is quite unique and my boss is more than happy to give me a lot of free rein over the accounts because he knows that my priority will always be our company. I have a great boss and we get along very, very well. I'm totally happy in my job and that makes me really lucky because not many people can say that."

She stopped and bent down to re-tie the lace on her boot, which had come undone. When she'd finished, she stood up, placed her hand back on Pete's arm, and continued to talk as they walked along

"Now, this next bit may be a bit uncomfortable for you to hear, you being the quiet, shy and humble little creature that you are..." Once again she gave him a gentle nudge so he'd know she was just messing with him. She'd realised he was still getting used to her style of humour. "I need to tell you about Elsa. We've known each other since we were kids and she is my absolute, best friend, in the whole wide world. We're more than sisters to each other and I would do anything for her."

"And why might this be uncomfortable for me to hear?"

"Because, for reasons *totally* beyond my

comprehension, she thinks that you, Pete Wallace, are the very best thing since sliced bread and fancies you something chronic!"

Pete stopped in his tracks and looked at Sukie. "Seriously?"

"Yup, seriously! I have tried to talk sense into her but she won't listen."

Pete shook his head in mock dismay. "That poor, poor girl!" he said. "Have you tried medication? Therapy? Hitting her several times around the head with a sledgehammer?"

"All of the above but nothing has worked. I even went as far as to paint red, felt-tip zits all over your face on a couple of her posters, in the hope the fright of such ugliness would snap her back to her senses."

"Did it work?"

"Nah! The dozy baggage simply didn't talk to me for two whole days, until I apologised. I have come to accept that she is mentally afflicted and the best I can do is support her through this madness until she, one day, realises what an abomination you truly are!"

"You really *are* a good friend to have, Sukie McClaren. I cannot express deeply enough how honoured I feel to know you are also my friend. I'm quite sure, however, that I will genuinely live to regret the day I asked you."

"Oi, sunshine, are you trying to muscle in on my territory of abuse and sarcasm? We'll see about that!"

And, with those words, she let go of his arm, ran over to a nearby bench and grabbed a handful of snow. Two seconds later, Pete received a snowball in the gut and Sukie was already rolling her next missile. Within minutes, there were snowballs flying back and forth and the two of them were squealing and shouting like children.

An elderly couple, walking past, smiled first at their antics and then at each other as they remembered back to the early days of their courtship when they too had indulged in such fun.

Chapter Twenty-One

Eduardo di Santo stood outside the doors of the Physiotherapy Room. Through the window, he could see Angeliqua putting Sofia through her paces. After all this time, the two had developed a close friendship and Angeliqua now knew exactly when it was right to bully Sofia into pushing her limits a bit further, and exactly when she'd had enough and to go easy on her. Some days her young patient was in high spirits and able to take the extra moments of the gruelling punishment needed to try and fix her broken body, other days she struggled to raise a smile and couldn't cope with the pain her daily exercises brought on.

Today, however, was a good day. The doctors felt some advancement had been made and had said there was a good chance she'd be allowed home for the holiday period as long as Angeliqua was happy with her progress in physio. So, she was going all out to impress and to make sure she got a good report card. No matter how friendly they were, Angeliqua gave no quarter when it came to Sofia's welfare, and she was not going to risk undoing the developments made thus far.

He could see Sofia biting her lip in determination, as she carried herself along the parallel bars. As he stood watching, one of Sofia's doctors, Doctor Manto, came walking down the corridor and, seeing Eduardo standing there, turned towards him and stopped. He stood at the doors and also watched Sofia through the windows for a couple of minutes. He then spoke quietly, "Sofia's on form today. The thought of getting away from here for a time has certainly cheered her up."

Eduardo replied, "It will be good to have her home. The apartment is very quiet with just Mamma and I – we need Sofia to bring back the laughter. She needs to be at home where she belongs, with Mamma and me."

Bonito Manto looked at him. "Eduardo, would you care to join me for a coffee?"

"I have one." He lifted his arm to indicate the plastic vending machine cup in his hand.

Bonito looked at it, grimaced and replied, "I think it takes a very good imagination to even get close to calling that abomination 'coffee'! I was thinking more along the lines of the little café, just along the road, which does the most excellent espressos and some very tasty biscotti. Sofia is going to be busy in there for at least another hour so we have plenty of time. You'll be back before she is done."

Eduardo looked at the young doctor. He had assessed him to be maybe a year or two older than himself but this did not detract from the care and assistance he'd given Sofia over the last two years, since he'd taken over her care. He suspected Sofia might have a small crush on him as Doctor Manto was always the one able to cheer her up on her down days, the one she listened to when told they would find ways to make her better and the one she turned to when she had questions or needed reassurance. He was a good man and Eduardo respected him for all he'd done for his sister.

"Ok, why not." He gave the plastic cup a shake. "You are correct. It would take an excellent imagination to call this dish-water 'coffee'," and he tossed it into a nearby waste bin.

Five minutes later, they were seated at a table by the window in the small café. It was busy with people taking a break from their Christmas shopping and they'd been lucky to find a seat. The air was thick with the rich, heavy scent of freshly ground coffee beans. Once they'd given the waitress their order, Eduardo sat back and looked out of the window but didn't see the pretty little piazza across the way, however, or the shining Christmas tree standing there. No, his head was still in the hospital, seeing Sofia going through her moves.

Bonito leant on the table. "Eduardo, I asked you to join me for coffee as we need to have a talk and I thought it would be easier to chat away from the hospital."

Eduardo's felt his stomach begin to churn. He was about to be told that they could do no more for Sofia and this was as good as it was going to be for her. His heart sank with grief as he tried to think how his sister would cope with this news.

"Let me guess," he replied. "You can do no more for Sofia and you wanted to tell me first so I can be there when you break the news to her."

"I'm sorry, what?" Bonito looked confused but then realised what Eduardo was thinking. "Oh! No, no... This has nothing to do with Sofia. This is about you."

It was now Eduardo's turn to look confused. "Me? I don't understand."

Bonito sat watching him, knowing his next words were very likely going to cause a bit of friction but they had to be said, for the sake of his young patient. He hesitated for a few seconds then drew in a deep breath and took the plunge.

"Eduardo, I know that you adore your sister, and love your mother, very, very deeply. And that is right, you should. Family is important and we should always look after each other. I can't help but feel though, that your focus on your family is becoming somewhat detrimental for you."

Eduardo said nothing, the expression on his face giving nothing away. Bonito carried on, "Since Sofia's accident, you've been to visit her every day she has been in the hospital. You haven't missed a single daily visit. Often, you stay for several hours and only leave to go to work. It's also not unusual for you to pop back in to see her when you finish your shift, before you have even been home to sleep or have breakfast. In the early days, this was understandable, but now, more than two years later, it is worrying. You've put your life on hold and this is not healthy. Not for you, not for your mamma and most certainly not for Sofia."

Just then, the waitress returned with their coffees and slices of nadalin. Bonito sat back in his chair to give her space to put them down on the table. Eduardo was still looking at him but had said nothing. Once the waitress had left, he continued talking.

"Eduardo, I know how much you have looked after your family through the years, Sofia has told me. She's explained about how hard you have worked to keep them housed and fed and from such a young age. She appreciates that she has had a good life thanks to your love and dedication. But, she also now feels the time has come for you to step back from your familial duties and find a life for yourself. She tells me you have never had a long-term relationship, never had a holiday that did not include her and your mamma, that you have never had anything just for yourself."

Eduardo replied in a tight voice. "I am the head of the family. It is my place to look after them both. That is my role as the only man in the house."

Bonito paused for a few seconds before he answered. "Eduardo... When Sofia was too young to be left alone, and your mamma had to stay at home with her, the support you gave would have been invaluable. I suspect your mamma says prayers of thanks every day to have been blessed with such a caring son. But you need to loosen your grip a little. Give them both some space to be themselves and do their own thing. I understand your mamma wanted to go back out to work, when Sofia was twelve and had moved up to senior school, but you told her she couldn't. You were adamant that she wasn't to do so."

"I wanted Sofia to come home from school every day to a warm, loving welcome from our mamma. When I was younger, and Mamma had to work to ensure we could eat, I hated coming home to an empty apartment. It would be cold and unwelcoming. A mamma should always be there to give her children hugs after school."

"Do you not think your mamma would have liked some time away from the apartment, to have a life where she was not your mamma all the time but a woman in her own right?"

Eduardo stared hard at Bonito. "I'm not sure I'm getting what you are trying to say here."

Bonito sighed inwardly. He had known Eduardo was a proud man. He'd summed him up within the first few minutes of meeting him. It had been evident from the behaviour he'd displayed and the manner in which his questions were asked. Bonito had, at the time, also had some suspicions that he was quite domineering over the two women who shared his life. His subsequent chats with Sofia had only cemented this belief. She'd told him of the many occasions where he'd played the role of her father, instead of her brother, and had dominated her all her life. She understood this had come about due to their own father being such a waster, and Eduardo having to take on so much responsibility at such a young age but, now she was older, she needed some freedom and Eduardo would not allow it. She'd also confided to him that, had Eduardo allowed her to attend the Pete Wallace concert with her friends, she wouldn't have been in such a rebellious frame of mind and wouldn't have drunk the alcohol which had led to her error in judgement and, subsequent, catastrophic fall. She didn't blame him for her accident but did hold some resentment towards him, believing his over-bearing nature had contributed to it. She'd also admitted she would never, ever tell Eduardo this but she, somehow, had to find a way of getting him to stop behaving like her father and become her brother instead.

Bonito had wondered, at the time, if Sofia was being a little melodramatic, the way some teenagers can be, but Eduardo's earlier comment on how Sofia *'needs to be at home where she belongs'* had made him see that she'd not exaggerated at all. They may now be living in the twenty-first century but Eduardo's way of thinking was very much in the nineteenth and, for a young eighteen-year-old girl, it was too hard to deal with.

Bonito decided to try a different approach to put his concerns across. "Don't you wish you had some more time for yourself? Some time to take a young lady out for a drink or a meal? Or a visit to the cinema? Don't you want to go out with your friends – maybe to a football match or on a camping trip? Or holidays? Surely you must wish, sometimes, that you could shed the responsibility of your family, for just few hours, and have the freedom of being a young man with no ties?"

As Bonito talked, Eduardo could feel the anger at his words growing inside him. How dare this man say these things to him, like he knew anything of what he'd had to deal with growing up. Mamma and Sofia were HIS family, HIS responsibility and it was HIS right to care for them as HE saw fit. How *dare* this man tell him what his family needed, when he already gave them everything they wanted. He swallowed down hard because he knew he was close to losing his temper.

Eduardo growled at him, "You seem to be suggesting that my family are some kind of a burden to me. Well, let me assure you they most certainly are not!"

Bonito looked at Eduardo and could see the fury building within him. However, having come this far, he knew he had to finish what he'd set out to discuss. So far, most of the conversation had been a lead in to what was coming next. He'd hoped, but not really expected, their meeting to have been more open and responsive which would have made the next part easier to say but clearly that was not going to happen. But, this needed to be said, and he only hoped that, once the dust had settled, Eduardo would come to understand this discussion had been purely for the benefit of him and the family he was so desperate to protect.

"Eduardo, I would never make such a suggestion. I know you love and care for your family but I also feel you need to take a step back and re-evaluate your own life. You need to stop living for them 24-7 and give yourself some of your time. I also think, however, this may be difficult for you to come to terms with as you have lived this life for so many years. It is possible you won't know how to detach. So, to help you through these changes, I'd like to suggest you consider speaking with one of the counsellors at the hospital."

He reached into his pocket and took out the business card he'd picked up a few days ago, in anticipation of this conversation, and handed it over to Eduardo. "Delanna Conti is an excellent doctor. I really believe talking to her would assist you when considering the life changes you need to make."

Eduardo took the card from Bonito and read it. He then, very slowly, ripped it into several pieces which he proceeded to drop into Bonito's coffee cup. He stood up, leaned over the table and grabbed Bonito by the collar. Pulling him up from his seat, Eduardo pushed his face up close and hissed, in a cold, flat voice, "If you *ever* speak about me, or my family, in such a way, *ever* again, I will bring down the pain of all the gods upon you. You have one job, and one job only – you fix my sister. You do *not* have an opinion on me or my family, how we live or what we do. That is *not* your concern and it never will be. Do you understand me? Cross this line again and you will know how it feels to be sliced open and disembowelled without the benefit of anaesthetic. Nobody tells me how I live my life and certainly not some jumped-up little doctor who knows nothing about me. Nod, if I am making myself clear."

Bonito just about managed to move his head in a downward motion, so tightly was Eduardo twisting his collar.

"Good!" With that, Eduardo released his hold and Bonito fell back into his chair.

Eduardo glared down at him before turning on his heel and marching out of the café, slamming the door wide open as he walked out.

Conscious of the other diners looking his way, Bonito ran his fingers around his collar and straightened his tie, while signalling to the waitress to bring his bill. He'd expected to encounter some friction and anger from

Eduardo, because a proud man, such as Eduardo was, would never take kindly to the proposal of seeing a counsellor. When Eduardo had pulled him out of his chair, however, Bonito found he had another reason to be concerned. The anger he'd seen in his eyes was not a shock but the hint of madness behind the anger most definitely was. This he had not anticipated and it was a discovery which was now a cause of worry to him. If Eduardo was able to hide this side of his character so well, how long would it be until it took over completely and turned the man into a monster?

Chapter Twenty-Two

Saturday morning and it was still raining in London. Beth and Laura came out of Tottenham Court Road underground station and did battle with one of their umbrellas, trying to get it up while being jostled by other tourists and passengers attempting to do the same. They agreed that sharing one brolly would be better than putting up one each. Oxford Street was already crowded and an extra umbrella was a hassle they could do without. Cosied up under Laura's bright pink and white offering, they made their way along the pavement towards Oxford Circus.

The trip to London was a last-minute decision by Laura, who needed to brave Hamleys on Regent Street to get her little grandson an extra special Christmas present. The problem was she didn't know exactly what that extra special gift was and so needed to go looking to find it. Her daughter Eleanor had been no help at all when she'd asked for suggestions. "Mum, he's barely two years old," she'd said, "He'll be more interested in the wrapping than the gift inside. Just get him anything."

"Pfft," said Laura, "as if I would get my, so far, one and only grandson just 'anything' for his Christmas." When she'd asked Beth if she'd like to join her, Beth had jumped at the chance. Despite the crowds, and the murky weather, she loved London at Christmas. She might be in her fifties but she still got a thrill when she saw the Christmas lights over Oxford Street and Regent Street, the tree in Trafalgar Square, the beautifully decorated shop windows and felt the festive buzz in Covent Garden. This year, as a special treat for them both, she'd secretly booked some tickets for the Ice Sculptures Display at the Winter Wonderland event in Hyde Park. Sukie wasn't going to be the only one visiting the glorious German Christmas Markets. She hadn't told Laura they were heading there yet. Laura had a deep dislike of the cold and would never enter the equivalent of a giant deep freeze with any kind of willingness. However, after hearing one of the girls at work raving on about her visit there the week before, Beth knew she had to see it for herself. Just like her daughter, she loved all things wintery and Christmassy. She wasn't quite sure if Sukie had inherited this love from her or had been brainwashed by it all from a young age. Either way, it was something they shared and they always tried to make Christmas special, even if it was just the two of them. This year, however, had been knocked off kilter by Sukie going over to Austria but, she was due back tomorrow night, so they still had a few days to make some plans and put them into action. She was looking forward to seeing Sukie on Monday night. It was rare for them to be apart for this long. They didn't live in each other's pockets the way some mothers and daughters did but they would talk on the phone every few days and meet up a couple of times a week. She was very proud of Sukie's independence, it was how she'd brought her up after all, but it did occasionally come back to bite her when she didn't quite agree with some of the things her daughter did with her life. Like still being single and unmarried at thirty-six. When she listened to Laura talk about her little grandson, it always tugged at her heart. She would love to be a Grandmother and hold a baby in her arms again. There again, having arrived outside the 'Finest Toy Shop in the World', and taken in the long queue waiting to get inside, she quickly decided that she was happy for Sukie to wait a few more years before settling down and becoming a mother.

Forty-five minutes, and several elbows in the ribs later, Laura and Beth were spat back out onto the heaving Regent Street pavement, looking – and definitely feeling – rather the worse for the experience. Laura had eventually found the perfect gift and had wisely chosen for it to be delivered next week. Now they had the rest of the day in front of them to soak up the atmosphere.

"Shall we head towards Covent Garden from here," suggested Beth "and then on towards Piccadilly and Hyde Park?"

"Sounds like a plan to me," replied Laura, quite happy for Beth to lead the way. "We could have a coffee and some cake in the market square. I hope the string-quartet is performing this year, they really do add to the ambience."

Chattering away about this and that, they made their way down to Piccadilly Circus and through Leicester Square, admiring the various street artists they passed and looking at some of the funfair rides which were currently sleeping but would be full of screaming teenagers and young adults in a few hours' time.

"Do you remember when we were young and the biggest thrill was being whisked round and round by the cute fairground boys on The Waltzer?" reminisced Laura.

"Oh, yes! You wouldn't get me on those now though, they make me feel ill. And you wouldn't get me on any of those, new-fangled, white-knuckle, things either. These days, I'm happy to stick with a nice gentle carousel."

They arrived at Charing Cross Road and Laura pushed the button on the crossing to change the traffic lights in their favour. Beth turned to speak to her but was suddenly jostled really hard from behind and would have lost her balance had she not grabbed Laura's coat sleeve. She spun round and saw a short, stocky man behind her, roughly pushing his way through the crowd who'd gathered to cross over. "Oi you!" Beth yelled after him, "ever heard of the words 'Excuse Me' you bad-mannered little oik? Clearly you were dragged up, not brought up!" The man glanced back at her as she delivered her scathing words but said nothing and, still hurrying, carried on his way.

The lights changed and, as they crossed, Laura

declared, "And *that* is why visiting this city just once a year is more than enough for me!"

Jordie glanced down at his watch again as he rushed down Charing Cross Road to meet Daniel Cleary at his preferred pub near St Martins Lane. The meeting with the record company, in Soho Square, had over-run and now he was against the clock to arrive on time. Jordie hated being late, loathed it in fact, and it always left him feeling out of sorts when it happened. Pete often teased him over his need to be early for all appointments but Jordie liked those few minutes to collect his thoughts and prepare himself for whatever he was about to face or deal with. Being late put you on the back foot and this was not a good place to be when you were in negotiations over new contracts or agency deals.

He pushed through the door and, running up the stairs of The Chandos, he saw that Daniel was already seated in one of the booths, reading something on his phone. He arrived at the table, pulled off his wet jacket, hung it on the wooden post of the booth and sat down.

"Sorry I'm late, mate, my last meeting went on longer than it should have done and then I had to deal with all the bloody tourists around Leicester Square and Charing Cross Road. I nearly had my eye taken out by two daft birds with a stupidly bright pink umbrella. If I hadn't pushed one of them out of the way, I'd be sitting here with one good eye and doing an impression of your bloke over there on his column!" He gestured with his thumb towards Trafalgar Square as he made reference to Lord Admiral Nelson and his well-known eyepatch. "And then," he continued, "to add insult to my almost injury, one of them had the cheek to turn round and give me a mouthful of verbal! Would you believe it? Honestly, this city does my head in at the best of times but, at this time of the year, I really do hate it! Anyway mate, what can I get you to drink?"

Jordie used the few minutes of waiting at the bar for their drinks to settle his jarred equilibrium and prepare what he needed to say to Daniel. Once he'd been served, he took the glasses back to the table, put them down and then seated himself back in the booth. These booths were the reason he liked this pub – they provided a nice degree of privacy when an informal business meeting was required.

After drinking about half of his pint, and exchanging the usual pleasantries, Daniel got to the point and asked the question, "What do you need to see me for, Jordie? I know you haven't asked me here to chew the fat over what to get the missus for her Christmas?"

Jordie looked at him and tried to think of the best way to put his request across. He knew he was most likely going to sound very stupid but he needed to do this. His gut told him he needed to see this through. "Pete's met a woman."

"Oh aye?"

"I don't like her and I don't trust her? I suspect she has an ulterior motive but I can't find any way of proving it."

Daniel got out his little notebook and opened it to a fresh page. "So, would I be correct in thinking you want me to dig deeper and see what comes up?"

"Yes please, if you have the time."

"For you, Jordie, you know I will always have the time. Sure, I'm busy but I can do this for you. Will there be surveillance?"

Jordie thought for a moment. "Maybe... She's currently in Salzburg with Pete but flies back to the UK tomorrow night. She lives in, or near, Oxford. Well, I'm guessing she does as the company she works for is based there and, when I called last week to verify her story, they advised me she was away on a business trip. This fits in with what she's told Pete."

"So what's your concern?"

"I really don't know." He took a drink of his pint. "It's a gut feeling. I thought it might be because we got off on the wrong foot when we first met, but..." he hesitated again. "I can't explain it, Dan, I've tried but... it's just my gut keeps saying something isn't right. I know I could be completely wrong but at least I will be wrong knowing I've looked into her thoroughly and left no stone unturned."

"Fair enough, give me what you've got and I'll see what I can find for you."

"I'll tell you now, Dan, it's not a lot." He handed over the little he'd been able to piece together including a couple of photographs he'd taken when neither Pete nor Sukie had been paying him any attention. "I'm guessing she'll be flying into Gatwick Airport as she was on the same flight as the press junket last week and I know they came out of there. I've looked at the flight times and I think it will either be the 1.25 pm flight or the 3.30 pm. I'll send you a text to confirm as soon as I know."

"No worries." Daniel looked quickly through the file Jordie had given him. "You weren't joking when you said it was bare bones. It's barely even that!" He looked at Jordie and grinned. "I've worked with less than this. I'll have a bloke at the airport when she arrives and we'll take it from there."

With his business now concluded, Jordie was able to relax. "Fish and chips for two?" he asked.

"That sounds good to me. Here, I'll get them. Another beer?" Daniel nodded towards Jordie's almost empty glass.

"Oh, yes please." That was the other thing he really liked about The Chandos, they had an excellent line of home brews. And, as he had a few hours to kill before his flight back this evening, he had every intention of enjoying some more.

Chapter Twenty-Three

"Oh wow! Oh wow! Oh wow!" Sukie's head could've been on a swivel, as she twisted and turned, every which way, to take in all she was seeing. Pete had surprised her this morning by arranging a chauffeur-driven car to take them both out of Salzburg in order for her to see some of Austria's other wonderful views.

First on the list had been Mondsee, where she had been delighted to find the very church used for the wedding scene in 'The Sound of Music'. The thrill of walking down the same aisle Julie Andrews had walked, had her bouncing with joy. She'd even allowed him to take some photographs of her standing at the foot of the steps which led up to the altar.

The town itself had been stunning with its beautifully painted and decorated buildings. The cafés had been open and, even in the cold winter weather, had been doing a reasonable trade with customers sitting at the tables outside on the pavement, enjoying the weak December sun.

They were now heading towards St Wolfgang. Pete had recommended it as a beauty spot and he was also friends with the manager of a hotel there, so could guarantee some privacy when they stopped for lunch.

Pete looked at Sukie as they drove along. Her eyes were shining with happiness and excitement and her cheeks were still glowing from her walk around Mondsee. Her chestnut curls were bouncing all over the place as she moved about, craning her head up to see the tops of the snow-covered mountains as they passed by.

"Oh, Pete, this is all so amazing! I really am starting to be lost for words. I'm running out of ways to describe all this awesome scenery. Damn! I've just used up another one!" She grinned in his direction. "Thank you so very much for doing this. I can't begin to say how much I appreciate it." She leaned across and planted a noisy kiss on his cheek. "Seriously, I really am hugely grateful to you for arranging it all."

He smiled back, pleased to see that his surprise trip had made her so happy. He'd really enjoyed being in Sukie's company the last few days and wanted to thank her for allowing him to tag along on her forays around Salzburg. He'd guessed that seeing the Basilica St Michael would be a fitting end to her holiday and had not been wrong. He'd sneaked a couple of photographs of his own, when she'd asked him to take some of her beside the altar steps, so he too would remember this day and how much he was also enjoying it. He thought of where they were heading next and mentally prepared himself for the onslaught of her happiness again. Mondsee was very pretty, and it did have the advantage of the Sound of Music church, but St Wolfgang – in his opinion – was off the scale when it came to being stunningly beautiful. No matter how many times he'd been there, the views always left him breathless. The clarity of the water in Lake Wolfgangsee meant the mountains were reflected as though in a mirror. He had a photograph on a wall in the schloss which his father had taken many years before. Andrew had framed the sight of the mountains, water and reflection within one of the arches looking out from the piazza and, it had looked so good, his mum had gotten it enlarged and framed. It served to remind them of the good days they'd had there. Pete felt the familiar tug of pain inside him when he thought of his parents. He took a deep breath, pulled his shoulders back and forced a smile onto his face – today was Sukie's day and he was not about to spoil it by being morose and sad. The chauffeur was pulling into the car park and he knew he could do this. It was the first time he'd been back since the death of his parents but, with Sukie's joy and enthusiasm over the delights she was about to see, he knew her happiness would override any sadness that might threaten to engulf him.

"Oh, Pete, this place is magical! Just as I thought I couldn't be any more surprised, amazed, or awe-struck by the beauty of this country, you bring me here and I go through all this again. How is it possible that each town or village can be even more beautiful than the last?"

They were standing on the piazza, looking at the

shining lake and snow-covered mountains through the walled arches, in the middle of the little town.

Pete looked at Sukie and felt the darkness hovering inside him slip away. How could one feel downhearted when standing beside someone who was appreciating, so fully, the beauty and delights in front of her? He leaned down and whispered in her ear. "I put in a special order of pretty churches, towns and villages, just for you. It's amazing what you can buy on the internet these days!"

Sukie burst out laughing at his words. "Believe me, if this could be 'bought' on the internet, I'd have it all fully installed back home, although I would struggle to fit it into a two-bedroom flat!"

He looked at his watch. "Are you hungry? I've got a table booked at a hotel just around the corner if you'd like to eat."

"I am starving," was Sukie's reply. "It's a good thing we've done so much walking and climbing because I've eaten nearly triple my usual daily intake while I've been here. This fresh, clean air might be good for body and soul but it would play havoc with my waistline if I lived here permanently."

She looked Pete's slim build. "How do you manage to keep in shape with all this gorgeous food around you?"

"Lucky genes," he answered. "It runs in the family. I also have a reduced appetite, living mainly on coffee, and that helps too. Sally, my housekeeper, keeps trying to tempt me with all sorts of delicacies but, luckily, I resist otherwise I think even my skinny genes would struggle."

He held the door open for Sukie and they walked into the dark interior of the hotel. It was in keeping with the traditional aspect of the town with dark wood furniture, log-cabin effect décor and a roaring fire over in the far wall. As Sukie took off her gloves and hat, a dark-haired, young man came over to them.

"Peter my friend, how are you? It is so lovely to have you back to visit. It has been too long." With his words, he grabbed Pete and pulled him into a bear hug. "And today, you also bring a beautiful friend." He turned to Sukie and treated her to a small bow. "It is a pleasure to look after such a beautiful lady. Please allow me to take your coat."

Pete rolled his eyes. "Sukie, meet Lars. This is his family hotel and we've known each other since we were kids. Lars, you can knock off the performance, Sukie won't be taken in by your antics."

"Oh, I wouldn't be so sure about that," Sukie replied with a grin. "Very few women object to being treated so finely, once in a while. You carry on, Lars, it's nice to be appreciated."

"And appreciated you most certainly are, Fraulein." With these words, Lars made a show of taking Sukie's hand and placing the most exaggerated, noisy kiss upon the back of it.

Sukie took her hand back and laughingly turned to Pete. "Now *that* is how you look after a woman."

"If you two have quite finished slobbering over each other, is it possible we could be shown to our table?" For some reason, he was irritated by Lars' behaviour.

Lars looked at Pete and then nudged Sukie gently in the side and gave her a wink. "I think the big pop star does not appreciate the competition I give him. That is why he makes me stay here, he knows all the women would see me and forget about him."

As he walked them to a secluded window table in the Terrace Café, which looked out over the beautiful lake, Sukie quickly appraised Lars' appearance. He was slim, almost to the point of skinny, his shoulder-length brown hair was parted to one side and shorter at the front. He had slightly pointed features but these were softened by his bright, laughing brown eyes and full smiling lips. There was no way he'd eclipse Pete's drop-dead appearance but she liked the way he was prepared to take the piss out of his celebrity friend in this way. She decided she like Lars, he was her kind of person. Not in awe of Pete or his fame and happy to treat all people as equals. As she sat down in the chair he had pulled out for her, she looked at Lars and, returning his wink, said, "I think you could be right there, Lars, I think you could be right."

"Oh, dear, what I would give right now for an elasticated waist on these jeans," groaned Sukie, as she ran a finger around the inside of her waistband to help ease the tension around her middle. "Once again, I've eaten more delicious food. The size of those portions was obscene!"

Pete looked over and replied, "I think Lars likes you, I don't remember being fed like this before."

Sukie looked at him. "Are you ok? You've been subdued since we got here. Lars was only teasing, you know. You are definitely better looking than him, much as it pains me to say that to you." She gave him a smile.

"Yeah, I'm fine. Being here has brought back some childhood memories and they've knocked me for six a bit." No way was he going to admit he'd had twinges of jealousy as he'd watched Lars and Sukie messing about. Sukie was a friend and he wasn't comfortable with the possessive feelings he'd had swirling around inside him. This was something new to him and he wasn't sure what to make of it. He forced a bright smile onto his face and decided it would be better to change the subject. "Can you believe that a week today is Christmas Eve? It seems to have come around so quickly."

"I know, although I seem to say that every year. I'll need to pull my finger out when I get home to sort things out. Being away for over a week has played havoc with my usual run-up-to-Christmas routine."

"Do you have big family celebrations with a house full of people then?"

Sukie smiled. "No, it's only Mum and I, just the two of us. But we still go the whole hog. Mince pies and posh coffee for breakfast, get dressed up for the full Christmas dinner with all the trimmings, eaten after the Queen's speech, of course, fight over the purple ones in the chocolate tin, and indulge ourselves with a few bottles of fizzy wine. I take the cats over and stay with her for a couple of days. It's very relaxing and chilled out. What about you?"

He thought for a moment. "Rather like yourself although with less of the tradition thing going on. It'll be quiet with just be the three of us at the schloss – Sally, Jordie, and me. Kara will go off somewhere with her fiancé, Gareth. They're always invited to stay and join us, but Kara calls that a busman's holiday and says she'd rather get away properly."

Sukie thought for a few seconds. "I can't remember the last time we had a big family Christmas. I think it was probably when I was about twelve or thirteen when my grandparents were still alive. My grandmother died when I was fourteen and Grandad went into a care home. He'd been developing dementia for a few years and couldn't manage on his own after my nana died. My mum tried to bring him to ours the first Christmas after my nana passed but, he got so distressed in the car, she had to turn around and take him back. It's been just the two of us ever since."

"Hmmmmmm..." was Pete's reply, as he stared at Sukie.

"What?" she asked. She looked behind her to see if Pete was looking at something, or someone else, but she couldn't see anything or anyone. "Pete, why are you staring at me like that?"

Still Pete stared and didn't answer.

"PETE!" she hissed at him and pushed his leg under the table with her foot. "Stop staring at me like that, it's weird. What's up?"

Pete started and blinked at her when she hit his leg. "Oh, I'm sorry," he answered. "I didn't mean to upset you there."

"Well you did. What's going on? You were staring right through me and I don't know why."

"Again, I'm sorry." He hesitated for a few seconds and then continued, "As you were talking, I had an idea and I was, firstly, thinking it through and then, secondly, trying to decide if it was a good one or not "

"And what did you decide?"

Pete smiled at her. "I reckon it's a pretty brilliant idea actually."

"Well… Care to share or shall I just sit here for the next few hours trying to guess what it is?"

He looked at her and took a breath. "Would you and your mum like to join us at the schloss for Christmas and New Year?"

"Excuse me?" It was now Sukie's turn to stare. "Did you just invite my mother and me to come over here for Christmas? To stay, at the schloss, with you, Sally, and Jordie?"

"Ermm… Yes." Pete nodded, still smiling but finding it slipping a bit as Sukie had yet to give him an answer.

"Wow!" Sukie sat back in her seat and took a drink of her wine as she tried to think of the best response to give him.

On one hand, it was a fantastic offer but, on the other, it would be a big change to her usual Christmas routine. This didn't bother her but her mum may not take so well to it. "It's a bit sudden, Pete and completely unexpected. I don't know how my mum would feel about it and, even if she's up for it, trying to get flights organised at such short notice would be a nightmare." Even as the words came out of her mouth, Sukie was inwardly cursing her ever practical nature. Could she sound any more square?

"Ah, flights are not a problem, I can sort that!"

Sukie opened her mouth to protest that she could not

allow him to pay for them to come out to Austria but he put up his hand to stop her. "I wasn't finished speaking."

She let out a sigh. "Ok, finish then!"

"Thank you. I was about to say, there's a small private airfield less than fifteen kilometres from the schloss which I co-own with a local chap. I put up the finance and he runs the airfield and charter company. In return, I have full access to any private charter flights I require. Therefore, if I need two young ladies picked up from the UK on Christmas Eve and brought to Austria, I can arrange it. All I need to know is your location in Oxfordshire, in order for me to advise him on which private airfield to make arrangements with."

Rather dazed with the turn the conversation had taken, Sukie murmured "Um, we're in the north of Oxford."

"Great. I can let Fredrich know and he'll sort everything out. Now, would you prefer to come out late on the Friday evening or early on Saturday morning?"

"Whoa! Just back it up a minute there, sunshine!" Sukie was shaking her head. "I haven't agreed to this, and I can't until I speak with my mum. It involves her too you know. If she doesn't want to do this, then it won't happen. I won't come out without her."

"Of course not," replied Pete. "I wouldn't expect you to. The point of asking you both is so that we could all, hopefully, enjoy a slightly more fun-filled and exciting Christmas. A bit more of a 'family bash' than either of us usually have at this time." The more he thought about it, the more excited he became. He just had to hope that

Sukie's mum would fancy the idea too. "Do *you* want to do it?" he asked. "Does it float your boat?"

"Well, as suggestions go, it's not the worst idea I've heard. In fact, the more I think about it – now that I'm getting over the surprise of being asked – I do think it would be fun." Sukie was really beginning to warm to the idea but knew she could not accept it until she had discussed it with her mum. And that had to be a face-to-face conversation. She couldn't just drop this one on Beth in a telephone call. "I'm seeing my mum on Monday night so I'll talk it over with her then. I'll be able to let you know on Tuesday. Is that ok?"

"Of course it is. In the meantime, I'll let the airfield know the details so they can begin making the preparations. I'll advise them it is still to be confirmed."

"Ok." Sukie put her head to one side and looked over at Pete. "There is one other small detail, which might just help my case a bit when I'm trying to sell this extraordinary suggestion to my mother."

"What's that?" asked Pete.

"Where *is* your schloss? Where exactly do you live?"

Chapter Twenty-Four

"Mum! That was the doorbell. I think the car has arrived." Sukie walked over to look out of the bedroom window and let out a groan as she saw the shining black, stretch limousine blocking up the road outside. "I do *not* believe that guy! I'm going to throttle him when I see him. I told him to bin that idea when we discussed all this."

It was just after eight in the morning on Christmas Eve. Much to Sukie's total shock and surprise, Beth had fully embraced the idea of an Austrian Christmas. In the end, it was Sukie who had come across as being the more reluctant of the two. As she quickly put her make-up bag inside the suitcase, and battled to get the zipper closed, she thought back to Monday night when she'd arrived at her mum's after work.

Sukie let herself in and called through to her mum in

the kitchen, as she took off her coat and boots. "Hi, Mum, I'm here!"

She bent down to put her boots in the little shoe cupboard, straightened up and got the biggest of surprises. Her mum was standing in front of her, looking completely different. Gone was the long hair which she normally wore up in a top-knot. Now, Beth was sporting a long, sleek, shoulder-length bob which had taken years off her. She was also wearing tailored jeans and a fitted T-shirt with a loose, colourful, oversized shirt over the top.

"Mum! You look fantastic! When did you have this done?"

Visibly preening at her words of approval, her mum filled her in on her decision to make some changes in her life, as they walked into the kitchen. Beth poured her a glass of chilled, white wine and she took a large gulp as she sat down at the table.

"Do you like it?" Sukie asked, still gobsmacked by the vision in front of her. She couldn't recall ever seeing her mother with short hair before. It had been a very long time since she'd even seen her wear it loose.

"Yes, I do," Beth replied. "I feel very liberated. It's difficult to explain but I feel as though I'm a new person and I seem to have this urge to go out and do lots of new things and try new experiences." Beth shrugged. "I'd almost go as far as to say that I feel rather rebellious!" She grinned at Sukie's shocked expression as she went over to the cooker and bent down to take the casserole dish out of the oven. In a moment of wickedness, she said over her shoulder, "I've made a nice lentil casserole for dinner, are you okay with that?"

Sukie's mouth fell open. "You've made *what*?"

"Ha, ha! Only kidding! It's steak pie, as usual." Beth put the dish on the table, in front of Sukie.

"Thank goodness for that!" Sukie gave a loud sigh of relief. "I'm more than happy for you to change your appearance and become a rebel. I'll even post your bail if you get arrested. But, if you start messing with steak-pie Monday, we're going to be having words!"

After dinner, Sukie shared the plethora of photographs she'd taken in Salzburg. As they were going through them, however, Beth began to wonder who'd taken the ones where Sukie was in the shot. She'd noted the different outfits Sukie was wearing so knew they were not taken on the same day. Eventually, she asked the question and Sukie finally spilled the beans on her new BFF. She wasn't really sure who Pete Wallace was, so Sukie brought out her laptop and found a few of his videos on YouTube.

"He's a bit of alright, ain't he? I could fair fancy him myself!" She gave Sukie a lecherous look, at the same time digging her in the ribs with her elbow. Sukie looked at her in sheer horror which resulted in Beth cracking up with laughter. "It's alright, uptight daughter of mine, I'm pulling your leg, although, he's certainly a good-looking chap!"

"Well, Elsa seems to think so," Sukie sniffed in reply. "He's crap at snakes and ladders though – I whooped his butt three times!" and smiled as she recounted the first night they'd had dinner to her. It sounded like it had been fun,

"Anyway Mum, there's something I have to run by you…" Sukie began filling her in on Pete's invitation.

"Oh my! For real?" Beth, just as Sukie had been, was quite taken aback by this proposal.

"Oh yes, Mum, for real!" Sukie nodded vigorously. "This is not a wind-up."

Beth thought for a moment and then replied. "Well, it would be very rude not to accept. Please tell Mr Wallace we would be delighted to join him and his friends for the festive season. Now, what do I need to buy and can you help me choose which of my new outfits would be suitable?"

Sukie stared at Beth, her mouth hanging open.

"What? Why are you looking at me as though I've just grown two extra heads?

"I'd been expecting to have to talk you round to the idea and yet, here you are being exceptionally decisive and already talking about new clothes and what to pack."

"It's the new me, love. New hair, new clothes, new outlook on life!"

"Mum, are you sure you're okay with being away for Christmas? I mean, this is totally outside our usual routine. What about all of our little traditions?"

She turned to Sukie, took her hands in hers and, looking at her daughter's slightly pensive face, she put a hand gently on her cheek and said, "Sweetheart, it was only ever a routine because we didn't have many other options. If I could've afforded to take you away to snow-smothered winter locations each year, I would have done so." She stood up, and moving over to the dresser in the corner where she kept her important documents, carried on talking as she began rummaging through the drawers. "This is a wonderful and very kind invitation Mr Wallace has extended to us and I think it would be bad manners to decline it. From what you've said, if there are only three of them over there, then he will enjoy our company every bit as much as we will enjoy his. And as for our little traditions, well we can still indulge in some of them. And maybe we will make some new ones by sharing them with other people."

"But there's so much to arrange and sort out. What about your work? Will you be able to get the time off?"

"I see you've forgotten that my office will be closed until the beginning of January this year, just like yours, so time off will not be a problem for either of us."

"I also have to make arrangements for the cats. And it's such short notice. Maybe we could look instead at going after Christmas or something?"

"Sukie McClaren, you can stay here if you wish but nothing is going to stop me from getting on that plane. Now hurry up and decide on what you want to do because, if we are both going, I have stuff that needs to go in the freezer! Ah, here it is!" Beth turned around and waved her passport at Sukie. She placed it on the coffee table and stood with her hands on her hips, her chin jutting out in, what Sukie described as, her 'no-nonsense stance'. "Well?" she demanded.

Sukie replied, in a bemused tone of voice, "It looks like we're going to Austria then. I'll call Pete and give him the details."

And so now, here they were on Christmas Eve morning, being chauffeur-driven towards Oxford Airport where their chartered flight was waiting to fly them over to Austria, to spend the next ten days as the guests of a world-famous rock star who, only two weeks previously, had been just a name in the media and a face on the TV.

Chapter Twenty-Five

Pete and Fredrich were chatting in the air control tower when one of the engineers called over, "Landing in five."

Fredrich turned to Pete. "I'll ask Walter to drive you back to the hangar and we'll taxi the plane straight there. That will ensure you have total privacy to greet your friends. It's very busy here today and the last thing I need to deal with is mob control, should it get out that you're on the premises."

"That suits me just fine," replied Pete. "Sukie would punch my lights out if she ended up splashed over the pages of the press."

"Sounds like a feisty lady," said Fredrich with a smile.

"Oh, she's certainly that. She knows her own mind, no doubt about that. And has no time for all this celebrity nonsense either." Pete smiled to himself as he recalled some of the colourful expressions she'd injected into her comments whenever they'd discussed his fame.

"Right, Pete, you gotta go and I gotta get back on the case here. I'll see you soon and have a very Merry Christmas." Fredrich gave him a firm handshake and a thump on the back.

"A Merry Christmas to you, Fredrich, and also to Helena and your girls. I hope Saint Nicholas brings you much happiness."

Pete called on Jordie, who was standing over by the coffee machine, scrolling through his phone. Putting it away in his pocket, he walked across to Pete. They followed Walter down the stairs and out of the terminal to where the ground crew buggies were kept. They jumped aboard and Walter drove them both back to the hangar where they'd parked the Land Rover an hour earlier. This was Pete's preferred hangar as it was the one nearest to the back entrance to the airport and, as such, afforded him the most privacy whenever he went on his travels.

"You alright?" he asked Jordie, bumping him with his shoulder.

"No, I am not and fine well you know it!" was the harsh reply he got back.

Pete sighed. He'd hoped Jordie would've come round by now. On Monday night, when he'd received the text from Sukie, letting him know that it was all systems go for their visit, he'd told Jordie of the change to the Christmas arrangements. As he'd expected, Jordie had gone off like a Bonfire Night rocket.

"You've done WHAT?" Jordie had looked at him with abject horror on his face.

"You heard me the first time, I'm not repeating myself!"

"Let me get this right – you've invited Sneaky AND her mother to join us for Christmas and New Year. Without discussing this with me first! Are you out of your tiny mind?"

Pete had looked up from his phone, and the text he was sending to Fredrich to confirm their discussion from the night before. "Jordie, we need to get a few things straight here. Firstly, her name is SUKIE and I *don't* appreciate your alternative take on that. Secondly, they are MY guests, here at MY invitation and, if you have a problem with that, then maybe you should make other arrangements for the ten days of their visit. Finally, this is MY home and I neither need to discuss, nor get your permission, to extend invitations to my friends. And like it or not, Sukie is my friend so you had better get used to that and do it quickly!"

"But Pete, you don't know this woman or her agenda. How can you trust her not to be selling her stories to the press? Or not to have already made a deal to tell them everything when she returns? You've fought so hard over the last few years to win back some form of privacy and keep your name scandal free, and my concern is that you could lose it all and be right back in the public eye for all the wrong reasons."

"Jordie, I get the reasons for your concerns but I trust Sukie. Look at how she manipulated Aggie Wilson into changing her whole interview and photograph session in my favour. She didn't need to do that but she did."

Jordie looked at him with an expression of mutiny

still on his face. "A ploy to gain your trust. And it most certainly worked."

With a huff of exasperation, Pete replied, "Well, she's had plenty of time to give the press the lowdown on the days out we had last week, and tell them about the time we spent together, but she hasn't. There's been nothing in the press about any of it."

Jordie looked at him. "Just what level of stupid are you on, Pete? Of course there have been no press reports yet because, if there were, you'd cancel her trip over here and they wouldn't get the big scoop on where you hide out when you're not in the UK, or the location of the schloss, and all the deep dark secrets you no doubt plan to share while she's here. It's a long game being played here, I'm telling you!"

"ENOUGH!" Pete yelled, as he stood up and walked over to where Jordie was sitting. He placed his hands on the arms of the chair and put his face close to Jordie's. "Enough!" he said again, quietly. "For whatever reasons you have, you've clearly taken firmly against Sukie and that is your choice. I wish you'd change that view but I can see you're not prepared to. Fair enough, if you want to be a pig-headed, stubborn sod, then go right ahead. *However*, I like her, really like her, and I trust her completely. She hasn't given me one single reason to doubt her sincerity and integrity. It may also have escaped your notice that good, true, friends are something I don't have many of. The life I've lived, and the lifestyle I've led, has only served to either push away those who were once close or attract those who hope to shine as they stand in my shadow. I have no one who is a friend simply because they like me for the actual person that I am. Have you got ANY idea just how lonely that is?"

He straightened up and walked over to the fireplace and stood looking into the flames for a few seconds before turning back to Jordie. "I have been far happier in the last five days, than I've been for the last ten years. And that's all because this kind, funny, intelligent and caring woman has bypassed all the bullshit that is my life and can see *me*. The *real* me, the person behind all the glitz and fame!"

"But Pete—"

He put his hand up to stop him. "No, Jordie, I don't want to hear anything more on the matter. If it transpires that Sukie is the back-stabbing, conniving bitch you suspect her to be, then so be it. I will live with the consequences and learn a lesson. But, until such times as she gives me a reason not to trust her, she is my friend and will be treated with respect by all those who are living under this roof. Have you got that?"

"But Pete—"

"I said, have you got that, Jordie?" he asked, interrupting Jordie a second time.

"Fine! If that's how you want it." Jordie threw his hands up and got out of his chair. "But just remember that I tried to warn you about her when it all goes tits-up and also remember who it is who always ends up having to sort out the shit when it does." And with that, he stormed out of the room, slamming the door behind him.

Five days later, here they were, driving into the hangar where Sukie and her mother would be arriving in a few minutes and Jordie was still in a major strop He'd barely spoken to Pete since Monday night and the thaw didn't look like it was going to set in anytime soon.

As they got down from the buggy, Pete grabbed Jordie by his arm and whispered in his ear. "Grow up and get over yourself! I'm sick of this attitude you've had all week. It's Christmas – the time of cheer and goodwill to all. So, I suggest you get some goodwill on that face of yours PDQ because, if your bad grace and attitude spoils their holiday, believe me when I say you will live to regret it!" Then, letting go of his arm, Pete walked over to the plane that had just taxied in, and waited for the door to open.

Chapter Twenty-Six

Jordie bit his tongue and took a deep breath. No, he didn't want to spend the next ten days in the company of these women but, short of holing himself up in his room for the duration of their stay, he had no choice but to put on a face and make it appear as though he was happy for them to be here. An email from Dan Cleary had just arrived in his inbox when Pete had called him to go to the buggy, so he hadn't yet had the chance to read it. He'd do so once they got back to the schloss. In the meantime, he plastered a smile on his face and tried to look welcoming.

The aircraft's engines were now silent and the door was open. Another few minutes to sort out the steps and there she was – Sneaky! Dammit, he thought to himself. I must stop calling her that or, as sure as eggs are eggs, I'm going to end up saying it to her face. And while the confrontation that would follow would not bother him, he'd get it in the neck from Pete, so best to rein it in if he could. He watched as Sukie looked around the hangar and then, seeing Pete at the bottom of the stairs waiting, gave him a big grin and a wave before turning to speak to someone behind her. As she began to descend the steps, an older woman came through the door and followed her down. Jordie inhaled sharply when he saw her. She didn't look anything like the blowsy, unkempt harridan he had, for some reason, been expecting. She was younger than he'd anticipated and certainly far more attractive. In fact, she was very attractive indeed. Slim built, and with her shining silver hair cut in a long, shoulder-length bob, she certainly didn't look old enough to be Sukie's mother. He noted that Sukie kept glancing behind her to check the woman – he was going on the assumption it *was* her mother – wasn't having any problems with the metal stairs. He, very grudgingly, gave her some credit for her obvious thoughtfulness. He walked over to stand beside Pete and they waited for the ladies to speak with Walter as he checked their passports. Once they'd been cleared, they could all finally get together and head back to the schloss.

"Tweety Pie, how are you?" Sukie skipped over to Pete, threw her arms around him and planted a big kiss on his cheek. She gave him a tight hug then let go and stepped back. When she saw Jordie, she stuck her hand out and nodded. "Jordie."

Jordie noted the cool note in her voice and responded the same. "Sukie."

He gave her outstretched hand the briefest of shakes. In his head, only a guilty person would behave in such a manner. Sukie stepped back beside her mother and wrapped her arm around her waist as she introduced her.

"Pete, this is my mum Beth. Mum, Pete Wallace."

Beth stepped forward and shook Pete's hand, smiling widely at him. "It's lovely to meet you, Mr Wallace, and thank you so much for extending this gracious invitation to join you for Christmas. It's very kind of you."

Pete returned Beth's warm handshake. "Please, call me Pete, and it's my pleasure to have you join us. I hope you have a very enjoyable time."

Beth then turned to Jordie as Sukie said, "Mum, this is Jordie, Pete's manager. Jordie, this is Beth."

"Nice to meet you, Jordie." A frown crossed her face. "Have we met before? You seem vaguely familiar."

As Jordie returned the firm, warm handshake Beth gave him, he found himself looking into a pair of extraordinary cornflower-blue eyes that were twinkling with the excitement of her trip. Given Beth's silvery-blonde hair, and petite stature, it appeared Sukie had most likely gotten her colouring, and height, from her father. However, when they both stood side by side, you could see Beth's sharp bone structure and chin-tilt replicated exactly in her daughter.

"I'm very pleased to meet you, Beth." Jordie found his smile less forced as he let go of her hand. "I don't believe so, I'm sure it's something I'd remember."

He glanced behind the ladies and caught the wave of the porter, letting him know the plane was unloaded and their luggage could now be collected. He looked back at Beth and smiled again, "I do believe your luggage is now ready for collection. Let me help you with it," and he walked with her towards their bags and cases.

Sukie and Pete fell into step behind them. It didn't take long for them to pack up the Land Rover and, a few minutes later, they were in the car and heading out of the airport.

"How long is the journey from here to your schloss, Pete?" asked Sukie, from behind him. With Jordie behind the wheel, Pete was free to twist round and address his reply to both of his guests in the back seat. "It's about fifteen or twenty minutes, depending on which route you take. We're taking the slightly longer road today as it's very scenic and brings you to the front of the schloss. As this is your first visit, I wanted you to see it in all its glory."

"May I ask how old the schloss is?" asked Beth.

"Of course," he replied. "It was originally built in the 1400's and has been added to by successive generations over the centuries. These 'add-ons' have also turned it into a bit of a warren, so don't worry if you find yourself not where you'd expected to be. It's been a long-standing family joke to advise first-time visitors to allow themselves an extra ten minutes to get to the dining room for the evening meal. They invariably get there more by luck than judgement."

"And no one thought that some signage would be a good idea?" asked Beth.

"My understanding is that previous masters of the schloss considered it a good way to test the intelligence of their guests. As they'd often be invited there in a business capacity, this helped my ancestors to ascertain the problem-solving skills of potential business partners. In later years, the suggestion was made to my oma. She, however, thought signs would be tacky and advised us it was her home, not a hotel."

"So what does it look like?" Sukie leaned forward as she asked her question.

"Ah... Now that is a question I will not answer. You'll see her for yourself very soon. I don't want to ruin the surprise."

"Spoilsport!" retorted Sukie, as she sat back in her seat and stuck her tongue out at him. He grinned back and pulled a face. He loved his little Austrian castle and didn't want Sukie to have any pre-conceived notions which might spoil her first impression of his home.

A few minutes later, Jordie turned the car off the main road and headed into the dense forest area they'd been driving alongside for the last ten minutes.

"Are we there yet?" came Sukie's voice from the back seat.

"Almost," Pete said, "just another few minutes. This land is part of the grounds of the schloss but it's been left as open common ground for many centuries. We have approximately sixty-five acres but most of that is open for common use. We only have twenty acres closed off for the private use of the household residents. We'll be going through the gates in a few seconds, so I'd like to ask you, if you don't mind, to close your eyes."

Sukie and Beth looked at each other and then closed their eyes as he'd requested. The car carried on a bit further before slowing to a halt and he turned back to check the ladies still had their eyes closed. "Now then,

I'm going to ask you to trust Jordie, and I, to guide you out of the car to a point where you'll get the best view. You need to keep your eyes closed until I say so. Is that ok?"

"As long as that *is* the plan, Pete Wallace, and you're not planning to drop me in a ditch or anything," laughed Sukie.

"Darn it woman, you've sussed me out again!" They were both laughing as he stepped out of the car and went to help her down.

Jordie did the same with Beth. He opened her door and helped her to swing her legs round and placed her feet on the ground. "Beth, please give me both of your hands and keep your head down. I'll guide you round to the front of the car."

With her eyes still closed, Beth placed her hands into Jordie's and let him guide her along, only stopping so he could kick some debris out of the way.

Once Beth and Sukie were in situ, Pete said, "Okay, you can open your eyes now."

"This is just like an episode of a home improvement show we watch," said Beth. "I hope you're not about to change into the presenter from it, Sukie has a crush on him!"

"Oh, Mum! Shush you!" Sukie's voice came from her right-hand side. She took her mum's hand and said, "Right, let's do this."

Sukie opened her eyes and took in the view in front of her. She was glad Pete hadn't said anything because she honestly felt that no description could possibly have done his home any justice.

Jordie had stopped the car on a rise and they were looking over the top of the schloss, down in the valley. Behind it was a lake, so clear and still, it gave a perfect, mirrored reflection of the two large, black, snow-covered mountains that rose majestically into the sky. Her first thought, on seeing them, was that they were protecting the beautiful building beneath them. Her eyes moved back to the schloss and she took in the quite simple design, appreciating how well it fitted into its surroundings.

She studied the structure of the building and decided it looked like a capital 'E' that had fallen over onto its back. The middle 'stroke' was clearly the original castle. Very medieval in design, it had smaller windows and boasted a beautiful battlement on the rooftop.

Pete leaned in to her and pointed with his finger. "The building has been extended twice since it was built. The original castle keep is in the middle. The winged extensions along the front were added in the 1700's when a fire caused a lot of damage to the old building. The second extensions, the long, vertical wings going up to the lake, came along in the mid 1800's when people were vying with each other to display their great wealth. The architect was paid handsomely to work to the previous remit of the 1700's extension. This has kept the building uniform in design and, in my opinion, more aesthetically pleasing. I've seen a few castles where the architects were given free rein and the end result was not pretty!"

Sukie, however, thought the most 'aesthetically pleasing' things were the two turrets at either end of the side wings. These were sitting on the edge of the lake and looked out to the mountains opposite. The architect had chosen to add battlements to the top of these and, in doing so, he had balanced the building beautifully, pulling the old keep, and the later additions, together as one.

The schloss was a pale, yellow-cream in colour, inlaid with white painted woodwork struts and topped with the same green-coloured, copper roof she'd seen on many of the buildings in Salzburg. The main doorway was set in the middle of the original keep. It was a large, solid, white-painted, archway with equally large, double wooden doors set in it. The window frames, on the extensions, were also white brick arches and all had matching wooden shutters with, what looked like from up here, wooden window boxes. It was three storeys high and the smaller windows at the top were almost hidden under the eaves of the roof. A wall, in the same creamy-yellow shade, and level with the house front, ran away from each side, disappearing into the trees framing the gravelled area in front of the door. The top of the wall reached as high as the sills of the first-floor windows, thus giving complete privacy and protection to those on the other side. From this height, they could see some of the gardens on the other side. To the left, Sukie could make out a walled garden area and she suspected this may be an old kitchen garden. Beyond that, there was a variety of outbuildings. To the right, there was a small maze and a path wandering off into the forest. The areas directly behind the front of the schloss, in between the side wings and the old keep, had been landscaped with small box hedges. She guessed that, in the summer, these gardens were most likely a riot of colour when all the plants were in bloom. For now, however, they were a muted dark brown with only some small patches of snow, which had managed to hide from the melting sun, giving them any release from the dark shades of the earth.

In the pale, bright, winter sunlight, the schloss looked like a small golden ingot nestled against a backdrop of black and white, rugged, fierce mountains.

"Oh, Pete, it is beautiful."

Pete looked at her face and saw her words were genuine. "It's not as big, or as opulent, as many of the German and Austrian castles and villas you'll come across," he replied.

"It's perfect as it is. It's gorgeous and you have every right to be proud of it. I've just got one question though, aren't castles supposed to be high up so they could keep an eye out for raiders and such?"

"Many are, but some were also built on the side of lakes to protect from intruders coming in via the water."

"Ah, that makes sense," replied Sukie.

"I agree with Sukie," said Beth. "It really is very, very, beautiful. I would describe it as regal, rather than majestic. It's classy. I can't wait to see the inside."

"Thank you," replied Pete, with no small amount of pride in his voice. "So, are you ready to carry on?"

"Oh yes!" Both Beth and Sukie replied in unison.

They returned to the car and Jordie set off down the winding driveway. A few minutes later, he pulled up on the gravel in front of the large doors which, when viewed this close up, were very imposing indeed.

Still making sounds of appreciation, Beth and Sukie

got out of the car Pete walked them to the door and, mentally crossing his fingers, hoped they liked the inside as much as they did the outside.

Chapter Twenty-Seven

Pete needn't have worried. When Sukie and Beth walked into the large, open hallway, they both let out exclamations of appreciation. The high ceiling gave an immediate sense of grandeur, as did the twin staircases running up either side of the hallway to a beautiful galleried walkway connecting them at the top. The off-white colour of the walls enhanced the gilt cornice that ran around the ceiling. All the woodwork was pale oak and this lent warmth to what could otherwise have been a rather austere room. The gleaming, cream marble floor was enhanced by a large, thick rug in the centre. The final touch, which made the room extremely welcoming, was the massive, open fire, roaring away in the hearth to their right.

Pete was convinced, however, that Sukie had yet to notice the décor as she hadn't taken her eyes off the huge Christmas tree he'd had placed in between the staircases.

On Tuesday morning, knowing that Sukie would be here within five days, he'd had Kara on the phone, trying to find a professional company to come and decorate the schloss in all things Christmas related. Almost every room had a decorated tree in it, including the bedrooms. Every nook and cranny of the house was filled with little Christmas surprises, which could be anything from a nativity scene, a nutcracker soldier, or a winter scene with robins and small animals. He was sure he hadn't yet found them all. It had cost a fortune to get it all done at such short notice but it had been worth every penny. Christmas hadn't been celebrated at the schloss since his parents had died. Strangely, Pete sensed the building was happy with the effort he'd put in. When Jordie had questioned him about 'trying to impress that lass', he'd sharply reminded him it had nothing to do with impressing and everything to do with making this a Christmas to remember. Seeing Sukie's rapt expression, as she drank in the glorious, fifteen-foot, real pine creation in front her, he knew he'd done the right thing, regardless of what Jordie thought.

He walked over to her side. "Do you like it?"

When she turned and looked at him, her eyes were shining with joy. "Oh, Pete, I have no words. It's glorious. It really is. It's stunning."

"I'm so glad you like it. I had it put up to make you happy but, the truth is, seeing it there each day has made me happy too. For many different reasons, Christmas hasn't been special to me for a long time. This year is different. I am so looking forward to it all. So thank you, yet again, for being here, it really means a lot."

"Hey, you're all here! Welcome, welcome. Pete, Jordie, why aren't you showing these ladies to their rooms and giving them a chance to freshen up? There will be plenty of time for them to admire the décor once they've had some lunch and recovered from the journey."

Pete turned around. "Beth, Sukie, please meet Sally. Officially, she's the housekeeper but, really she's more of a surrogate mother and chief commandant. She rules the roost here and I learned a long time ago that I have a much easier life if I don't argue with her."

After another round of introductions and handshakes, Sally instructed Jordie and Pete to take the luggage up to their rooms while she pointed out to Beth and Sukie where to find the lounge. "Once you are ready to join us, please come down and I'll get lunch served up. Everything today is being done very informally as we're pushing the boat out for tomorrow. I am so looking forward to it."

Beth returned Sally's open, happy smile and replied, "We are too."

Sally then guided them towards the staircase on the right, just along from the fireplace. At the top she walked them along a number of corridors, chattering away as she did so – asking them how their flight had been, had they been up very early, and how was the weather back in the UK. She also informed them that a heavy snowfall was predicted for that night so they could be waking up to a nice, white Christmas morning which pleased Sukie very much. As they walked, Sukie kept a close eye on the route they were taking – remembering Pete's story from earlier, about the lost guests, she was determined not to be one of them. Or two of them, if she included her mother, as they would very likely go back downstairs together. At least for the first time anyway.

They turned yet another corner and met Pete and Jordie coming out of the two doors at the end.

"All luggage deposited," said Pete smiling, "I just hope in the correct rooms."

Sally moved to the door next to Jordie, opened it and turned to Beth saying, "This is your room, Beth."

Beth walked in and couldn't help but express her admiration. The room was large and bright, thanks to the winter sun shining in through the three enormous windows directly opposite the door. The warm yellow walls and white woodwork was beautifully accessorised with dark, midnight-blue curtains, window swags and cushions. A vast carved wooden bed took centre stage between two of the windows. Over the top, it had a matching wooden canopy, adorned with the same midnight-blue curtains as those on the windows. In the corner, in front of the third window, was a small, round dining table with two chairs on either side of it. Both were upholstered in a yellow and blue striped material. To the left of the doorway, the cream marble surrounded fireplace had a fire flickering merrily in it. A cosy seating area, consisting of two armchairs and a sofa, upholstered to match the dining chairs, and a coffee table was in front of it. The alcove to the right of the fireplace housed a twinkling Christmas tree, beautifully decorated to complement the colours of the room. The alcove on the left had a white built-in cupboard. Sally walked over and opened the cupboard doors. A small kettle and coffee machine sat upon the middle shelf. Below the shelf was a fully stocked fridge with milk, bottled water and some bottles of wine inside. Above it was everything Beth would need for a nice cup of tea or coffee, along with crockery and glasses. Turning around and pointing to a doorway in the corner diagonally opposite, Sally advised Beth that she would find the bathroom behind it.

Pete turned to Sukie, "Why don't I show you to your room, while your mum settles herself in here?"

"Are you ok with that, Mum? Shall I meet you here in about an hour to go back downstairs? Will that be enough time for you?"

Beth smiled at her daughter's array of questions. "The answer to all of those is yes, that would be perfect."

Sukie followed Pete, Jordie, and Sally out of Beth's room and closed the door behind her.

"I'll leave this one to you, Pete. I need to get back to the kitchen to check on everything." Sally smiled at Sukie. "I'll see you in the lounge in about an hour."

Jordie gave them both a sharp nod and, with a grunted "See you later", caught up with Sally and walked back along the corridor with her.

Sukie turned to Pete "Well, c'mon then, where's my room? I need to get my feet out of these boots and into something comfier."

Pete smiled and replied, "This way." He turned to the door next to Beth's room and put his hand on the door handle. Before opening it, he looked to Sukie at his side.

"I've... erm... given you a bit of a special room. It's quite different from your mum's. If you don't like it, please say so and we can move you to another one."

"Ok," she replied. "I'm not that much of a fussy mare though, so I'm sure I'll like it. Unless it's a room in the dungeon! I might raise an objection to that."

"I really do wish you'd stop guessing what all my surprises are!" Pete grinned at her. "You're no fun at all!"

"Just get on with it, will you, before my feet really start to ache."

He opened the door and walked through. Sukie followed behind him and found herself at the foot of a spiral staircase.

"This way," said Pete, and he began to climb the stairs.

As she walked behind him, Sukie tried not to admire the rather cute, tight, bottom encased in a pair of skinny black jeans that was right in her eye-line. She thought of how many women around the world would give anything to swap places with her right now. Once again, she was very glad she felt no physical attraction to Pete, because, it didn't take a genius to work out, that that way trouble lies!

They arrived on a small landing and Pete opened the only door before stepping back to allow her to walk in first.

Sukie stepped into the room but stopped short as she stared around her. She was in one of the turret rooms and it was beautiful. Two of the walls were straight but the other two were a combination of straight and rounded. The rounded section, the turret itself, had windows all the way round. The walls on either side also had large windows so the room was filled with light. The walls were painted a rich vanilla cream and the windows were dressed with big, thick, dark red curtains. The windows in the turret had small cream shutters and the walls there were dark red which made it appear very cosy. The large bed was placed there and it practically filled the space. There was just enough room for a small bedside table. On the right-hand side of the inner turret wall, a thick heavy red velvet curtain hung down, held in place with a huge cream tie-back. Looking up, she noted the rail which allowed the curtain to be pulled across to close the bed area off from the rest of the room. To the left of the turret was another Christmas tree and, just like Beth's, it was decorated to match the colours of the bedroom. She turned around and saw the bathroom, with the door slightly ajar, was situated in the corner nearest the bedroom door. It was then that she noticed, in the opposite corner, behind the bedroom door, a black, cast-iron, spiral staircase, which led up to an iron walkway attached to the outer wall, above her head. She stepped back into the middle of the room, and looking up, saw a closed door at the end of the walkway. She glanced at the stairs and then at Pete who nodded for her to go up.

Like a small child, she felt the excitement growing inside her as she ran up the stairs, all thoughts of her sore feet now forgotten. When she reached the door, she pulled it open towards her and found another small flight of wooden stairs behind it. She walked up them and, as she neared the top, she was unable to contain the gasp that slipped out. She climbed the last few steps, entered the room and found she was now at the very top of the turret. The room was completely round, and filled with bright, winter sunshine. She tilted her head back and gazed up into the pointed roof area where she saw three large skylights. A long, black, cast-iron ceiling lamp hung down from the centre point. The ceiling, walls and floor were all covered in wood cladding and this had been painted the same rich vanilla-cream as the bedroom below. Three arched, floor to ceiling French windows added to the open, spacious feel of the room. She felt as though she was floating high up in the clouds. Pete walked over to the middle window, opened the doors and, once again, stepped back for her to walk through. She did so and found herself standing on a small balcony overlooking the lake far below and staring at the snow-covered mountain peaks straight ahead. A couple of tall ceramic pots held some box hedging and these made the balcony feel welcoming, a place where you could happily sit awhile on balmy summer days. Today, however, being Christmas Eve and anything but balmy, there was a sharp icy wind which had her turning and walking back into the room a bit more swiftly than she'd normally have done.

Pete closed the doors behind her and turned to face her. "So, is it okay? Do you like it?"

She looked around her for a moment before replying "Nah! Could you show me the dungeon room instead?"

The look of shock on Pete's face was too much for her. She burst out laughing and said, "Oh, Pete, you are so easy to wind up. You really are. Of course I like it. I absolutely love it and I'm so grateful that you were thoughtful enough to know I would. How could anyone not adore a room like this? Thank you." She flopped down on the red velvet sofa and looked out of the windows. She gazed at the stunning view and continued, "I reckon you'll see very little of me over the next few days, as leaving this will be nearly impossible."

"At least I'll know where to find you."

"You sure will."

"Well, I'm going to head back downstairs now and leave you to get yourself, and your poor feet, all sorted and settled. I'll see you in about forty-five minutes?"

"Yeah, I'll see you then…" She was still taking in the stunning view in front of her and didn't turn to look at Pete. "Forty-five minutes," she answered distractedly.

Pete walked back down the stairs, through the bedroom and out onto the little landing, closing the bedroom door behind him. He was so happy that Sukie had liked his surprise and even happier that he'd correctly guessed she would. He ran down the stone steps and arrived back outside Beth's room. He had a warm, buzzy feeling inside and it felt good. As he walked along the corridor, he found himself humming the James Brown song he'd heard on the radio that morning and realised he was smiling like the proverbial Cheshire Cat. Yeah, he really *did* feel good!

Chapter Twenty-Eight

Sukie slept much later on Christmas morning than she would ever have done back home. She stretched in her bed and was surprised when she looked at her watch to see that it was after ten. Clearly the early rise and long journey of the previous day had caught up with her, although she reckoned the biggest contributor to her long and deep sleep was most likely the fresh mountain air. It had been snowing heavily when she'd gone to bed and she hadn't been able to resist keeping a window open so she could smell the snow as she slept.

Once showered and dressed, she wandered downstairs and found everyone in the lounge where they'd all relaxed and unwound the night before. Pete's dogs were both laid out in front of the open fire but, having made friends with them last night, which had included lots of fussing and cuddles (well, they were beautifully fluffy, how could she resist them?!) they quickly got up and came over to her as she entered the room.

She bent down and, petting them both vigorously, said, "Hey there, boys. How are you guys today? Aren't you both so gorgeous. I could snuggle you all day long."

"Well, that's very kind of you to say so but I don't think Jordie is big on the snuggling thing. I'm game though if you are!"

She looked up to see Pete walking over with a big grin on his face. She grinned back. "I think I'd rather stick with the dogs, their breath is less smelly!"

"Ouch! Once again I am cut by thy rapier tongue!" Pete placed a hand on his chest and made a playful stagger. "How can such a pretty face hide such a cruel and wicked soul?"

"Oh, away with you, you daft prat!" She gave him a playful push.

"Come here, you." He pulled her into a tight hug. "Merry Christmas, Sukes."

She hugged him back. "A very Merry Christmas to you, Tweets."

"Darling, Merry Christmas." Beth walked over and took her daughter in her arms. "Did you sleep alright? I slept like a log. I only came down myself about five minutes ago."

"Merry Christmas, Mum." She held Beth close for a few seconds, breathing in the Issey Miyake perfume she always wore on special occasions, and kissed her cheek. "I had a great sleep too. I couldn't believe the time when I woke up."

She let go and walked over to Jordie, who stood up

as she approached. "Merry Christmas, Jordie," she said and, without giving him a chance to move or complain, she gave him a hug too. Jordie stood stiffly for a brief second before he relaxed and hugged her back, saying "Merry Christmas to you too, lass, Merry Christmas."

Sally came in just then and, after more hugs and festive wishes, asked them what they wanted to do about breakfast, taking into consideration that it was only five hours until they'd be sitting down for Christmas dinner.

Everyone just looked at each other until Beth took charge. "If I may make a suggestion… How about we have some mince pies with tea or coffee and open our Christmas presents?"

This was unanimously agreed upon so Beth went with Sally to the kitchen to help her bring things through.

Once everyone had their drinks and plates of pies beside them, Pete went over to the Christmas tree in front of the windows and began gathering up the presents which had all been laid underneath it the night before. He brought them over to the coffee table and placed them on it.

Sally picked up a present from the pile and passed it to Beth. Beth, in turn, located her gift for Sally and handed it over with a smile. They opened their gifts together and, upon seeing the contents, burst out laughing. The gorgeous, deep russet, chiffon scarf Sally had given Beth would do absolutely nothing for her pale complexion. The delicious scarlet and cream stole Beth had bought for Sally, was going to clash with Sally's deep red hair something chronic.

"Shall we swap?" asked Sally, still giggling.

"I think that sounds like a perfect solution," replied Beth, handing Sally back her gift with a smile.

Beth then picked up a small package and handed it to Jordie. "It is very difficult to buy gifts for people you've never met, and know very little about, so I hope this is ok."

When he un-wrapped the small gift, and opened the box inside, Jordie was stunned to find a pair of silver cufflinks in the shape of the Tyne Bridge in Newcastle.

"Oh my! They're lovely." He took one out for a closer look. "These are really great." He smiled over to Beth and said, "This was very thoughtful of you. Thank you."

Beth blushed slightly under his warm gaze. "You're welcome. I know they're not an item everyone wears these days but I hoped that, with some of the events you must attend with Pete, you may have a use for them occasionally."

"I know I will have several occasions to wear them. I'll make sure of it." He then carefully placed the box by his side.

"This is also for you, Jordie," said Sukie as she passed her gift to him. She watched him carefully while he opened it. Sally had already exclaimed with joy at the new Mary Berry baking book she'd given her, but Jordie was a different matter. Their relationship was still strained and she didn't want to create any bad atmosphere today.

As Jordie peeled back the tissue paper underneath the gift-wrap, he was most surprised to find two pairs of very nice, soft, leather gloves – one black pair, the other brown, He looked at Sukie, the surprise evident on his face. "How did you know I needed gloves?"

"Kara mentioned you'd lost yours the day you went to London," she replied, a bit shyly.

"Well, they are very nice and exactly what I need. Thank you." He pulled the black pair on and he continued with a smile, "And a perfect fit too." He took in the thoughtfully chosen gifts Beth and Sukie had given him and looked more than a bit guilty as he watched them unwrap the two bottles of perfume he'd quickly grabbed from the pharmacy in the town.

"Here, Sukes, got this for you." Pete handed over his gift.

She un-wrapped it and let out a gasp. "Oh, Pete, it's fabulous. I love it, thank you." In her hands, she held a medium sized snow globe. Inside was a miniature replica of the Sound of Music gazebo, which she'd been so excited to find the first day she'd gone out with Pete. Eyes shining, she gave it a shake and watched the snow gently fall and swirl around the little monument. She adored it already.

"I've got you something else, too," Pete said, and he handed over a second present.

"What, more? But this is more than enough. Nothing could be as perfect as my snow globe." She opened the second present and found a square, silver bangle with little diamantes studded along it.

"But... this is the bangle you asked my advice on because you wanted to buy it for Kara." She looked at him in confusion.

Pete laughed. "No, I only said that because I wanted

to check you really did like it. I saw you looking at it in the shop window each time we passed by but I needed to be sure."

"But Kara...?"

"Kara doesn't do jewellery. She's got vouchers for a spa weekend she's planning with her mum and sister. She made sure to tell me exactly which spa resort to get them for too!"

"You tricked me," she smiled at him, "but I'll let you off on this one occasion as I really do adore it." She slipped the bangle onto her wrist and then leaned over to pick up the remaining two gifts on the table and handed them to Pete. "For you, from me," she said.

Pete opened the first present and let out a roar of a laugh. He held up the DVD he'd found inside – Looney Tunes Sylvester and Tweety Pie. "Good one, Sukes! That is brilliant! Thank you!"

She grinned back at him. "I thought you could both sing along together although I know he'll sound waaaay better than you!"

Pete grabbed a nearby cushion and threw it at her. "Always with the abuse!"

"Too right," she laughed. "If I gave you a break, you'd think it was Christmas."

Still laughing, Pete opened up his second gift. "Oh, my goodness! I don't believe it! Where on earth did you find this?"

She couldn't help laughing again as Pete took out the watch she'd given him – a watch with a picture of a winking Tweety Pie on its face.

"The internet is a wonderful thing, dear chap. It's

amazing what you can find."

"Clearly! I think it's absolutely fantastic." As he spoke, Pete removed the very expensive Omega watch he usually wore and replaced it with Sukie's gift. "I'm never going to take it off. I will wear it always."

Sukie was sitting on her bed, looking out of her turret windows. It was Christmas night and the snow was falling in gentle swirls. It was incredibly pretty and very hypnotic. The lights were off in the bedroom to enable her to see the night more clearly, but Pete had had some twinkling fairy lights strung across the turret ceiling and these were on, adding to the magical atmosphere. It had been a busy, fun-filled day but Sukie wasn't tired. Not yet. She thought about the rest of the day as she pulled back the quilt to get into bed. Sally's Christmas dinner had been excellent. Everything had tasted exquisite. The duck had been cooked to perfection and melted in the mouth. The vegetables had been perfectly crunchy and the roast potatoes had been to-die-for, crispy on the outside and fluffy-soft on the inside. She'd eaten far more of those than she normally would and knew she was going to feel the pinch in her jeans the next day. What was most amazing, however, was finding out that Jordie and her mother *had* met before. Well... not 'met' exactly but most definitely had bumped into each other – quite literally!

It had come about after the main course when Sally

and Beth had been clearing the table for the dessert. Jordie and Pete had just sat back, fully expecting the ladies to wait upon them. Well, Beth was having none of that and had said as much. "Come on you two, on your feet and get those serving bowls picked up and through to the kitchen. Chop-chop!"

Jordie had looked up in astonishment as he wasn't used to pitching in with clearing up. Sally normally got on with the task and never asked them to help. "Excuse me, are you talking to us?" he'd asked.

"Well, I'm not standing here flapping my gums to create a breeze so I guess I must be!" had been Beth's sassy reply to him.

Something in Beth's tone had sparked a memory at the back of Jordie's mind and, narrowing his eyes, he'd stared at her for a moment. Suddenly it came to him. "Pink umbrella!"

"You what?" Beth had looked at him, wondering what was behind his strange comment.

"Do you own a pink umbrella?" he'd asked her.

"Err… Nope! A black one. Why?"

"Were you in London last Saturday? Near Covent Garden?"

"Um, yes, yes I was. I was with my friend Laura…Who owns a pink umbrella!" Beth had had her own light-bulb moment as it came to her in a flash why Jordie had seemed familiar when she'd first saw him yesterday. "You were the moron who pushed me onto the road when we were waiting to cross at the lights." She'd glared at him as the memory came rushing back, remembering how, if she hadn't grabbed Laura's coat sleeve, she'd have gone flat on her face in front of a bus. "You could have killed me that day, you stupid idiot!"

"Killed you?" Jordie had stood up and glared right back at her across the table. "Do you realise how close you came to half-blinding me with that pink monstrosity you were carrying? If I hadn't pushed you away when I did, one of the spokes would have been right in my eye."

Everyone else in the room had gone quiet as the two of them squared up to each other across the table.

"Seriously?! We nearly poked you in the eye?" asked Beth, her tone suddenly more conciliatory.

"Yeah, seriously! Another fraction of an inch and Sukie here would've been buying me eye-patches for my Christmas, not gloves."

"Oh gosh, I am so sorry. I thought you were just another rude Londoner who couldn't be bothered to say 'excuse me' to the tourists."

"Well, that explains the gobby mouthful you gave me." Jordie had begun to smile as he recalled Beth's fishwife antics that day. He'd looked at Sukie. "Your mum can sure stand up for herself when she needs to!"

She'd grinned at him. "Of course she can. Where do you think I got it from?" She'd turned to her mum. "And may I ask what you said to him?"

Beth had blushed as the words she'd hurled at Jordie's retreating back that day flowed back into her mind. "No, you can't. Jordie, once again, I'm very sorry that you had to take such evasive action. Although I still think trying to put me under a bus was a bit drastic."

Beth had given him her apology but she still expected one back from Jordie. He wasn't an innocent in all of this either, even though he might like to think he was the only injured party.

Jordie had cottoned on quickly to her expectation and, given how quickly Beth had apologised to him, felt it would be most churlish of him not to reciprocate. "I too, am very sorry for pushing you as hard as I did. It was not my intention to put you in the way of harm, merely to keep both my eyes in working order. Still friends?" He'd put his hand out across the table.

Beth had taken a hold of it and given it a firm shake. "Of course we are. But that doesn't get you out of helping to clear the table so get those bowls picked up and into that kitchen otherwise you will find out how much of a fishwife I can really be."

Still smiling at the thought of her mum giving Jordie a mouthful of abuse, Sukie switched off the fairy-lights and snuggled up to go to sleep.

In her bedroom, Beth had run herself a bubble-bath and was enjoying the soak with a cup of tea on a small table at the side. She'd had a delightful day in the company of very lovely people. She still couldn't get over that she and Jordie had previously crossed swords. It really was a small world, she thought, as she took a sip of her tea – a really small world indeed.

Downstairs in the lounge, Jordie and Pete sat in front of the fire, staring into the flames, both nursing a tumbler of fine malt whisky.

"I'd say today has been a wonderful day, wouldn't you, Jordie?"

Jordie thought for a moment before replying. "D'you know what, Pete, I'd say it has. In fact, I'd say it has been a mighty fine Christmas Day indeed."

They clinked their glasses together and said, in unison, "Merry Christmas."

Sitting back, they resumed their silence, once again staring into the hypnotic flames and reflecting on the day they'd shared.

In a bedroom, in Verona, Eduardo di Santo sat watching Pete Wallace concerts on his computer. By his side lay a large writing pad and pen. Every so often he would jot down some notes.

Notes that would help him to assess the weak spots in Pete's stage performances. Notes that would help him to know when to make his move.

Notes that would help him to get his revenge.

Chapter Twenty-Nine

"Eduardo… Smile! Why always with the grumpy face huh?"

Rosa di Santo looked at her son as they sat watching a Christmas comedy on the television. Once he'd been a happy child, but after his father had walked out, he'd changed and it was now quite rare to see him either relaxed or hear him laugh. He'd had to grow up fast and, as a result, had become a very serious young man who thought having any kind of fun was a frivolous waste of time. As she looked at him tonight, she could see her maternal grandfather in him. He'd always had a stern demeanour about him, both in nature and appearance, and she'd been rather scared of him when she was a child. Eduardo could have been his twin with his solid, thick eyebrows, heavy-lidded, brown eyes, long, patrician nose, sharp cheek-bones and strong jawline. They even shared the same thick, wavy, brown hair although Eduardo chose to keep his very short. She believed they called it a 'buzz-cut'? Whilst the stark hair-style suited him, and accentuated his excellent bone structure, it only served to enhance his intimidating persona. This was probably not a bad thing within the security business but he was never going to meet a young lady if he carried a perpetual scowl on his face. She'd tried to tell him many times that no girl wants her dark and mysterious man to be that way *all* the time, even if it was what had attracted her to him in the first instance. He'd simply glared at her – no surprise there, he glared at everyone, all of the time – and had informed her he had no interest in meeting girls and certainly no time to be bothered with silly nonsense like that.

Since Sofia's accident, he had become increasingly distant and more intense. Rosa could understand that he felt helpless. He'd so often been the 'fixer' within their little family unit and now he was faced, very starkly, with something outside of his fixing abilities. Sofia's poor health was something he could not control and, for someone who could only be described as a control-freak, this was very hard to accept. She'd witnessed, only today, his inner conflicts as he'd had to help, or carry, Sofia around the apartment. It pained him to see his sister stripped of all dignity as he had to lift her in or out of the bath or assist her when she needed to visit the bathroom. She tried to help as much as she could but she lacked the physical strength needed to help Sofia with these tasks.

Rosa watched him now. She could see his mind was elsewhere and that he was not taking in any of the television show he was staring at. As much as she loved her son, and she did, fiercely so, she was under no illusion that he was a flawed character. His temper was terrifying and his brooding intensity was very intimidating. As he'd grown older, his controlling nature had worsened. She'd tried to stand up against him – she was his mother after all – but the ensuing dramas had only served for her to realise that she and Sofia had a quieter, better life if she allowed him to be in charge. She also admitted to herself that, had it been just the two of them, she'd have taken a stronger stand against him but, with Sofia to consider, she'd had to take the path of least resistance. She was not going to have her youngest child grow up in a disruptive atmosphere – she'd given up too much to have her daughter and she wanted her to have the best life possible. Between her and Eduardo, she'd known they could do that. Sadly, with the benefit of that wonderful thing called hindsight, she could now see that, by not reining Eduardo in, she'd created a controlling monster and, if it hadn't been for his overly strict household rules, Sofia may not have felt a need to rebel that night, may not have drunk too many of those silly alcopop things and may not have stupidly thought, in her inebriated state, that she could leap from the stand in the concert hall onto the stage. Rosa felt a tear slip down her cheek and she discreetly wiped it away. Tonight was not the first time she had cried over the fact that, by doing their best to protect Sofia, they had, in all likelihood, contributed towards the error of judgement which had changed their lives so profoundly.

Eduardo could feel his mother's eyes on him as he

watched the television. Contrary to what Rosa thought, he was actually watching the programme that was on, he just didn't find it funny and considered the slap-stick antics to be stupid and boring. Sofia, however, was giggling at them so he was prepared to carry on watching for her benefit. In the back of his mind though, he was mulling over the next step in his plans. The Wallace gig in June still had to be confirmed although they'd been told this was merely a formality and to begin the procedures required to provide the level of security which would be needed for the event. With this information, he was now looking at ways to move forward with his intentions.

He no longer considered his fixation for revenge to be unnatural. It had been in his head for so long, he'd convinced himself this was how it worked. If you messed with his family, he'd make you wish you hadn't. Some people would say this was a very Mafioso-style mentality but they wouldn't be brave enough to say it to his face – that was for sure!

He needed to come up with a few options though to make his pay-back a reality. He'd downloaded a number of videos of various Pete Wallace gigs from his last tour, which he'd watch later. Thank goodness for all-singing and all-dancing mobile phones – people just couldn't resist filming these events and loading them onto the internet. This would make it so much easier to find the weak spot that would enable him to put his plan into action. All he needed to do now was sort out the plan.

Chapter Thirty

Sukie couldn't get to sleep. After tossing and turning for about an hour, she sat up and switched on the bedside lamp. She knew what the problem was – she needed a book to read. Every night, without fail, she'd read for about half an hour and this habit always ensured she got a decent night's sleep. She'd stupidly, however, put her e-reader into a handbag which she'd decided at the last minute not to bring and had forgotten to take it out again.

She was surprised she hadn't fallen asleep as soon as her head had hit the pillow. After the long Boxing Day walk she and Pete had taken around the grounds of the schloss, she'd expected to go out like a light as soon as she'd lain down but her mind wouldn't switch off. She was wondering on the best thing to do when she recalled the room Pete had said was the library when he'd given her and Beth a quick tour. Hopeful of finding something there to see her through the next few days of her visit, she got up to go for a look. Not having expected to be wandering around the schloss at night, she hadn't packed a dressing gown. Her thick cotton pyjamas were certainly modest enough but she really didn't feel comfortable at the thought of walking the corridors in just them and nothing else. She looked around her room and the only thing she could see that would suffice was her coat. Since no one else was likely to see her, she gave a mental shrug and pulled it on. She opened the bedroom door and stepped out onto the spiral staircase but, seeing how dark it was below her, and uncertain exactly where the light switch was, she went back to pick up her mobile phone. She had a torch facility on it and, for the first time, it was about to come in very handy.

She made her way down the stairs and past her mother's bedroom. She gave a small shiver and was glad she'd brought both the torch and her coat. The heating had gone off and it was quite chilly. It also appeared as though the lamps which usually lit the corridors in the evenings were on timers as, they too, were switched off and the corridors were now voids of deep, heavy blackness.

She continued down the main stairs into the hallway and paused at the bottom to get her bearings while trying to remember which door led to the library. She loved to read and it had been her intention to explore the library in more detail but hadn't yet had the chance to do so. Now that the schloss was in darkness, everything felt, and looked, very different and it was not so easy to establish where she needed to go. She closed her eyes and tried to visualise the daylight tour she'd had. This helped and, opening them again, she turned right under the staircase she'd come down and walked along the corridor till she came to the third door on her left. She was sure this was the room she wanted. She pushed the door open slowly and quietly and, when she walked in, felt around for the light switch on the wall to her left. But it wasn't there. Oh, for goodness' sake, she thought to herself, where is it? She groped about some more but couldn't find the switch. "Dammit!" she muttered aloud. Vaguely, she recalled seeing a desk or a table on the other side of the room, near the window, and she was sure there was a lamp on it. She held her phone out in front of her and used the feeble ray of light to try and find her way.

Suddenly, from the furthest corner, a voice said, "What the hell do you think you're doing?"

With a sharp scream, Sukie dropped her phone, which skittered across the polished, wooden floor and disappeared underneath one of the sofas, plunging the room into total darkness.

Pete switched on a nearby lamp and looked down to find Sukie scrabbling around on the floor, trying to locate her phone. "I said, what the hell do you think you are doing?"

Sukie looked up at him, as she thrust her arm under the heavy piece of antique furniture. "Hmmm… Let me see. What am I doing? Am I checking under your sofa for dust bunnies? Or am I trying to get a hold of the phone I dropped when you scared the living SHIT out of me? Which do you think it might be?"

"Why are you tiptoeing around my home, in the dark

and in the early hours of the morning? What do you want? What are you looking for? Are you hoping to dig up some dirt on me?" Pete stood over her, anger written all over his face.

"Hey, steady on, Pete. Just back up the thinking there a minute! What are you accusing me of here exactly?" Sukie found her phone, stood up and stared back at Pete, her own anger beginning to rise. She'd just had one heck of a fright and here was her so-called friend accusing her of… well, she didn't know what he was accusing her of exactly but she was far from happy about whatever it was.

"I asked you first and I repeat – Why are you tiptoeing around my house, in the dark, in the middle of the night? Please answer me." Pete was seething. Jordie had been right after all, Sukie was just another opportunist, out to get all she could from him.

"I was, as you put it, 'tiptoeing around in the darkness' so as not to disturb anyone because, as you have pointed out, it is the early hours of the morning and I expected most people to be asleep," Sukie replied, every word dripping in sarcastic disgust. "And…" she put her hand up to stop him interjecting, "what I was doing was looking for a book to read. I stupidly left my e-reader at home and I can't sleep without reading for a bit beforehand."

"You didn't need one last night or the night you arrived."

"No, I didn't, because I was shattered on both of those occasions. I'd expected to be the same tonight, after our long walk today, but I must be acclimatising to the mountain air because I'm not as tired as I thought I would be."

"So, why the phone and the coat?"

Sukie sighed and explained, with no small amount of exasperation. "The coat is because I didn't bring a dressing gown with me and the phone because its pitch black when the lamps are all switched off. I couldn't see a thing and I didn't fancy falling down the stairs and breaking my neck. I know I said I wanted to visit all the local sights but I wasn't including the local hospital on that list!"

Pete rubbed a hand across his face. Sukie's explanation made perfect sense but he couldn't let go of his suspicions. "Why didn't you put the light on when you came in here then? How were you going to find a book with that?" He nodded towards her phone.

"I *tried* to put the light on when I came in but couldn't find the switch. I was aiming for that table lamp," she pointed behind her, "when you decided to check out my heart function by scaring the absolute crap out of me. Thanks for that, by the way. Highlight of the holiday so far!" Sukie hadn't yet dropped her sarcastic tone. She'd had such a fright and she was still shaking from the shock of it. An interrogation was not what she needed right now.

"The light switch is behind the door, so I don't get how you couldn't find it."

Sukie looked at him in disbelief. Was he for real? "Oh, the light switch is *BEHIND* the door, is it? Well, silly me for not knowing that. After all, most of the places I've been to, the light switches are just *inside* the door where you open them. Perhaps if I'd lived here for two *years*, and not just two *days*, I'd have known that!"

Pete realised how wrong he'd been and slumped down on the chair next to him. "I'm sorry. I really am. I didn't mean to frighten you. I saw the phone in your hand, you appeared to be sneaking about, and I thought the worst."

Despite her coat, Sukie was growing colder and her teeth began to chatter as she replied, "I th-thought we had g-gotten past th-that?"

"Oh, you're cold," Pete exclaimed. He jumped up, pushed the chair he'd been sitting on closer to the fireplace and led Sukie to it. "Let me put the fire back on." He moved over to the cold grate.

"P-put the f-fire b-back on?" asked Sukie. "I th-thought it w-was a real one?"

"Crikey no!" Pete grinned at her as he fiddled about. "While they're fabulous to look at, the effort that goes into laying, cleaning and maintaining them is far too much and Sally would not thank me for the extra work involved. When the schloss was updated about ten years ago, the open fires were all replaced with these gas-effect things. They look just like the real thing but with much less effort. See?" and he sat back on his heels as the lovely orange flames quickly began to warm up both the room and Sukie's feet.

"I didn't realise you could get such large fires. Some of the ones in this place are massive."

"They are, but they look great and really help to keep the authentic atmosphere of the schloss. They didn't have central heating back in medieval times when this place was first built so it had to be kept as discreet as possible. Are you warming up now?"

"Yes, thank you," replied Sukie, but she pulled her coat around her a bit tighter.

"Didn't you have a jumper or a cardigan you could have put on?"

"None big enough to fit over the top of my jammies…"

Pete walked to the desk, picked up a jumper draped over the chair and brought it back to Sukie.

"Here, try this. I think it should be big enough."

She took off her coat, and pulling the jumper over her head, found herself swamped in a mass of thick, soft, cream wool. The sleeves were long enough to cover her hands and there was even enough room for her to pull her knees up to her chest inside it. A slight hint of citrus wafted off the fabric as she moved and she recognised the after-shave that Pete occasionally wore. "Oh, this is lush! It's so soft and definitely warm." She snuggled into it a bit more.

"You can keep it. You'll need a decent jumper if you're planning any more night-time forays." Pete smiled to let her know he was making a joke of the situation.

"Pete…" Sukie looked at him in her usual direct and forthright manner. "Why were you so quick to think I was up to no good? I thought we'd dealt with that in Salzburg."

He sat down on the sofa in front of the fire, at the end closest to Sukie's chair. "I know. Again, I'm sorry. It's just…" he hesitated for a moment before continuing. "It's just that I've had very bad experiences in the past

255

with people I've trusted letting me down. This is why I have so few friends. I found out the hard way not to put my faith in anyone because, the last time I did, it resulted in the death of my parents."

Sukie gasped and put her hand to her mouth. "Oh, Pete, I'm so sorry. That must have been awful for you."

Pete looked at her quizzically. "Didn't you read about it? It was in all the papers."

"I told you before, I don't read newspapers. Although, thinking about it now, I vaguely recall hearing something in passing. However, I really don't have the inclination for reading celebrity tittle-tattle so you'll have to forgive me for knowing almost nothing about you or your life."

Pete could see she was telling the truth. Sukie genuinely knew very little about him. "But your friend, the one who thinks I'm the bee's knees or whatever... Didn't she mention it?"

"Ah... Elsa! While she and I may be the very best of friends, with a gazillion things in common, sadly most of our musical tastes are now quite different. I like a bit of indie and hard rock whereas she prefers soft pop and disco'y funk stuff. Where she's all Simply Red and Jay Kay, I'm Simple Minds and Green Day. It was agreed a long time ago that we'd try to keep musical discussions to a minimum as we rarely agreed on anything. Except for Robbie Williams that is! We're both very much in agreement that he is sex on legs!" She grinned at the last bit. "So, at the risk of putting a massive dent in your ego, Mr Wallace, I am, genuinely, in complete ignorance about your past and most things about you as a person."

Pete didn't know quite where to go from here. It was a very rare thing indeed for him to be in this position.

Sukie sensed his confusion. "Look, I'll tell you what I know about you. You were in a boy band called The Astons. You were massively popular, had world-wide domination of the charts and record sales. The band split up – I don't know why – and it broke the hearts of almost every girl and woman between the ages of thirteen to thirty. Since then you've pursued a solo career which has given you continued success. And that's it! Oh… and you often appear in the media with a variety of gorgeous women on your arm but we've already covered that bit."

"Well, that is what you would call a short summation of my life in about what… five sentences?"

"As I said, Pete, I don't read the newspapers. Look, why don't you tell me about you. After all, who else is the best person to tell me the truth about you than you?"

Pete looked into the flames for a moment and then, turning towards Sukie, simply replied, "Okay."

Chapter Thirty-One

Pete turned back to look into the flames and began to tell his story.

"It all started as a joke. One night, I was at the house of my mate Ed. My other two friends, Danny and Buzz, were there too. We were aged between fifteen and sixteen and life was easy and simple. Ed's older sister Louise was watching Top of the Pops with a couple of friends when some boy band came on. Take That maybe? I can't recall for sure. Anyway, the girls were all squealing and excited over them and we began to take the mickey, pretending to prance about dancing as they were on the television, all the while saying they weren't that special and anyone could do what they were doing. We didn't mean any of it. It was just a means of winding them up. Anyway, the girls got quite annoyed with us and said, if it was so easy, why didn't we do it? The school we all attended held a talent contest every year and the winner, or winners, got to perform their act at the end-of-year school disco. Louise and her chums pretty much dared us to enter as a boy band. Well, have you ever met a sixteen-year-old lad who'd refuse a dare?"

Sukie shook her head. "No, I don't think so."

"Exactly! And we didn't. We put our names on the entry list the very next day and began practicing. We were determined to do it right and do it well. We got a hold of some karaoke backing tapes and took over Danny's dad's garage. Danny was an only child so there were no siblings to take the piss out of us when we rehearsed. The song we chose was the Elvis Presley number 'Return to Sender'. After a few teething issues, such as who was taking lead vocals and stuff, we really got to grips with it and began to enjoy what we were doing. We only had a couple of weeks in which to sort ourselves out – learn the song, work out harmonies and put a dance routine together – but we managed it and, the night before the contest, we were pretty confident we could pull it off the next day. There were only two things we hadn't sorted out – outfits and a name. When we compared our wardrobes the only item of clothing we all had in common were our football shirts. We all agreed we would wear those – two of us in the home strip, the other two in the away strip – and the band name stemmed from that. If we were going on stage, wearing Aston Villa shirts, then the natural and obvious choice for a band name was 'The Astons'."

He paused for a few seconds as he remembered back to those early days when they'd been all innocent and un-knowing of what lay ahead of them.

"To cut a long story a bit shorter, we went down a storm and won the contest by a landslide. We were asked to perform two songs at the disco so we set about finding something else which worked as well as 'Sender' did. We came up 'Wonderful World' – you know, the Louis Armstrong song."

Sukie nodded. "Those are unusual choices for sixteen-year-old boys, if I may say so."

"I agree, but we'd heard them so many times growing up we knew most of the words, meaning we were able to learn them quickly. Quite sensible actually, looking back on it now." He smiled and carried on. "The night of the disco came and we performed our two songs. And that's when it was supposed to end. That's where it *should* have ended but for one tiny little quirk of fate. Some of the parents volunteered throughout the year as helpers at the various school events. On this night, Karen Carmichael's mother, Trudy, having had a guilt trip at her lack of involvement that year, had come along as a helper. Her day job was a talent scout for one of the larger record companies. She saw us perform and, in her own words, knew she'd hit the jackpot. The next day, all our parents received a phone call from the school asking them to come in for a meeting. Due to our age, they had to give their consent for this to be pursued on a professional level. At this point, we knew nothing of this. It had to be a unanimous parental agreement before they would break the news to us. Danny's parents were the most resistant to the idea but Trudy Carmichael was a very persuasive woman and she managed to bring them round. The parents all stated the final decision lay with the four of us.

If we didn't want to do it, then the deal was off the table. That, however, didn't happen. In our youthful naivety, we had no idea of where it would lead and just thought it would be a bit of a jolly. With a bit of luck, we'd even get to snog some girls." Pete looked over at Sukie. "That was all we cared about then, getting to snog some girls!"

Sukie smiled at him. "Well, I think we can safely say you all achieved that ambition huh!"

"Didn't we just! Although it did take a bit of time – we were so wet behind the ears, it was like we had our own swimming pools back there! It was a big step up from performing in a school hall to performing in front of fee-paying punters. Every weekend we'd be in a van, heading off to some place or another, being the support act for goodness knew who at goodness knew where. But, it was the only way to learn the trade and get the experience we needed. That's where Jordie came in. With his knowledge of the music business, our parents wanted someone on the inside who would be looking out for our interests. The record company personnel around us only cared about their own jobs and reputations whereas Jordie ensured we were treated fairly. As our success began to grow, his role with us changed. He stopped being our roadie stroke driver stroke minder and became our manager. He always played it totally fair between the four of us. We all got equal shares of everything. When it became evident that Buzz and I were doing most of the song writing, he made amendments to ensure we got the writing credits. At the time, neither of us saw the merit in this, but – as time has passed and circumstances have changed – it was the right thing to do. We now come to the bit you know we ended up being very successful and had world domination of the music charts."

"So why did you split up?"

"The same old things that always splits bands... drugs, drink, bruised egos and arrogance. We were so young, and our success had come so easy, it was impossible to maintain a grip on real life. Once we were riding high, people couldn't do enough for us. It became a game between us to see who could make the most outrageous, extortionate requests and to see where the line would be drawn. Who would actually have the balls to say no to our impossible demands? Unfortunately, no one ever did and we got out of control. Jordie did his best to keep us on the right track – and when it came to doing our 'day job', we were always totally professional. We never missed a gig and attended every rehearsal, recording session or interview we were booked in for. We never swore or rebelled on television and we always acknowledged our fans for what their loyalty and support had given us. Behind the scenes, however, in our personal lives, we were all completely fucked up!" Pete stopped talking as some of the fights, and arguments they'd had, came back to him. He stared into the fire for several minutes, reliving those scenes once more in his mind.

"Finally, it all came to a head and we had a really massive row. It turned out that Danny and Ed were not so happy with Buzz and I getting more recognition than they did. You see, when we did the school stuff, those guys were really shy about singing solo, so Buzz and I had shared the lead between us. Danny and Ed were happy to harmonise and be backing vocals. Although they

262

eventually got to sing lead later on, it was never as often as Buzz and me. This fermented into a deep resentment which, when fuelled with drugs and booze, was going to explode one day. And, when it did, it took us all down a road from which there was no return. We could no longer work together. We managed to finish the tour we were on and then we went our separate ways."

"Have you seen or spoken to them since?" Sukie was genuinely interested. "Your story's so interesting, maybe because it's something I've never given much thought to before."

"No, I haven't. We came off stage after our last gig at Wembley, got into four separate cars and went our own way." Pete halted for a few seconds as he remembered those early days of loneliness. "In the first few months after we'd split, I felt very alone and rudderless. It was like floating in a vast empty sea, with no sign of land anywhere. For years, those guys had been my closest friends. We'd spent our early school years hanging out in each other's homes. When the band came about, we spent the next ten years living in each other's pockets. And then, suddenly, I was on my own. I didn't know where to go, what to do, even what to eat. Everything had always been done for us and there had always been one of the other guys around to hang out with. Now they were gone and I was alone. I hadn't been alone like that in my entire life. I had no one to turn to. Two years before the split, my oma became very ill and was dying so my parents moved from Birmingham to live here in the schloss to be with her. My mum couldn't wait to come back because she'd found the constant press intrusion hard to bear and it was causing rifts in the family. My twin sister refused to visit the house—"

"Woah! Stop there a minute. Twin sister?" This was the first time Pete had ever mentioned a sibling, never mind a twin! Sukie was flabbergasted.

"Yes, I have a twin sister but very few people know about her. And that's how she wants it to stay. When we were twelve, and moving up into seniors, she asked to go to boarding school. She's quite brilliant at maths and, with some testing, had shown an exceptional aptitude for the sciences. My parents never forced her in any way and allowed her to choose her own path in life. Having already decided she wanted to do forensic science, she found a school that had produced excellent results in their science department and wanted to go there. Our parents agreed it would be to her benefit and off she went. Her brilliance meant she qualified for university a year before her peers. This all happened around the same time the band was becoming successful. Just like you, she loathed the idea of being in the newspapers or the public eye and so, with my parents' blessing, she changed her surname and started university under a different name. She always made sure to tell people her brother was called Peter and no one ever made the connection. It also meant visiting our parents at home, however, became virtually impossible because the risk of the connection being made was too risky. While we're not identical twins, there is enough of a resemblance that some sharp-eyed journalist would make the connection. I've always respected her desire to stay anonymous and never mention her in any interviews."

"Wow!" Sukie didn't know what else to say.

"Yeah, indeed! So, because Claire would visit so rarely, Mum moved herself back to Austria as soon as she had a good reason for doing so. Caring for my oma gave her the excuse she needed. The Austrian press are a bit less intrusive than those in the UK."

Pete got up and went over to the little coffee machine in the corner. He selected a couple of pods and made a hot chocolate for them both. Reliving all this again was hard and he needed a few minutes to collect his thoughts and quell some of the emotions whirling around inside him.

As he sat down and handed Sukie her drink, she could see how drained he looked. She stood up, went to sit beside him on the sofa and, putting her hand gently on his, said softly, "Hey, you ok? I didn't mean for you to get upset over this. Please stop if you're finding it hard. I don't need to know your past. I'm friends with you now, what happened then is not important."

Pete gave her hand a squeeze. "Thank you. This is the first time I've ever sat and told someone the full story of my life. People have always known some part or another of it but very few know everything. It's refreshing to speak to someone with no preconceived ideas. It's also making me visit times in my past I'd almost forgotten about, along with remembering people I haven't thought of for a very long time. Now that I've gotten this far, I may as well finish."

"Well, only if you're sure. There's no need to carry on for me."

"I think I need to carry for me though," he replied.

He took a deep breath and resumed talking. "As I've already said, the months immediately after the split were really tough and my use of drugs escalated. I always stopped short of the hard stuff – heroine and crack – but I was popping and sniffing just about everything else I could lay my hands on. Downers, uppers, cocaine, ecstasy... I was a mess and the media went to town on it. Every time I set foot outside, the paparazzi were there, taking photographs and making up all sorts of wild stories to accompany them. To this day, I still cannot believe that no one questioned the authenticity of what the papers were printing or that people were so gullible as to believe what they were reading."

"Anyway, one morning my cleaner walked in to find me lying on the floor, curled up in total agony. She called for an ambulance and I was whisked off to hospital where I underwent urgent surgery for a ruptured appendix. The newspapers, however, printed that I'd taken a massive drug overdose and was close to death. You see, three months prior to this, I'd become mates with a bloke in the local pub. His name was Stan and he was about six years older than me. We just hung out, shot some pool, played some darts and drank beers in front of the footie on the television. When the media was reporting the 'breaking news' that Pete Wallace had been rushed to hospital, Stan decided to sell them a story giving them 'the dark truth of my friendship with Pete Wallace'. Well, he sold them a pack of lies. He said we'd had many nights of heavy drinking, taking drugs and entertaining 'ladies of the night' – if I may use the politer name for the profession. The papers lapped it up and didn't even try to find anyone to corroborate his story. When Jordie tried to find him, in order to disprove what had been written, he'd disappeared. Stan – if that was even his real name – had taken his fee and done a runner. We haven't seen or heard from him since. Jordie has a friend who's a private investigator but even he drew a blank."

"Anyway, while I was lying in hospital unaware of what was being printed, some 'well-meaning' person..." Pete stopped talking. It was always hard for him to even think about this never mind say the words out loud. He swallowed hard and carried on. "Someone saw this on the news and called my parents to tell them I was dying. To this day, I've never found out who it was. Anyway, in a state of panic, they pretty much rushed out the door and drove towards Salzburg with the intention of getting on the first UK-bound plane. They never made it. There'd been an accident on the main autobahn and it was at a standstill. We believe they came off it and were trying to get to Salzburg via the back roads. Their car was found three days later at the bottom of a ravine. We don't know what happened. There were some skid marks which matched the tyres on the car but the police were never able to ascertain if my dad had taken the bend too quickly, or swerved to avoid something – a deer in the road perhaps – or if another car was at fault. I got out of hospital in time for the funeral."

He stopped to wipe his eyes as tears were now streaming down his face. Sukie picked up the box of tissues from the coffee table in front of them and handed it to him. She was tempted to stop him from talking any further but her gut was telling her to let him finish. She sensed he'd held all this inside for a long time and it would help him to get some release. Instead, she just gently rubbed his arm as he blew his nose and took another breath to steady himself before continuing.

"It was a small funeral. Jordie, Claire, myself and some local people who'd worked at the schloss. Mum was an only child, Dad's older brother lives in Australia and wasn't able to get here. Afterwards, when the three of us had returned to the schloss, Claire and I had a massive row. She blames me entirely for the accident. I told her that I'd been hospital for a genuine medical reason, nothing to do with the drugs overdose the media had reported, but she wouldn't back down. Her reasoning was I had a history of taking drugs and being drunk. So, when our parents were told I was in hospital with an overdose and close to death, they would've believed the story and panicked. They would've been out of their heads with worry and terrified I'd die before they got to me. And this would've been why they tried to take a shortcut to get to the airport quicker. Had they known it was appendicitis, while still worried, they'd have been more rational and called Jordie for information. They'd have found out I wasn't in a life-threatening state and wouldn't have been in such a panic to get to the airport. Well, I couldn't argue with that. She spoke the truth. Their deaths were my fault."

"No, Pete, it wasn't your fault. It was a really horrible accident. You can't blame yourself." Sukie looked at Pete, utterly aghast that he was carrying so much guilt over something that was clearly not his fault.

Pete looked at her and said, ever so quietly, "Yes, it

was and I will never forgive myself for that. They died thinking I might have killed myself. They died trying to get to me, so they could hold me and talk to me and be with me. They died because of me, Sukie and that fact will never go away." With those words, the pain became too much for him and he collapsed into her, his sobs muffled against her shoulder as she wrapped her arms around him.

Chapter Thirty-Two

Jordie was sitting in the lounge, relaxing in front of the fire. Bosie had his head on his lap and Jordie was absentmindedly stroking the top of it, staring into the fireplace, completely lost in his thoughts. He was thinking back over the last few days and accepting that he'd found them far more enjoyable than he'd been expecting. Sukie and Beth's presence had certainly livened the place up. It had felt almost family-like. The schloss had always been too big for just the three of them – he always said they rattled around the place – but, simply by having two extra people there, it had become homelier and the atmosphere around it was much warmer and pleasing. He liked it. He'd also, finally, had the chance last night to print off the email Dan Cleary had sent him on Christmas Eve. He'd been unable to find anything slightly untoward about Sukie. The only small detail he'd dug up was that her birth name was Suzette but she'd been known as Sukie since her late teens. Other than that, she was as clean as a whistle thus far. He'd asked if he wanted him to carry on with the surveillance after the New Year but Jordie had decided to knock it on the head. Now that he'd spent more time in Sukie's company, he'd come to realise she was totally upfront. No one was that good an actress and no one could have kept up such pretence, in these close quarters for this length of time, without slipping up once or twice. Furthermore, having met Beth, he could see she was a good woman, with a good, kind heart, and there's no way she could have raised a daughter who'd be two-faced or conniving. He had to admit that on this occasion, he'd been completely wrong and was actually happy about it.

He was also trying to come to terms with the fact that he was finding himself attracted to Beth. With the kind of life he lived, always travelling around and looking after Pete, he didn't have the chance to meet nice women and develop relationships. He met women, of course, but all too often they were trying to use him to get to Pete. He'd once been badly let-down by a girl he'd met, who he'd thought had liked him for himself, only to catch her trying to get into Pete's room wearing nothing more than a hotel bathrobe. The outcome of this was he now tended to keep women at arm's length. Any involvements he had now were purely on a one-night only basis.

But… there was something about Beth he found very appealing though he couldn't put his finger on what it was exactly. She was very attractive but… it was more than that. She had a great personality but it wasn't that either. He could see she was a kind and caring person although bolshie enough when she needed to assert herself. But that wasn't the appeal either. She just had something about her that was pulling him in and he was trying to figure out if he could resist it. Or, if he even wanted to…

He let out a small sigh of contentment and, closing his eyes, put his head back to mull over what to do next when…

WHAM!

The smack to his jaw nearly took his head off. And there was the very woman he'd just been dreaming of, standing in front of him, shaking with fury and pulling her arm back to put another punch on him.

She was shrieking like a banshee, screaming over and over "How could you? How could you? We trusted you! You bastard! You lying, sonofabitch, bastard!"

He managed to duck in time to avoid the second punch but he wasn't quick enough to miss the slap that followed from Beth's other hand or the kick in the shins either. He wriggled, in an awkward, sideways movement, and managed to get out of the chair, quickly moving to stand behind it as he tried to put some distance between them, at the same time wondering what the hell had brought this on.

Sukie woke up and stretched out. This bed was so comfy, and the quilt so snuggly, that she didn't want to get up. She curled up under the covers and thought about

Pete's story. After he'd cried on her shoulder for several minutes, he'd wiped his face and apologised for getting so upset. She'd told him firmly that he had absolutely nothing to apologise for. Crikey, he was talking about the death of his parents and the part he felt he'd played in that. He had every right to be upset. They'd continued talking for another couple of hours as he'd told her how, unable to cope with the grief and the guilt, he'd lost himself in his music by day and the drugs by night. Somehow, in amongst all the chaos, he'd managed to record his first solo album and it had gone straight into the charts at number one and had remained there for several months. A world tour then followed. He couldn't recall most of it because he was wasted every day. He still didn't know how he was able to go out every night and put on a show. He sure as hell didn't remember any of them... Until they'd gone to Italy!

He'd done a gig near Verona where there'd been an incident. A young girl had tried to jump from a side stand onto the stage. He had this set showpiece thing he did whereby he'd pull some pretty girls out of the audience and dance with them on the stage. It turned out this girl, Sofia, had realised that, by being in the stands, she wouldn't be picked. Being a bit drunk, she thought she could jump from the stand to the stage. Unfortunately, she'd grossly misjudged both the distance and the drop. She'd landed on top of some stacked metal packing crates and the impact had broken both her legs. From there, she had fallen a further eight or nine feet to the ground, landing on her back and causing serious damage to her back and pelvis. He'd found out the next morning how badly she'd been injured. Jordie had advised him to visit her in hospital a few days later – the press had gotten a hold of the story and it would be in Pete's best interest to meet her. It took seeing her – this beautiful young girl, just fifteen and with all her life ahead of her – lying broken in a hospital bed, waiting to find out if she'd ever be able to move or walk again, that made him wake up to what he was doing to himself. This girl had only had a few drinks, it was the first time she'd drunk alcohol, and look at what had happened. Yet he, who was abusing his body every single day, in almost every possible way, would be the one walking out of the hospital, intact and carrying on with his life.

He'd promised himself that day to end the abuse. He managed to get to the end of the tour, there had only been a few weeks left, on the bare minimum of drugs. 'Enough to hold the withdrawal symptoms at bay but not enough to put me out of it' was how he'd described it to her. He hadn't told anyone what he was doing, not even Jordie. When the tour was over, he moved into the schloss – he'd hoped that by being in the family home, it would give him some focus when things were really bad – and went cold turkey.

Pete didn't go into any great detail on that except to say he owed Sally his life as she'd looked after him through those dark days and had been the rock and the crutch he'd needed to stay true to his intentions. Finally, almost six months later, he started to feel like a human being again. He hadn't touched drugs since and hardly ever drank alcohol. There were days when he still had a desire for them but he'd remember Sofia, who was still trying to get her life back together, and that gave him the push he needed to stay strong.

Sukie pushed back the quilt, got up and made herself a coffee using the pod machine in the corner. She was becoming quite used to these and was thinking about looking for one in the January sales when she got home. She wandered up the stairs to the turret room above and opened the French windows for a blast of cold, frosty, but wonderfully fresh air. She sat down, looked across to the solid black mountains and was reminded of her little black fur-balls back home – strong, silent and always nearby. Admittedly, the mountains were a bit bigger than Tony and Adam but their presence gave her the same comfort her cats did.

When she realised what her train of thought was conjuring up – she'd be the first one to tell you there were times when, if anyone could see the nonsense that went around her head, she'd be certified – she gulped down the rest of her drink and went back downstairs to take a shower. As the hot and cold jets brought her to full wakefulness, she thought of how difficult it must have been for Pete to face up to himself in such a cold, hard way. How much strength of character did one need to put yourself through such pain and torture in order to exorcise the poison from your body? Her respect for him had shot up massively and she now did feel quite honoured that he trusted her as a friend. After all he'd been through, she could now understand why that trust was not so freely given.

When she was showered, dried and dressed, Sukie made her way down to join the others. She'd just stepped off the bottom step of the stairs and turned towards the lounge when she heard a loud commotion coming from that direction. At the sound of her mother's shrill screeching, she hurried to see what was happening. She arrived on the threshold and her eyes took in the sight of both Pete and her mother shouting loudly at Jordie. Jordie had a livid red mark on his face and Pete was holding her mother by her upper arms. It looked as though he was trying to restrain her from hitting Jordie who was shouting, just as loudly, back at Beth and Pete.

"What is going on?" Sukie asked.

Beth caught sight of her daughter, pulled herself free from Pete's grip and rushed over to her, waving a folder in front of her face. She screamed, "He had you followed. That bastard had you followed."

Strangely, she didn't really take note of Beth's words. She was more shocked by the fact Beth was swearing. Beth never swore. She was always very correct when it came to the use of profanity so, for her to be using such language now, meant she was beyond furious. Sukie couldn't recall ever seeing her mother this mad. She blinked with confusion. "What? Followed? I don't get you?"

Beth dragged her over to where Jordie was still standing behind the chair and, waving the folder in Sukie's face again, shouted once more, "That bastard there had you under surveillance. He's been having you watched!"

Beth's words of anger prompted Jordie to shout back

at her and then Pete shouting once more at Jordie.

"BE QUIET! NOW! ALL OF YOU!" Sukie yelled at the top of her voice and with all of the authority she could muster.

Suddenly, there was silence as they all turned to look at her.

"But Sukie— Beth started again

"I said *be quiet*, Mum. That includes you." She looked around her. "Right, who wants to tell me what's going on here? Mum, you start."

"I found *this*," Beth waved the folder in her hand once more, "in Jordie's room. It has pictures of you and all your movements from last week listed down."

"What were you doing snooping in my room? Don't you know that people who snoop never find anything good?" Jordie spoke in raised tones but did manage to refrain from shouting. Sukie was at least grateful for that.

"I wasn't snooping!" Beth visibly tempered her voice so that, she too, was no longer shouting. "I asked Sally if I could help with some housework seeing as how she had extra guests to clean up after and the usual daily staff had been given the festive period off work. She asked if I'd mind hoovering the bedrooms and corridors and gave me directions on which rooms to do." She looked at Jordie. "One of them was yours. This folder," she thrust it towards his face, "was on the edge of the coffee table. I caught it with the hoover and it fell on the floor. As I bent to pick it up, the papers inside fell out and I was looking at pictures of my own daughter. Clearly, they were taken without her knowledge. So, it's a bit rich for you to be accusing me of snooping!"

Pete held out a hand to Beth. "May I have a look please?"

Beth handed the folder over to him but continued to glare at Jordie. Pete walked off and quickly flicked through the contents before turning back to face Jordie.

"Why?" he asked. "Why did you do this? I told you to trust me. Why didn't you just leave things be?"

Jordie looked at Pete and replied, "I was only looking out for you, Pete. I could see you getting close to this girl–"

"THIS GIRL? THIS GIRL IS MY DAUGHTER!" Beth started screeching again and would've moved to lay a few more slaps and kicks on Jordie had Sukie not stepped in front of her and held her back.

"ENOUGH, MUM!" She loosened her grip and held her mum's arms gently. "That's enough, mum. Sit down now. Please."

Beth sat in the armchair Sukie had guided her to and felt the fight go out of her. She quietly began to weep. Sukie leant down and gave her a big hug. "Hush now, Mum. Everything'll be okay. Shhh... It's okay."

She straightened up and looked around the room. "As I seem to be, unwittingly, at the centre of this commotion, I think I should take a look at this folder. Pete... Please."

Pete walked over to give her the incriminating paperwork her mother had found. She took it from him and stepped over to the window to read it through. When she'd finished, she looked out of the window for a few moments as she thought about what she'd just read. She also thought about her conversation with Pete the night before and this helped her come to a decision. She turned back to face the room. "Well, I think this has proved quite conclusively that I lead a very dull and boring life! Also, that coat is so *totally* unflattering – it's going straight to the charity shop when I get home!"

"But Sukie—"

She lifted a hand to stop her mother short. "Mum, I truly understand why you're so mad. I really do. I also fully understand why," she turned to face Jordie, "you did it." She stood looking at both of them. "I can see this from both sides. Yes, Jordie, I really should be mad with you but I know you did this for all the right reasons. Pete and I had a long talk last night and he shared a lot of stuff with me. I now get why you work so hard to protect him. You needed to be sure I wasn't a phony intent on causing trouble. And, Mum, I know why you're so mad too. You want to protect me and you're furious that someone should think your precious baby girl is not a fine and upstanding person who should be trusted without question. Both of you are just looking out for the people you both care deeply about. The funny thing is that, if all our roles here were reversed, and I was the famous person, we'd most likely still be having this conversation because both of you," she pointed to Jordie and Beth, "would've probably done exactly what the other did. It's all about looking out for those we love, and that's not a bad thing."

She walked over and stood in front of Jordie, looking him square in the eye. "Are we cool now?"

Without any hesitation, he replied "Yes lass, we are. We're cool."

She leaned in and gave him a tight hug. In his ear, she whispered, "Thank you for always looking out for him."

Jordie hugged her just as tightly as he whispered back, "Thank you for forgiving a silly old man and for being Pete's friend. He needs you."

"He needs us both,"

She let go, moved over to her mum and wrapped her arms around her. "Thank you, Mum for still wanting to fight my battles. I love you for that."

After she'd released her mother from her bear hug, she looked at them all and said, in an attempt to break the tension, "Is there any chance of getting some bacon butties around here? I am starving!"

Chapter Thirty-Three

Jordie was standing on the attic terrace, leaning against the balustrade at the edge, looking over to the big black mountains across the lake. He'd really cocked it up big time. With hindsight, he could see he'd been an idiot to put Dan Cleary onto Sukie but he'd had such a downer on her after she'd made him look a fool that first night at the hotel, and he hadn't been able to get past that. Both Kara and Pete had told him he was barking up the wrong tree but he'd been too damn stubborn to back down and look where it had gotten him – in the doghouse with everyone! He knew Pete would take a long time to forget this. And Beth, the first woman he'd really wanted to impress in such a very long time, now saw him as some kind of small-minded, interfering asshole. He'd seen the way she'd continued to glare at him throughout the day. That was why he'd escaped up here to the roof, to get away from the censorship in their eyes. It was with no small amount of irony, that he acknowledged that the only person who didn't seem to want him tarred and feathered was Sukie. Where the other two had pretty much removed themselves from him, she'd come in closer and had been very sweet and kind to him all day. He was a stupid, stubborn old man and he'd managed to break up his friendship with Beth before it had even had a chance to get started. "You idiot!" he muttered aloud, as he kicked the stonework in front of him.

"You will be if you break your toe kicking that heavy concrete."

He turned around to see Beth standing with two mugs of something warm and steaming in her hands. "Pete told me where to find you. I brought some coffee to warm you up. I also added a little nip of whisky."

"Trying to get me drunk so you can exact your revenge by pushing me over the edge?" he asked gruffly, as he took one of the mugs from her.

"You know, the thought never crossed my mind, but now that you've mentioned it, it does sound like a very good idea. So be a good chap and drink up so I can get the gruesome task over with quickly."

"Don't bother yourself. The way I feel right now, I'll jump and save you the trouble. After all, can't risk you chipping that pretty nail polish of yours, can we?"

"Oh, hush there! What satisfaction would I get from you doing that? At least if I push you over I can say my family honour has been avenged. Chipped nail polish can always be repaired."

"Sorry, love but my conscience just won't allow me to let you carry such a burden. I'll do it myself just as soon as I've finished this cuppa."

"Oh, for goodness' sake, you'll be dead, so your conscience will be of no consequence. And it will not be a burden. I shall declare my action with pride. Once I've repaired my nail polish, of course!"

"But it *will* be on my conscience and I'll be stuck to this earthly plain for all eternity because I'll have unfinished business and won't be able to move on to a heavenly paradise. I'll have to hang around here and haunt you every Wednesday night."

"Why every Wednesday night?"

"No EastEnders on Wednesdays. If you think I'm giving that up to come and haunt you, then you've got another think coming, lady!"

"Hmmph! Well, seeing as we can't seem to come to an agreement over your imminent demise, maybe we should just give it up as a bad job and move on. What do you think?"

"Well, if you insist. I'm quite happy to throw myself on my sword... well rocks and concrete actually, if it helps you to obtain closure over the whole sorry state of affairs I created."

"Nah, you're good. Besides, the more I think on it, I realise just how much mess you'd make when you land and then there would be the hassle of cleaning it up. You really would be a blot on the very beautiful landscaped gardens. No, we'll leave it for now until we come up with an alternative, more practical option."

"Fair enough! I like the way you think. One doesn't want to be a bother. I've bothered enough for today. It wouldn't be fair to add to that."

Beth moved over to sit on one of the loungers on the terrace. She tapped the one next to it. "Come and sit down, Jordie. We need to have a chat."

He picked up his cup did as he was told. Beth lay back on her lounger and looked up at the sky, watching as the stars began to appear in the late dusk of the day.

He copied her actions and waited for her to talk.

After a few minutes she said, "This terrace is quite something. The view is breath-taking and the silence is so peaceful and soothing. It's just what one needs to ease away one's troubles. When you look at the majesty of the mountains, and the vastness of the sky, it puts your life into perspective. We humans are so good at thinking we're the big main picture when, in actual fact, we are tiny, little, insignificant, dots in an unfathomable universe."

"We most certainly are," he agreed. After a few more minutes of quiet contemplation, he spoke again. "I really am very sorry for upsetting you and Sukie. My actions are inexcusable and I'll never be able to apologise enough for the distress I've caused you."

Beth kept her counsel for a minute or two and then replied, "If Sukie is prepared to forgive you, and it was her life you intruded upon, then it would be churlish of me not accept her wishes and do likewise." She paused for a few seconds. "I also need to apologise for hitting you the way I did. Is your face okay?"

He rubbed his jaw, which still smarted a bit under his touch. "My face is fine and no apology is needed. You were a mother protecting her child, your reaction was understandable."

"I guess Sukie was correct in her assessment. If we were both in the other's shoes, the chances are we'd have taken the same course of action. We're just a couple of old ducks keeping an eye on our little ducklings and trying to protect them the best we can."

"That's a good way of putting it."

They both continued to watch as the sky changed from dark grey to dark blue to black and the stars multiplied until they had become a massive network of twinkles, extending as far as the eye could see.

Jordie eventually broke the silence. "The ducklings are visiting some of the ski resorts tomorrow. I was wondering if you might like to go to Salzburg for the day. I'd be happy to take you – unless you'd prefer to spend more time with your daughter, of course."

Beth responded immediately. "I think a day out in Salzburg sounds lovely. I love Sukie very, very much but, after four days, I need some time out. Thank you for the offer, I accept it with gratitude."

A few more minutes of silence had passed when Beth said, "This really *is* the most perfect spot. Whose idea was it to do this? I can see it's not part of the original structure."

"You're right. It is a recent addition. Andrew, Pete's dad, had always had the idea that something like this would be good..." and Jordie went on to fill her in on how the attic terrace came to be.

Chapter Thirty-Four

Beth found herself, once again, sitting on a roof-top terrace with Jordie. This time, however, it was at the top of the Riley Mirabelle hotel and the whole of Salzburg lay beneath them, laid out in all its frosty, twinkling, glory. She looked over to her right and could see the sunlight reflected in the River Salzach. She reckoned she'd fair walked the legs off Jordie this morning. They'd set off quite early to allow them to make the most of the day and had arrived in Salzburg just after ten a.m. Four hours later and this was the first time they'd sat down since then. Poor Jordie hadn't complained but she smiled as she recalled the look on his face when she'd suggested grabbing a burger from the market area so they could eat as they walked. She'd been pulling his leg but he didn't know that. She'd really had to bite the inside of her lip to prevent herself from laughing when he'd turned his rather pained expression upon her and stated that he preferred to sit to eat. She was still smiling to herself when he sat down at the table.

"So, what do you think of Salzburg?"

She turned her smile on to Jordie, completely unaware of the effect it would have upon him, "Oh, it is stunning. I can fully understand why Sukie is so in love with this city and I know I've only seen a fraction of it."

Their first port of call, when they'd arrived, had been a visit up to the Fortress which was such a dominant presence on the Salzburg skyline. Unlike Sukie, however, they'd taken the lift up to the castle. Jordie had argued it would take too long to walk and, having seen some of the steep pathway through the window of the lift on the way up, she was happy she had taken up his suggestion. Afterwards, they had wandered through Old Town where she'd admired the beautifully decorated shop windows and their stunning ironwork signage, the Christmas markets and the fabulous yellow exterior of the Mozart Museum.

"So, you're not a Sound of Music fanatic then?" Jordie asked her.

"Not as much as Sukie. When she was a child, we used to snuggle up together whenever it was on the television and sing along to the songs. For a child, it is very appealing and I suspect that's why she's so enamoured with it. Now I've seen this splendour with my own eyes, I know I'll view it quite differently when it's next on."

As she spoke, a waiter came out with the two hot chocolates Jordie had ordered and advised them their BLT sandwiches would be ready in ten minutes. Once he'd placed the mugs on the table and retreated to the warm interior of the bar, Jordie picked his up and clinked it against Beth's, saying 'prost' as he did so. Beth returned the greeting, took a large sip and declared it to be the nicest hot chocolate she'd ever had. Once he'd taken a drink from his own mug, Jordie sat back and, looking directly at her, announced, "This very table is where it all started."

She looked at him in confusion.

He continued. "Sukie and Pete's friendship was born right where we're sitting now. He'd stormed out here in a strop, wearing only a T-shirt. It was bitterly cold and Sukie was concerned for his health so she brought him a coat to put on."

"Why didn't you do that?" she enquired.

"Because I've lived with Pete's temper for many years and experience has taught me that, when the lion is roaring, it's best to leave him alone in his den. Eventually he calms down and wanders back out and that is when sensible conversation can resume. Your daughter, however, did not know this and, unknowingly, walked out here, right into the face of a Pete Wallace special."

Her eyes widened. Sukie hadn't gone into the finer points of how she became friends with Pete, only that they'd met and they got along well. "So, what happened?"

With a wide smile on his face, Jordie replied, "What do you think happened? Your gobby daughter didn't take any of his crap, gave him a mouthful and put him in his place!"

Beth threw her head back and laughed. "Yup, I can

see Sukie doing just that. She wouldn't have cared who, or what, he was, she'd have given it to him straight. That's my girl," she finished, with pride in her voice. She picked up her mug and asked, "So, how did you and Sukie come to be at loggerheads with each other?"

"Bad timing and a misunderstanding," he replied before explaining about the press week and how Sukie had, inadvertently, gotten caught up in the midst of it. "For the purposes of security, and because of the large press contingent arriving that Saturday night, we'd agreed with the hotel that, for one night only, it would be closed to non-residents. An agreement which didn't come cheap, by the way! Sukie had flown in on the same flight as the press crew so arrived here at the hotel just as they did. When the doorman was checking his list, for all the new arrivals due in that evening, her name wasn't on there. I immediately suspected her of being a groupie – they crop up everywhere – or, even worse, an uninvited press journalist, un-vetted by myself and trying to get dirt on Pete. Both of these are guaranteed to put me in a bad mood. As it happened, her name *was* on the doorman's list – or should I say, her *company's* name was on the list. Had she known to give that detail, well, I doubt we'd be here now."

"Why do you think that?"

"Pete witnessed our verbal exchange and she piqued his interest. She put herself on his radar. She was different."

Beth took in a deep breath of the clean, crispy air. "Well, however it came about, I'm not complaining. This holiday has been wonderful and getting to know you,

Pete, and Sally has been so lovely. I've had a glorious time and I'm grateful to you all for sharing it with us."

"The same goes for us, or me, anyway. You and Sukie have made this a very special Christmas for Pete. It's been too long since he's let himself relax as he has done the last two weeks. It reminds me of when he was young and all this same stuff wasn't even in his head. Those were the days."

"You've known him a long time then?"

"Yes, his dad and I were best friends. He was a truly decent man. His mum Katya was an angel – both in looks and nature. Everyone who met them liked them. I've known Pete since he was a babe in arms."

"His parents died in a car accident Sukie said…?"

Jordie took another long drink from his mug and stared into the distance for a moment. She watched him take a deep breath before he began talking again and explained to her the basics of what had happened.

When he'd finished, she put a hand over his. She could see it had taken a lot for him to tell her Pete's story. "In a sense, you've become his surrogate father, I suppose."

Jordie cleared his throat and nodded. "I guess I kind of am. Not long after he was born, Andy and Katya asked me to be his legal guardian, you know, in the event of anything happening to them. I was happy to agree. The legal guardianship expired a long time ago but, in my heart, I will always be there to look after him, just as any father would, because that's what his parents would have wanted."

Still holding his hand, she gave it a tight squeeze.

"You're a very kind man underneath all that bluster, Jordie Ray, a very kind man indeed."

Jordie swatted away the compliment. "Oh no, I'm not really, just doing what anyone would've done. You seem to have forgotten that I push women with silly pink umbrellas into busy, traffic-filled roads when they get in my way..." He gave her a mock, evil leer as he spoke.

"Oh yes, that little nugget had slipped my mind." She saw the waiter coming through the door with their lunch. "Therefore, as soon as we've eaten the mammoth sandwiches that are coming this way, you can make it up to me by escorting me around more shops."

Jordie let out a groan of despair but, secretly, he was looking forward to it and felt a little skip of joy in his chest. For every minute that passed in the company of this delightful woman, he wanted to spend another ten with her. It looked like his 'love 'em and leave 'em' status was about to take a mighty tumble and, right now, he couldn't have cared less.

Sukie had just gotten showered and changed from her day out when there was a knock on her bedroom door. When she opened it, she couldn't contain the look of surprise on her face at seeing Jordie there, looking quite unsure of himself. He asked if he could have a word with her so she invited him in and closed the door behind him. She wasn't daft and had a suspicion as to why he'd come to see her. She said nothing and waited to see what he came out with.

Jordie stood looking around the room, trying to think how to word what he wanted to say next. As he glanced about, he noticed how tidy the bedroom was – no clothes strewn about the floor, the bed was neatly made with Pete's snow globe present on the table next to it, and her make-up was stacked tidily on the dresser. He really had summed Sukie up all wrong and she was turning out to be nothing at all like he'd imagined her to be. He turned to face her, wringing his hands together in a nervous manner, as he tried to think of the best way to make the apology he'd come to make. Although he'd apologised the day before, in front of everyone else, he felt it was the decent thing to give her a private, and personal, apology without witnesses. She had the right to give him a hard time but he didn't need for that to be public.

"I… um…" he hesitated. He coughed to clear his throat and tried again.

"I need to… um…. that is, I feel I have to… erm…" He stopped again. Jeez, why was he finding this so hard? Silly question, he knew exactly why. His deepening feelings for Beth meant he had to make things right with her daughter. He'd have said sorry even without the added impetus of her mother but he knew that the outcome of this conversation could potentially impact on his relationship with Beth. This was making it harder for him to get the words out correctly.

"Look, why don't I make us both a coffee from the wonder-machine there and we can sit upstairs in the comfort of the turret?" Sukie smiled gently at him.

He readily agreed to her suggestion and, once seated with the mug of hot liquid in his hands, found it much easier to say his piece. Sukie thanked him for coming to see her and repeated her previous comment regarding her understanding of why he had felt the need to take such action. She took his hands in hers, and looking into his eyes, said firmly, "Now I know more about Pete's past, and all the stuff he's had to deal with, I genuinely don't blame you for having me checked out. In fact, I'm almost glad you did because you now have peace of mind knowing that I've no agenda here; I have no dirty plan to cause trouble. All I want is to be the best friend I possibly can to someone who's very lonely and needs more people he can trust in his life. I can tell you that I'm a very loyal person and no one will ever hear any kind of gossip about Pete from me. I'd say you can trust me but I hope you'll realise that, over time, for yourself."

He gripped her hands tightly, and trying to speak past the choked up feeling in his throat, replied, "We'll protect him together, eh lass?"

Sukie gave him her sweet smile – a smile that was so like her mother's – and said, "We sure will, Jordie, we sure will."

"Ok, for the yellow cheese, and the game, Sukie McClaren, you have to answer this history question correctly."

They were playing Trivial Pursuit at the large dining

room table and Pete had donned a quizmaster voice in which to ask the question that may win the game for her and Jordie. The table, a long, single piece of dark oak with beautiful carvings around the thick sides, was large enough to seat twelve, and so the four of them – Sally was away for a few days staying with friends – were rather swamped by it. At one end, were the plates holding the leftovers from their quick buffet style dinner. No one had been in the mood for cooking when they'd all returned from their day out, and so, after a quick raid on the freezer, they'd cobbled together a buffet of finger food – mini pizzas, sausage rolls, chicken nuggets, mini spring rolls and oven chips.

Sukie and Jordie sat next to each other, in the middle of the table, with Pete and Beth sitting opposite. As they ate, they'd exchanged the news of their respective days out, with Sukie calling her mum a wuss for not doing the walk up to the Fortress. Sukie filled Beth in on her day in Zell Am See, regaling her with descriptions of the little town which she'd thoroughly enjoyed visiting. The Christmas Market had still been in situ, there was snow on the ground, and the decorative Christmas lights straddling the little streets and alleyways had made the place truly magical.

Each day she spent in Austria, the more she was falling madly in love with it. She'd always known that, once she'd made her first visit, she would be inordinately fond of the country but she'd never anticipated that the thought of leaving could almost reduce her to tears. She was dreading the day when she had to leave and go back to the stark, boring, reality of home.

Jordie gave her arm a little pat and said, "I have every faith in you, lass. Go on, wipe that smirk off his pretty boy face."

She looked at Pete and smiled. "Well, come on then, what are you waiting for? I'm ready!"

Pete waved a yellow triangle in front of her before continuing. "Ok, here goes. What did Samuel Pepys famously bury for protection during the Great Fire of London in 1666?"

She burst out laughing. Could the question have been any easier? She looked Pete in the eye, and with a smug smile on her face, replied, "Why, his Parmesan cheese, of course."

"Dammit!" Pete said, as he chucked the yellow wedge over to her. "How on earth did you know that?"

Beth answered for her. "History was Sukie's best subject at school. She loved it. I knew we were done for when I realised that was the subject for the final question."

Jordie leaned in and gave Sukie a quick hug. "Well done, lass, I knew you'd get it."

She hugged him back as she replied, "Hey, you weren't too shoddy yourself. I'd never have gotten most of those sports questions and you're pretty hot on the old sciences and wildlife. I reckon we're a pretty good team." He gave her a smile of genuine fondness, knowing he was very lucky she had such a forgiving, and understanding, nature.

She put the game back in its box, stood up, gave a big stretch and, with a large yawn, announced she was off to bed. "It's been a long day and I need some sleep. I'll see you guys in the morning." They were all spending the following day together in Vienna and she wanted to be bright-eyed and rested for the trip.

With good-night wishes ringing in her ears, Sukie left the room as Pete and Jordie voiced their intentions for an early night also. Beth stacked the plates at the end of the table and said, "I'll just clear these away before I head up myself."

Jordie quickly came to her side with an offer to help but Beth insisted on doing it herself, explaining she'd like a little time by herself.

"Just to unwind after our busy day. My mind is still buzzing and I need to relax. Washing and putting away the dishes will help me to do that." She picked up the plates, leaving Pete and Jordie in the dining room as she walked down the hallway to the kitchen.

She placed the plates at the side of the sink, walked over to where Sally hung her aprons and put one on, looking around the kitchen as she tied it. It was a lovely, big, bright room in the daytime. It was positioned on the outer corner of the schloss and had one large window looking out towards the front of the house – so the cook could see when the master of the house returned she supposed – and two others on either side of the large chimney breast which still dominated the room. Inside the chimney, was an enormous cream, range-effect, gas cooker. Sally had told her that, when Pete had renovated the room a few years earlier, he'd fancied putting in a genuine Aga but Sally wanted none of it. They were great to look at but not always so easy to cook on, she'd said. So, they'd compromised on a cooker that looked like an old-fashioned range but worked like a modern appliance. The units on the floor, and along the walls, were also in cream and with a traditional design. The worktop was an unusual dark green marble. In the middle of the room, was Sally's pride and joy – a large cooking island which housed all of her baking trays and utensils in deep, smooth-closing drawers. The room was also high-ceilinged, which could have made it seem cold and soulless, but Sally had asked for an old-fashioned wooden pulley to be installed and, from it, she hung the various herbs she collected from the garden to dry. As such, they not only gave the room a beautiful combined smell of lavender, rosemary, sage and thyme but helped to create a cosier ambience by making the ceiling height appear reduced. This was finished off with the addition of cookery books, pots of flavoured tea-bags near the stainless-steel kettle, and, when not in use, a large jug of flowers or foliage on the centre island. Currently it was a display of holly and gold ribbon in the old double-handled jug.

As she washed and dried the plates, Beth thought about her day out with Jordie. She'd enjoyed it, and his company, very much. Given how long it was, since she'd been in any kind of a relationship, she no longer had the desire, or the inclination, to go through all the hassle involved with meeting someone new.

With Jordie, however, she didn't know what to think or feel. She could tell he was sweet on her – it was the best word she could think of to describe his attentiveness to her. The way in which they'd all been thrown together meant she was pretty much forced into getting to know him better and it was turning out to be a lot less hassle than she'd previously been used to. There had been none of the waiting for phone calls, or getting ready for a date, or trying to agree on a place to meet that normally preceded new relationships and she suspected the more relaxed atmosphere of everyone being under the same roof had helped to remove some of the defences she normally put up.

She'd been absolutely furious with him, however, when she'd found the surveillance folder he'd had on Sukie and he'd seen her at her very worst as she'd given him the full brunt of her rather vicious temper. It was a temper she usually kept well under control but, finding a folder like that on her daughter, had been too much and she'd lost it in style. Her apology to him this morning had been brushed away as he said he fully understood and it was he who should apologise to her. She supposed, as she hung the tea-towel up to dry and switched off the under-unit lighting, plunging the room into darkness, that if Jordie was still prepared to make advances on her after that, then maybe he'd be worth trying on for size after all.

Chapter Thirty-Five

Beth closed the kitchen door behind her and walked along the corridor towards the main hallway. The schloss was quiet with only a few lamps still on to light her way. She switched these off as she passed by. Upon reaching the hallway with the central staircases, she was about to turn into it when she noticed a light shining out from the open door of the library – believing herself to be the last person out of bed, she went to switch it off and, as she threw the door open wider, gave Pete quite a fright when she walked in.

"Oh, Pete, you surprised me there!" she stated, as she took a deep breath to help slow down her racing heartbeat. Pete was bending over, picking up his guitar which had fallen from his lap when she'd marched into the room.

He grinned over to her as he straightened up. "I think we just about did for each other, Beth!"

Feeling she had to explain herself, it was Pete's home after all, she replied, "I thought everyone was in bed so, when I saw the light shining out, I thought it had been left on by accident and came to switch it off. I wasn't snooping or poking about."

"The thought never crossed my mind, Beth, and thank you for being so vigilant. I appreciate it."

"Vigilant? More like habit I'd say. I always had to run around after Sukie, switching off room lights – she was a bugger for leaving them on when she was younger. I really hope she's improved now she has her own place otherwise her electricity bills are going to be massive!" She smiled back at Pete. "So, not in bed yourself then?" She knew he had trouble sleeping, after what Jordie had told her earlier that day.

"No," he replied. "I like this time of day, or night I should say, to do some writing. For some reason, the stillness of the night helps me to be more creative."

"Then far be it for me to interrupt the musical genius any further. I will leave you to it. Goodnight."

"Goodnight, Beth. And I promise to switch the lamp off before I leave the room."

She smiled at him and made to leave. As she did so, she stopped and looked at him again. This young man who was more vulnerable and lost in himself than anyone realised. Who was beating himself up every day for consequences which had been beyond his control – believing he was responsible for the death of his parents even though he'd been lying unconscious in a hospital bed many miles away.

"I need to say something to you, Pete, and I ask you

300

to forgive me if I'm speaking out of turn." She walked over and sat next to him on the sofa.

Pete looked at her curiously. "Ok…"

She cleared her throat. "I'm going to come straight out and say this to you. You are not responsible for your parents' deaths and you must stop berating yourself over it. It's not what they would have wanted."

This was the last thing Pete had been expecting Beth to come out with. He'd thought she'd been about to ask him more on his friendship with Sukie, nothing could have prepared him for this. His shock made his reply more abrupt than he intended.

"What makes you so sure about that?"

Beth looked at him as she replied gently, "Because I am a mother."

She took his hand and said, "Look at me, Pete. Please."

When he'd lifted his head and was looking her in the eye, she continued. "Sukie is my life, as you would have been to your parents. If anything was ever to happen to me, the very last thing I want is for Sukie to carry any kind of guilt on her shoulders. No matter what she may have done, I would always love my daughter more than anything and the thought that she may be unhappy would make me very sad. The one thing all parents want, more than anything, is for their children to be happy. They may wish success, riches, good fortune upon them but, for most, happiness is always what they hope for above all else. The hardest part of being a parent is seeing your children hurting and not being able to take away, or protect them, from the pain they're experiencing. There have been times when I felt as though my heart was being gouged out with a blunt spoon because Sukie was in my arms, sobbing heavy tears over some waster of a bloke who'd let her down. I can't begin to describe the helplessness I felt when she broke her arm and was lying in a hospital bed – a tiny little slip of a thing, only nine years old – and I believed it was my fault for not protecting her enough."

She squeezed Pete's hand tightly and, lifting her free hand, placed it softly against his cheek. "I can assure you, with every fibre of my being, that your mother and father would never, ever have wanted you to put yourself through the agonies that you do, every day. They would never have wanted you to take the responsibility for their decision upon yourself and to carry it around the way you do. They loved you and were on their way to see you, to prove that love to you. At the moment of their deaths, their hearts were filled with their love for you. And now you must let go of the hate you feel for yourself and let that love from your parents take its place. The very best way for you to honour your parents' memory, is to break away from the dead-weight of guilt holding you down and to learn to fly high with freedom. Let their love be the wings you need to soar again and let the joy of living replace the pain of their loss. Just let go and be happy."

As Beth quietly spoke her, soft, gentle words, Pete felt the heavy, painful, weight he'd carried for the last six years shift inside him and slowly begin to ease away. Counsellors had told him he needed to learn to forgive himself before he could begin to heal but they were wrong. What he'd really needed was forgiveness from his parents for all the pain he'd heaped upon them in the last few years of their lives. It came to him, as he sat there with Beth, that he'd taken their deaths as a rejection. In the depths of his grief, he'd twisted their loss in to being their punishment for him. He was such a bad and horrible son, that they'd rather be dead than be with him.

It had taken this sweet, kind, woman to see what was really causing his pain and, with her gentle explanation, she'd given him the release he needed. He could see now that his parents hadn't left him, they'd been coming for him. They'd always loved him no matter what. They'd never have left him through choice. It had taken a mother to explain to him how his mother would have felt, to tell him what his parents would have wanted for him because it was exactly what she would've wanted for her own child. He was allowed to live outside the shadow their deaths had cast upon him. By the time Beth had finished speaking, he was crying – noisy, wailing sobs which sounded as though they were being pulled out of the very core of him. He was crying as he'd never cried before. With every tear he shed, he could feel himself getting lighter as more of the pain was being washed away. Finally, he was unable to cry anymore and he just lay within the circle of Beth's arms as she stroked his hair, patted his back and muttered sounds of comfort. He could remember his mother doing the very same thing when he was young. He wondered if mothers all across the world had the same mothering skills and, by bestowing some of hers upon him, Beth had managed to give him the release he'd been unable to find by himself. In a few days from now it would be New Year's Day – the perfect time to make a fresh start. With Beth, Jordie, and Sukie in his life, he knew he could do it. And he would do it in a style that would've made his parents very proud of him. Very proud indeed!

Chapter Thirty-Six

Sukie sat, for the last time, sipping a coffee in her little turret room. As always, the French windows were wide open and she was saying her goodbyes to the mountains. She was going to miss the sense of peace she felt whenever she looked upon them. "Look after my new friends, guys," she whispered to them. "Keep them all safe for me. I'm going to miss you all so much." It was the second of January and the time to say good-bye had come. Sukie and Beth had to go home.

She closed the windows for the last time and made her way back downstairs to her bedroom. It didn't feel like ten days since they'd both arrived but, here they were, packing their bags again and checking they hadn't left anything behind. She carefully wrapped her precious snow globe inside the gorgeous cream jumper Pete had given her to wear that night in the library. With a final glance around her room, she picked up her luggage and headed down the little winding staircase to see if her mum needed any help with hers.

Jordie came out of Beth's room with the larger of her suitcases in his hand just as Sukie arrived in the corridor. Beth followed him out of the door and was surprised to see Sukie there. "Hello, darling, are you all ready to go?" She walked over and gave her a quick hug, hiding the guilty blush she'd felt rush across her face when she realised Sukie had seen Jordie leaving her room. Nothing untoward had been occurring but that didn't stop her feeling as though she'd been caught getting up to no good. All they'd been doing was talking and saying goodbye. Okay... they may have also swapped phone numbers and email addresses but there was nothing in it. They'd simply become friends.

Ach, who was she kidding? She already knew this was more than just a passing friendship but she wasn't ready to think more on that right now. She'd do that once they were home and she had the benefit of distance to give her some perspective. She was a bit long in the tooth to be having some kind of holiday romance!

The journey to the airport was subdued as everyone was lost in their own thoughts.

Sukie was trying to take in the events of the last month and get her head around the fact that one of the world's biggest, and most famous, rock stars was now her new best friend. She also couldn't stop worrying about how she was going to break the story of all this to Elsa.

Jordie was keeping his eyes firmly on the road. It

helped him to focus away from the weird feelings he had inside him. He didn't know exactly what he *was* feeling and he wasn't too sure if he wanted to. He suspected he might be falling in love with Beth and had to work out if this was something he wanted to pursue. He'd done a good job of avoiding that particular pitfall for most of his life – was he ready to jump in now and give it a go?

Beth was having the very same thoughts about Jordie. Was she ready for something more? Did she *want* something more? She liked her independence but was she clinging to that as though it was some sort of security blanket? Was her independence actually her excuse to prevent the risk of being hurt again, as she had been all those years before when her husband had left her? Was she brave enough to let it go and give this man a chance? The nearer it got to the moment when she'd have to say goodbye, the more of a maelstrom her emotions became.

Pete was the most relaxed of them all. He was thinking about how you just never know who is going to come into your life and, in an instant, turn everything on its head. Three weeks ago, these two women were complete strangers to him. Now they were the dearest of friends and he knew he was going to miss them very much. Beth had given him her phone number and email details, along with very firm instructions that he should call her any time he felt he needed to chat. Her words 'I know I'm not your mother but that doesn't mean I can't share some of my mothering with you. I have plenty of motherly love inside me and I'm sure Sukie won't mind if I give some to you' still resonated in his head. He really hoped the hug he'd given her had let her know just how touched he was by her sweet, generous offer. One he had every intention of taking up. And as for Sukie... He quickly glanced at her as she stared out of the window. How was it possible that people you've known most of your life could still be strangers to you and yet someone you've known for no time at all could feel as if they've always been a part of your life? This was how Sukie felt to him. Her open, guileless, generous nature had drawn him in like a moth to a flame. She didn't judge him, she asked nothing of him and she had given him her friendship and loyalty simply because he'd asked her. He felt a small flame of something flicker inside and he realised what it was. It was happiness. Pure and true happiness! Not drug-based or alcohol-based happiness but genuine happiness. Something he hadn't felt for a very long time. Oh yes, this was going to be a great year for him. He could feel it in his bones. This was the year he was going to begin living again. Bring it on!

Chapter Thirty-Seven

Eduardo di Santo scrawled his name on the rental form and thrust the clipboard back towards the young estate agent. He threw enough cash on the desk to cover the rent for the next six months, grabbed the keys from her hand and, without a word of thanks or a goodbye, strode out of the office and got into his car. Twenty minutes later he parked up outside a disused warehouse on an old, isolated, industrial park outside Verona.

He stepped inside and let the metal door slam behind him. The echo reverberated around the vast empty building. He smiled as he looked around. He *really* smiled. This place was exactly what he needed. He had six months to prepare and assess which of his options would be the most effective.

Six months to decide how Pete Wallace was going to die.

PART TWO

Chapter Thirty-Eight

February, Oxfordshire

Sukie was sitting in her chair, looking out into the garden. Snow had begun to fall but it wasn't lying. Not yet anyway. The forecast had been for light flurries but there was a chance of something heavier if the wind changed direction. She smiled as she looked down at Tony and Adam, hitting the windows with their paws as they tried to catch the snowflakes landing on the glass. On the table beside her chair stood the Sound of Music snow globe Pete had given her. Every so often she would reach across and give it a shake, watching absentmindedly as the little silver flakes settled inside.

She looked at her watch and saw she'd have to get a move on if she was to be ready on time. She was taking Jenny, her neighbour upstairs, out for a meal to say thank you for looking after the cats over Christmas, when she'd been away. Jenny had tried to decline, saying it had been no trouble and she'd been happy to help – "It wasn't like I had any great plans lined up so it was no inconvenience," she'd replied but Sukie was adamant.

Sukie didn't know too much about Jenny's personal life other than she'd never been married, she worked at the Bodleian Libraries within Oxford University and she had a brother who she couldn't stand the sight of, so they took it in turns each year to spend Christmas Day with their parents. It had been his turn this year so Jenny had shared Christmas with Sadie next door and visited her parents on Boxing Day. She also had a massive crush on Tony and Adam and, whenever she popped down for a girlie evening, she'd have a bottle of wine in one hand and a packet of their favourite cat treats in the other.

Sukie often wondered about the things Jenny hadn't told her but didn't want to pry. She'd always felt that, if folks wanted you to know their life story, they'd tell you. Otherwise, keep your beak out.

As she looked out at the snow again, she thought back to her own Christmas. Was it really six weeks ago? In one respect, it felt as though it was only yesterday when she'd been sitting in the turret, looking out over the mountains but, equally, it felt like ages ago.

Just then her mobile phone buzzed. She'd received a text:

R U dressed up yet? Want to see.
Do you look like CoCo the Clown?
TP x

Damn him! This was the fourth text from Pete in the last two hours. She'd made the mistake of telling him she was going to one of Oxford's finer restaurants and would have to make more of an effort to dress up for the occasion. He'd been teasing her ever since. So far, he'd asked if she looked like a bag lady, a dog's dinner or something the cats had dragged in! She was really beginning to regret telling him that she didn't do 'dressing up' and, as she got older, the more she disliked it. She hadn't minded so much in her teens and twenties but, these days, comfort was really beginning to win out over style.

Oh poop! She caught sight of the time on her phone and saw she was going to be late. She needed to get ready now! Fingers flying, she did a quick internet search and, finding the picture she wanted, attached it to her text, typed back a reply, hit 'send' and put the phone on silent. She already knew there would be a barrage of abuse when he read her response.

> I look like Aunt Sally.
> Pity U not here. With your face, U
> could be my Worzel Gummidge.
> WL x

Pete felt his phone vibrating in his pocket. He smiled as he pulled it out. This was the first time Sukie had replied to his texts today. He knew he'd been winding her up but it had been fun. He didn't doubt for a minute that she'd look very nice when she went out this evening. He opened her text, read it and then burst out laughing. "The cheeky baggage!" he exclaimed.

Kara and Jordie looked over. The three of them were in the lounge going over the itinerary for the next few weeks They were due to decamp from Austria to the London house in three days. Pete was performing a two-song set at the BRIT awards next week and, after that, it was back into the melee that came with releasing a new album and going out on tour – interviews, final stage constructions to ensure what had worked on paper would also work in reality, and then the rehearsals would begin for the tour which was due to kick-off mid-April. Six weeks of touring in the UK and Ireland before going to Europe for the various summer festivals.

On one hand, he was looking forward to it but, on the other, he was scared. Three years completely off the circuit was a long time and he'd gone through a lot while he'd been away. For a start, there'd be no illegal substances to back him up and keep him going. He hadn't been this 'clean' since he was about eighteen and they'd been allowed to add alcohol to their riders. He'd also have to ensure the Italian incident didn't play on his mind and affect his performance – he didn't want to be constantly watching the audience, looking for potential accidents. He'd been aware of doing that during the remaining gigs he'd played at the end of the last tour. He was sure it had affected his performance although Jordie was adamant it hadn't.

He handed his phone over to Kara so she, and then

Jordie, could see what Sukie had written. For some strange reason, he delighted in their verbal sparring and that she never held back from giving him abuse. He supposed it was because that's how real friends speak to each other and it was a constant reassurance to him that she was a real friend.

Kara leant across the coffee table to hand the phone back to Pete, smiling as she did so, and asked, "So when are you two meeting up again?"

As the weeks had passed, Kara found herself liking Sukie more and more and hoped to meet her again when they were back in the UK. Not only was she good for Pete, which in turn was good for her because Pete Wallace in a good mood made her job so much easier, but she'd been easy company to be in on the few occasions they'd crossed paths in Salzburg, and she was hoping Sukie would make it to a few of the upcoming gigs. While there were other women on the tour crew, they tended to hang out with each other and Kara never felt she really fitted in with them. It's difficult to bitch about the boss when his PA is sitting next to you. Her position as Pete's right-hand woman could be rather lonely at times.

"In two weeks," Pete replied. "She's coming down to London for the weekend."

"Is she now?" Kara gave Jordie a knowing look. "Did you know about these plans, Jordie? Do you think it's all as innocent as he keeps making out?"

Pete sighed. "Oh, will you two just stop that! For the umpteenth time, there is nothing going on between us.

317

We are just friends!"

"Yeah, yeah… You honestly expect us to believe that?" Kara was grinning widely as she teased him. She knew the relationship between Sukie and Pete was purely platonic but hoped it would grow into something more.

Pete growled his reply, "Yes I do. Now, either get back to what we were discussing, or get out of my space, lady!"

With a wink at Jordie, she raised her hands in feigned surrender and quickly got their thoughts back to the lighting plans.

Chapter Thirty-Nine

Jordie walked along the corridor to his suite of rooms in the schloss. Since Pete had moved in here permanently, it had become Jordie's home too. He could've carried on living in the UK but he'd chosen to be near Pete. He'd seen he was in a bad way and thought it prudent to stay close at hand. He also felt that this is what Andrew and Katya would have wanted, for him to keep an eye on their son.

It had never really bothered him where he laid his head each night. Since leaving Newcastle all those years ago, he'd become quite the nomad. When you lived your life on the road, touring the world with different bands, it was par for the course. He'd rooted himself for a few years when he'd been running the pub in Birmingham but, when The Astons had become an almost overnight success, it hadn't been too painful to uproot himself once again and go back out with the boys. Since then, he'd been mostly on the road – first with the band and then with Pete. In the early days, when he was between tours, he'd take out a short-term lease on a flat. About eight years ago, however, at Andrew's suggestion, Pete had invested in a large house in the Notting Hill area of London, along with some other smaller properties around the capital which were rented out. The Notting Hill house had since become the crash pad whenever Pete, Jordie or Kara needed to be in the UK. Lately though, Jordie had begun to think the time may have come to put his wanderings behind him. He wasn't getting any younger and he knew the forthcoming tour with Pete was going to be knackering. The big ones always were, no matter how young or old you were.

He closed the door of his suite behind him, pulled out a Dean Martin CD and, once it was playing quietly, he poured himself a large whisky and stretched out on the sofa, trying to get his turbulent thoughts in order. He picked the glass up from the coffee table next to him and took a large swallow. The burning sensation as it slipped down his throat was comforting. Since waving goodbye to Beth and Sukie last month, he'd been feeling unsettled. The only time this eased was during his conversations with Beth. They spoke every night – sometimes on the phone, sometimes via Skype – and they'd also text each other a couple of times throughout the day. Jordie had finally admitted to himself that he'd fallen for Beth in a big way. They say it's the ones you don't see coming which hit you the hardest. And boy was that ever the truth here! If anyone had told Jordie on the 1st December that, by the end of the month he'd be madly in love, he'd have laughed so hard, after which, he'd have booked them into a clinic to have their head seen to. He hadn't been looking for love – didn't want it, didn't crave it, did not need it. And yet, here he was, watching the clock as he waited for the phone in his hand to ring and for the most amazing woman in the world to speak with him again. He couldn't wait to be back in London, knowing that Beth would only be an hour's drive away. They hadn't discussed meeting up yet, it was – so far – the elephant in the room. He was waiting until Pete had confirmed his plans with Sukie, for her visit to London, and then he'd suggest to Beth that they get together at the same time. With Sukie away, Beth might feel more comfortable about taking their, currently, very good friendship to the next level. He really hoped so because anything less than a total commitment for him was no longer an option. He had to know if Beth felt for him the way he felt about her.

Almost nine hundred miles away, the object of Jordie's affection was walking through her front door and kicking off her dancing shoes with the greatest of pleasure. The Salsa Bar had been busier than usual tonight and Beth had been danced off her feet. Or, she thought, as she rubbed her poor toes, her feet had been danced off her. She padded through to the kitchen and relished the cold of the tiles on her hot, swollen tootsies. A nice cup of tea was needed before she did anything else. She glanced at the clock above the door, as she switched on the kettle, and noted it was later than when she normally got in. Her and Laura had been having such a good time, they'd left the bar far later than they usually did. She couldn't believe she was getting home after 1 a.m. in the morning. She was supposed to be calling Jordie but, adding on the time difference, it was almost 2.30 a.m. in Austria and she was reluctant to disturb him at such a later hour. While pouring the hot water into her mug, she heard her mobile phone beep in her handbag out in the hallway. Once her tea was ready, she walked into the lounge, picking up her bag as she passed by. When she was seated, and had taken a couple of refreshing sips from her mug, she fished the phone out and read the text she'd received:

Hope you're ok. Bit worried at not hearing
from you. I hope you're having lots of fun
and everything is fine.
Hope to speak with you soon. Jx

Beth read the message twice, touched by Jordie's obvious concern. Well, she hoped it was concern and nothing more sinister. She caught her thoughts and pulled herself up short. "Stop that right now," she told herself, speaking aloud. "You are not going to over-think this one like you have done with all your previous encounters. You need to trust and stop looking for the pitfalls. If they come, they come and you'll just need to deal with them. Thus far, Jordie has done nothing to make you question him, so behave yourself and enjoy the moment."

With her pep-talk still in her head, Beth called Jordie.

Jordie saw Beth's name come up on his phone and

let out the breath he had been holding since sending his text. With a deep breath, he hit the 'answer' button and let the relief wash over him as he heard her voice in his ear.

"Hey, you, what are doing out of bed so late? You're not such a young thing anymore." He could hear the smile in her voice as she spoke.

"You're a fine one to talk." he replied. "I'm not the one out dancing till the wee small hours you know."

"I think I'll be paying for it in the morning. My feet feel like something you see in cartoons – ten times the size they should be and throbbing away like big, red, lighthouse beacons!"

"So you had a good time then?" He had to push down the hard lump of jealousy that had formed in his chest.

"Oh yes, it was fun. Much busier than usual and I'm really bad at saying no when I'm asked to dance. It feels so rude. So I kept saying yes. The result of my good manners may be that I can't walk properly for several days!"

"Glad to hear it. I mean… that you had a good night out, not that your feet feel like they're shredded to ribbons." He rolled his eyes. Why did he always manage to say the wrong thing and then sound really awkward and gawkish when he tried to correct himself? "By the way, please don't think I was checking up you. I was just concerned and worried not to have heard from you. You hear horror stories about things happening and women going missing after nights out and…" He stopped. To his ears, he sounded like a sad, crazy, old man so how on earth was this coming across to Beth. "I was just worried, that's all," he finished meekly.

Beth smiled to herself. The concern in his voice was clear and she found it gave her a lovely warm feeling inside. She felt quite cared for and it was nice. She curled her feet up underneath her as she proceeded to tell Jordie about her night. For the next hour, the two of them chatted, both happy to hear the other's voice and not really caring what they were talking about.

One floor below Jordie, Pete was lying on his bed, talking to the other McClaren woman in their lives. Sukie had sent him a selfie of herself in all her war-paint (her words) and wearing her favourite dress. He'd found himself looking at it several times throughout the course of the evening. With her hair piled up on her head, and wearing a red, calf-length, fitted, mandarin dress and black, patent, stiletto-heeled shoes, she'd looked utterly stunning. He'd caught his breath when he'd opened the text and seen the picture. This he had not been expecting! Had he been asked, he'd have described Sukie as pretty with nice hair. Their friendship was such that she'd never had to really dress up when with him and he would, in all honesty, have been a bit suspicious if she'd done so. Seeing her like this had brought home the fact that she was actually very beautiful and he was trying to work out why this made him feel uncomfortable. He dragged his mind back to the conversation and tried to pay attention to the story Sukie was telling him about an incident her friend had had at work the day before.

"So, Jenny was telling me about this young student who she'd noticed was coming into the library every other day. Very sweet and innocent looking – all glasses and big eyes. On his first visit in September, when term started, he'd asked her to point him in the direction of the Art History section, which she did. Anyway, yesterday, she was putting some books back on the shelves when she noticed him sitting at the furthest away, most secluded, table in the building. He had his back to the rest of the library and was facing out the window. Thinking he might be lonely, being young and still new, she went over to speak to him. It was only as she got closer she realised he had the art books open at the pages with the naked ladies on them and his arm was moving up and down at a great speed. He was only jerking himself off!"

"No way! You are kidding me!"

"That's exactly what I said to Jenny," Sukie replied.

"So, what did she do?"

"Also exactly what I said," said Sukie with a laugh. "Well, she just walked up to the table and sat down opposite this lad. She made a show of peering over to look at the books and said, "Ah, you're studying Rubens, I think we have a few other books that'll give you a deeper insight into his works. Let me just go and find them for you." At which point she got up and walked away. When she returned a couple of minutes later, he was gone. Scarpered! The books were still lying open on the table but he'd legged it. She doesn't think he'll be back for some time."

"That poor boy! He'll be scarred for life now."

"Jenny said it happens most years with the new intakes but it was the first time she'd come across it herself – if you pardon the pun! I got the impression she was more shocked because he didn't seem the type. If he'd been more of a 'lad' she would have kept a closer eye on him."

"So, you had a good night then?"

"Yes, it was very nice. Food was lovely and the company was good. What did you get up to?"

"Had a meeting with Kara and Jordie to finalise details for our return to the UK next week."

"On a Saturday night? Wow, what a rock-star life you lead! I'm so jealous…"

He grinned at her jesting. "Oh, be quiet you. I've been there, done that and designed the T-shirt. This quieter life suits me just fine. Anyway, to sustain a rock-star lifestyle, one occasionally has to be a rock star and that takes a lot of organising. And, talking of organising, are you coming to London a week on Friday like we talked about?"

Sukie let out a sigh. "I don't know if I can. I've got to think of the cats. I don't like leaving them all the time. They're not used to me going away this often – I hardly saw them in December – and they're just about getting over that. Besides, I don't want to keep leaving them. I miss them when they're not around me. I am disappointed that I won't get to see you but my boys are my priority and I won't put them second to anyone. Not even the world's most sought-after musician."

"So, bring them with you then. I don't mind. Do they travel ok?"

"Seriously?" The idea of taking Tony and Adam to London hadn't even crossed her mind.

"Of course I'm serious. I want to hang out with my friend and if that means she brings her menagerie with her, then so be it. Tell me what I need to get in for them and I'll get it sorted."

"No need for that, Pete, I'll bring their stuff with me."

"Sukie, I'm hoping you will be a regular visitor whenever I'm in London so it makes more sense for me to get whatever stuff cats need and then it can stay there, ready for any future visits you make."

"Well, if you're quite sure, that would be great. What I'll do is place an online order and it can be delivered directly to your address. Would that be ok?"

"Of course it's ok. That's perfect. Now, what time should the driver pick you up?"

"Err... Pete, I can drive myself you know. I'm a big girl now and they have let me loose with a driver's license so I think I can make my own way down."

"Oh, Sukie, I have no doubt you're a great driver but there's a reason for this. Once it's known I'm back in the UK, the paparazzi will be clogging up the pavement outside my house. Anyone going in and out will be photographed. And if it's a beautiful woman, such as yourself, walking through the front door, I can assure you that your picture will be in every gossip column within two hours of your arrival. In order to avoid that, I have a trusted driver who I use a lot. He'll pick you up and bring you in via the underground car park, which the paps don't know about because it's in another street, and no one will be any the wiser that you're here. This is all about protecting that privacy which you cling to so dearly."

"You just called me beautiful."

"Eh?"

"I said, you just called me beautiful."

Pete had a fleeting few seconds of panic as he realised what he'd let slip. He hadn't meant to say that. "Well, when you walk around wearing your balaclava, you certainly do turn heads. Which is better than the stomachs you turn when you don't!"

He punched the air as he realised he'd got in his comeback for her Worzel Gummidge insult earlier and, hopefully, had deflected away how much she'd affected him with her photograph.

"Oooooohhhhh! Such a mean boy. I can see I've trained you well!"

They exchanged a few more insults and retorts before saying goodnight. Pete was really looking forward to being back in London again. Something he'd never thought he'd say in a million years.

Chapter Forty

Elsa placed her tray on the table and moved her plates onto it before sitting down. A moment later, Sukie arrived and did the same. She placed the empty trays on the seat next to her, looked at the plates of food in front of them and laughed. "Well, Elsa, even on our girlie day out, you can't let go of the salads, can you?" She surveyed her own plate, which was laden with all sorts of yummy Chinese nibbles, and was glad she'd spent two hours in the gym the night before. "I suppose that's the great thing about these buffet style restaurants, I get to indulge and you can still maintain your tight-body routine." She smiled at Elsa, letting her know she was only teasing, although, since Harry's death, she had become fastidious about what she ate – it all had to be organic, no refined sugar and minimal fat. She'd never said anything but she suspected Elsa put some of the blame for Harry's death on the lifestyle they'd lived. Lots of takeaways, a bottle of wine every other night and not making enough use of the gym-membership they'd allowed to renew every January when their New Year's resolution, along with half of the world's population, was to get fit and be more health conscious.

The doctors had told Elsa that the brain tumour Harry had developed was extremely rare and it was highly unlikely he'd done anything untoward to cause it. It was one of those horrible flukes of nature where there was no rhyme, nor reason, behind it. As the neurologist had explained to them both, it had been a one-in-a-million disease and Harry had just so happened to be the one on that occasion. Once she'd gotten past her initial stage of grieving however, Elsa had thrown herself into the health and fitness regime she now lived by.

Sure, she looked great on it, but Sukie did wonder if she maybe clung to it a little more tightly than she should. On the odd occasion she'd suggested getting a burger and chips from a certain, well-known, American fast-food joint, Elsa's protests against the idea were a bit more heated and high-pitched than would be considered normal. Sukie knew she'd have to tackle Elsa on it sometime soon but not today. They hadn't been out together for ages and she didn't want to spoil the day by having an argument.

"So, tell me everything you've been up to," said Elsa. "We've not had a good old natter since you went to Austria."

"I know. I'm sorry. That trip netted me the promotion I'd been hoping for but the workload is far greater than I'd expected so it has been more late nights than I'd have liked. And then, with you seeing Glenys most weekends... How is she doing, by the way?"

Elsa let out a sigh. "Not so good I'm afraid. She's not getting over the stroke as well as we'd hoped. The doctors think she's giving up. She's not really making any effort to try and get well."

Glenys was Elsa's mother-in-law and they'd always been close. Harry had been a late surprise for her and her husband Malcolm – they'd been told many years before they would not be able to have children. Harry had been their only child and they had, understandably, doted on him. When he'd died, their whole world had shattered. Malcolm lasted six months without his son when a severe heart attack reunited them. Glenys had said it was a broken heart that had taken him from her, not a faulty one.

She'd appeared to be coping. Elsa and her mum visited several times a week but, the week before Christmas, she'd fallen quite badly and tests had revealed she'd suffered a stroke. The doctors didn't believe it to be a bad one and had expected Glenys to make a reasonable recovery but it was looking now as though she had other ideas on that. She'd been sent home from the hospital in mid-January but needed almost round the clock care. Elsa and her mum were working alongside the carers who came in throughout the day and night to help.

"She responds to Puddle, when he sticks his nose in her hand, but the rest of the time she's very uncommunicative." Puddle was the Golden Labrador Elsa and Harry had bought for his parents, with a view to keeping them active from walking him each day. The name came from his love of splashing in any puddle of water he came across.

Sukie gave Elsa a sympathetic look. "That's got to be tough on your mum and you. It's really something that both of you are giving her so much care."

"You do what you need to do. Anyway…" Elsa sat up straight, pulled back her shoulders and put a big smile on her face, "I'm not here to moan about how things are in my life right now. I've got a whole day off, thanks to Glenys' lovely next-door neighbour, and I'm here to catch up on girlie gossip, forget about my responsibilities and have a lovely time with my best mate. So now, I want to hear ALL about Salzburg and how you ended up going back there for Christmas."

Sukie chewed her bite of pancake roll a bit longer than necessary. She'd been dreading the moment when she'd have to tell Elsa about meeting Pete and, having just heard the latest update on Glenys, she knew she couldn't do it now either. It was a revelation which needed to be broken gently and a busy buffet restaurant in the middle of Oxford was not quite what Sukie considered to be the best location for the task.

Finally swallowing her mouthful and taking a sip of her drink, Sukie grinned at Elsa and said "ALL of it? Are you sure?"

"Ok, the finer details you can keep to yourself. Was it what you hoped it would be? Did it disappoint in any way?"

"It was fantastic! I loved it! The scenery was amazing, the city is so beautiful and the air is so clean and crisp – it was very hard to leave."

"So how did you end up going back again for Christmas?"

Ok, here goes, thought Sukie. She'd thought of an 'out' to buy her some time and she was now about to put it to the test. She crossed her fingers under the table and said, "I met some Brits in the bar at the hotel. They actually live in Austria but were staying in the city for some business meetings and we got along very well. Peter kindly came with me on a couple of my sight-seeing ventures and, on my last day, invited Mum and me to join them for Christmas. I hadn't expected Mum to go for it but she surprised the socks off me when she not only accepted but even talked me into going. She was totally up for it. So we went and had a wonderful time. I won't, however, talk about it non-stop as it doesn't seem right given your Christmas was more subdued."

Before Elsa could say anything else, Sukie quickly changed the subject. "Oh, by the way, have you seen that Bare Faced Minerals have some new face products out? I need more foundation. Will you help me to choose one?"

"Oh, have they? Nice. I could do with some new eye shadow. We can go over to the shopping centre when we're finished here."

Sukie breathed an inward sigh of relief. Elsa had taken the bait and moved away from the subject of her holidays. She'd gotten a reprieve for now but she knew she was living on borrowed time. The longer she held back from sharing the news about Pete, the harder it was going to be.

Chapter Forty-One

Sukie let out a sigh. Pete looked over at her and asked, "Are you okay?"

She glanced away from the extra-large television screen, where Jason Bourne was doing his thing, looked at him and answered, "Yes, why?"

"Because that's the third big sigh you've done in the last fifteen minutes. If you don't like the movie, we can put something else on."

They were both sprawled out in the lounge on the large sofa-bed which Pete had unfurled for their viewing pleasure. When she'd walked in, after checking Tony and Adam were settling in without any problems, she'd done a double take at the sight of it and couldn't prevent the surprised expression appearing on her face.

"It goes back to being on the road," Pete had quickly explained. "Often, you're so hyped up from being on stage that it can take ages to come down, unwind and go to sleep. Some nights we'd party, but most of the time, we'd go to our rooms and simply watch films until we dropped off. I got so used to watching films in bed I now find it difficult to watch them unless I'm lying flat out. I'm hoping the sofa is large enough for you to crash out beside me, but if it makes you uncomfortable, I'm happy to pull the chair around for you. It's not a problem."

She'd looked at the expanse of sofa-bed in front of her. It was massive. You could probably fit half of the England rugby team on it! "I think there's plenty of space there for us both to fit on comfortably."

And there was. Even with a huge bowl of toffee popcorn in between them – it turned out that Pete had an extremely sweet tooth – there was more than enough room for both to feel comfortable lying there together.

Sukie was quick to reassure him. "No, it's not the film. I do like the Bourne movies. It's just…" She hesitated, not sure if she should really be laying her problems out to him. Sukie was someone who would happily help others when they were in trouble, or needed to talk, but was very bad at opening up herself and allowing her friends to help her.

"Sukes, just spill it. You've been distracted all week. Get it off your chest and then, hopefully, you can relax for the rest of the weekend."

He was right, she thought. She'd been out of sorts since seeing Elsa last week. Not telling Elsa about her new friendship with Pete was really beginning to lie heavy on her and, the more she was dwelling on it, the worse she was feeling but she just couldn't see a way of breaking the news that didn't have the potential to upset her dearest friend.

She drew in a breath as she decided that she did need to share this. Maybe the old saying of 'two heads are better than one' might just prove to be right. After all, she was coming up with sod all on her own. Before she could allow herself to change her mind, she blurted it out. "I haven't told Elsa about our friendship. I don't know how to tell her and, the longer I keep quiet, the harder it's becoming."

Pete looked at Sukie as he grabbed a handful of popcorn. "Can I ask why you haven't said anything yet?"

"Do you remember me telling you about the rather big crush she has on you?"

"Yeah, but I don't get why that would be a problem? She's an adult isn't she? It's not like you're schoolgirls and you've snogged her boyfriend is it? Not that we've snogged or anything," he added hastily.

"There's kind of a bit more to it than that." She filled him in on Harry's death and why the situation was so delicate. Even as she spoke, she felt she was being disloyal to Elsa by sharing her personal pain with another person. She'd only ever discussed Elsa's situation with Beth and that had been purely for the purpose of her mum advising her on how to support her grief-stricken friend.

When she'd finished, she looked at Pete. "I hope you can now see why it's so hard for me."

He nodded that he did. "I do and I totally understand how telling her is not going to be easy. It's one thing having a safe crush on someone you believe you are never likely to meet. It's quite another when your best friend turns round and says 'Hey, guess who I met when I was on my hols and now speak to about six times a day'?"

"I think you mean 'who annoys the crap out of me by texting and calling me six times a day'," she retorted.

"Yeah, yeah, whatever! I haven't heard you complaining. Let me have a think about this."

Pete turned his attention back to the action on the television as he thought about Sukie's problem. He was touched by her concern that she may upset her friend. It reassured him that his own trust in her was not misplaced. After a few minutes, an idea began to take shape. He let it work itself out a bit more and then thought to himself that it might just work. He turned back to Sukie and asked, "When's Elsa's birthday?"

"Middle of May," said Sukie.

He took his phone out of his pocket and scrolled through the calendar. "Not perfect but doable." He smiled at Sukie and said, "I think I've got it. You can blame me. I'll take the flak for you!"

With a frown on her face, and a confused shake of her head, Sukie asked him "What? How?"

"It's really quite simple. As you know, I'm touring from the middle of April and I'm playing in Birmingham at the end of April. So, take her to the gig – an early birthday present – and bring her backstage afterwards. Introduce me as the friend you met in Austria."

He saw Sukie was about to interrupt him. "Let me finish. When Elsa looks surprised at this news, I will then apologise for you not telling her sooner by saying that '*I*' had asked you not to tell anyone about our friendship. I will then go on to explain, truthfully, I might add, that I find it hard to trust people and had asked this of you as a favour to me. I will then proceed to sing your praises by saying the fact you didn't tell her is what makes you such a good friend to the both of us. The way I see it, even if she's pissed off at you for not telling her sooner, she will, hopefully, accept I was a secret you'd been asked not to share."

Sukie took a moment to think over what Pete had said. "You would do that for me?" She looked at him in astonishment. "I was expecting you to tell me not to be so daft, just tell Elsa or something 'blokey' like that. I didn't think for a moment that you'd come up with a workable solution.

He answered her question in a gentle tone. "It's not 'for you', it's 'for us'. We're friends and, as far as I know, friends help each other. You truly don't realise how much of a difference you and your mum have made to me by becoming a part of my life. Being able to give you something back really means a great deal to me. I'm also hoping that Elsa and I can be friends. You clearly think very highly of her and care for her deeply. I don't want to be the one to put your friendship in jeopardy. I think this could work and is probably the best way around what is a rather sensitive situation."

Sukie pondered some more on Pete's suggestion. "Do you think this could work? I certainly haven't been able to come up with a way of telling her about you that isn't going to be really awkward." She looked at him and smiled. "Ok, we'll try it. But only if you're sure you don't mind being the fall guy."

He returned her smile. "I'm quite sure."

"Well, in the absence of any other options, it's worth a shot. I don't feel comfortable with the thought of just blurting it out to her and, given the circumstances, I can't see a way of breaking it to her gently. Hopefully, meeting you will be enough to bring her to her senses. When she sees what a prat you actually are…" Sukie ducked as a piece of popcorn came flying her way.

"There is, however, one thing which needs to be done." Pete's expression was serious as he looked at Sukie. "I need to ask you to do something for me please."

"Sure, what is it?"

"Could I ask you, for now, not to mention our friendship to anyone. It's just as we're getting to know each other better. You know I have trust issues so, if you could bear with me on this, it would mean a lot."

With another smile, Sukie replied "I can do that. It's no problem at all."

"Good! Now you'll not be lying to your friend and your conscience is clear. The timing may be out but you can look her in the eye and tell her, truthfully, that I've asked this favour of you."

Sukie leant across the expanse of the sofa-bed and gave him a hug. "Thank you," she whispered. As she rolled back to her spot, she picked up a handful of popcorn and, giving Pete a cheeky grin, said, "Who knows, maybe you'll meet Elsa, fall madly in love with her, get married and have lots of babies. That way, it would all work out quite nicely."

Pete's blood ran cold at the thought. "Err, no!"

"Why not?" asked Sukie. "Elsa is lovely. She's a

sweet, kind person who is also rather gorgeous to look at. She's the full package."

"I'm sure she's all that, but I'm equally sure I'm not the person who can mend her broken heart. A basket case like me is the last thing she needs to tie herself to."

"Good point, well made," said Sukie, laughing. "A bampot like you is something she definitely doesn't deserve!"

This time, she didn't duck fast enough and the popcorn hit her square on the face.

While they'd been talking, the film had finished so Sukie took the opportunity to pop up to her rooms to see how Tony and Adam were. Pete had, very thoughtfully, done some research online and had noted that cats like 'safe rooms' when they go to new places so he'd put Sukie in the suite of rooms up in the attic, where her boys had plenty of space to run around but where they could also feel safe and relaxed. It was a very pretty suite with white painted floorboards, white wooden cladding covering the bottom half of the walls, sloped ceilings and dormer windows. The bedroom contained a lovely cast iron bedstead and free-standing wardrobe, and the small sitting room was furnished with a brightly patterned sofa, a matching chair and a circular rug on the floor gave it a lovely, homely feel. There was a further, smaller, box room, which could have been a second bedroom if required but, instead, Pete had put the cats' toys and scratching tree in there, along with some squishy beds Sukie knew they'd never use. Pete had still to learn that small fact about cats – they'd rather sleep in the boxes the beds were delivered in! She walked in the door and was happy to see them both curled up together on the sofa. Noting they had eaten some of the food she'd put out for them, she was satisfied they were content. She gave them both a kiss and went back down the stairs to the lounge.

"How are they? Not too fazed I hope." Pete had met the cats earlier when Sukie had arrived. They'd been more interested in sniffing out their new space and hadn't really bothered with him. He knew very little about cats and was anxious to get to know them better but had read during his research that it was often better to wait for them to approach you than to force yourself upon them. He was hoping they'd be more interested in him tomorrow.

"They're good, thank you. All curled up asleep on the sofa. I put a couple of their throws from home over it so they've got a familiar smell around them. That helps."

Sukie reclaimed her spot on the sofa-bed, and noting that Pete had refilled the bowl with more popcorn, she grabbed the remote control. "My turn to choose," she said, as she flicked through the film menu on the screen. "I think we need something funny and light-hearted. Ah, there we go. That will do very nicely. I love this film."

Pete looked at her selection. "Casper? As in, Casper the Ghost?"

"Oh yes, the very one."

"Is that not a kid's movie?" Pete wasn't so sure about this. He liked his films to be full of guns, explosions, car chases and high drama. This sounded a bit boring to him.

"It's a good movie, trust me. Anyway, it's my turn to choose and this is it. So be a good boy and just watch it." Sukie gave him another cheeky grin as the opening credits began to role. "Furthermore, one of my favourite 'magical movie moments' is in this film, just so you know."

"Magical movie moments?"

"Yeah, you know… those bits in movies that give you goosebumps. Moments such as Michael Caine in 'The Italian Job' – "you were only supposed to blow the bloody doors off!" Or, in 'Love Actually', when Colin Firth proposes to his Portuguese housekeeper."

"Ah yes, I get you. So when does that happen in this one?"

Completely focused on the screen now, Sukie replied, "Oh, you'll know when, you can trust me on that."

Pete couldn't concentrate on the film. He was trying as it did seem to be better than he'd expected and Sukie had been giggling quite a lot at the various antics of the comical ghostly trio. He could see she was more relaxed now that it appeared her problem with Elsa had been resolved.

Elsa… He was still trying to work out why Sukie's joke about him falling in love with her had filled him with such revulsion. He hoped it hadn't been too obvious to Sukie, the effect her words had had on him. She'd given no indication of anything untoward so he must have covered himself pretty well. But why had he reacted like that? Why did the very thought of being in love with someone make his insides churn? Maybe, emotionally, he wasn't ready to make that commitment after all he'd gone through. His recent self-forgiveness was still very fresh and perhaps he needed more time to adjust. But... the adverse reaction to Sukie's comment had been *so* intense. It was that which was puzzling him the most. He'd actually felt sick at the suggestion.

Just then, Sukie's arm came across and her hand landed on his wrist, gripping it lightly. "This is nearly it, my little magical movie moment..."

He stopped questioning his earlier reaction and gave his full attention to the film. This he had to see. The young girl in the film – Kat – was in bed and Casper, the ghost, was floating around talking to her, telling her about his life and how lonely he'd been until she'd come along.

I can identify with that, he thought, giving Sukie a quick glance.

When Casper realises Kat has fallen asleep, he leans over her and whispers in her ear, "Can I keep you?"

As he uttered these words, Sukie gave a tiny little squeal and drummed her heels lightly on the sofa-bed. She looked at Pete. "That was it, my magical movie moment. Don't ask me why I love that little segment so much, I just do. It turns me to mush every time." She gave him a big happy smile, took her hand off his wrist and returned her attention to the movie.

And, in that small exchange, Pete found the answer to his question. Why had he felt so repulsed at the thought of falling in love with Elsa?

Because he was already in love with someone else... And that someone was Sukie!

343

Chapter Forty-Two

It was Saturday morning and Beth lay in bed, looking at the sunlight shining through the window. It may look glorious outside but, as it was only the last weekend in February, she'd bet her underwear on it still being blooming cold. The thought of the chilly outdoors made her snuggle further into her soft, warm haven. Just then, the doorbell chimed. Before she could move, Jordie walked out of the bathroom and gave her a smile. "Stay put, I'll get it."

A moment later he was back, wheeling in the trolley delivered by room service and full of delicious breakfast treats. He picked up the coffee pot, poured her a cup, added some milk and brought it over to her bedside table. As he put it down, he leaned over her and gave her a long, deep kiss. "Would madam like her breakfast in bed or on the table by the window?"

She pulled his head back down for another kiss and

murmured against his mouth, "It depends on what's being offered for breakfast."

Jordie straightened up and removed his bath robe. "Allow me to show you, madam."

She cast her eyes hungrily over his well-toned body and his quite obvious excitement. "Hmm... that all looks very tasty. Very tasty indeed!"

Jordie swiftly threw back the quilt, got into the bed beside her and pulling the quilt up over their heads, said, "I hope you enjoy your breakfast, madam," as he began to kiss her throat, working his way slowly down to her breasts.

Arching her back with desire, she replied, "Oh I think I will..."

Beth was standing in the shower, letting the hot water wash over her as she thought about how wanton, and desired, she was feeling. She hadn't been with a man sexually for a long time and, being in her mid-fifties, she'd thought it was all behind her. Jordie had very much proved her wrong on that one. She smiled as he once again entered her thoughts – not that he was ever far away from them these days. When she'd left Austria last month, she'd fully expected the small spark between them to peter out but Jordie had had other ideas. When they'd landed back in the UK, and she'd turned her mobile phone on, it had beeped immediately. The text had been from Jordie, asking if they'd gotten back okay and how the flight had been. That same night, just before she got into bed, he'd sent her another text, wishing her sweet dreams and how he hoped her first day back at work wasn't too arduous.

From there, they'd grown into speaking, texting and Skyping every day. They'd talked so much, covering everything from their childhoods, to their teenage years, to seeing their hopes and desires change over time as life had thrown curve-balls their way. Beth felt she now knew Jordie better than any other person in her life. Even Sukie had secrets which she'd never share with her mum but Beth expected that. It worked both ways – there were some things in her life which she never intended to share with her daughter. But Jordie… She wanted to tell him everything and hear everything about him in return.

She turned off the shower, and stepping out to dry herself, wondered why this relationship had taken off when so many previous attempts had failed so dismally. She guessed it had, most likely, been the distance between them both that had made it work. With all those miles between you, all you can do is talk and get to know each other. People seemed to move so fast with their expectations these days and, if you hadn't jumped into bed with each other by the third date, the whole thing was considered a disaster and everyone moved on. No one did courting anymore. It seemed the anticipation of waiting for the first touch, the first hand-hold, the first kiss, was no longer thrilling enough. Beth preferred the slow approach and she knew this was why she'd spent more time ending relationships than being in them. After all, how could she be expected to be intimate with someone she barely knew?

She wrapped herself in the lovely, fluffy bathrobe and walked back into the suite Jordie had booked for them. When he'd first suggested they meet up, she'd been unsure whether to accept or not. She'd ascertained from their conversations that he wanted their relationship to develop further but she was scared that, by doing so, she'd lose his friendship if it didn't work out. She'd finally shared her fears with Laura.

Laura, bless her soul, had taken those fears and stamped them to dust. "You, lady," she'd said "need to stop worrying about everything. Just go with the flow and stop being so uptight. Meet the bloke and see what happens."

Well, she thought with a smile, she'd certainly taken Laura at her word and then some. Jordie had been the perfect gentleman and had booked two rooms – well, a luxury suite and a deluxe room – in a very upper-class, city centre, Birmingham hotel. When they'd met in the hotel lobby, they'd greeted each other with a hug and a kiss. The kiss, however, turned into something more than just a hello – her toes still curled up when she thought about it! When they'd finally pulled themselves apart, they'd both known where they were headed.

Jordie had whispered to her, "I've got two rooms booked."

She'd whispered back, "Cancel one of them!"

The porter had barely closed the door before they were in each other's arms, quickly removing the clothing getting in their way. Their love-making had been fast and furious as the desire which had been slowly building over the last seven weeks had overtaken them. The second occasion had been more leisurely as they'd taken the time to find out what the other liked. The third and fourth time… She caught sight of her face in the bathroom mirror as she blushed at the thought of how daring she'd been. But, oh boy, had it been good or what!

She walked out of the bathroom and saw Jordie looking at his phone.

"I've just had a text from the ducklings, they're going out sightseeing today. What do you fancy doing?"

She walked over to him, removed the phone from his hand, straddled his lap and, as she undid her robe, she kissed him deeply before whispering, "Let *me* show *you*…"

Chapter Forty-Three

Eduardo di Santo stood looking at the chalked-out stage plan on the floor of his rented warehouse. His job had made obtaining this information so much easier. Providing security for the summer festivals meant his company had access to all the details pertaining to the local venues and all their planned events. He'd curried favour with his boss by, not only offering his services as Head of Security for the Pete Wallace event but, also, from saying he was more than willing to take on extra tasks on the run-up to the concert if it helped to ensure everything ran smoothly on the night.

Fabio Mancini had been delighted with Eduardo's offer. Only that morning, he'd been advised that IL Divo were now going to be performing at the Teatro Romano on the same night as the Pete Wallace gig at the Stadio Bentegodi. With two such big acts in town on the same day, plus the festival's Opera Spectacular in the Arena,

Verona was going to be crammed with concert goers and tourists. Fabio was concerned they may not have enough manpower to cover the extra security needed for these events and still be able to provide for his long-standing, day-to-day, cliental. He was going to have to discuss this with Head Office so, being able to delegate the Stadio workload to Eduardo, was a godsend. He'd said as much as he'd pulled the Pete Wallace file from the filing cabinet and handed it over to Eduardo. "If you do a good job on this one, it would really help you to move up to the next level. You're due for a promotion and this will help me to convince Head Office to give it to you. I know you won't let me down."

It had taken every ounce of restraint Eduardo had not to grab the file from Mancini's hand and begin reading it there and then. He'd smiled his thanks, left Fabio's office and had practically run back to his own. When he'd gone through the file, and had read the stage set-up requirements, he'd punched the air with glee.

He'd initially considered four possible options which would have done the job of taking Pete Wallace down, but the logistics of carrying them out were either too difficult, too awkward, or too risky. A small selection of explosives in the Marshall-stack speakers would be difficult as it would be virtually impossible to get close enough to them. He'd considered poison, as most acts stated their preferred food choices on their riders, but all Pete Wallace wanted was sealed bottles of mineral water in his dressing room, so poisoning him was a no-go. A third option had been to arrange a falling lighting rig but the risk of others also being hurt was too great. He only wanted to eliminate Pete Wallace, no one else.

This left him with his last, and final, option. It was the choice he'd always preferred, but he knew it paid to be thorough by always going through every possibility.

He was going to shoot Pete Wallace.

He'd noted, as he'd trawled through the endless hours of Wallace videos on the internet, that Pete usually had a period in his shows where he'd climb on top of the large speakers at the side of the stage and lead the audience in a singalong. It appeared as though he'd always done this – first when he'd toured in the band and also on his last solo tour – so Eduardo was fairly confident he'd stay true to form and carry out the same little ritual on this coming tour.

The plan, so far, was that Eduardo would place himself in the security area in front of the stage barrier. As he'd be Head of Security that night, this would be easy. While Pete always climbed the speakers on both sides of the stage, he had a tendency to favour the stack to the audience's left, so Eduardo intended to take up his position near there. However, and going back to still being thorough, he would be practicing his moves from both sides to see which was most effective and which was most comfortable for him.

This was why he was creating a mock-up of the stage lay-out. He was leaving nothing to chance. He also wanted to practice shooting at different areas of the stage, just in case Wallace changed his routine. There was no harm in covering all eventualities. He looked at his watch. Where were those deliveries? They should be here by now.

A loud bang on the metal door a few moments later told him they'd just arrived. Within ten minutes he was standing in front of his purchases, trying really hard not to whoop with joy. The sixty packing crates would become his substitute stage and speakers. The job lot of ex-display shop mannequins were his substitute Petes. Finally, to bring in a degree of reality, and to ensure he stayed focused on his task, he'd also bought a load of soft cardboard, tie-on, Pete Wallace face masks.

After all, when you plan to blow someone's brains out, you need to know exactly where to aim.

Chapter Forty-Four

April

Pete, lying on his bed in his hotel room, read the text he'd just received from Sukie, letting him know she and Elsa were on the train and would soon be in Birmingham. He wouldn't see them both until after the gig as he'd be sound-checking when they arrived. He was pleased about this because it gave him a few extra hours before he had to put on the act of his life.

He hadn't hung out with Sukie since that weekend in February, when he'd realised he'd fallen in love with her, although they still spoke on the phone several times a day and Skyped most evenings. He'd hoped his feelings were just a blip and that, once he'd started rehearsing and then touring, they would fade. Life out on the road was a very different creature to the real thing and it was easy to lose yourself in the monotony of same crew, same gig,

353

different towns and cities. Your life became a cocoon and it was usually easy to forget those outside of the little world you and your fellow travellers were sharing.

Except… forgetting Sukie was proving to be impossible. Whenever something funny happened, she was the first person he wanted to share it with. He found himself taking photographs of amusing billboards, or shop signs, and texting them to her to make her laugh. As his tour bus ate up miles of motorway each day, taking him all around the country, he'd spend the hours trawling the internet, finding cute kitten videos he knew she had a soft spot for.

And then, at night, wound up and wrung out after yet another gig, they would talk on Skype and she would help him to relax and unwind by chatting about her day in the office and the various forms of office politics she had to deal with. She often joked that hearing about her job was enough to put even the worst insomniac to sleep.

It felt as though, the more he'd tried to keep his feelings at arm's length, the more they were intent on wrapping themselves tightly around his heart. She had become everything to him and he wanted to be everything to her.

In the five months since they'd become friends, Sukie had never once given him cause to think her feelings for him were anything more than platonic. Whenever they'd hugged or kissed, it was always evident that these signs of affection were nothing more than just a part of their friendship. He'd been with enough girls and women over the years to know when hugs and kisses were just hugs and kisses or when they were a suggestive

354

precursor hoping to lead to something else.

One night, he'd decided to test the waters and see if there was any chance Sukie may harbour stronger feelings for him but she soon burned him on that score. The memory of that chat still had the ability to make the blood rush to his cheeks. When he'd asked her, in a jocular manner, if she'd ever fancied him herself, her answer had been brutally honest. "Good grief no! Not ever. You are soooooo not my type."

Not content to leave it there, however, his sadistic little heart had forced him to push it further by asking, "So, what is your type?"

"I'm not quite sure but I do know it's *not* pretty boys like you who are all teeth, cheekbones, and floppy blonde hair," were the words she'd slashed him with. His mother's wise words had come back to him that night – 'Don't open the can of worms if you can't swallow the contents'. How he wished he'd paid more heed to them now. Unrequited love is easier to live with if you think there may be a chance of it one day being reciprocated. When you know there is absolutely no way the object of your affections will ever love you back, it is nothing short of a living hell.

The sharp knock on the door, and Jordie's head popping around it, quickly dragged him away from his navel-gazing. "Ten minutes till we head over to the arena, Pete."

He dredged up a smile and gave Jordie a thumbs-up. "I'll be with you in five."

When the door had closed again, he got up off the bed and went into the bathroom. As he splashed cold water on his face, he looked at his reflection in the mirror and said out loud, "You need to pull this one off tonight, dude. After all, a little bit of Sukie is way better than no Sukie at all!"

And therein lay the rub, because he already knew that having her as a friend was painful enough but it was nothing compared to how he would feel if she wasn't in his life at all.

"I'm very sorry, Miss McClaren, but I'm afraid we're overbooked on the deluxe twin room you reserved. The Pete Wallace gig tonight has filled us to capacity. I hope the upgrade we've given you compensates for any possible inconvenience this may cause."

The hotel receptionist had been well drilled by Kara on what had to be said when Sukie booked in.

Sukie had almost had her first argument with Pete over this arrangement. She'd been quite insistent that she'd pay for their accommodation, he was adamant that she should not.

"I can't help but feel this friendship is becoming a bit one-sided, Pete," she'd said. "So far, you've paid for Mum and me to go to Austria, you paid for the driver to pick me up for London, and bring me back again. You've sorted out the tickets for the gig, you won't let me pay for those, and now you insist on taking on the expense for our accommodation for the night. It's too much and I'm not comfortable with it. I'm beginning to feel like a sponger and I don't like that at all. I pay my way!"

"Oh, Sukes," he'd replied, "It's not like that. I explained to you I'm a partner in the airfield company so flying you both over wasn't really an extra expense. The driver is on a monthly retention fee so there was no additional cost there either. I pay him the same regardless of how many trips he makes. The tickets for the gig are part of our rider – we're given an allocation of seats for friends and family – and, finally, Kara will book the rooms as part of a block booking for myself, the band and other crew members. These are written off as work expenditure. So, you see, the only thing I have really paid for was the takeaway pizza we had when you came down to London. If it makes you feel better, you can stand the next one. Okay?"

She'd felt slightly mollified after this. "That's a deal. You'd better be telling me the truth now. I will be really pissed off if you've lied to me."

"I promise you, I'm not lying," he'd assured her.

Pete promised that she and Elsa would be treated like royalty and had stressed the importance of Elsa being unaware of his involvement in the plans for the evening. Not wanting to discuss Elsa's personal issues, he'd only given Kara need-to-know information, telling her that it was a special surprise for Elsa and an unexplained, rather posh, bedroom might give the game away early.

As she took in the delight on Elsa's face at the beautiful suite they were now standing in, Sukie was glad she'd let Pete take the reins on putting this trip together. There was no way she could've afforded a room like this.

She was feeling quite apprehensive about introducing Elsa to Pete later and knew Pete was doing all he could to help butter Elsa up beforehand. She still felt guilty about the subterfuge they were both involved in but she was deeply grateful to Pete for helping her out. She was just keeping all her fingers and toes crossed that Elsa's normally sweet, forgiving nature would not suddenly do a runner tonight when she found out the truth behind this trip.

Jordie saw that Pete was now fully occupied on the stage, so he stepped out into the foyer to give Beth a quick phone call. He'd given Pete some excuse about meeting his old friends in Birmingham last night and that he'd be staying over with them. He'd told him he would meet him at the hotel today. The truth was he'd been in Oxford, having dinner with Beth. They'd managed to meet up on a few occasions and, when he'd kissed her goodbye this morning, he'd realised it was becoming more and more difficult to leave her. They stole every moment they could to be together.

"Hey, how's it going?" He could hear the noise of her office in the background.

"It would be better if I could stop yawning," she replied. "I can't operate on three hours sleep anymore." Their physical need for each other was still as strong as that first weekend and they'd proved this to each other again last night. "I'm not complaining," she continued, "I just wish I was young enough to cope with the lack of shut-eye a bit better."

"If it helps, I feel just as knackered. And I won't see my bed until the early hours of the morning either."

"How's it all going? Is everything ok? Do you think Pete suspects anything?" They hadn't mentioned their relationship to Sukie or Pete yet. It had been discussed but they'd both decided to wait until they themselves knew where they were headed.

"It's all going well. Pete's sound-checking now and everything's ok. He's too excited about seeing Sukie tonight, and meeting Elsa, to notice anything about me. So stop worrying," Jordie replied, reassuring Beth that their secret was still a secret. Suddenly, there came a loud bang from the auditorium. "Damn! Looks like I spoke too soon," he said.

Sure enough, just then, one of the doors into the foyer opened and Bob, the assistant sound engineer stuck his head out. He looked around until he spotted Jordie and started walking towards him. Jordie held a hand up to stop him and turned his back to finish his call. "I'm gonna have to go, pet. I'll catch up with you later, after the gig. I love you." He hit the 'end call' button on his phone and shoved it in his pocket as he walked over to Bob, completely unaware of his last words to Beth.

Beth, however, was fully aware of what Jordie had said before he'd hung up. Slowly putting her mobile back down on her desk, she replayed the words in her mind. It was the first time they'd been said and Beth was pleased to note that she was okay with hearing them. In fact, the more it sunk in, the more she realised she was very okay with it indeed. The initial, small glimmer of uncertainty had disappeared and, in its place, was a lovely warm glow and it was spreading through her rapidly. She knew Jordie hadn't realised he'd just declared to her how he felt, but that made the words all the more special as they'd come from him naturally. Better still, hearing them had answered the question she'd been asking herself for the last few weeks – did she love Jordie? Well now she knew. She absolutely did! Feeling a bit giddy and light-headed – blimey, at her age? – she pulled the mountain of filing on her desk towards her. She'd been putting off doing it all week but now, she felt like she could climb Everest, and looking at the pile of paperwork in front of her, she figured this was probably the next best thing.

Chapter Forty-Five

"Oh my God! Oh my God! Oh my God! He was AMAZING!" Elsa grabbed Sukie and pulled her into a massive bear-hug. "Thank you so much, Sukie. This has to be the best birthday present EVER!"

"Hey, it was my pleasure. I'm glad you enjoyed it so much." Sukie returned the hug and pushed back down the feeling of guilt which had risen up at Elsa's words. This had been the easy bit. It was what came next that had her palms sweating and her stomach churning. She'd been able to push it to the back of her mind while Pete had been on the stage. As distractions went, he'd turned out to be a rather good one. She'd never seen him perform live before and, she had to admit, he was a great showman. She'd been more than a little impressed.

"Did you see him looking at us? I'm sure he was looking at us. And I'm even *more* sure he pointed at me when he was singing 'Always the Girl for Me'. What do you think, Sukie?"

She looked at Elsa's shining eyes and glowing face and agreed that she was equally sure Pete had sung part of his song to her. In fact, she *knew* he had sung it to Elsa as he'd winked at her afterwards and flashed the cheeky grin he always gave when he was winding her up or teasing her. She'd get him for that later.

Just then, her mobile phone vibrated in her pocket. She counted the rings – two – then it stopped. A few seconds later, it did the same again. This was the signal to say Kara was making her way to the side of the stage to meet them and take them backstage to Pete. She bent down to gather up their jackets and handbags. When she straightened up, she smiled at Elsa and said, "Right, now for the next part of your birthday surprise. Come with me and don't ask any questions."

"Why? Where are we going now?"

"Seriously, Elsa, which part of 'don't ask any questions' did you not understand?" she asked laughingly, as they walked away from their seats.

Elsa followed behind her. "Of course I'm going to ask. As soon as you said 'don't ask', it was clear that I would."

Sukie saw Kara waiting for them, and gave her a wave as she hurried across to where she was standing. The security guard moved the heavy steel barrier to one side and let them through. Kara gave Sukie a hug and then stuck her hand out towards Elsa. "Hi," she said, "you must be Elsa. Very pleased to meet you. I'm Kara, Pete Wallace's PA."

Elsa, looking completely bemused, returned Kara's

friendly handshake. "Hello. Yes, I am Elsa. It's nice to meet you too." She turned to Sukie. "Sukie, what's going on?"

Before Sukie could reply, Kara smiled and said, "Ah! That would be telling! Now, before we can go any further, I need you to put these on please," and she handed them each an 'Access all Areas' pass.

Elsa looked down at hers. "This has my photograph on it. How did you get my photograph?"

Kara didn't answer but instead said, with a smile, "Right, now we can proceed. Follow me please, ladies."

Elsa grabbed Sukie's arm as they walked behind Kara and hissed, "Sukie McClaren, you'd better tell me what is going on right now, if you know what's good for you."

Sukie's stomach was now churning like a washing machine on a fast spin but she managed to smile as she said, "Elsa, we're backstage, we're wearing band passes and we're following Pete Wallace's PA – what do you think is going on?"

"No! No, no, no, no, no! We're meeting..." Elsa wasn't able to finish the sentence as her head finally absorbed what was happening. She grabbed Sukie's arm again and pulled her to a stop.

"Sukie, I can't meet Pete Wallace! I don't want to meet him. This cannot be happening." Elsa's voice began to shake and she started to tremble as she explained, "This is the worst possible thing ever. It's one thing to have a massive crush on the bloke when he's a fantasy inside your head, it's quite another to stand in front of him and turn him from a fantasy into a reality."

Sukie took Elsa's hands in her own and looked her in the eye. With her most gentle tone of voice, she said, "Elsa, I get that this may be a bit more of a surprise than you'd expected but I'm afraid you do need to meet him. There's more to this than you realise. I'm sorry. It'll all become clear very soon but, for now, you need to trust me and do this. Ok?"

"Why? What do I need to know? Why can't you tell me now? Sukie, what is going on?" Elsa was trying to gulp down some air as her throat closed up with panic.

Sukie gripped Elsa's hands tightly within her own. "Please Elsa, just trust me. Can you do that for me? Please?"

She watched as Elsa hesitated for a few more seconds, continuing to draw in deep breaths to calm herself. Finally she looked at Sukie and nodded. "Okay, I'll do it. But only because I'm more intrigued as to what else is going on."

"Thank you," said Sukie.

Elsa took another long intake of breath and closed her eyes. After a few seconds, she exhaled and turned to Sukie, saying, "Right, before we move another step, I want to know one thing – is my lipstick still on?"

Sukie gave her dearest friend a hug. "Elsa, you look as perfect as you always do."

"Good. Then let's get this thing done!"

Kara, looking back, saw that Elsa and Sukie had stopped. She noticed how pale Elsa had become. Pete had given her the gist of the situation and she made a note to let him know that Elsa appeared to be as fragile as Sukie had feared she might be.

When she saw them walking towards her, she smiled and continued to lead the way backstage.

Pete saw Kara stick her head around the dressing room door. He caught her eye and she gave him a quick nod before withdrawing and closing it again.

"Okay guys, time out. Let's pick this back up later at the hotel." He shoo'ed his backing band out of the room. "I'll see you all in the bar." They always did a post-mortem after each gig to go over anything that may have occurred during that night's set or which might need reviewing. He quickly pulled on a clean T-shirt before the door opened again and in walked Kara with Sukie and Elsa. He did a quick double take when he saw Elsa; Sukie hadn't been joking when she'd described her as gorgeous. She really was a stunner. When he looked at Sukie, however, his heart did a quick double-flip. No matter who she stood beside, she'd always be the most beautiful woman in the room where he was concerned.

Kara walked back to the door. When Pete looked over to her, she raised her eyebrows high. They'd worked out a couple of secret signals so she could bring him up to speed on how Elsa was taking this without it appearing obvious to her. Kara had just made him aware that Elsa was not too sure about it all and that he had to tread carefully. He walked over to Sukie and gave her a quick hug. "Hey, fancy seeing you at a Pete Wallace gig. Will the Death Metal fan club revoke your membership after this?" he teased.

She punched him on the arm as she replied, "Nah! I'll tell them it was a research trip and I can confirm you are definitely shit!"

Elsa stood gobsmacked as she watched their exchange. Before she could say anything, however, Sukie turned to her and said, "Elsa, this is Pete. Pete, meet Elsa."

Pete stuck his hand out. "At last we meet. Sukie has talked about you so much."

Elsa shook Pete's hand while replying dryly, "Has she indeed, because she's told me sod all about you!"

"Remember I told you I'd met some people in Salzburg? And that I was spending Christmas with them? Well, Pete, Kara, and Jordie, Pete's manager, were those people." Sukie's expression was very sheepish as she spoke.

Elsa stared at Sukie, as she tried to comprehend what she was hearing.

"Are you telling me, Sukie McClaren, that you've known Pete Wallace since December, spent Christmas with him, clearly speak with him frequently enough to be able to organise all *this*," she swept her hand around, "and yet, at no point, thought it might be something worth sharing?"

Before Sukie could say anything, Pete stepped in. "Elsa, please don't blame Sukie. It's my fault. I asked her not to tell anyone. I don't get close to many people and I find it very hard to trust. It takes time for me to let my guard down due to so many bad experiences in my past. Please don't be upset."

Elsa bit her lip to prevent herself from saying anything. Upset? Angry more like. In fact, bloody furious would be even better. She was trying very hard to stay calm but failing dismally. She felt duped, stupid and let down. Sukie knew how she'd been carrying on about Pete all these years, how he'd always been the main man in her stupid fantasies. Good grief, how many times must she have wittered on about him to Sukie since January alone, never mind before then? They'd been laughing at her, she knew it. How could Sukie have done this to her?

"Are you two an item?" she felt compelled to ask. She had to know.

"What? No! Absolutely not!" Sukie could not have sounded any more shocked.

"I can assure you, Elsa, that we are not romantically involved in any way." Pete backed up Sukie's refusal.

Elsa looked at them both for a few more seconds before turning to Sukie and speaking through gritted teeth said, "I'd like to go back to the hotel now please."

"Of course! No problem!" Sukie handed Elsa her jacket and put her own on.

"Will I see you both in the bar later? I'll be there in about an hour or so." Pete looked at Elsa. "I'd like the opportunity to get to know you better. You could tell me some of the stories about Sukie that she refuses to share."

"That is unlikely to happen. Goodnight." Elsa's reply was as stony in tone as the look on her face. She turned away, flung the door open and walked out. Sukie looked to Pete and shrugged. "I need to go."

Pete nodded. "Hopefully, I'll see both later. Good luck."

"Thanks. I think I'm going to need it." With that, Sukie closed the door and turned to follow Elsa down the corridor.

Chapter Forty-Six

Elsa didn't speak a word to Sukie as they walked back to their hotel. Well, she marched and Sukie did her best to keep up. For a little thing, Elsa could walk very fast, especially when she was brimming with anger. Her fists were balled tightly as she tried to contain the trembling that was surging through her. She didn't think she'd ever been so angry. Even when Harry had died, she hadn't felt such consuming rage. In her head, she kept replaying the scene where Sukie and Pete had hugged and teased each other. How dare they lie and tell her they weren't in a relationship. It was as clear as day that they were. She'd have thought more of them if they'd only been honest with her – knowing they'd lied to her about that meant she didn't believe anything else they'd said. She knew Sukie had told him all about her crush on him. The sad little widow, who played out fantasies about rock stars in her head, because it was easier than dealing with the pain of being alone. The thought of Sukie's betrayal kept slicing into her like a knife.

By the time they walked into their hotel room, she'd worked herself into a total fury. The door had barely swung shut before she whirled round and verbally laid into Sukie.

"You bitch! You fucking bitch! Who the hell do you think you are, humiliating me like that? Did you get some kind of weird kick from it? Was it fun? Are you and your boyfriend going to have another good laugh at my expense? How many have you had so far? 'Oh, the poor little widow, fancying the big rock star!' I must have kept you both entertained for hours."

Sukie looked at Elsa, totally aghast at what she was hearing. "Elsa," she said calmly, "we're not in a relationship. We're just friends. I'm sorry. I expected you to be angry or upset with not having been told of my friendship with Pete sooner but you are way off the mark here."

"Stop lying to me, you bitch," Else screeched back. "I'm not fucking blind you know! I could see it with my own eyes. The two of you must have thought it was hilarious – I'm the one with the crush on him and you're the one who bagged him. Ha-fucking-ha!"

Sukie tried again, "Elsa, I repeat, we are NOT a couple. We *are* only friends, just like you and I."

"Oh no, you are not my friend, Sukie McClaren. That has been made very clear tonight. You're a back-stabbing, lying cow and, if I never see you again, it will be too soon. You have betrayed me, and our friendship, with what you have done."

369

"Elsa " but, before Sukie could continue, Elsa came flying towards her and slapped her hard across the face. "I HATE YOU, I HATE YOU!" she screamed hysterically.

For a few brief seconds, Sukie was slightly stunned from the blow. Then... she slapped Elsa back, just as hard.

Elsa drew up short. Sukie's slap had been every bit as effective as a bucket of cold water being thrown over her. She stood still, breathing heavily. Sukie took a firm but gentle hold of her wrists, and backed her up until the calves of her legs were against the end of the bed. With a small push, Sukie sat her down.

Still holding Elsa's wrists, Sukie spoke to her sharply. "Stop it! Just stop it right now. How *dare* you accuse me of betraying you! If, after thirty plus years of friendship, you think so little of me, then you are not my friend." As she spoke, Sukie could feel her own anger rising. In fact, *she* was now absolutely livid. All the times she'd sat with Elsa, comforting her after Harry had died, came rushing back and, before she could stop herself, her own anger came spilling out.

"Elsa, you are nothing but an ungrateful little brat. How many nights did I sit with you, holding you in my arms as you cried rivers of pain and sadness? Did it ever cross your mind that I was missing Harry just as much? He was also my friend for twenty years but no one ever asked me how I was coping with the loss. I loved him too you know but people always forget about the friends. It seems they're not allowed to grieve. No, only families are allowed to do that. But because you needed me so much, I

370

had to deal with it alone. Did I ever once refuse when you said you needed me with you? No, I didn't. I was there for you, every-single-time! I held your hand, I dried your tears. I cleaned up after you on those nights when you decided it was easier to get stinking drunk and then vomit everywhere. Did I ever reproach you? Did I ever tell you to 'get over it and move on'? No, I fucking didn't, And do you know why? Because you are the most, dearest, friend I have. I would have walked to the ends of the earth and back again if it could have taken away your pain. When you started having your fantasies about Pete, I didn't worry about it like other people did. I was glad that you seemed to have moved to a point where you could think of another man like that, regardless of who he was. And you have got NO idea how much I wanted to tell you everything about Salzburg but I was so scared of upsetting you that I kept quiet. The only thing I am guilty of is quite simply, not knowing the best damn thing to do. For you!"

Sukie let go of Elsa's wrists and walked away to gaze out of the window.

"Sukie—"

"No, Elsa, you've had your say, now it's my turn. I like Pete." She turned away from the lights outside and looked at Elsa. "He's my friend. I worry about him in the same way I worry about you. I give him the same level of loyalty I give you. But I can ASSURE you that we are not, and never will be, anything more than friends. We're not a couple and we have NEVER laughed at you. He's been really looking forward to meeting you and do you know why? Because I talk about you! A lot! When I share childhood stories, you're always there in them. Yes, he does know about Harry and, I'm sorry to say, he's knows about your crush on him. I had to tell him because he couldn't understand why I was becoming agitated about breaking the news to you."

She walked back over to the bed, where Elsa was still sitting, knelt down in front of her and looked into her eyes "I repeat... We have *never* laughed at you, and I never would. You also know I would kill anyone who did. I love you, Elsa Clairmont. You ARE my BFF. My Best Friend Forever."

Elsa looked down at Sukie kneeling in front of her. All the fight and anger had drained out of her when Sukie had slapped her. They never fought or fell out. She couldn't believe she'd hit Sukie like that. "Oh, Sukie," she said, as her eyes welled up with tears. "I still miss him. Every. Single. Day. The pain feels as though my heart is being dug out of me." By now, the tears were pouring down Elsa's face. "I put on a brave face because, after all this time, it's what people expect but, the truth is, I really don't think I'm any better now than I was when he left me. I'm so sorry I hit you. I know you would never do the things I accused you of but, for the last few months, I have felt all this anger building and building inside me. I'm afraid you got the full brunt of it tonight. I am so sorry. I really, really am."

Sukie pulled Elsa into her arms and, once again, held her as she sobbed over the loss of her husband. All this time she'd led everyone to believe she was coping and moving on when, the truth was, she was still where she'd always been – still grieving and still trying to deal with the pain of his death.

Sukie swallowed hard as she, herself, tried not to cry from the sadness of knowing there was nothing she could do for Elsa except be there for her. As she always had been and always would be.

Pete was standing at the bar with Jordie when Sukie and Elsa walked in. Sukie, seeing him there, gave him a wave and they made their way over.

"Hey there, really glad you came down." He smiled at them both. Up close he could see Elsa had been crying but she returned his smile.

"Hello again," she replied shyly. "Can I just say how very sorry I am for my behaviour earlier this evening, it was inexcusable. I was very rude, please accept my apologies."

Pete put a hand gently on her arm. "Elsa, there's absolutely nothing to apologise for. Please don't think there is. Everything's good and I'm delighted you've decided to join us for a drink. What can I get you?"

"I'll have the same as Sukie please."

As he was placing the order, Elsa noticed he hadn't asked Sukie what she wanted to drink. Interesting, she thought to herself. Before she could dwell on this any further, Sukie grabbed the arm of a short, stocky man walking past.

"Elsa, let me introduce you to Jordie, Pete's manager. Shall I tell Elsa about our first encounter Jordie or shall I leave that for another time?" She gave him a nudge and wink.

"I think we can leave that one in the bank for today," he answered gruffly. "No need to bore the lass."

"Oh, I won't be bored, please tell me."

"Let's just say Jordie's looking a lot smarter tonight than he did the first time we met." With a pointed look at his suit, Sukie continued. "I think it would be fair to assume you didn't pick that up in a charity shop?" She'd also noticed his recent haircut and clean-shaven appearance. "In fact, Jordie, without a word of a lie, you scrub up rather well. Who are you trying to impress?"

"Such a cheeky brat! Your mother would be so ashamed."

Sukie laughed as she replied, "No she wouldn't, and you know that fine well. So why are you dressed so smartly?"

"Because I'm working, that's why. Now come, I'll introduce you to some of the band. Your smart gob should keep them busy for a time, they like a challenge." He placed a hand on the small of her back and gently guided her to the other side of the room.

Pete watched them for a moment and then looked at Elsa. "Is your drink okay?"

"It's perfect, thank you." She took a long sip of her spritzer to prove her point.

He cleared his throat. "Look, Elsa, please don't blame Sukie for earlier, and not telling you, it really was all down to me—"

"Pete, I know the full story," she interrupted him. "Sukie told me everything, including how you offered to take the blame for her not telling me sooner. It was very kind of you to step up like that to help her out."

"She's been a good friend, even though we've only known each other a short time, and I was trying to be a good friend back. She's very loyal to you, you know."

Elsa nodded. "She's very loyal to all those who are close to her but, a word of advice, don't piss her off because then she can be bloody vile. I've seen it happen and it ain't pretty. No siree!"

"Oh, I know that. The first time I saw her she was putting some bloke back in his box. He was being a bit of an idiot though so he deserved all that he got. It was quite something to watch." Pete smiled as he recalled the first time he'd set eyes on Sukie and he looked around until his eyes came to rest upon her again.

"Sukie has also assured me that you are both just friends and nothing more. I'm very sorry for getting that so wrong."

"Yes, she's right, we're just friends." Pete quickly glanced down at Elsa as he spoke but his eyes were soon dragged back to Sukie, laughing with his band.

Elsa followed his gaze and saw Sukie was right in his line of vision. She looked back at him and caught the brief softening of his face. Oh yes, she thought. Just friends, are we? My ass you are!

It was very clear that Pete was in love with Sukie – he couldn't stop watching her. She looked over at Sukie and could see her friend was oblivious to Pete's feelings as she happily flirted with the boys in his band. Elsa cast her mind back to when they'd greeted each other in Pete's dressing room after the gig. The more she thought about their interaction together, and the ease of their bantering, the more she became convinced that Pete's affection was not one-sided. It was simply that her dear friend hadn't yet come to realise she was also in love with Pete.

She leant back against the bar and took another long sip of her drink. A small smile played on her lips for she knew life was going to be rather interesting over the next few months.

Now it was her turn to keep a secret.

Chapter Forty-Seven

<u>*May*</u>

"Well done, Eduardo, this has got to be one of the highest scores any of our employees has ever achieved. You must have been putting in plenty of practice." Fabio passed Eduardo his certificate from his recent fire-arms accuracy test.

Eduardo glanced down and saw he'd achieved 98.5% accuracy. He looked at Fabio and smiled. "Well, if I'm hoping for a promotion after the summer, then I need to ensure there are no reasons for it to be declined. I thought a good score on this would stand me in good stead."

He *had* been putting in a lot of hours on the gun range but not for the reason he'd just given Fabio, although it was certainly an added bonus. No, he'd been doing it solely as an excuse to acquire the extra ammunition he needed for the practice he'd been doing in his warehouse. He'd spent quite a few hours there too, as the broken, shattered, mannequins would attest to.

Fabio put a hand across the desk to give Eduardo's a congratulatory shake. "From what I have seen so far, you appear to have the organisation for the Wallace concert well under control. I reviewed the file the other day and liked what I saw. I would say promotion is definitely on the cards."

"Thank you, Fabio." After returning the handshake, Eduardo left his manager's office and returned to his own. He shoved the certificate carelessly into his desk drawer, logged off his computer and closed it down. He had the weekend off and he planned to share some of it with Sofia and his mamma. He felt he'd neglected them recently with the amount of hours he'd been spending on improving his shooting skills. A day out to Lake Garda had been promised for tomorrow. Sofia had always enjoyed the boat trips on the lake and he felt she deserved a treat for all the effort she had been putting into her physiotherapy.

He started up the car, pulled out of the parking lot and headed home, still thinking of Sofia. She'd been home from the hospital for a few weeks now as her last operation appeared to have been successful. There had been two previous failures but a newly developed technique looked as though it was the breakthrough they'd been hoping for. If this particular method of bone grafting worked, then there was a good chance the next two operations could, if successful, see Sofia fully mobile with only a walking stick to help her balance. There was even hope that she'd be able to do away with that in time. After all the pain and struggle, it was a pleasant relief to know there was, potentially, some light at the end of the tunnel.

This progress, however, had not reduced his desire to exact revenge on Pete Wallace. Oh no! The need to eradicate that manipulative Lothario from society continued to be as strong as it always was. He could not allow another young girl to suffer as his little Sofia had suffered. And now that Wallace was back out touring once more, the chances of it happening again had increased. His anger was further flamed by Sofia's insistence that she was going to his gig at the Stadio next month. He'd told her, in no uncertain terms, she would not be attending but Sofia was adamant and, as she was now eighteen and, therefore, technically an adult, he was hard pressed to find a way of preventing it. He'd pointed out that she had to avoid crowds and wouldn't be able to stand. She'd just laughed and said, "I'll be in my wheelchair. For once, the damn thing will actually be useful. And I'll get a much better view from the disabled bay."

Sofia's determination to be more independent was another thing he blamed Pete Wallace for. If she hadn't spent so much time in hospital, away from his brotherly guidance, she'd be a far better behaved young lady and would be doing what she was told. How could he possibly look after her if she refused to accept that he knew best? After all, look at what had happened the last time she'd disobeyed him.

He soon arrived home and drove the car into the

garage. He switched off the engine and sat there for a few minutes, thinking. He had to come up with a means of preventing Sofia from attending that gig. If the worst came to the worst, he'd lock her in her bedroom if he had to. She would not disobey him this time.

Chapter Forty-Eight

June

"Ah, Sukie, c'mon… You know you'd love it. And it's about time you had a holiday. When was the last time you took a proper break, huh?" Pete was trying to talk Sukie into joining him in Italy when he arrived there in three weeks. "We'll be in Rome Saturday through to Monday and then driving up to Verona on the Tuesday. We're staying there until Sunday. The gig is on Saturday night so there'll be plenty of time for some sightseeing. We could even go to Venice for the day…" He'd remembered a conversation where she'd mentioned how much she wanted to visit Venice and so had used it as his trump card.

"Oh, Pete, I don't know…" She sighed heavily. "Leave it with me. I'd love to join you. I just need to see what I can do about taking the time off."

Pete bit his tongue as he refrained from lecturing her about looking after herself. He didn't think it would go down too well but he was concerned at the hours Sukie had been putting in over the last few months. Too many of their conversations were happening when she was at the office. On the few occasions he'd spoken to her at her flat, the chances were she'd taken work home with her and was still hard at it.

"Please try, Sukie. You need the break. You're exhausted."

"I will. I promise. You had me with Venice. I'm not going to miss that opportunity if I can help it. Catch you later."

Sukie ended their call and looked back at the spreadsheet on her computer screen but she wasn't seeing it. Instead, her head was filled with all the pictures of Venice she'd seen in books and movies. After Salzburg, it had always been the place she'd most wanted to visit. She sighed again as she picked up her mouse and tried to focus on her work. She *had* been working non-stop and, the truth was, she really could do with a vacation. There just never seemed to be a good time to have one. As fast as she got one project cleared, another landed on her desk and always seemed to require the same immediate action.

"Blimey, that was a sigh and a half, Sukes. What's up?" Elsa came through the door and placed another pile of files on Sukie's desk.

Sukie looked at them in dismay. "What are those?"

"These are the files for Ellis Houghton Ltd. William needs them reviewed and re-checked as their five-year contract is coming up for renewal next month. He says he needs them back as soon as possible."

"Oh, would that be the same 'as soon as possible' he applied to the Haslett files, the Walter Bearings files and the Samson Jones files?" She glared at Elsa. "Exactly how, and when, does he expect me to do all this? I'm already putting in about sixty hours a week. I'm shattered!" With her elbows on the desk and her head in her hands, she stared down at her keyboard.

Elsa sat on the chair opposite. "I'm sorry, Sukie. I know it's a lot. We're so busy right now and, with the expansion into the USA going live in six weeks, everyone is snowed under."

Sukie sat up and came to a decision. Pete was right – she did need a proper holiday before she had a breakdown. Two mid-week days off, for his gig in Birmingham, could not be considered a holiday. She rummaged in her desk, pulled out a holiday request form and filled it in for the week Pete would be in Italy. She was going to see Venice and God help anyone who said no.

As she checked the dates, Sukie told Elsa about the conversation she'd had with Pete. "And I've decided… I'm going." She signed her holiday form with a defiant flourish.

"Good luck with getting that signed off. I don't think William is going to go for it. I know he's already refused a few of the other managers who've asked for leave recently."

"Oh, he'll be signing it, Elsa. You can be assured of that." With her words hanging in the air, Sukie marched out of her office.

William looked at the form in front of him and sighed. "Sukie, I can't agree to these dates. You know how hectic it is right now. You're needed here." He looked up at her. "I'm sorry."

Sukie, standing on the other side of his desk, glared back at him. "William, did you have a nice two-week break in France with your family at Easter?"

"Err… Yes, I did, thank you. Why?"

"Because, when you were relaxing and quaffing the local vino, I was here in the office working… sorting out all the paperwork for Hamilton & Clarke Ltd. The only day I didn't work was Easter Sunday and that was because I was spending it with my mum."

"I get that you've had to do some extra hours and they are appreciated—"

She leant forward, placed her hands on the desk, and interrupted him. "No, William, you *don't* get it! 'Some extra hours' – are you having a laugh? You got to enjoy the two bank holidays in May plus chilling out in Cornwall over the half-term. I didn't! I was, unsurprisingly, buried beneath a pile of files that were, yet again, "very urgent"." She flicked the quotation marks in the air, a mere inch away from his face. "Everything that comes across my desk is 'urgent' and I'm expected to turn it all around within a few days. Well, I have had enough. I want a holiday. I NEED a holiday and I am going to have that one," she pointed to the form in front of him, "before I end up having a breakdown from exhaustion."

William looked up at Sukie. He saw the dark circles under her eyes and the tiredness on her face. He hadn't stopped to think about the hours she'd been doing, he'd just taken it for granted that she was coping with the extra workload. It hadn't occurred to him either that she hadn't taken any holiday in six months. He picked up his pen, authorised her request and handed it back to her.

"Just make sure all the files are cleared before you finish."

"No, William, I will do as much as I can before I finish but that's all. I'm not putting that pressure on myself. Furthermore, when I return, we're going to talk about bringing in an assistant because I'm not prepared to carry on working as I have done up till now."

She left his office with her head held high and a weight off her shoulders. As soon as she got back to her desk, she was going online to order a few travel books on Venice.

A few days later, Sukie was having dinner with her mum. She'd barely seen her since January.

"I'm really sorry I've neglected you, Mum, I didn't realise just how much I was letting it all get to me. I guess I was trying to prove I was up to the job and show I deserved my promotion. I didn't realise that the more I proved how good I was, the more work would be piled upon me. I plan to make up for it though, I promise."

Beth leaned over the table and patted her daughter's hand. "It's fine, love, honestly. I do understand. I'm just glad you've realised and sorted it out. I was more worried about you overdoing it than me being neglected."

What she didn't say was that, by being so busy and focused elsewhere, Sukie had made it easier for her and Jordie to meet up and spend time together. She usually shared all the details of her various outings and activities with Sukie and, had Sukie not been so absent of late, she'd have had to either lie – which she *really* wouldn't have liked – or be evasive in her comments which would surely have made Sukie suspicious. She and Jordie hadn't yet shared the news of their relationship with the outside world.

"So, what are your plans? And what's happening with the boys?"

Sukie leaned forward, excitement on her face. "Well, I've booked the whole week off. Elsa has said she'll house-sit for me – the lure of my garden in the summer I think – and she'll come over on Sunday. I'm going to drive down to Surrey to see Kym on the Monday and stay with her until Wednesday. She's said I can leave my car at her place and she'll take me to the airport. She's also going to pick me up again on Sunday. That'll save me a packet on car-park fees."

"How is Kym doing? Is she coping ok?"

Sukie thought of her friend and smiled. They'd met when Sukie had worked in London for a few years and had become instant friends. Her busy life meant they didn't get to meet up as often as they would like – two young children and a third on the way kept her on her toes – but, when they did get together, they had the best of times. "She's doing well," Sukie replied. "Although, I think she's getting the pregnancy blues. Her words, when

I asked, were 'I feel like a beached whale that has swallowed a beach ball!'"

Beth smiled. "I can remember that feeling. I'm sure she'll enjoy seeing you though. You can take her mind off things for a while."

"I'll do my best. But anyway, getting back to Italy, I was wondering if you fancied coming along? I can make up some of the time I've missed with you over the last few months."

Beth almost dropped the serving dish she was carrying. Thankfully, her back was to Sukie so her slip went unnoticed. "I can't, darling," she replied. "Annie in the office has already booked that time off."

"Oh! That's a pity. I'm sure you'd have enjoyed it."

She stood at the kitchen sink and took her time washing the dish she'd managed to get there in one piece. What Sukie didn't know was that Jordie had already asked her to join him in Italy and she'd been giving his suggestion some serious consideration. It was now a moot point as she'd have to decline. While they'd been chatting, she'd realised she still wasn't ready to tell Sukie her secret. Maybe, when she'd returned from Italy, she'd feel the time was right.

Chapter Forty-Nine

Jordie and Pete walked down the quiet corridor, their footsteps echoing on the tiled floor as they looked for Sofia's private room. They should have been visiting her at home but Kara had received a tearful phone call from Rosa, Sofia's mother, the night before, informing her that Sofia had had a fall at home and was back in the hospital.

"I hate these places," said Pete.

"Can't say I'm a fan of them myself," was Jordie's caustic reply. "Ah, here we are."

He knocked on the door and walked in when they heard Sofia call out.

"Hey, you, what's all this? Are you still trying to get a job as a pyjama model huh?" Pete had a big smile on his face as he walked over to the bed and leaned down to give Sofia a hug. Jordie did the same as Pete walked around the bed to greet Rosa. After she'd kissed him on both cheeks and told him he still needed a good meal inside him, he pulled over a chair for Jordie while he sat on the bed beside Sofia.

"I hear you had a fall, what happened?" Pete's concern was genuine. He liked Sofia a lot and was always upset whenever he got news of setbacks in her recovery.

"Oh, it was one of those stupid fluke accidents, not even my fault. Eduardo slipped on the kitchen floor and bumped into me. I was doing my physio exercises, using the kitchen worktop as a barre. My crutches had been placed out of the way so I had no means of keeping my balance when he hit me. I went down and thumped my hip on the floor when I landed."

Rosa let out a snort which she quickly covered up as a cough. "Let me go and get you both a coffee," she said, standing up. "I need some water. These rooms get so stuffy. Sometimes it's difficult to breathe."

She picked up her bag and walked out of the room.

Rosa made her way along the corridor, in the direction of the café, her mind was once again replaying the events of the night before. She'd been walking into the kitchen just as Sofia had fallen and she knew she'd seen a smile on Eduardo's face when Sofia had let out her cry of pain. As she rushed to help her daughter, she'd asked what had happened. Eduardo said he'd slipped on some water on the floor yet, when she'd looked afterwards, the floor was completely dry. She was still unsure if her son had purposely hurt his sister but she knew he was quite adamant Sofia was not going to Pete's concert on Saturday. Would he really go to such lengths to prevent it? He knew how fragile Sofia was and that it wouldn't take much to set her recovery back.

Rosa stood in the queue to be served and forced herself to look at Eduardo's behaviour and moods over the last five or six months, as she waited.

Since Christmas, he'd grown more aggressive and his constant bad temper had gotten worse. She'd had to buy several new coffee mugs and dinner plates because he kept breaking them. He spent hardly any time at home – often coming in just long enough to sleep, wash and eat, before heading back out again. Whenever she asked him where he was going, he'd shout it was none of her business and go into vicious rants in which he called her and Sofia all sorts of horrible names. This would frequently end with him throwing whatever came to hand at the nearest wall before storming out, slamming the door and leaving two very scared women behind him.

Rosa paid the cashier, put the bottle of water in her bag with one hand while placing the coffees in a cup holder tray with the other, and walked slowly back to Sofia's room, trying to work out what she should do. Eduardo hadn't actually hit her or Sofia, although she was now worried that last night could be the start of that happening. She had no one she could talk to – Eduardo's nasty temper and tantrums over the years had made it difficult for her to keep any friends. She couldn't report him to any authorities because she had no proof. Right now, she felt very isolated, very alone and more than just a little bit scared.

When she arrived back at Sofia's room, she opened the door and walked in to the sound of laughter and merriment. She couldn't help but smile at the happiness she saw on Sofia's face.

Sofia saw her standing in the doorway and called over, "Mamma, good news. Nothing broke when I fell. Everything is okay."

She rushed over the bed, put the coffees on the bedside table, leaned in and hugged her daughter tightly, delighted to hear this news.

"I do have a great big bruise," Sofia continued, "and they want me to stay in for two days for observation, but Dr Manto has promised me I can leave on Friday morning." She turned to Pete, "I'll be able to go to your concert after all."

"Sofia, I wouldn't have let you miss it. You'd have been there, one way or another," Pete said. The doctor had explained to them how happy he was with this news himself. The new form of surgery had clearly worked and it gave them hope that, with the other couple of operations they had scheduled, Sofia stood a very good chance of being able to finally walk unaided.

As Sofia passed on this news to Rosa, her relief was overwhelming. At last, they had hope and seeing her daughter walking properly again was all that she'd wished for since the accident had occurred. At the back of her mind, however, she couldn't shake the thought of how Eduardo would take the news. He would not be happy his plan had backfired and that Sofia still had every intention of going out on Saturday night. Maybe, when Pete and Jordie had left, she'd suggest to Sofia that they kept the news to themselves for the next few days. She was not prepared to take the risk of Eduardo coming up with something more dangerous to ensure Sofia stayed at home over the weekend.

Chapter Fifty

Sukie was getting out of the cab when Kara came rushing out of the hotel. "I'm so sorry I wasn't able to meet you at the airport. Some issues came up with the next venue and I simply couldn't get away." She pulled Sukie into a big hug as she spoke.

"Don't worry about it," Sukie replied. "It amused me to hear all about the Pete Wallace concert on Saturday and how all the local girls are getting so excited. I forget just how much of a phenomenon he is."

"Sometimes I wish I could," said Kara wryly. "The requests we get – for radio interviews, television interviews, charity visits, to name just a few – are off the scale. And making sure he does the ones which give maximum publicity, with minimal effort, is a minefield."

"How does he manage it, Kara? All those questions, the photographs, his personal life being picked to pieces by all and sundry – how does he cope and stay sane? I couldn't do it. It was bad enough having my photograph in the company magazine when I was promoted, the thought of my face being plastered all over the media would send me into a meltdown." She shuddered at the thought.

Kara picked up one of Sukie's bags and they walked towards the hotel foyer.

"He hates it, we all do, but it's a necessary evil and part of the business. When Pete renewed his contract with his record label, part of the deal was that we took full control of all press interviews and media-related issues. As such, we've managed to control it better on this tour and we've been more selective. Making Pete more exclusive has worked in our favour."

They walked into the reception area and Kara put down Sukie's bag. "Let me just get your room key. Wait here."

They'd both been so busy talking that Sukie hadn't paid much attention to her surroundings. As she looked around her now, she delighted in the traditional décor the hotel had maintained. When she'd looked it up on the internet, she'd read that the building dated back to the 1600's and the current owners had carefully restored it to its former glory eight years ago. Taking in the beautiful gilding, the Renaissance paintings and stunning marble floor and pillars, she'd say they'd done a fantastic job.

Kara saw her admiring it when she walked back over. "It's breath-taking, wouldn't you say? I love how it looks so grandiose and yet maintains a homely, cosy feeling," she said, handing over Sukie's key. "You're in the suite across from Pete's on the top floor."

"I've got a suite? Oh, that's too much, an ordinary room would do," she protested. She wasn't used to such luxury and wasn't sure she was comfortable with it.

Kara smiled. "If you weren't in that room, it would be empty. There are only two suites on that floor and Pete's in the other one. There's no way we'd put the band or the crew in there — they'd expect such luxury all the time and that's never going to happen!"

"But, what about you? Or Jordie? Surely it would be better for one of you to have it?"

"I'm afraid not," Kara replied. "I'm in and out so much I need to be on the first floor and Jordie likes to stay near the crew to make sure they don't get into too much mischief. Anything untoward reflects on Pete so Jordie keeps a tight rein on them. Stop beating yourself up and enjoy it. Pete's told me how hard you've been working this year so just relax and soak it up."

She turned and pointed to the concierge. "The porter is waiting to take your luggage upstairs. Enjoy a soak in the Jacuzzi to get over the journey. Pete's organised for the four of us to eat in his suite this evening but please feel free to order anything from room service if you're hungry. I need to go now but I'll see you later." And, with another hug, Kara rushed away down the corridor, leaving Sukie to make her way across to the porter who stood smiling behind his desk.

Sukie groaned when her alarm went off. 6.30 a.m. had seemed okay last night, when Pete had informed her the coach to Venice was leaving at 7.30 a.m. That, however, was before they'd polished off three bottles of wine between the four of them over dinner. It now felt like a really bad idea!

She sat up and groped around the panel of switches at the side of the bed. She pushed the one for the curtains and they slowly opened, letting in the glorious sunshine from outside. If she had to be awake at this ungodly hour, she was at least going to enjoy the weather with it. She threw back the bed clothes, got up and shuffled towards the bathroom. A good ten minutes under the power shower would soon have her back on track.

Forty-five minutes later, she walked into the reception area and saw Pete, with Kara and Jordie, standing by the door. He waved her over to join them.

"Good morning. You're looking fine and fresh today." He glanced down admiringly at her pale blue capri pants, loose-fitting white cotton shirt, and lightweight walking sandals. She had a matching blue cardigan thrown over her shoulders. Her still-damp, chestnut waves were tied up in a high ponytail. With her usual minimal sweep of make-up, Sukie looked like she'd stepped out of a 1950's poster advertising the merits of clean living. Pete had to exercise every tiny bit of willpower he had to prevent himself from gathering her up in his arms and going back up to his suite where he could have her all to himself.

"Looks are deceiving. I am shattered really," she muttered back, "but I am grateful for the compliment." She looked him up and down and took in his own casual attire – he was sporting a pair of quite natty, loose-fitting, knee-length shorts and an untucked, pale denim shirt, with a pair of sunglasses hooked into the front. A pair of denim espadrilles on his feet finished off his dressed-down look. "You're not looking too shoddy yourself, if we're exchanging compliments. No disguise today?"

Pete unfurled the baseball cap in his hand and showed it to Sukie. Sewn on the inside was the same false red hair he'd sported in Austria. She smiled as she looked back up at him. "What about the contact lenses?"

He flicked the sunglasses on his shirt. "I'll have these on for most of the day so I should be okay."

Kara turned around just then, "Right guys, time to get on the coach if we want to get ahead of the traffic."

As they walked out of the reception, Sukie asked Pete, "Do I still need to call you Karl?"

"Probably best if you do," he replied, "just in case anyone is astute enough to make the connection."

"I never thought to ask, are you okay with being on boats and on water?" Pete looked at Sukie with concern. They were waiting for their pre-booked water taxis to transport them from the Venetian coach park to Saint Mark's Square.

From behind her sunglasses, Sukie saw his concern for her and was touched by it. He was always so considerate towards her welfare. She assured him he had nothing to worry about just as their taxis arrived. She pulled her cardigan around her a bit more tightly – the breeze off the water still carried the morning chill – and stepped into the boat, making her way inside the little cabin area where it was more sheltered. Pete followed behind and sat beside her. He took the baseball cap off and ran his fingers through his hair. His fringe flopped forward over his forehead in his usual style.

"I hope you have your camera with you," he said, "I hear the view of the Basilica and the Campanile from the water is quite stunning."

"You bet I have!" She dug it out of her bag and waved it in front of him. "I even have an extra memory card for good measure."

Pete grabbed the camera from her hand, "Selfie time!"

"No! Give that back, you monster. You know I hate photographs." She tried to retrieve the camera but Pete's extra height meant she couldn't reach even though they were both sitting down.

Pete handed the camera over to Kara who'd sat down opposite them. "You can have it back as soon as Kara takes our photograph. I don't have any of you and it would do me good to remember how ugly you are. It's always such a shock when I see you again." He laughed at the indignation on her face. He wasn't about to tell her he still had the photograph she'd sent him the night she'd gone to dinner with Jenny. He also, most definitely, wasn't going to tell her that he looked and stared at it several times each day.

"Whereas I'm never lucky enough to forget how dodgy you look as your face is plastered almost everywhere I go these days," retorted Sukie.

Kara quickly took a few shots, while they bantered and they were unaware of her doing so. "When you two have quite finished insulting each other, I'll take this piccie…"

Pete pulled Sukie so tightly to his side she was almost sitting on his lap. He wrapped one arm across the front of her shoulders, just below her neckline, and the other around her waist, enclosing her in a warm embrace. His head was pressed against the side of hers and he could smell a hint of citrus and watermelon from the scent that she wore. Everything about her was always so fresh and clean and it turned him on far more than any of the heavy, musky scents so many women chose to wear, thinking it made them sexy.

"C'mon, Sukie! Smile! You look like you're one step away from the guillotine!" Kara glanced over the top of the camera as she spoke.

Pete whispered in Sukie's ear, "I do love your perfume. I never knew the smell of horse dung could be bottled so well."

Sukie burst out laughing at his words and Kara clicked the camera.

Kara knew she'd just taken a very special picture. She'd had an inkling for a while now that Pete had finally realised he'd fallen in love with Sukie, but had said nothing. It was better to let these things come out in their own good time. She knew her suspicions had been correct, when she saw them together like this. She was pleased for Pete as he'd been on his own for far too long and it was clear that Sukie was the perfect person for him.

The problem was, she couldn't work out if Sukie felt the same way. Kara hoped that she did because, as couples went, these two really did belong together.

"Get in there, you stupid thing!" Sukie was trying to change the memory card in her camera and was cursing at how fiddly it was. "There, sorted!" She smiled as it clicked into place and she closed it up.

They'd stopped for lunch after pounding the walkways and alleyways around Venice for most of the morning. When she saw how quickly the Piazza San Marco had filled with other tourists, she was glad they'd arrived so early. It meant they could explore the rest of the city away from the bustle as it appeared everyone was descending on the island of San Marco. Once they'd crossed over the beautiful Rialto Bridge, the atmosphere had immediately changed to one far more peaceful. Sukie had soaked it up lovingly. Thus far, Venice had lived up to all the hype and she'd taken so many photographs as she tried to capture the essence of the areas that were less publicised but felt more real.

While they'd been walking through the maze of small alleys and tiny streets that made Venice so unique, the smell of hot tomato sauce and herbs had suddenly assaulted their noses. They'd strolled around a corner and came across a little trattoria serving up large bowls of delicious looking pasta in a wisteria covered courtyard. They'd both decided they were famished and should stop for some lunch. A small, plump woman had come over and, with a wide smile, welcomed them to sit and relax and she would feed them her special pasta for the day.

Sukie had been glad to rest her feet and have a breather. The downside of being here for only a day meant they were trying to cram in as much as they could. She couldn't help but hope that one day there would be the opportunity to return for a longer visit and she could do her sightseeing at a more leisurely pace.

When it had arrived, the pasta was every bit as tasty as it had looked and the large glass of red wine had gone down very nicely. Now they were just relaxing in the peaceful atmosphere, sipping coffee, before moving on and eventually making their way back to San Marco and the arranged meeting place.

She picked up her phone, quickly clicked a picture of Pete, framed by the wisteria above him and sent it to Elsa, writing above it:

I thought Venice was supposed to be beautiful?
Well, not from where I'm sitting! Lol.
S xx

She showed it to Pete before hitting the 'send' button, laughing as she did so.

"Always such a cheeky baggage," he smiled across at her. "You know, it wouldn't hurt for you to say something nice to me once in a while. Not all the time, maybe just once a month or so."

"What? And have you getting big-headed? Not a chance! I'm your friend and, as such, it is my job to keep you grounded and prevent your head from swelling so large, it could be viewed from the moon. There are plenty of groupies to boost your ego if that's what you need." She made sure she gave him a big grin to take the sting out of her words.

The truth was that, as time had passed and their friendship had deepened, she'd found Pete becoming more attractive and likeable. He was an exceptionally kind and caring person, very considerate to those he cared for and highly intelligent. He was witty and incredibly self-effacing. If she'd met a normal bloke with all these traits, she'd have found herself hankering for a date with him and probably hoping for something more. Unfortunately, Pete was as far removed from being a 'normal bloke' as it was possible to be and that put any chance of their friendship becoming anything more completely off the table.

In a sad twist of fate, having finally found a man who possessed everything she wanted, he turned out to be the one man she wasn't able to have.

She pushed her thoughts to one side, stood up to gather her belongings together and looked down at Pete. "Well, c'mon on then, let's get a move on. You need to work off all that pasta otherwise your fans will need cameras with wide-angle lenses!"

Pete burst out laughing and stood up, smiling his thanks to the little Italian lady as he followed Sukie out of the courtyard. Her comments had been no less than he'd expected. She never sugar-coated anything and he loved her all more for it.

Chapter Fifty-One

Eduardo di Santo stood in the middle of the Stadio and watched Pete Wallace go through his sound check, up on the stage. It was Friday morning. In thirty-six hours, Pete Wallace would be dead and he would finally be rid of this black heavy weight which had been upon him since Sofia's accident. He'd let her down then, but tomorrow night, he could hold his head up again, safe in the knowledge that Sofia and other impressionable young girls like her, had been saved from the evil influence of this man. He knew this deep-rooted anger inside him stemmed from his inadequacy to keep Sofia safe from harm. Retribution was the only way to bring closure. Once Pete Wallace was dead, he'd be able to move on with his life.

Not once did the consequences of his actions cross his mind. He'd given no thought as to what would happen to his family after he followed through on his plan. His focus was solely on destroying the man who'd destroyed his sister. Eduardo believed he would be a hero. He'd be recognised as the man who'd saved many families from the pain and upset both he and his mamma had gone through with Sofia.

He made a pen mark on the paperwork he had attached to his clipboard. To anyone looking on, it would appear as though he was taking notes for his security detail the following night. In actual fact, he'd made a long list of the various moves Pete had incorporated into his stage performance over the years and he was ticking each one off as Pete went through his rehearsal. He needed to be absolutely sure Pete was maintaining the same routines as those he'd watched for hours on the internet. His plan depended on it. Although, being the perfectionist that he was, he'd also put in place a plan B *and* a plan C – just in case – but neither of them would be quite as effective as his plan A.

He stood and watched as Pete walked over to the large Marshall stacks on either side of the stage. When Eduardo had arrived at the stadium a few hours earlier, the first thing on his agenda had been to check the stage set-up still matched that of the plans they'd been given. He'd been delighted to see they did. Everything was going well so far. He watched Pete and waited to see if he would climb up onto the speakers but, instead, Wallace called over some technicians and was talking to them while pointing up at the speaker tops.

He made his way towards the stage and waited for the technicians to finish talking to Pete. When they came down off the stage he approached them. "Excuse me, is there a problem with the speakers? You were having a big discussion on them."

One of the men stopped and looked at Eduardo. "What's it to you, mate?" he asked.

The aggressive tone got Eduardo's hackles up and he straightened himself up to his full height. "I am in charge of security and it is my place to know every last detail in this stadium. If there are problems with those speakers which could cause harm to anyone – such as them falling over into the crowd – I need to know about it."

"Ah, sorry, didn't mean to be rude." The technician smiled at him. "The speakers will be firmly battened down and totally secure. You have nothing to worry about."

"I saw you pointing up at the top of them. Is there a problem there?"

"No, everything is fine. Pete likes to climb onto them and we were just discussing the lighting requirements."

He feigned a look of shock on his face. "He climbs all the way up there?"

"Yeah, that's one of the highlights of the show. It really gets the crowd going. You'll see for yourself tomorrow night. The fans love it."

"Oh, okay then. Thank you for the information. I'll look out for that." He bid the technician goodbye and walked away, putting another tick on his list as he did so. Oh yes, he thought to himself, this really *was* all going to plan indeed.

Chapter Fifty-Two

"O Sukie, Sukie, wherefore art thou Sukie?"

Sukie heard Pete's voice calling as she stepped out onto the Juliet balcony. She looked down at him and replied, "I'm up here, ya daft plonker. And that's supposed to be my line!"

"Well, it was taking you so long to appear, I was getting bored."

"We're not the only tourists here you know, I had to wait my turn. Now get up here and see for yourself how amazing this house is."

She was feeling very relaxed and chilled out despite the density of the crowds on the streets of Verona. While Pete had been sound-checking that morning, she'd enjoyed the spa facilities at the hotel. The restorative powers of a Jacuzzi, the steam room and a good massage should not be underestimated. She felt great. The tension which had built up from so much work over the last few months had melted away as the knots in her shoulders and back had been worked out. By the time Pete had returned to the hotel, she'd been champing at the bit to get out and do more sightseeing.

Upon arriving in the city, they'd headed straight for the Casa di Giulietta as her guide books had advised it was one of the busiest tourist spots in the city. They'd not been joking either. When she and Pete had arrived, the Casa was absolutely heaving and they'd been discussing whether to wait to go in or move on. As luck would have it, however, a large coach party had come out as they'd been talking and they'd been able to get in pretty quickly. It had been Pete's idea to attempt the re-enactment of William Shakespeare's most famous love-scene. She should have known better than to trust him to be serious about it. She was still smiling to herself when he arrived at her side. He put an arm around her waist, took her camera from her hand, whipped his sunglasses off and whispered once again, "Selfie time."

"Oh, will you stop that! I've never had my photograph taken as often as I have in the last two days." Even as she admonished him, she smiled into the camera. She knew she was fighting a losing battle but she didn't want Pete to think he was getting his own way too easily.

Pete slipped his shades back on quickly before anyone recognised him and handed her back the camera. "Come on, let's move. I want to see the big stone arena thing we passed on our way here."

She rolled her eyes, knowing he was being deliberately obtuse. "It's an amphitheatre, you moron," she told his back, as she followed him down the stairs and out into the sunlight.

They walked back to the stunning Roman amphitheatre which had dominated their view as soon as they'd stepped out of the taxi. Pete held tightly onto her hand – his reasoning was they could easily lose each other in the crowds. She could see the sense in this and didn't argue. Also, if she was being *really* honest with herself, holding his hand felt quite nice but she didn't care to dwell on that right now.

A short time later, they were sitting on the pink limestone steps at the top of the structure, the warm afternoon sun beating down upon them. Sukie was filled with awe at the deep feeling of history surrounding her. Despite the venue now housing so many modern-day items to assist in the operatic performances put on most nights, when she closed her eyes and blocked out the sounds of the other tourists nearby, she could sense the majestic age of the stones seeping into her bones. She'd visited many old castles and stately homes in her life, although none as old as the arena, but she couldn't recall any ever having such an effect upon her. She drew in deep breaths of the balmy air and felt its warmth in her chest. How different, she thought, from the fresh, crisp air in Salzburg which was so cold it left icicles inside your lungs. When Pete tapped her arm and suggested they move on, she was in an almost trance-like state, her mind lost in the past as she imagined some of opera's best known historical stars performing here in centuries gone by. She blinked rapidly in the strong sunlight as she came back into the current century and stood up to leave. When they made their way towards the exit, she looked back, knowing that this structure had left a little piece of itself in her heart. She promised herself that she would return. Aware that she'd been dallying, she hurried to catch up with Pete, put her arm through his and pulled out a guide book to see where else they could visit before they had to return to the hotel.

Pete glanced at Sukie's face, took in her wide smile and saw she was absolutely glowing with happiness. He was glad this break was doing her so much good. He'd been shocked by how shattered she'd looked when she'd arrived on Wednesday. She was now back to being the girl he had fallen in love with – carefree and enjoying the new experiences surrounding her. He wished he could ask her to join him full-time on the tour, there were so many new places they could visit together, but he knew he couldn't. She relished her independence and would not give up her job or her flat to be kept by him. She'd told him how proud she was to have her career, and to have purchased her flat, all under her own steam. There was no way she would leave it all behind to follow him around the world, no matter how he presented it to her.

Nope, for now, he just had to try and deal with them remaining friends and doing most of their talking on Skype. The thought filled him with dismay and he had to quickly bite his lip to prevent the large sigh which had risen up inside him from escaping. His love for Sukie was his problem to deal with and he wasn't about to burden her with it. Although, how long he could carry on like this, was another issue altogether.

Jordie hit the 'end call' button and closed his computer. He lay back on his bed and tried to work his way through the emotions he was currently feeling. He'd just been talking to Beth on Skype and had finally told her of his decision to hang up his managerial boots at the end of this tour. She'd been both shocked and surprised in equal measure and had asked him if he was absolutely sure. He'd been quite emphatic in his reply that he couldn't be more sure and, seeing the pleasure his words had given her, written all over her face, had been enough to convince himself that his decision was the right one. He wanted to spend the rest of his life seeing that look on the face of this woman who he loved so intensely. He'd gone on to voice, quite thoroughly, his feelings for her and how he wanted to spend every minute in her company. He'd been on his own for far too many years. Now he had finally found the woman he loved, he didn't want to waste time being away from her.

As he reflected on the conversation, he realised he felt a bit dizzy and light-headed. He was finally doing something for himself and it felt good. For too many years he'd been at the beck and call of other people or shouldering their responsibilities. He loved Pete as though he was his own son, and he would always be there for him, but the time had come for Jordie to let go.

He thought about how he'd been beside Pete through the darkest time in his life. The loss of Katya and Andrew had been so hard for both of them, but they'd supported and helped each other through it and had come out the other side scarred but still alive and able to move on. Well, now he was going to move on big time. There was another six months left on this tour – although that felt more like six years right now – and that was it. He was going to marry Beth, buy a nice house in some quaint English village, and live a lovely quiet life. Okay, he had yet to run *that* bit past Beth but he was sure he could talk her round to the idea.

But, going back to Pete, he had grown up considerably in the last few years – coming off the drugs had finally allowed the man he was meant to be to come out. For a time, Jordie had worried that the loss of his parents would consume him to the point of killing himself but, in the end, it transpired Pete was made of stronger stuff. After years of floundering, he'd picked himself up and was living his life again. His friendship with Sukie had put the light back into him and everyone could see how she brought him alive. He'd also noticed the way Pete bloomed whenever she was around. Everyone could see the difference. Like Kara, however, he was unable to tell how Sukie felt about Pete. He'd discussed it with Beth but she didn't know either. The vibe Beth kept picking up from Sukie was that she genuinely only saw Pete as a friend and there was nothing to suggest Sukie had any kind of romantic notions towards him.

He was really hoping Sukie would fall in love with Pete as it would make it easier for him to break the news of his retirement. He knew this was a selfish desire but, with Sukie on the scene, he knew Pete would be in a better place to hear what he had to say.

Deciding he'd done enough thinking for one day, he got off the bed and walked towards the bathroom for a shower. He reminded himself, as he stopped to pour a quick whiskey on the way, that no matter how much you tried to plan the events in your life, all too often they will go awry. As Robert Burns wrote 'The best laid schemes o' mice an' men…'

He would do well to keep that in mind.

Chapter Fifty-Three

Sukie closed the door of her suite, stepped across the hallway and knocked on the door to Pete's, directly opposite. After all their walking today, she was rather hungry and looking forward to dinner.

Pete opened the door and stood back to let her in, admiring her outfit as she passed by. "That's a very nice dress. You look lovely."

"Dare I say 'what, this old thing?' even though that is exactly what it is," she replied with a smile. "I've had it for years and it remains one of my favourite outfits. Being linen, however, does mean its days out of the wardrobe are few and far between." She smoothed down the skirt of the vintage 1950's dress. The deep scarlet colour complemented her fresh complexion. It had a ruched, sleeveless bodice and the high waistband was smooth and fitted against her midriff which enhanced the fullness of the circular, ballerina skirt. A chunky midnight-blue necklace, which perfectly matched her blue kitten-heels, completed the outfit. She'd let her hair dry in its natural, soft, wavy style and had simply pulled the sides up with some clips.

"I'm glad I chose to wear my dressier looking chinos rather than my jeans." Pete's white cotton shirt was tucked in, but with his collar open and the sleeves rolled up, he was certainly more casual than smart.

Sukie wandered into the lounge area. "No Jordie or Kara?" she questioned, as she looked around.

"No, not tonight, we're all alone." Pete pulled a lecherous face which made her laugh. "Kara has gone to meet Gareth from the airport and Jordie fancied a quiet night on his own. Drink?" He held up the bottle of Prosecco which he'd had room service deliver earlier.

"Oh, that would be nice. Thank you. Some bubbles are the perfect end to this perfect day. So, Kara's Gareth is in town. How lovely for her. Is he staying a few days then?"

Pete handed over the chilled glass of wine as he replied, "He's joining the tour crew from Monday. He finished his latest contract this week so is now free to re-join my lot. I'm glad because he's one of the best sound and light engineers in the business." He walked over to the French windows. "Shall we sit outside until dinner arrives?"

"That sounds like a plan." Sukie walked through the open doors, sat down at the small table on the balcony and closed her eyes, tilting her head up to catch the warm rays of the evening sun. She could smell the scent of the geraniums in the pot nearby and hear the hazy sounds of birds chirruping in the trees and hedges below in the hotel gardens. "Oh, this is blissful. I could stay like this forever…"

Pete admired the smooth neckline opposite him. The urge to lean across and run little butterfly kisses up it, until his lips landed upon hers, was so strong that, to prevent himself giving in to it, he had to stand up and walk away to the opposite side of the balcony. As he looked across the rooftops of the houses nearby, he made a decision. Tonight, he was going to take the bull by its proverbial horns and tell her exactly how he felt. His stomach churned at the thought but it had to be done. He couldn't keep his feelings to himself any longer. They were eating him up and the time had come when he had to know, one way or another, how Sukie felt about him.

"That was delicious but I couldn't eat another thing." Sukie left the dining table and flopped onto the nearby sofa. Pete pressed the discreet button for room service to come and clear the used crockery away before joining her there.

"The salmon was cooked to perfection," he said as he refilled their glasses. The Prosecco came from a local vineyard and was equally as perfect.

"Oh gosh, I really shouldn't have any more wine but this one is by far one of the nicest I have tasted. It's very difficult to refuse." Sukie took a long sip from her glass. She was feeling quite light-headed, most likely due to her earlier glass being consumed on an empty stomach. She hoped that, having now eaten, she would sober up again soon. Although, she wouldn't if she kept on drinking, would she now? Ah sod it, she thought. When was the last time she'd been a bit squiffy? It was so long ago, she couldn't remember. It wouldn't do her any harm to let her hair down a bit.

She picked up her glass and chinked it against Pete's. "Saluti!"

With a smile, he returned her greeting, "Saluti."

He downed a large swallow of his wine and took a deep breath, ready to lay his soul bare to Sukie, but before he could speak, she placed her glass on the coffee table and, turning to him, wrapped her arms around him in a massive hug.

"Pete Wallace, I just want to say a really big thank you for asking me to meet up with you here in Italy." She pulled back and looked into his eyes. "I really needed this break and I've had a fabulous time, I really have. It has been wonderful! There are not enough words for me to tell you just how much. Thank you, thank you, thank you!"

He didn't have a chance to reply before she'd placed her lips on his to give him a thank you kiss. She'd caught him unawares, however, and, unable to stop himself, he folded his arms around her, pulling her closer to him. He felt her hesitate slightly but then she was returning his embrace, holding him as tightly as he was holding her. Her lips moved beneath his and then parted. His tongue slowly made its way into her warm mouth. The taste of her was like nothing he'd experienced before. The heat of her tongue against his was sending his senses reeling. He'd heard people speak about getting high on love but this was a first for him. Tentatively, Sukie's tongue slipped into his mouth and he couldn't contain the moan that escaped from him. Months of waiting for this moment and finally it was happening. He was delirious with desire and it had never felt so damn good.

He tore his lips away from hers and moved his kisses down her throat, just as he'd wanted to do earlier. He could feel her breath on his ear and it was making him even more aroused. Working his way upwards, he gently nipped her earlobe with his teeth and then whispered, "I love you."

Suddenly, there was a loud knock on the door and the words "Room service" were uttered on the other side of it.

Sukie's eyes snapped open and she pulled back from him as though she'd had an electric shock. The look of sheer panic on her face immediately deflated Pete's happiness.

"No," she said. "No, no, no. This is not right. We can't do this. *I* can't do this." She reached beneath the coffee table, grabbed the shoes she'd slipped off when they'd sat down, and rushed to the door, just as it was knocked upon a second time. She yanked it open and pushed past the waiter with his trolley. Pete rushed after her but the waiter had begun pushing his trolley through the doorway. By the time he'd managed to pull it out of the way, Sukie's suite door had slammed shut behind her.

He covered the short distance in three long strides and banged on her door.

"Sukie," he called through the wood. "Speak to me. We need to talk about this. Please open the door." The door, however, remained resolutely shut and there was no sound from within. He tried again. "Please, Sukie, speak to me. I didn't mean to upset you."

Still there was no response. Pete touched his forehead against the door, unable to accept how fleeting his moment of happiness had been. His chest was tight with the pain of his upset and the sadness rapidly poured into every corner of his being. He whispered quietly, more to himself than to Sukie, "Please don't do this to me. Please don't leave me. I love you."

But the silence stretched on.

Eventually, he straightened up, walked back to his suite and closed the door. He sat back down on the sofa, where he'd been in seventh heaven only a few moments earlier, put his head in his hands and cried.

He'd lost her.

The intensity of the pain squeezing the inside of his chest was so severe he wondered if this was a loss he couldn't survive.

When she heard Pete's door closing from her position behind her own door, Sukie slid down and slumped onto the floor. The tears were pouring down her face and she finally let out the sobs she'd been holding in. She'd heard Pete's words and she had heard the pain in his voice as he'd begged her to talk to him. She was distraught at having caused him to feel that way but they could never be together, surely he would see that. She could never live in his fishbowl of a life, everyone peering in and thinking they owned you. She loved him. In every way possible, he had slipped quietly into her heart and her soul. She finally admitted to it herself – she loved him!

However, she hated the public ownership of him. The subterfuge needed just to have a day out sightseeing. Trips to the cinema or out to restaurants had to be planned with near-military precision. It was a lifestyle she knew she could not cope with and which would eventually drive them apart. She acknowledged, however, that it was impossible to have Pete without the celebrity trappings that came with him. She had no choice – she had to walk away.

One day, she knew she would finally be able to live with her decision but, right now, her tears would not stop flowing and it felt as though her heart was being ripped out of her chest.

Chapter Fifty-Four

Sukie quietly slipped the envelope under Pete's door and made her way to the elevator, carrying her little suitcase to ensure the squeaky wheel did not alert him to her departure.

She'd already spoken with reception and a taxi was now waiting downstairs to take her to the airport. Her return ticket was for the following day but she was hoping to exchange it for a flight today. She'd tossed and turned for most of the night and knew she couldn't face seeing Pete right away. She needed to get away and return to her normal life where people didn't need a disguise to go to the shops or bodyguards when they went to work. She wanted to be able to look out of the window and not worry if the paparazzi on the pavement were taking, and selling, photographs of her without make-up to some tabloid newspaper which would then rip her apart for having a spot on her chin.

She arrived in the reception area, dropped her key into the key box and hurried out the door before anyone saw or stopped her.

While the driver put her suitcase in the boot of the taxi, she slipped on her sunglasses to hide her red swollen eyes and got into the back of the car. Had she looked up, she would have seen Pete standing on his balcony, looking down at her as her letter, in his hand, flapped in the gentle morning breeze.

Pete watched the taxi pull away out of the hotel grounds. He was still wearing his clothes from the previous evening. He hadn't gone to bed and had lain curled up on the sofa for most of the night, trying to understand how it had come to this. He'd been going over and over in his head all the times they'd spent together and how perfect they had been. He accepted that Sukie had never given any indication whatsoever that she viewed him as anything more than a really good friend but, if *he* could see how well suited they were together, why couldn't she?

He must have finally fallen asleep because, the next thing he knew, the sun was streaming in the window onto his face and the soft shuffle of her letter on the carpet had woken him up.

When he'd read it, his heart broke all over again when she admitted she did love him but, regrettably, his very public life was something she could never cope with. She had also asked him to respect her wish to go home earlier than planned and to give her time to come to terms with the shift in their relationship. She would call him once she was ready to talk about it.

When he could no longer see her cab, he turned on his heel and walked back inside. He threw her letter down onto the coffee table, where her glass from last night still sat, and headed towards his bedroom. Regardless of how he felt, he still had a gig to get through tonight and he needed some decent sleep.

He swallowed down one of the mild sleeping tablets the doctor had prescribed for him – having been assured they were non-addictive – stripped off his clothes and got into bed. As he waited for the sedative to kick in, he repeated the age-old show business mantra in his head – the show must go on, the show must go on, the show must go on…

Jordie let himself into Pete's rooms. It was almost midday and they needed to begin getting everything together before heading off to the venue in a few hours. Traditionally, Pete always liked to be on-site several hours before he was due on stage. This gave him the opportunity to watch the other acts perform and to gauge the mood of the crowd. It was one of those strange quirks of the music business – just because people had paid to come and see you perform didn't mean they were always going to make it easy for you. Some locations *were* easy and you could almost feel the love as the fans poured in through the doors. Others, however, arrived with the view that, having paid a good wedge to be there, you had to earn your crust and be sure to entertain them. Sometimes you could almost feel them crossing their arms while thinking, 'Well bring it on! Amuse me!'

He walked into the room and his eyes fell on the two wine glasses on the coffee table. Oh aye, he wondered, was last night the night when the ducklings had finally gotten it together? He felt his spirits lift at the thought – his life would be so much easier if they had. As he drew nearer to the table, however, he saw Sukie's letter lying on it. He picked it up and quickly read the contents.

Oh shit!

He put it back down, headed towards the bedroom to find Pete and, seeing him sleeping soundly in the bed, he closed the bedroom door and went out onto the balcony, dialling Kara's number as he walked. When she answered, he rapidly explained the situation. Kara was equally dismayed to hear that things had gone pear-shaped between Pete and Sukie. She informed Jordie she'd speak with the hotel reception and report back. Two minutes later, she called to confirm Sukie had indeed checked out early that morning. She had settled her bill and taken a taxi to the airport. He thanked her, ended the call and let out a groan.

Six months ago, this news would have given him cause to celebrate but, having lived with a much happier and more stable Pete in that time, and knowing it was Sukie's influence behind it, he was surprised to find himself quite upset they hadn't been able to get their relationship off the ground. His own, new found, happiness with Beth had woken him up to the importance of having someone special in your life and he had dearly wished it for Pete and Sukie.

Beth!

Oh crap! He'd better call her and let her know what had happened.

He sat down in the same chair Sukie had sat in the night before, found Beth's name on his phone and pressed 'Call'. Knowing she'd harboured the same hopes for Sukie and Pete as he had done, telling her this news was not going to be easy.

Chapter Fifty-Five

Sukie closed the door of the hotel room behind her, put her suitcase in the enclave next to it and walked wearily over to the bed. She flopped down and lay across it for several minutes. What a shitty, shitty, shitty, shitty day!

Her great plan to head back home to the UK had very quickly hit the wall when she had tried to change her flight home from the next day. The customer services desk for her airline had quickly informed her that all flights to the UK were fully booked. The young clerk had gone on to explain this was due to the Verona Festival now being in full flow. When she'd enquired if it was worth checking the other airlines – if she had to pay for a new ticket, and lose the cost of the one she had, then so be it – the assistant had advised it was worth trying but suspected she would encounter the same problem. In the meantime, she had offered to put Sukie's name on her standby list in the event of any no-shows or last minute cancellations. Sukie had accepted the offer before walking off to speak to the other airline desks nearby.

Thirty minutes later she was back. All the other airlines were saying the same thing – completely booked up, no seats available on any UK flights. It seemed her only option was to sit, wait, and hope. She whiled away some of the time by loading the photographs she had taken in Venice and Verona onto her tablet. She'd been looking through them when she came to the pictures taken by Kara on the water taxi and her breath had caught in her throat. Zooming in, it was easy to see that she and Pete looked very much like a couple in love. She hadn't realised Kara had taken a few natural shots of them, when they'd been messing about, and there was no mistaking the underlying love flowing between them. Had other people seen what she hadn't, she wondered. When she'd looked at their posed shot, she'd almost started crying again. Happiness shone on both of their faces. They looked like a couple in every way. She was surprised to notice she had wrapped her arms over Pete's when he'd held her. She couldn't recall doing that, but looking at the photograph, the embrace was completely natural. She'd stared at the image for quite a time before switching the tablet off. There was no point in torturing herself further. As she sat waiting, however, her mind kept replaying the events from the night before. Round and round the scenes went in her head, as though they were on a perpetual loop.

She could still feel the sensation of Pete's lips upon her own. Just thinking about it made her toes curl with desire. Every nerve ending in her body zinged with electric energy as she recalled his hot breath on her throat. She had been completely lost in his kiss and she didn't like to think how the night may have panned out had room service not arrived when they did.

She refused to dwell on how everything had unravelled after that – she couldn't bear to think of the desolation she had heard in Pete's voice as he stood on the other side of her hotel room door, begging her to speak to him.

Finally, at five o'clock, the customer services clerk had come over. She'd advised Sukie that all the expected passengers for the last flight of the day had checked-in. There was nothing more she could do to get Sukie home today. She had, however, made a few phone calls and had been able to find Sukie a room in one of the hotels nearby. This was almost a miracle in itself, but she'd called in a favour and secured her a place to sleep for the night. Sukie had expressed her gratitude for all the help the clerk had given her and accepted the compliment slip with the hotel details on.

So here she was, stuck on her own in Verona, in a hotel room which had cost far more than half of the holidays she'd ever been on. She just wanted to get home where she could curl up in her own bed with the furry bodies of Tony and Adam beside her, and cry until the pain went away.

She picked up her mobile and sent Elsa a text, asking her to call when she got home from visiting her mother-in-law. She needed to talk to her oldest friend and hoped she would phone soon.

In the meantime, she was going to have a good, hot shower and wash the stale airport smell from her hair while she waited for Elsa's call. She peeled herself off the bed, took her pyjamas out of her suitcase and made her way to the bathroom.

Jordie knocked on the door of Pete's dressing room and walked in. "How are you doing?" he asked.

Pete looked up from the sofa he was crashed out on. "I'd be a lot better if people would stop asking me that."

"We're just concerned about you. That's all."

"I know, I know. It would just be easier for me if people carried on as normal. We've got a show to put on an hour from now. Let's all just focus on that, eh? We can do the broken-hearted psychoanalysis tomorrow."

"Okay. Right, checklist time!" Jordie assumed his managerial persona and looked down at his clipboard. "Are you still happy with the set-list? Is there anything you want to change?"

"Yes, I'm still happy, no, there is nothing I want changed."

"Good." Jordie walked over to the hanging rail in the corner and quickly counted the freshly ironed T-shirts, shirts, waistcoats, and jeans which Pete would change into through the course of the evening. Finding everything in place, he marked it off his list. He turned back to Pete and said, "We've done a second check on the speaker stacks and they are totally secure. Gareth is going to stand with the lighting techs to ensure all the angles are correct on the spotlights and you don't get blinded. The last thing we need is you having your retinas burnt out when you're standing twenty-odd feet up in the air."

"Well, that's reassuring," came Pete's sarcastic reply.

Jordie shot him a look but bit his tongue. "Finally," he continued, "it looks and sounds like we've got a good crowd in tonight. They've been singing along to the other bands throughout the day and giving them hearty cheers and applause."

"Great stuff! Tell the boys I'll be out shortly, I'm going to shower now and get dressed." Pete sat up and swung his feet to the floor. Just as Jordie was opening the door, Pete spoke again quietly. "Jordie... Thank you."

Jordie looked back and the misery on Pete's face made his insides twist. There was nothing he could say right now to make him feel any better so he simply nodded, left the room and closed the door quietly behind him.

Pete stood up and walked into the bathroom. All he wanted to do right now, was curl up in a ball and forget the world existed. But he couldn't. The final support band had almost finished their set and he could hear some of the crowd beginning to chant his name. Somehow, he had to drag up a smile and go out there looking as though he didn't have a care in the world. His fans were waiting for him to make their night special and the professional within him knew he would never let them down. As he waited for the water to warm up, he repeated the words that had gotten him through the day. The show must go on. The show must go on. The show must go on…

Chapter Fifty-Six

Artie Baggio tugged on his florescent tabard as he stood looking over the crowd in the stadium. He still couldn't believe his luck in getting this job. His friend's older brother, Danilo, had suggested he try *RussoRicci* when Artie had mentioned he wanted to get a summer job before going off to university in the autumn. Danilo had said that, with his sturdy, rugby-playing body, he would be a shoo-in for a role as a security bouncer. He himself had worked for them when he'd been at university and they always needed extra staff during the summer months. If you did well in your first season, they kept you on file for future years.

At his interview, Eduardo di Santo had discussed the requirements of the role with Artie. He must have been pleased with his answers for he'd been offered a job on the spot. And now, here he was, standing behind the stage crash barrier in front of the crowd, at the Pete Wallace gig. When Eduardo had given him the details for his first night, he had expected to be outside the stadium, doing crowd control or something similar. He had certainly not expected to be front of house. Full of pride, he pulled his shoulders back and straightened himself up to his full six-foot – a movement he instantly regretted as the tabard tightened across his chest. He tugged at it again. He'd been slow off the mark to pick his tabard up and, by the time he'd gotten to the box, all the extra-large sizes were gone. He had squeezed himself into a large but would see Eduardo later about getting a bigger one for next time.

He quickly glanced to his right to make sure Eduardo hadn't noticed him fidgeting. Eh! That was strange. Eduardo had his back to the crowd and was staring at Pete up on the stage above him. Not wanting to be caught being lax in his own job, Artie resumed his stance of watching the crowd but, as he did, he recalled the instructions given out by Eduardo, to all the security staff, earlier in the day.

"You are here to work, not enjoy the show. Focus on the role you've been given. You must concentrate on your job and not be distracted by the bands on the stage. People's safety depends on you doing your job and doing it well. Those of you on crash barrier duty – you need to be extra vigilant and ensure the people at the front are safe and are not being crushed by the crowd behind them."

He stole another look at Eduardo and saw he was still standing with his back to the audience, watching Pete intently. He didn't know what to do – should he say something or mind his own business. Eduardo was his supervisor and it would not do well to antagonise him on his very first day.

Just then, the crowd began going wild. The opening bars to 'Right Up Here in Heaven' were being played. Artie's younger sister had filled him in on everything he didn't really want to know about Pete Wallace but was being told anyway. Due to her instruction, he knew this was when Pete climbed up onto the speakers and got the crowd to sing along with him. It was also when he was known to get some ladies from the crowd up on the stage for a dance and that was why the girls in front of him were becoming excited. Artie smiled at their antics as they hoped they would be the lucky ones.

He sneaked a fleeting look over his shoulder and saw Pete clamber up onto the Marshall speakers furthest away from him. Soon, the crowd were singing their hearts out as Pete waved his hands in front of him, conducting them as though they were an orchestra.

A few minutes later, whilst he kept a close watch over the screaming women in front of him, Artie heard Pete run across the stage above his head and begin to climb the speakers behind him. He glanced over at Eduardo again and was shocked to see him still standing with his back to the stadium crowd. He was staring at Pete as he began his second upward climb. The look on Eduardo's face was one of pure hatred. By now, Artie had forgotten about watching the crowd and was giving him his full attention. Eduardo was so engrossed in watching Pete, now standing up on top of the speaker stacks, that he was oblivious to everything else around him.

Artie's eyes widened and disbelief coursed through

him as he saw Eduardo's hand go for his gun, pull it from its holster, and point it up towards Pete.

What the hell…?

Not stopping to think about his actions, he launched himself at Eduardo and pulled him down, using one of the hard rugby tackles that had won his school team many honours. He heard, and felt, Eduardo's gun fire just as he knocked him off his feet and looked up to see Pete Wallace fall backwards off the speakers. The screams of the fans began to fill the stadium behind him.

Sitting astride Eduardo's back to stop him getting away, Artie looked down and was horrified when he saw Eduardo smiling widely. Just then, he felt Eduardo's body begin to shake and, thinking he was having some kind of fit, he was about to move off him when he realised Eduardo was laughing. And the laughter got louder as two policemen rushed over, pulled his hands behind him and handcuffed him. By the time they'd gotten him upright, and were walking him away, Eduardo's laughter had become hysterical.

Chapter Fifty-Seven

Sukie reached out groggily towards the bedside table where her mobile phone was ringing. She picked it up and, prising one eye open, she saw Elsa's name on the screen.

"Hmm, hello," she muttered drowsily. Her restless night and long day had caught up with her and she'd fallen asleep while waiting for Elsa to call.

"Oh, my goodness, Sukie, where are you? How's Pete? Is he okay? What's happening?"

Still half-asleep, Sukie missed the panic in Elsa's voice. "I'm in a hotel room. I was sleeping until you woke me up." She ignored the questions about Pete. She needed another couple of minutes to get her head together before she could talk about him.

"Sukie, what do you mean you're in a hotel room? Why aren't you with Pete? What is going on?"

She pulled herself up the pillows into a sitting

position and yawned widely before replying, "The short version? We fell out, I left, sat in the airport all day and am now in a hotel because there were no seats available on any flights to bring me home."

"Oh, Sukie…" Elsa hesitated, "You don't know what's happened, do you? Sukie, Pete's been hurt."

"What? How?" She was immediately wide-awake and scrambling around, trying to find the remote control for the television.

"The reports are hazy; some are saying he fell off the speakers – you know how he climbs up them – others are saying he fell because he was shot."

As Elsa talked, Sukie flipped through the channels on the television, trying to find a news report. Eventually she found one. The commentary was in Italian but she didn't need to understand what was being said. The picture on the screen was that of a body on a stretcher being put into an ambulance. Just then, Jordie came on the screen, pushing people aside as he climbed into the vehicle.

For several seconds, she was unable to speak or think. A heavy, ice-cold sensation swept through her body. She could actually feel it as it rushed from her head all the way down to her legs. She just stared at the television, watching the ambulance doors close and it speeding away. The face of a local reporter then filled the screen, talking directly to the camera, but Sukie was no longer watching. She spoke into her phone as she got off the bed, "Elsa, I have to go."

She hastily pulled some clothes from her suitcase and got dressed, gathered up the few bits and pieces she had lying around the room, shoved them into her case, switched off the television and rushed out of the door, dragging her luggage behind her.

A few minutes later, she flew out of the elevator and ran over to the reception desk. She had to find out which hospital they were taking Pete to and then she needed to get a taxi over there.

"Scusi, Scusi. Please help." She looked up briefly at the man already standing at the reception desk, talking to the receptionist. "I'm sorry to interrupt but this is an emergency." She hoped he understood English.

She turned back to the receptionist and spoke very quickly, trying not to cry as she did so. "Pete Wallace has been hurt and is going to hospital. I need to know where they've taken him."

She spoke so quickly, however, the young receptionist was unable to keep up with her. "I am sorry but I do not understand. Please say again."

Sukie repeated herself although, by now, she had begun to really panic and was struggling to breathe properly. "Pete Wallace, hospital, where?" she gasped.

The receptionist still had a puzzled look on her face. Just then, the gentleman she had practically pushed aside spoke to her in perfect English. "Take a deep breath, and tell me what is wrong. I will try to help you."

His voice was deep, calm and soothing and it helped Sukie to focus. She took a few deep breaths and tried to explain in a more rational manner. "Pete Wallace has been shot. They've taken him to hospital and I need to know where he is as I need to be with him."

The man looked at her and asked, not unkindly,

"Why do you need to be with him? He will have his friends and family there at his side."

"I'm his friend. He is my friend. He's my…" Sukie stopped as it hit her, what she had been about to say. She took another deep breath and finally gave in to accepting the reality of what Pete had become to her, and his place in her life. She looked the man in the eye and replied firmly, "He's my boyfriend."

The man looked at her and, with no small amount of cynicism in his voice, replied, "Of course he is."

Rolling her eyes, she exclaimed, "Ah jeez, why does this keep happening to me? I am *not* a groupie! See for yourself!" She opened up the front pocket of her suitcase and pulled out her tablet. A few seconds later, having made some quick swipes on the screen, she handed it over to the man. There, in front of him, was the picture Kara had taken in the water-taxi. She leant over and swiped a few more times, letting him see the other photographs of her and Pete together.

The man looked at them for a moment. There was no doubt she telling the truth. The pictures clearly showed a couple very much in love. He handed the tablet back to Sukie, turned to the receptionist and spoke to her in rapid Italian. She immediately nodded her understanding, picked up the phone and began punching in numbers.

The man then took Sukie by the elbow and gently walked her over to the sitting area nearby. When she'd sat down, he introduced himself. Putting out a hand, he said, "My name's Jeff, what's yours?"

"Sukie," she replied while shaking his outstretched hand.

"Right, Sukie, I've given the information to the receptionist and she's now making a few calls to try and find out where he's being taken."

"Thank you, you are very kind."

"It's no problem."

She looked at her helpful saviour. There was something very familiar about him but she couldn't quite put her finger on what it was. He must have caught her giving him a funny look because the next thing he said was, "Clint Eastwood."

She blinked in confusion. "I'm sorry?"

"You're looking at me and wondering if you know me because I look familiar. I'm telling you I look like Clint Eastwood."

As soon as he finished his explanation, she could see the man in front of her did, indeed, bear a very strong resemblance to the famous Hollywood actor.

With a smile, she replied, "I'm guessing from your explanation that you get it a lot then."

Jeff nodded. "You could say that. It started in my mid-twenties and I've had to deal with it ever since." With a glance around him, he leant over and whispered, "I've even had to give a few autographs too as some folk refused to believe I wasn't him." He winked as he sat back in his seat.

Sukie let out a small giggle at his revelation. She could see how it could happen though. With his swept back, thick, sandy-coloured hair, strong, craggy jawline and piercing blue eyes, Jeff could easily pass for the actor in his younger days.

"Err... Hasn't Clint Eastwood got green eyes?" Her

mum had a soft spot for the actor and had often mentioned his 'dreamy green eyes'.

Jeff smiled. "He has, but how many people do you think actually know that? He's also quite a bit older than me but people seem to forget he's aged. It's just one of those things."

"That's so true," Sukie said. She glanced over to the receptionist and, seeing her still on the phone, looked down at her watch.

"If it's not too personal," Jeff said, "may I ask why you're here? Why were you not at the concert?"

She looked at Jeff for a moment before answering. "We fell out. We're not really a couple. He wants us to be but I don't. Or I didn't."

"Why not? You clearly love him."

She sighed. "It's the 'fame' thing. I can't stand it. I don't want people watching me all the time. I like my privacy. Unlike some, I have never hankered to have my face all over the media. I'm very happy being the person nobody knows."

Jeff nodded. "I know exactly what you mean." He paused for a few seconds before continuing. "It can be managed though. It needn't be such a big thing if you do things right."

"And you know this how?"

"Do you remember the actress Brenda Barker?"

Sukie nodded. Brenda Barker had been very popular when she was growing up and had starred in some of the biggest Hollywood blockbusters.

"She's my mum."

Sukie's eye's widened. "Wow! Really?"

Jeff smiled. "Yes, really! But she was very good at keeping her work and family separate. Her stardom has never intruded on our family life and she ensured the media and the press knew we were off limits. My father is like you, a very private man. Apart from some film premiers, you will struggle to find any pictures of him in the public domain." Jeff paused and smiled as he thought about his parents. "I promise you, Sukie, you will be able to work it out. I suspect you've developed such a fear of this celebrity factor that it's grown out of all proportion in your mind. I'd say now is as good a time as any to push it into a box. Don't allow it to influence your life. You rarely get a second chance with true love. Don't throw it away."

Jeff turned and saw the receptionist walking towards them. He stood up and listened intently as she handed over a piece of paper. He thanked her and turned back to Sukie. He handed the paper to Sukie and said, "This is where they've taken Pete. A taxi is now waiting for you outside and has been instructed to get you there as quickly as possible."

Sukie stood up, put a hand out to Jeff and, shaking his again, said, "Thank you, Jeff, thank you so much for helping. I would now be a blubbering wreck on the floor if you hadn't stepped in. You have been very kind."

"Now, now, you are stronger than that. Don't put yourself down." He put his hand in his pocket, pulled out a card and passed it to Sukie. "This is my business card. It has my mobile number on it. If you have any problems, call me. I mean it. Call me."

She gave the card a quick glance.

'ROWLANDS'
Galleries of Art
Mayfair, Knightsbridge
London

There was also a mobile number, just as Jeff had said. She put it in her jeans pocket, gave him a hug and thanked him again. She leant down, picked up her handbag, grabbed a hold of her suitcase and smiled her goodbye before walking quickly to the door where the hovering taxi driver took her case from her and guided her towards the car.

Jeff Rowland watched her leave and hoped things worked out for her and Pete. When he saw the time, he walked back to the reception to finish checking in. After this little drama, he needed a couple of malt whiskies to help him relax and unwind.

Chapter Fifty-Eight

Sukie sat in the back of the taxi and pushed the 'redial' button again. She was trying to get a hold of Kara but, unsurprisingly, the call kept going through to her voicemail. She'd left a message to say she was on her way to the hospital and to call her if she got the chance. She'd also tried Pete's number but was not surprised when it just rang out before also going to voicemail. She hadn't expected it to be answered but, with no other options, she'd felt she had to try.

She looked down as her phone began to ring in her hand. It was her mum. She answered and tried hard to keep the panic out of her voice. "Mum, hi."

"Sukie, where are you? Are you ok? Elsa called me and told me what happened."

The tears welling up again as she replied, "I'm in a taxi on my way to the hospital. Well, I hope I am. I can't get hold of Kara to confirm if I'm going to the right one and I don't have Jordie's number." A small sob escaped her as she spoke.

"Which hospital are you going to?"

When Sukie had read out the name the receptionist had written down for her, Beth said, "Give me five minutes. Stay off your phone and wait for my call."

Four minutes later, Beth called back. "Right, I've spoken to Jordie and he says you have the correct details. He's advised you to drive past the main doors as there's a heavy police presence there, holding back the press, and the fans, both of whom are now arriving in their droves. You'll never get through them. He said to go around the back. There's a small fire door underneath the fire escape. He'll meet you there. When we come off the phone, I'll text you his number. I've already given him yours. Don't worry, sweetheart, everything will be fine."

"I hope so, Mum. Thank you for sorting this out." Just then, a thought hit her. "Err... Mum, how do you come to have Jordie's mobile number?"

Beth hesitated for a moment. "Ach, you had to find out sooner or later! Jordie and I are in a relationship, darling. It started in January and I have to tell you it's serious. We love each other."

Sukie smiled in the darkness. She'd talked with Pete a few times about trying to get Beth and Jordie together. It seemed, however, the two of them had managed quite well without their help. "Mum, now is not the time, so we'll talk about this when I get back. However, I am happy for you both. Well done."

She saw the taxi was now approaching the hospital so quickly said goodbye and gave the driver the instructions Beth had passed on. As he drove past the melee at the front door, Sukie's phone pinged again. Her mum had sent over Jordie's mobile number. She dialled it to let him know she was here and would be at the back door in a couple of minutes.

Jordie opened the fire door as the taxi driver was getting her suitcase out of the boot. When she tried to pay him, he refused her money, telling her the hotel had sorted everything for her. There was no charge. Instead, she had to make do with giving him a generous tip for getting her to the hospital so quickly. It had taken less than fifteen minutes.

Jordie took her suitcase from the driver, led her inside and made sure the door was closed securely behind them.

"How is he Jordie? What happened?" She couldn't stop the tears this time.

"Hush there, pet, don't cry until we know we have something to cry over. Save your tears." He put a comforting arm around her shoulders and walked her to the service elevator where one of the hospital porters was waiting for them. As they stood, heading upwards, Jordie continued, "He's in surgery right now. The news reports are correct – Pete was shot. The bullet hit him in the chest. The paramedics couldn't tell us any more than that and he was whisked straight into the operating theatre when we arrived. I know nothing more."

The doors of the lift opened and they walked out into the hallway of the Intensive Care Unit. She saw Kara and Gareth sitting in the waiting area opposite. When she reached them, Kara stood up and gave her a big hug. Sukie awkwardly hugged her back. Surely they must be wondering why she'd left so suddenly that morning.

Kara patted her on the arm. "It's okay, Sukie, Jordie's explained everything so, please, don't feel awkward. Despite what we see on all these reality shows, and in the newspapers, not everyone wants to live in the limelight. Most people want to go about their daily lives in relative obscurity. We fully understand. What's far more important is you're here now when Pete needs you. That is more than good enough as far I am concerned."

"Yes, I'm here, Kara, and I won't be leaving him again. Stuff the media, Pete is way more important to me than them. I'm here to stay – for good!"

"Well, you make sure you tell him that, yeah?"

With a small smile, she replied, "Oh, I will, you can bet on it. I will tell him every single day until he's sick of hearing it and, even then, I'll keep on telling him."

Jordie overheard her words as he returned with the coffees he'd picked up from the nearby machine. Now they had to hope Pete would survive to hear her say them.

Four hours later, the ward doors swung open and Pete's surgeon walked through, the porters pushing Pete's bed behind them. The doctor walked towards them as the porters and the nurses took Pete into the room beside the nurses' station. Sukie knew this was not good as they always put the most critical cases nearest the nurses. She stood up, along with Kara, Jordie, and Gareth, and tried to concentrate on what the doctor was saying.

The surgeon explained that, while the bullet has

445

missed Pete's heart, it had brushed against it, causing some deep bruising to the delicate muscle. It had also inflicted a considerable amount of trauma within the chest cavity before lodging itself in Pete's shoulder blade. The bullet had been removed and was with the police. At this time, however, the doctor was more concerned with Pete's head injury which he'd sustained in his fall. He'd been unconscious when the paramedics had gotten to him and the scans had shown he currently had a bleed on the brain. They were keeping him sedated for the moment and he was being observed every ten minutes. He'd also broken his left leg but this was currently the least of their concerns. There was nothing more they could do for now. They just had wait and hope the brain injury didn't become more severe.

"Can we see him?" Jordie asked.

"Yes, but only one person at a time. He has a lot of machinery around him, so we can only allow one person in with him."

Jordie turned to Sukie. "You go in first."

Sukie was surprised. She'd expected Jordie or Kara to go in before her. "Are you sure? Shouldn't you or Kara go in?"

Jordie put his hands gently on her shoulders. "It's you he loves Sukie, not us. It's you he needs beside him right now. We'll be out here though. You won't be alone. Now go in and speak to him. Tell him what he needs to hear. Bring him back to us, pet."

Sukie walked in and balked when she saw the machines beeping around Pete and heard the hiss of the pump that was currently helping him to breathe. The

446

doctor explained this was to ease the pressure on his lung, which had also been damaged by the bullet.

Looking down at him, Pete simply appeared to be sleeping. His silly, floppy fringe was swept back off his forehead. He had no bruises on his face that she could see although the breathing tube in his mouth hid quite a bit of it. As her eyes moved along his body, however, it was a different matter. His chest and left shoulder were covered in bandages and his left leg was raised up slightly, resting on some pillows.

She pulled up a chair and took hold of Pete's right hand which was lying on the bed. Slowly, and hesitantly, she began to tell him how she felt. She said she was sorry for walking out on him and for not being there when he needed her. She told him that, from now on, she would always be beside him, she would always be there for him and she would never leave him again. She apologised for being so stupid, for being so hung up on his celebrity status it had blinded her to how deeply she loved him. On and on she spoke, through the night, hoping he could hear her words and hoping they would encourage him to keep fighting.

Chapter Fifty-Nine

It was three days later when Pete's doctor and the head nurse came into his room and asked Sukie to step outside. Thinking they were merely doing more observation tests, she did so and was surprised when Jordie came over with a big smile on his face. He gave her a hug and said, "Great news, the bleed on his brain has stopped. They suspected it had last night but wanted to wait a further twelve hours before confirming it. The build-up of blood has begun to disperse. The doctor thinks he's going to be okay."

She looked over to see Kara and Gareth walking back onto the ward and guessed, from the smiles on their faces, that Jordie had already called them with the good news. The last three days had been difficult. Kara, Jordie, and Gareth had taken turns in staying at the hospital with her. She'd refused to leave and had used the bathroom of Pete's private room to shower in when Kara had told her she was getting a bit smelly. She'd eaten nothing that first day but Jordie had pretty much dragged her down to the cafeteria on the second, when they had taken Pete away for another scan. "I told your mother I would look after you, and that is what I am doing. So, come on, move it."

It was this comment which had sparked her curiosity about their relationship and saw her following behind him. Once they'd been sitting at a table, Jordie with some lasagne and she with a cheese sandwich and a portion of chips, she questioned him on his intentions regarding her mother and also how the relationship had begun.

After a few mouthfuls of food, Jordie had replied. "I felt something move inside me when your mum first stepped off the plane in Austria. As I got to know her over the week, I realised for the first time in my life, I might actually be falling in love. I knew I was in love on the day you both left. Saying goodbye to Beth made me see I never wanted to be away from her. After that, we spoke almost daily on the phone and on Skype. I visited as often as I could. I'd find reasons to be in the UK – some were genuine, some, I confess, were fabricated. Each time I see her, it gets harder to walk away."

Sukie nodded as she'd popped a chip in her mouth. "So, what are you planning to do, going forward?"

Jordie had taken another bite of his lasagne before answering. "We've discussed a few options and I know Beth wants to talk to you about them herself so forgive me for not going into further detail right now. All I will say is this – I intend to be by your mother's side for as long as she wants me there. I hope you are okay with that but tough if you're not. I'm going nowhere."

Sukie noted his defiant expression as she'd chewed on another chip. She'd swallowed it down, taken a sip of her water, cleared her throat and replied, "Nah, you're good. If you make my mum happy, then it's all alright by me." She'd smiled to let him know she really was happy for them both.

Now the four of them were waiting for the doctor to finish with Pete and update them on his progress. Kara and Gareth stood quietly, holding hands. Jordie paced up and down while Sukie sat staring at the closed door, willing the doctor to hurry up and come out. A few minutes later, he did. He walked over to them, smiling, and imparted his news. "As you know, the bleed has stopped and the blood in the brain cavity is less. This is very good but it will be better once it has dispersed altogether. We have to monitor this very carefully though to ensure it does not go to other places where it may cause some harm. So, he is not out of the woods just yet. We have removed the breathing tubes and he is now doing this unaided. This is also good. We are, however, keeping him on the heart monitor for a little longer. We'll check this to see if he is functioning okay without the other machinery helping him along. He is no longer being sedated and, we hope, he should begin to waken very soon."

"Thank you for this news, doctor, it really is great. May I go back in now?" Sukie was pleased to hear such good news but she was anxious to get back to Pete's side. If there was a chance of him beginning to wake up, she wanted to be sure she was with him when it happened.

The doctor smiled his consent. "Of course, of course!" He'd seen Sukie sitting at Pete's side all this time and was not going to keep her away from him any longer than he had to.

She walked back into the room and was surprised by how much bigger it appeared, and quieter too, now most of the machines had been removed. The heart monitor was still there, however, just as the doctor had advised. She'd dozed off to its constant beep several times over the last three days and it gave her a strange sense of comfort to hear it in the otherwise quiet room.

She made her way over to the bed, sat down and looked at Pete. He appeared more peaceful but also quite vulnerable now the breathing tube had gone. She'd gotten used to it being there and it was strange to see him without it.

She placed his hand between hers and began talking to him again. "Oh, Pete, can you hear me? The doctor's told us you're getting better. You're not quite there yet, but you're heading in the right direction. Kara, Gareth, and Jordie are all here, waiting outside and desperately wanting to hear your voice. They're not the only ones. I want to hear your voice too. I miss you so much. It seems that no matter how many times I tell you I'm sorry, it doesn't feel enough. I love you so much, Pete Wallace, and I want you to wake up so you can hear me tell you. I just want you to speak to me."

"I would, if you'd shut up for two minutes!" Pete's voice was nothing more than a croaking whisper.

"Oh my, you're awake. Hush now… Take it easy." She stood looking down at him, holding his hand tightly as he tried to speak again. "I need to call the doctor."

"No. Not yet." Pete looked up at her. "Just you and me... For a few minutes... Please." The effort of speaking those few words had left him breathless.

"Okay, but *only* for a few minutes. They need to check you over now you're awake."

She perched on the bed beside him, his hand still in hers, resting on her lap. She leant over and gently smoothed his fringe to one side. With a smile, she asked, "So, did you hear everything I said?"

"Oh yes." He gave a glimmer of a smile. "Every word!"

"Good! I meant it. All of it! I *do* love you and I will always be here for you. I promise I will never leave you again."

Pete was silent for a few seconds before he spoke again. "Sukie, can I ask you something?"

"Pete, you can ask me anything."

"Can I keep you?"

She felt her heart flip over at his words, and couldn't keep the smile off her face as she replied, "Of course you can. I am yours until the end of eternity."

Pete smiled at her reply.

Suddenly, he let out a gasp and his body went totally rigid. Sukie let out a scream and hit the call button at the side of the bed. "Help, somebody help..." she shouted. The doors to the room were flung open and Pete's doctor ran in, the nurses right behind him. He pointed at Sukie and said something in Italian. She didn't know what he'd said but one of the younger nurses had her arm around her and was walking her quickly to the door. "Leave. You must leave," she said, as she pushed her gently out into the corridor.

Jordie came running over and gathered her in his arms. "It'll be okay, it'll be okay. The doctor's there, he'll fix him. Shhh…"

She stood in his embrace, clinging to him as tightly as she could. Over his shoulder, she could see the doctor and nurses working over Pete's inert body.

Something else was wrong though.

What was it?

Her brain was screaming at her to pay attention.

The doors began to swing shut.

Suddenly she realised what was different.

The heart monitor was no longer beeping.

The dull, low, steady monotone was the last thing she heard as the doors closed tight.

Chapter Sixty

Eighteen months later

Sukie was sitting in her chair looking out into the garden. Snow had begun to fall but it wasn't lying. Not yet anyway. The forecast had been for light flurries but there was a chance of something heavier if the wind changed direction. She smiled as she looked down at Tony and Adam, their little noses pressed up against the glass as they watched a robin hopping around on the grass. Dusk was falling quickly, so he wouldn't be there much longer. On the table beside her chair, stood the snow globe Pete had given her. Every so often, she would reach across and give it a shake, watching absent-mindedly as the little silver flakes settled inside.

The CD player behind her was playing her favourite Pete Wallace track.

'I didn't know when we were kissing
Exactly what I would be missing
When you went away.
If I could have you here,
If I could bring you near
If only for one day
Then you would hear the words you never heard.
I'd say the words I never said.
I love you.'

She pulled a tissue out from her sleeve to wipe away the tears which had begun to fall at the sound of his voice. She missed him so much. She couldn't get used to him not being here.

She wrapped her arms across herself and let her chin fall down onto her chest. She still had the jumper he'd given her in the library and she was wearing it now. If she sniffed *really* hard, she could get the tiniest hint of his scent from it, but it had pretty much faded away.

It was difficult to believe it was two years since she'd first met him, sitting outside in the freezing snow, wearing a silly thin T-shirt. The same day she had named him Tweety Pie. She looked down at the watch sitting on her wrist. Pete had been wearing it the night he was shot. When he fell, the glass on the front had gotten smashed. It had taken until now for her to finally get it repaired. She wiped her eyes again and blew her nose.

"Are you crying again? What are you like?" a voice whispered in her ear.

"You're home!" She let out a squeal and went to stand up.

"What are you doing sitting here in the dark? Stay where you are. I'm going to put the light on. Close your eyes."

Sukie did as she was told and saw the light come on from behind her eyelids. She opened them slowly and looked into Pete's brilliant green eyes as he knelt in front of her.

"It wasn't dark. See, the moon is shining brightly tonight." She waved a hand towards the window. "Anyway, what are you doing home today? You're not meant to be back until tomorrow."

"The interview for tomorrow was cancelled and I didn't want to be hanging around in London when I could be at home with you. So I flew back early."

"Hmph! I'm still not happy I couldn't come with you." She pulled a sulky face to emphasise her words.

Pete laughed. "It's not my fault the doctor wouldn't allow you to fly. Is that why you were crying?"

"Nah! Don't be so daft. I was missing you like crazy, if you must know. Personally, I would like to blame the hormones but I can't. I was really missing you. This is the first time we've been apart for more than a day since 'you-know-what' and I've really felt it." She took his hand and held it to her cheek. "I don't like it when you're gone."

Pete leant in and gave her another kiss. "I don't like being gone either, my love. I hated not being here with you all, but I'm back now. And how are my little bumpies doing? Are they behaving themselves?" He placed two kisses on her swollen belly.

"They were until they heard your voice. Judging

from their kicks, I think I can safely say they missed you too."

"I'm going to go up and have a shower. Want to come and talk to me while I do? You could even scrub my back if you like." He winked suggestively at her.

"Tempting as that sounds, I think I'll wait here until you come back down." Being nearly seven months pregnant with twins, meant Sukie felt the size of the schloss, never mind a house. The thought of waddling her way up the stairs made her shudder.

"Okay, I won't be long." Pete placed a kiss on top of her head and walked out of the room. She watched his reflection in the window as he left and noticed the slight limp he occasionally had.

The broken leg had turned out to be more serious than the doctor had let on at the time. It had required pinning and a couple of other operations to get it right but it still had a tendency to play up in cold weather or if Pete knelt on it for too long. It was the same damn leg that had caused the problems on the day they'd ceased his sedation.

Several blood clots had formed around the fracture and one had broken off. The doctor had called it a pulmonary embolism. This, apparently, was not unusual with broken limbs.

Unfortunately, the clot had moved up towards his heart and had gotten lodged in one of Pete's coronary arteries and had caused a heart attack. It was fortunate Pete's doctor had faced such a situation once before and had been prepared for this possibility. Knowing there was a risk of clots from either the leg fracture or the brain injury, he'd ensured a scanning machine, syringes, and several vials of thrombolytic were kept in Pete's room. His precautions had saved Pete's life.

She couldn't bear to think of the alternative had he not taken this action. She looked down and realised she was twisting her wedding ring, something she now did whenever she was agitated or distressed – thinking about the shooting always caused both.

In an attempt to calm down – the bumpies didn't like it when she got stressed – she thought about their wedding. It had been such an idyllic day. The May sunshine had shone down on the beautifully decorated gazebo in the grounds of the schloss. Against all the odds, she'd ended up going for a full-on Cinderella-style dress. It had never been her plan to wear something so opulent but the lady in the shop had brought it into the dressing room as part of a selection to look through and she had tried it on for a laugh. Elsa and her mum had been egging her on to do so even though they knew she wouldn't wear anything in that style. They had stopped laughing though when she'd walked out of the changing area and, when she'd turned around and looked in the mirror, she saw why. It had been utterly breath-taking and Sukie knew then she had found her dress.

Despite Pete's very public, celebrity status, they'd managed to keep the wedding small, personal and private. She'd had four bridesmaids. Elsa, naturally, was her matron of honour. Pete's twin sister Claire had been asked and had accepted very gracefully. This had been one benefit from the shooting – it had helped to mend their relationship and brother and sister were now talking again. Claire also couldn't wait to be an auntie and had been delighted to find out they were having twins.

Her friend Kym, who'd ended up babysitting her car on her driveway for about three months, was her third bridesmaid. Sukie felt it was the least she could do to say 'sorry' and 'thank you' for the inconvenience.

Finally, she had asked Sofia. Sofia had been beside herself with joy when Sukie had called her and it was the incentive she'd needed to get her through the last hurdle of her rehabilitation. When she'd found out it was her own brother who had shot Pete, she'd been devastated. Once he'd been permitted more visitors, she had visited Pete every day in the hospital and Sukie had liked her from the first time they met. Not long after Pete had eventually been discharged, and flown home, he'd received a call from Rosa to say Sofia had been very down-hearted and her recovery was suffering a set-back as a result. It was no surprise she was upset though – the news coverage of her brother's actions had been intensive and both she and Rosa were bearing the brunt of it all.

After a time, the detectives working the case had come to see Pete to inform him Eduardo had been declared *'Non di Mente Sana'* – not of sound mind – and so would not be in a position to stand trial. Pete had breathed a sigh of relief. The last thing he had wanted was to see his mother and sister pilloried by the press – both at home and abroad. It was a case which would have attracted a great deal of media attention around the world. As it was, however, Eduardo was now in an establishment that would help him.

Rosa had confided to them at the wedding, that it had

459

transpired there was a history of mental instability on his father's side. She'd never known about it. Her ex-husband had only ever said his father was dead. He'd certainly never told her he'd died in the same building where Eduardo was now ensconced. The errant gene was passed down through the male line. It explained why he'd never wanted children.

Beth, on overhearing the conversation, had interrupted their chat, saying it was not the day to be talking about such things. It was a day of joy and celebration and she had led Sukie and Pete away as it had been time for the first dance.

Thinking of her mum, Sukie looked at the time on her watch and realised Beth and Jordie must have returned from their day out. Jordie had officially retired as Pete's manager and Beth had decided life was too short, so had taken early retirement and now spent all her time with Jordie. On Sukie's recommendation, Jordie had taken Beth to St Wolfgang for the day. She really hoped they'd enjoyed themselves. She wondered if Jordie had proposed again and smiled at the thought. Beth had confided to her that Jordie now proposed every Wednesday, without fail. When Sukie had asked why she hadn't accepted, Beth had smiled and replied, "Oh I will. One day. When I'm ready…"

She heard Pete's footsteps behind her, as he walked back into the room and began to heave herself out of the chair.

"Hang on, babes, let me help you…" Pete wrapped his arms around her and helped her to her feet.

"At this rate, we're going to need to hire a crane to

460

do that," she giggled.

Pete laughed, gathered his wife in his arms and whispered in her ear, "You're doing just fine. *We're* doing just fine." At that, he felt a kick in his abdomen. He looked down at Sukie's bump and said, "And you guys in there are doing absolutely fine too."

He put his arm around her waist as they headed towards the door.

"Oh, just one moment…" She stopped, walked back to the table by the chair, picked up her snow globe, gave it a shake and put it back down. With a smile, she turned around and walked out of the room, switching off the light as they left, leaving the little silver flakes to dance and float in the moonbeams shining brightly through the window.

THE END.

If you enjoyed 'A Rock 'n' Roll Lovestyle, the
second book in the series is now available in e-book
and paperback.

An Artisan

Lovestyle

*When falling in love is the only way to
stay alive...*

Elsa Clairmont was widowed barely five years after
marrying her childhood sweetheart. She has struggled to
come to terms with the loss and, six years later, has
almost ceased to live herself.
She does just enough to get by.

Danny Delaney is the ultimate 'Mr Nice Guy'. He's kind,
caring and sweet. A talented artist in his teens, his
abusive mother ruined his career in art and he turned his
back on his exceptional gift.
Now, he does just enough to get by.

On New Year's Eve, both Danny and Elsa are involved in unrelated accidents which leads to them having to make some serious lifestyle changes and face up to the consequences of their actions. They need to begin living if they want to keep living. Will they succeed in altering the paths of their lives?

Will they find love before it's too late?

An uplifting tale of second chances and appreciating every opportunity life gives you.

It reminded me of my favourite film, 'It's a Wonderful Life...'

★★★★★ *"A sheer pleasure from start to finish"*
Hair Past a Freckle Book Reviews

★★★★★ *"This book is one that has that 'wow' factor"*
Heartshaped Bluestocking

About the Author

Kiltie Jackson spent her formative years growing up in Glasgow but, when she was old enough to do so, high-tailed it down to London where she spent thirteen wonderful years in the Big Smoke before relocating to the Midlands. Those London years gave her many interesting experiences, many of which are now finding their way into her novels.

Kiltie now lives in Staffordshire with one grumpy husband and five cats who kindly allow her to share THEIR house. She's allowed to stay as long as she keeps paying the mortgage! Home is known as Moggy Towers where, despite plenty of moggies, there are no towers!

Kiltie likes reading, watching movies, and eating things she really shouldn't! She hates going to the gym!

If you would like to read more about Kiltie Jackson, and follow her progress in the world of writing, dealing with life and living with five cats and a grumpy husband, she can be found on the following:

www.facebook.com/kiltiejackson

www.twitter.com/kiltiejackson

www.kiltiejackson.com

Printed in Poland
by Amazon Fulfillment
Poland Sp. z o.o., Wrocław

57449494R00266